LIGHT
&
TRUTH

Volume Two
The Gathering

A Historical Novel
Based on a True Story

Visit us at www.harrispublishing.com.

Library of Congress Control Number: 2004111923.
ISBN: 0-9747376-1-5.

First printing October 2004.

Printed at Falls Printing, Idaho Falls, Idaho, U.S.A.

Dedicated to the memory of my father,
Reed Ingval Harris,
who treasured the family name.

The Gathering

"And ye are called to bring to pass *the gathering* of mine elect; for mine elect hear my voice and harden not their hearts;

"Wherefore the decree hath gone forth from the Father that they shall be gathered in unto one place upon the face of the land, to prepare their hearts and be prepared in all things against the day when tribulation and desolation are sent forth upon the wicked."

Doctrine and Covenants 29:7-8

The Prophet Joseph Smith taught:

"What was the object of *gathering* the people of God in any age of the world? The main object was to build unto the Lord a house whereby He could reveal unto His people the ordinances of His house and the glories of His kingdom, and teach the people the way of salvation. It is for the same purpose that God gathers together His people in the last days, to build unto the Lord a house to prepare them for the ordinances and endowments, washings and anointings" (*History of the Church*, 5:423–24).

Foreword

Light and Truth is a church history series of novels that tells the story of four ordinary people from England. The first volume, *The Field Is White,* is a missionary story. In that volume, the four main characters—Daniel, Elizabeth, Robert, and Hannah—rejected the religions of their parents to join the United Brethren congregation. That placed them in a group, organized by Thomas Kington and John Benbow, that sought the further *light and truth* of the true gospel of Jesus Christ. Guided by the Lord, Elder Wilford Woodruff, an Apostle of the Church of Jesus Christ of Latter-day Saints, found the United Brethren members and with help, taught and baptized virtually all six hundred members within a few months.

This second volume, *The Gathering,* is the story of how Daniel, Elizabeth, Robert, and Hannah find themselves caught up in a desire to heed the call to gather to Zion. They find that the gathering is both spiritual and physical. They have already been spiritually gathered, by virtue of their baptism. They have been gathered from the world into the kingdom of God on earth. Now they want to gather, or emigrate, to Nauvoo, where the main body of the Church is located. There, they are to participate in the building of a temple, where saving ordinances of the gospel could be administered to them.

I recently had a conversation with Elder Harold G. Hillam, a member of the First Quorum of the Seventy, who is serving as an Area President in England. I remarked, "Those early converts from Great Britain sort of saved the Church back then."

"Correction," he said. "Not sort of. They virtually *did* save the

Church."

How true. At every step during the restoration of the gospel, Satan did his level best to destroy the Church. There was only one place where the restoration could have survived on planet earth, and that was the United States of America, where a Constitution guaranteed basic freedoms. After the Church built up some initial strength, Satan used a nationwide financial panic to undermine that strength in 1837. Financial institutions closed their doors right and left. The distress affected the Church sorely.

The Prophet Joseph Smith described it this way: "At this time the spirit of speculation in lands and property of all kinds, which was so prevalent throughout the whole nation, was taking deep root in the Church. As the fruits of this evil, evil surmisings, fault-finding, disunion, dissention, and apostasy followed in quick succession, and it seemed as though all the powers of earth and hell were combining their influence in an especial manner to overthrow the Church at once, and make a final end...In this state of things, and but a few weeks before the Twelve were expecting to meet in full quorum...God revealed to me that something new must be done for the salvation of His Church."

Note that the Savior had a plan of his own to counteract the opposition of Satan. The Savior, in a revelation, commanded Joseph Smith to send members of the Quorum of the Twelve Apostles on a mission to England. On June 13, 1837, while the great crisis in the United States and in the Church was reaching a troubling crescendo, Heber C. Kimball, Orson Hyde, and Willard Richards departed on their missions from Kirtland, Ohio. Others followed, including Wilford Woodruff, Brigham Young, and John Taylor.

A great miracle happened. Volume One, *The Field Is White,* told of part of that miracle. Hundreds, even thousands of British people joined the Church, not only in England, but also in Wales, Scotland, and Ireland. Brigham Young recorded that by the end of 1841 the Church had been established in almost every noted town and city in Great Britain. Baptisms numbered between seven and eight thousand. The Book of Mormon and hymnbooks had been printed. And more than a thousand souls had already emigrated to Nauvoo.

Those who joined the Church from the British Isles were, as author Charles Dickens described them, the "pick and flower of England." Literally, the Mormon missionaries in those early days converted the best Great Britain had to offer. The Lord had prepared people for the gospel, and they joined as fast as they could be taught, and as fast as the Spirit witnessed to them the truthfulness of the gospel. The greatest example was the United Brethren.

President Gordon B. Hinckley has said that the opening of the British Mission was a bold declaration to the world, showing the great millennial vision of the Prophet Joseph Smith. It was also an expression of tremendous faith, a demonstration of personal courage, and a statement of everlasting truth. "The infusion of the blood of Britain into the weakened body of the Church in 1837 and in the years that followed gave much needed strength. From those isles came thousands of converts, many with great skills which became useful in building Nauvoo and, later, the communities of the western valleys" (Gordon B. Hinckley, "Taking the Gospel to Britain: A Declaration of Vision, Faith, Courage, and Truth," *Ensign*, July 1987).

It has been my intent in writing the second volume for the reader to vicariously live through what it must have been like to board a rickety wooden ship in 1841 and journey across the perilous Atlantic Ocean. And then leave that ship and board an equally dangerous steamboat for the trip up the Mississippi to Nauvoo. The doctrine of the gathering was a powerful force, but it did not immunize members of the Church against hardships, trials, and tribulations. You will read about fear, seasickness, violent storms, being blown off course, near shipwreck, lusty sailors, pirates, treachery, unscrupulous captains, and a long, drawn-out journey.

I have researched libraries, the Internet, Family History Centers, the Mormon Immigration Index, Church books, and numerous other sources to bring this story to you. I owe a debt to the many LDS historians and family historians who have compiled information that I accessed. And I thank those who gave advice, and read and proofread my manuscript. And I again thank Dr. Ben Bloxham, retired professor at Brigham Young University, who encouraged me to write this Church history series of novels, and for the access to his personal library.

This book is fiction based on a true story. Most of the characters are real, but a few are imaginary. The history of events is offered as accurate. No work of this scope can be free of error, but readers will discern, I hope, an arduous effort to give a true and full picture of an event called *The Gathering.*

This is a product of Harris Publishing, Inc., and is not an official publication of the Church of Jesus Christ of Latter-day Saints.

Principal Characters

All characters are real except those indicated with an asterisk. Bold face indicates main characters. Ages are as Volume Two opens in February 1841.

THE ROBERT HARRIS FAMILY
Robert, 29, the father.
Hannah, 25, the mother.
Joseph, 5.
Lizzy, 3.
William, 2

THE BROWETT FAMILY
Daniel, 28.
Elizabeth, 26, sister to Robert Harris.
Martha Pulham Browett, 55,
    Daniel's mother.
Rebecca, 21, Daniel's sister.

THE EAGLES FAMILY
Ann, 57, the mother.
George, 35.
*Henry, 33.
*Katherine, 28, Henry's wife.
William, 29.
Elias, 18.
Jane, 16.

THE BLOXHAM FAMILY
Thomas, 28, the father.
Dianah, 29, the mother.
Charles, 8.
Lucy, 7.
Tommy, 6.
Johnny, 4.

OTHERS
John Benbow, 40; and wife, Jane.
Jacob Kemp Butterfield, 28.
John Cox, 30.
John Cheese, 31.
John Davis, 28.
Mary Ann Weston Davis, 26.
John Hyrum Green, 39; wife, Susannah.
Joseph Hill, 34.
Orson Hyde, 36, Apostle.
Thomas Kington, 47.
William Pitt, 27.
Edward Phillips, 27.
*James Pulham, 31.
Nancy Eagles Pulham, 24.
Levi Roberts, 30.
Joseph Smith, 35, President of the Church
    of Jesus Christ of Latter-day Saints.
Wilford Woodruff, 33, Apostle.

CREW OF THE ECHO
Josiah Wood, captain.
Michael Heywood, steward.
Theodore Evans, first mate.
Bryant Adams, second mate.
John Poole, sailor.
Lionel Dana, sailor.
Harvey "Neptune" Crump, navigator.

PART ONE

The

Atlantic

1

Liverpool, England, February 1841

ANN EAGLES STEPPED OFF THE train at the underground Hargreaves Railway Terminal in a bitterly sour mood. She had not been able to sleep on the train. Her back hurt. Her head ached. Her nose was running. Her heavy winter coat was not keeping her warm.

"Do you see them yet?" Ann asked her daughter, Nancy. "Where are they? They're supposed to be here." Ann's words smoked in the frigid air. She sneezed into her handkerchief.

Nancy Eagles Pulham did not feel much better. "Patience, Mama. I'm certain they'll find us." Nancy scanned the railway platforms, looking for her sister, Hannah, and Hannah's husband, Robert. Robert was part of a seven-man presidency charged with the responsiblity of getting a company of new Mormon converts to America. Hundreds of passengers, clad in dark winter coats, scurried up and down the platforms.

"For a half a farthing I'd go back to Apperley right now," moaned Ann, her elderly bones aching. It seemed to her that every gray hair of her head ached, too.

"Oh, Mother. You'll be fine." The cheerful voice came from Ann's son, Elias, only eighteen. "You've got to think of this as an adventure."

I hope I survive this adventure, Nancy thought. Dizzy with morning sickness, she leaned on her husband, James. *Is it time I told him?*

Henry Eagles, a large swarthy man, and Ann's third oldest son, began unloading baggage. His mood was sour, too. But he was born that way. Henry didn't care if Robert found them or not. Henry could find the Liverpool docks on his own. There were a lot of people in the world that Henry hated. Robert Harris was at the top of his list.

Henry's new wife, Katherine, her most prominent feature being a dish nose, rose to the tips of her toes and pointed. "There they are," she said, waving her arms.

Ann's face broke into its first smile in two days as she watched Hannah, more than seven months pregnant, waddle toward her.

"Welcome to Liverpool, Mama," Hannah Maria Eagles Harris said, leaning over and wrapping her arms around her fifty-seven-year-old mother. "The children are being tended by Mormon passengers on the ship. How was your first train ride?"

"Dreadful," Ann answered honestly, wiping her nose. "I don't think I'll ever warm up. Practically everyone on the train had a cold. The stagecoach would have been faster, and warmer."

Robert politely kissed his bent-over mother-in-law on her wrinkled cheek. Second-class travel on England's new rail system was admitted near-torture. First-class was not much better. A sailing ship might be worse, depending on a lot of uncontrollable factors.

Ann flinched, rubbing her back. "I've never sat on a harder bench. And sometimes that terrible black smoke came right into our coach. Never again."

Sensing her mother's distress, Hannah wilted at what her mother might think of the ship they were about to board. She changed the subject. "Where're George and William?" Her two brothers were the only members of the Eagles family besides Henry who had not accepted Hannah's new religion, Mormonism. Everyone else was emigrating with her and Robert to a frontier settlement in America called Nauvoo: Ann, Henry, Katherine, Nancy, James, Elias, and Jane.

Elias answered for his mother. "They'll be here to wish us well in a couple of days, before we leave." With black hair and a bulky frame, he was beginning to resemble Henry.

Hannah understood. It's difficult for dairymen to be away from their cows.

With a nervous face twitch, Robert approached Henry and shook his hand. "Welcome to Liverpool." He still doubted the sincerity of Henry's decision to marry a Mormon convert, Katherine Hill, a sister of Robert's friend, Joseph, and join the emigration process.

Henry, the non-Mormon, grunted.

"Daniel is sorry he could not be here to greet you," Robert said, turning to face the others. "As leader of our company, he's quite busy right now. Our numbers have swelled to more than a hundred."

Jane, sixteen, twined her fingers with Hannah's. "How soon can we see the ship?"

"Soon," Hannah said, glowing. "The quay is not far from here. We slept on board last night."

"How exciting," Jane said, sending out a happy grin.

A throng of carters had surrounded the arriving passengers.

"Don't pay the bag carters more than six pence per cart," Robert directed, motioning. "We've had our problems with them. And watch out for groups of fast-talking sharpers. They'll relieve you of your baggage and currency quicker than a cat, and you'll never see it again. That's already happened to one of our Mormon passengers. The Brethren asked me to warn you."

Robert shook his head back and forth in a negative gesture. "We need four of you, that's all," he said to the carters. Robert dictated the price; they accepted.

Robert, Henry, and Elias helped the carters load the Eagles family's baggage on carts. Crates full of furniture and other personal belongings were dragged off a freight coach.

With Ann sneezing and coughing, Nancy hiding her wooziness, and Hannah waddling, Robert led the Eagles family and the carters north to Hilliar's Hotel. From there they took Moon's Ferry across the River Mersey.

Along the way, Robert explained what he knew about the history of the city, a benefit of his earlier arrival. It had been established by King John as a port in 1207 to send men and supplies across the Irish Sea. England had just conquered Ireland. It had a strategic access to the River Mersey. It got its name from old words, *lifer pol,* meaning muddy pool. Liverpool developed into a fishing village and market town during medieval times, with a population of about 1,000. Ireland developed into an important trading partner for Liverpool. The first docks were built in 1715, when the population reached 15,000. The city swelled to 77,000 by the turn of the century.

The sights along Liverpool's streets and docks stunned the gray-haired Ann Eagles, who had spent her entire life in the small Gloucestershire hamlet of Apperley. More than 300,000 Englishmen crammed together. Squalid, foul-smelling cellars where the poorest of poor lived. Beggars young and old, victims of England's severe economic depression. Thieves, with their evil eyes. Roaming prostitutes. Drunken seamen, toppling a fruit vendor's stand, and harassing an elegantly dressed woman. Building walls thoroughly placarded with sailing notices of packet ships. Unscrupulous "man-catchers" who received commissions from passenger brokers. Shouting, laughing, singing, cursing dockworkers, clamoring like ants to unload vessels. Massive warehouses, endless on both sides of the river. Bales of cotton and tobacco from America. Hogsheads of sugar, molasses, grain, tobacco, and cottonseed oil. Fresh fruit from the Caribbean and South America. Tea, coffee, spices, clothing, furniture, jewelry, and even fireworks from China. Export cargo of crockery and textiles.

Elias and Jane seemed charmed by the air of hectic festivity that prevailed everywhere. Loved ones waving at departing passengers. The music of flutes, fiddles, and bagpipes. Organ men and their monkeys. A campanologist playing "Home Sweet Home." Wails of children. Chanteys of sailors. Peddlers of ribbon and lace. Streetpatterers crying headlines of their newspapers.

Booking offices dotted the streets. "Thank your lucky stars you don't have to stand in line there," Hannah said. "The church has done your booking for you. Our berths are secure."

"That's the *Echo* over there," Robert said as his group neared a quay overlooking Liverpool's customhouse. "What do you think of her?"

He pointed to a 668-ton three-decked packet ship with an American flag flying from her spanker gaff. Her name was painted exquisitely in white letters on her bow and stern. Her figurehead was that of an eagle, and her elliptical stern was ornamented on one side with a gilded carving of an upper New York village scene, near the East River shipyards. On the other side was a gilded carving of the New York wharf, her port of hail. She had lost her three topgallant sails on a recent voyage to Rio, where she put into refit.

Ann Eagles gasped. Her tired old brown eyes scanned a wooden ship with masts that seemed as tall as the spires on the Gloucester Cathedral, near her home. The *Echo* seemed to be infected with an imminent departure as she creaked, rolled, and strained at her mooring lines. Frigid gusts of February winds pushed against her bow, and whistled across the decks. The mustiness of the ship, combined with the dank odor of the river, and the bleak cry of seagulls piercing the air, made Ann irksome.

"She's just beautiful," James Pulham answered, a sense of adventure stirring in him. He was fascinated by the ship, closing his eyes to imagine the creaking of the timbers during his voyage to America. Sailors tinkered at coils of rope, blasphemed, hammered, and bustled about.

"All that food for us?" Katherine asked. Her gaze fixed on ragged Irish and American stevedores loading sacks of flour and potatoes, net bags full of cabbages, gnarled and stunted vegetables gathered from storage cellars, bundles of dried fish, boxes of tinned food, and water casks. The men stretched hand-to-hand up the gangway, across the deck, and down the hatches.

Robert boomed a laugh. "No. That's all for the crew. Remember what we were told at our meeting in the Gadfield Elm Chapel a few weeks ago? We have to provide our own food. You'll have time tomorrow to shop. Get lots of fruits and vegetables, or you'll get that cursed scurvy."

Ann Eagles stood beneath the giant ship, wondering what she had gotten herself into. A muscle twitched in her face. She sent her son-in-law a sharp, searching look. "Is it really safe to travel across the ocean on one of these?"

Hannah laughed at her mother's absurdity. "Oh, Mama. I'm certain it is. Otherwise, I wouldn't have my things on board, let alone my children."

Henry's voice was a low growl. "But the weather…" Despite his brusque outward appearance, he harbored inner fears. He shrank at the thought that the *Echo* might depart Liverpool even in the cruelest winds, facing a murderous sea.

"The Brethren are confident," Hannah said, forcing a balmy smile. *You look less than brave, my bully brother.*

"Well, I'm *not,*" Henry retorted, turning his massive back against the wind.

Elias scanned the ship up and down, his eyes twinkling and his mind racing about his pending adventure. "Is this brig British or American?"

"Built in America only six years ago," Robert answered. "Can't you see the American flag? And she's not a brig. The *Echo* is classified as a ship because she has three masts. Her sails are mostly square. The triangular ones are called jibs, you know."

Henry scoffed inwardly at Robert's knowledge of ships, obviously gained in the two days he had been in Liverpool. Nevertheless, he followed Robert's pointing finger, and gazed upward.

James Pulham pulled his wife, Nancy, to his chest. "This is going to take us to Zion," he said.

"I know," she said, feeling a little better. "I can hardly wait. Living in a holy city like Nauvoo sounds like heaven."

"We'll have our own home," James said, dreaming.

"And we'll be together forever," Nancy added. She buried her head in her husband's chest and a tear came to her eye. "I love you."

"Ahoy there, mates!"

Robert cast his blue-gray eyes at a waving sailor, standing on the forecastle deck above them. "Ahoy!" he returned. "The rest of our family is here."

"That's Michael Heywood, the steward," Hannah told her mother, her voice chiming.

"I'll be right there," Heywood yelled. The young sailor bounded down the gangplank, and then stood before them wearing trousers made of clear white duckcloth, a handsome pair of black pumps, and a tarpaulin hat bright as a looking glass. A long black ribbon streamed behind the hat. He had a new royal-blue silk handkerchief tied around his neck, threaded through the single vertebra bone of a shark, highly polished and carved. A heavy wool overcoat covered his bright blue shirt.

Sixteen-year-old Jane Eagles was charmed and captivated by his presence.

"Michael Heywood of Farmington, Connecticut, United States of America, at your service," the sailor said, bowing.

"Not unless you've changed your system since I was here a few hours ago," Robert said, rolling his blue-gray eyes.

A puzzled look crossed Heywood's face.

Robert's tone was friendly. "Our steward is a remarkably helpful young man. But because we are steerage passengers, we're obliged to load our own luggage and fend for ourselves on board."

Ann Eagles cast a wary smile at the young sailor, who appeared to be about five feet nine inches tall, with dark brown hair, and hands that were severely scarred. Ann guessed the scars were from scalding.

Steward Heywood winked his green eyes at the elderly lady in front of him. "Well, I would certainly help you with your things if the cap'n, first mate, second mate, and the rest of the crew would let me. However, you Mormons seem to be pretty well organized. Help is all around you. Your own cap'n is coming." He pointed to Daniel Browett, arriving with his wife, Elizabeth, his mother, Martha, his sister, Rebecca, and his five other counselors.

2

DANIEL BROWETT WAS NO CAPTAIN, though the ship's crew called him that. He was the Mormon selected by his Church leaders to preside over a company of 109 Saints emigrating to Nauvoo, Illinois. He was dressed in a brown tweed suit. His blond hair well hidden by a dark brown cap pulled over his head, and a gray scarf wrapped around his neck, Daniel ambled up to the Eagles family, greeted them, then asked the steward, "Did I hear you say Farmington, Connecticut?"

"Sure did," the steward answered. Heywood had been raised there in a God-fearing home, where the Bible was always open, songs sung, jigs danced, long stories spun. He had the makings of a man of letters, but he wanted to explore the wider world. His restlessness turned into aspiration, and he opted for a life at sea, leaving Farmington as a teenager.

"Correct me if I'm wrong, Elizabeth," Daniel said from his bony, ramshackle frame, "but isn't that where Elder Woodruff is from?" Elder Woodruff had baptized Daniel and Elizabeth, along with six hundred other former members of the United Brethren congregation in southwestern England. As he spoke, John Cheese, David Wilding, James Lavender, William Jenkins, and John Ellison—Daniel's assistants—greeted the Eagles family and began the task of dealing with their baggage.

Her olive eyes beaming and her gloved hand tugging at her chin, Elizabeth said, "I'm quite *sure* that's right. Oh, I miss him *dreadfully.* I wish he were here with us instead of preaching in London. But, oh well, I suppose spreading the gospel there is *more important* than seeing some of his Gloucestershire converts off."

Daniel cut off his wife's prattling and placed a hand on Heywood's shoulder. "Did you know of a Woodruff family in Farmington?"

"I haven't been there for a few years, but I sure did," Heywood answered, pleased that he could remember. "I think the Woodruffs worked at the mill there. Why do you ask?"

"He's the reason we're all Mormons," Daniel explained, his blue eyes glistening. "Greatest missionary in the world." *We were converted by the Spirit, really, but you wouldn't understand that, yet.*

Heywood's smile was indulgent. His wandering eyes took in Rebecca, Daniel's twenty-one-year-old sister, her sinewy body covered with layers of winter clothing.

Rebecca dropped her blue eyes and blushed.

"Do you have time to show them the ship?" Daniel asked.

"Follow me," Heywood said. The spunky sailor leaped up the gangway.

With the new arrivals on the main deck with Robert and Hannah, Heywood pointed to another young sailor, also dressed in white duckcloth trousers and a bright red handkerchief tied around his neck. "That man is our second mate."

The mate, Bryant Adams, a tall man with a bronze complexion and visible tattoos on his hands and face, seemed to ignore the passengers, barking orders at his crew. "Lively up there men! Let's have that battered old lower topsail down on deck. Sing out when you're ready to lower away."

Hannah tapped her mother on the shoulder. "Look up, Mama."

Ann turned her gaze upward. Sailors were crawling like monkeys in trees on a complicated system of ropes and wires.

"Aye, aye, sir!" one sailor yelled, followed by others springing to their places along a foot rope, loosening various ropes, working quickly, knowing the mate's eye was watching them.

"There's a lot of maintenance goin' on while the ship is moored," Robert explained, gesturing.

"Been here only two days, and Mr. Harris is the expert seaman," Heywood joked. "But he's right. Our sailors are never idle. The discipline of the ship requires that every man be at work upon something when he is on deck. Not even in our state prisons back in America are the men more regularly set to work."

Adams concurred in a raspy voice. "A ship is like a ladies watch, folks. Always out of repair. We're overhaulin', replacin', and repairin' our rigging in more ways than you'd ever imagine. Several sails were ripped badly during our last crossing of the Atlantic."

It took a few seconds for the last statement to register in the mind of Ann Eagles. She gasped.

"Our ropes, too many to number, are constantly chafin', or wearin' down. You can see sailors using our chafin' gear, wormin', parcelin', roundin', and service of all kinds. Many of our ropes are made right on board." He pointed to a wheel and a spindle. "That's our spun yard winch right there."

"Do your ropes ever break?" Ann asked, still gasping, thinking of the implications.

"Only during exceptionally high winds."

Heywood could see the stunned look on the elderly woman. "Let's go up on the forecastle deck to get out of the way. From there we can get into the steerage compartment, where your berths are located."

The second mate's voice pierced the winter air. "Lower away handsomely, look out for her below. Look out, missy," Adams said to Rebecca, casting his furtive eyes at her.

Daniel moved Rebecca aside, and it was Henry who stood hypnotized as a huge sail tumbled down, fluttering like a crippled bird, straight at him.

Robert instinctively reached out, and with a powerful thrust pushed Henry out of the way. He grimaced, waiting for Henry's reaction. Depending on which personality was dominating his brother-in-law at the moment,

Henry might lash out in protest at the former pugilist, or politely thank him. For a split second Robert thought he detected a dark anger beneath Henry's greasy black hair and swarthy chest. He was relieved when Henry gave him a playful smile.

"I guess I was standing in the wrong place," Henry said.

The second mate was unapologetic. He summoned another sailor, giving him more orders. "Avast there, you old seadog. Not enough slush on that royal mast. Get up there and do it over again. That perfumed grease won't hurt you."

A pig-tailed slender sailor named Lionel Dana, his face terribly disfigured by a remarkable scrofula scar on his right cheek that contracted his eyelid and ran all the way down to his throat, grabbed an evil-smelling bucket containing some kind of greasy mixture and swung it past the new passengers.

Rebecca grimaced as the bucket slopped past her.

"A bonny lass you are, Ma'am," Dana told Rebecca, bowing slightly.

Rebecca felt a chill, uneasy with the attention she was receiving.

Heywood regarded Rebecca's puzzled look. "That stuff's made from boiling down salt beef. Quite the thick lobbered gravy, ain't it? The sailor is ordered to slush the main topmast with the galley grease so it won't dry out."

The pig-tailed sailor scampered up the rigging, dangling the bucket from an equally greasy rope handle. Rebecca moved away, in case the sailor dropped the bucket.

From round, searching eyes, Elias Eagles asked, "Are all your sailors from America?"

"No, not at all," Heywood said, shaking his head and turning thoughtful. "We have an international collection. We're still recruiting. The crew changes every voyage. I won't tell you which one, but we have a seaman who deserted a British frigate because of the way he was treated. The people's food on British ships, I'm sad to say, is always scanty and very bad. It's better on an American packet ship like ours."

A clinking noise caught Nancy's attention as the group moved toward the capstan and hard-pine bowsprit. Following the noise, she could see a sailor swung out over the prow in a bowline, hammer in hand, pounding away.

"He's chipping rust off the anchor," Heywood explained, pointing. "And this sailor is picking apart old ropes to collect what we call oakum, a loose fiber the ship's carpenter uses to make caulking. Caulking is used to fix small leaks."

"Leaks?" Ann Eagles asked in surprise, still not recovered from earlier revelations about the *Echo*. "Drats. This ship leaks?"

"Just small ones, here and there. The bottom and sides of the ship are covered with copper. There are no serious leaks, I can assure you of that."

Ann narrowed her eyes in disbelief.

Shaking off the woman's distress, Heywood pointed to another sailor, whittling at a large piece of wood. "During the time when we are not at sea, there's more time to whittle new belaying pins. The constant friction of the ropes wear the pins down."

Hannah's mother stared at a worn pin.

Next, Heywood pointed to a group of sailors beginning to mend the battered lower topsail that had just come down. "While we're in port is a good time to mend torn sails."

Ann blinked, paling at the words. "How did it get so torn?"

Heywood's answer was blunt. "High winds."

Ann inwardly cringed, and then keyed her worried eyes on the sailors. Five more sailors danced up the forecastle steps carrying a large tub of seawater, singing, and each brandishing buckets and short-handled brooms.

"Oops," Heywood said, "better get out of the way again. They're gonna swab and holystone the deck."

Henry stepped aside, staring at the prayerbook-sized chunks of sandstone carried by the sailors and the gleaming white pine deck, already meticulously clean. *What a wasted effort,* he thought.

Daniel's counselors slid by, carrying boxes marked "Not Wanted For Passage."

"Where do they store our belongings?" James asked.

"Way down in the cargo hold, below steerage," Heywood answered, motioning for them to follow. The cargo held pieces of furniture, and items like Robert's butchering tools and Daniel's carpentry tools. "The luggage you'll need goes into a compartment at the rear of the ship."

Ann shivered, suddenly chilled. She coughed long and hard, closing her eyes, wincing, and putting a hand to her chest. Her son-in-law, James, a medium-sized man with a square face marred by boils, patted her on the back.

"When do we get to meet the captain?" James asked.

"Ha!" Heywood laughed. "Probably not until the day we leave, which'll be Tuesday. While in port he's staying in the best room at Hilliar's Hotel, hobnobbing with Liverpool's wealthy businessmen and diplomats. He'll be having dinner in some posh oysterhouse tonight would be my guess, sipping on England's best Madeira wines."

Ann Eagles' mouth dropped. "How can a sailor afford to do all that?"

"Oh, ma'am, he's no ordinary sailor. A sailor makes fifteen dollars a month. Captain Wood gets a share of the ship's profits. I'd say he makes five percent of the income from the cargo, twenty-five percent of the passenger's fares, and the entire fee for the mail we carry. By the end of the year, he'll probably make five thousand dollars."

Hannah leaned toward her mother and whispered, "That's the same as a thousand pounds."

Ann grunted in disgust.

"Once we get under way, you'll see he earns his money," Heywood explained. "No matter how much authority he delegates to his mates, he's still responsible for the safety of the ship, and he must determine how much punishment she can take and still sail safely at top speed to keep on schedule. The captain is a man of profound knowledge and a lot of experience. That's how he got to be the captain."

Heywood's words shook Ann. *How much punishment she can take?* She grimaced again.

Heywood whirled, pointing. "What do you think of our staterooms?" He opened a door, revealing embossed crimson velvet upholstery and teak-appointed louvered doors.

A broad smile crossed Ann's delighted face.

"And how's about our dining room?" Heywood pushed open another door. Inside were twenty oak chairs surrounding an opulent oak table. Benches were set in the walls and glasses held in racks. Immaculately dressed passengers occupied a few chairs. *The gentry, no doubt,* Nancy assumed. *England's elite class.*

"This is where we'll eat? And I can have any stateroom I want?" Ann asked, her eyes gleaming now.

"Sorry, no," Heywood said, his face sobering. "I didn't mean to mislead you. You're a steerage passenger, remember? Staterooms are for first-class passengers only."

Ann's mouth curved downward. She coughed again. "Then what do our quarters look like?"

A sharp voice was heard before Heywood could answer. "I'm wanted by the mate. Mr. Harris and Mr. Browett can show you steerage quarters." Heywood excused himself and disappeared.

Robert knew by the look on his mother-in-law's face that Heywood had made a mistake by showing her the staterooms. "Down this way," he beckoned, striding onto the main deck where he opened a hatch. "Elias, help your mother down the ladder."

Descending into the gloomy space between the forecastle and poop decks, Ann gnawed on her lower lip. "You expect me to sleep in here?" she asked, choking in anguish.

Stunned, Ann strained in dim light to gaze at an open area surrounded by two tiers of rough-built, six-foot-by-six-foot wooden berths, fastened to the deck beams. There was a musty, dank smell. Down here, the ship's creaks and groans were amplified, terrifying Hannah's mother.

Bent over, Robert shrugged and gave a blunt answer. "This is steerage." The headroom was six inches shy of his six-foot stature.

As Ann absorbed her disappointment, Nancy asked, "How many people will be down here?"

"The mate says they have capacity for more than two hundred," Robert said, forcing a pained smile. "Passengers are still being booked. About half will be members of the Church."

Nancy bristled. "But where will we eat, if not in the first-class dining room?"

"Don't fret your eyelids on that score. We'll eat on the decks. There're two small galley stoves on the main deck. We'll have to take turns. We can't use the large stove. It's for the crew."

"Just two stoves for all steerage passengers?" Henry asked, whining.

Robert shrugged his shoulders again. "We are trying to get some cooking grates as well, and some coal to fuel them."

Henry's scowl deepened. "I see chamber pots down here."

"The ship provides them. Everyone will have to make certain they are taken up, and dumped overboard on a regular basis."

Rebecca recoiled at the thought of using a chamber pot with limited privacy.

"But I thought I saw water closets on deck," James said.

"For the first-class passengers," Hannah answered, pointing upward.

Robert lit a lantern. Walking, he illuminated one of the berths. "Not much head room, but the width is adequate."

"I should have brought my feather mattress," Ann scoffed.

3

NEXT MORNING, LATER THAN MOST, the widow Ann Eagles appeared on the main deck. Not saying much, rubbing her bloodshot and baggy eyes, she spooned mouthfuls of sticky oatmeal into her mouth, swallowing in pain. Her neck and back ached, both from the rickety train ride, and from the hard wooden berth in the steerage compartment she had shared with Hannah and Willie, the youngest child. Except for a couple of hours near twilight, sleep had evaded her. At first it had been Hannah's children, crying, wanting drinks of water, and needing to use the chamber pot. Then the rats kept her awake, scampering through the berths, rummaging through baggage. Newer berths, made of green wood, creaked horrendously during the night. She had dreamed of the feather mattress she had left in Apperley. Even the old corncob mattress she had slept on as a child would have been better. The single wool blanket she had wrapped herself in had not been nearly enough to keep her warm. She had coughed all night. Now, her throat seemed to be choking shut with bits of gravel.

Robert's constant kindness—cooking her breakfast, answering her questions, trying to cheer her up—did little to mitigate her squalid mood. She did not doubt her testimony. When she had been baptized last August, the Spirit had stirred her soul. Other doubts plagued her, however. She had delayed a decision on whether or not to emigrate to Nauvoo with Robert and Hannah, and James and Nancy, until December. The decision meant she would leave two married sons and their families behind. Between the two sons, they had seven children. Seven grandchildren she might never see again. And she had a proposal of marriage. Samuel Roberts, father of Levi Roberts, was waiting for her answer.

"More oatmeal?" Robert asked, sipping his tea, looking over the brim of the cup. "Plenty of time to eat until we have to leave for the orientation meeting."

Ann shook her head.

"Try some fried pork? Might be the last until we get to America."

She shook her head again, gesturing to her sore throat.

Ann set her bowl on the wooden deck and grimaced. On the other hand, if she returned to Apperley, she might never again see the three grandchildren Hannah had borne, Joseph, Lizzy, and Willie. Nor would she see those yet to be born to Hannah, and to Nancy.

"Sleep well?" Hannah asked.

Ann shook her head sideways, recalling how Hannah and Nancy resembled each other, almost as if they were twins. Both had silken auburn hair, dark narrow eyebrows, deep-set brown eyes gleaming with bold intelligence, and full lips circled by oval chins. Hannah was an inch shorter than Nancy and had a fuller figure after three children.

"You'll sleep better tonight," Hannah said. Starting tonight, crewmembers would enforce the rule that families would be berthed in the center of the steerage compartment, and single men would berth on one end, and single women on the other.

I doubt it, Ann thought. *I'll probably have to share a berth with a woman I don't even know. How will I endure six weeks of the smell of two hundred unwashed bodies in that cramped steerage compartment? Berths smaller than a dog kennel. Suffocation for want of air.*

Tears welled up in her eyes as Ann thought of her situation, a burden no matter how she looked at it. She dearly loved Hannah, and had learned to love

Robert although it had taken her six years to do it. At first his arrogance and pride had repulsed her. She remembered his altercation with Henry in the barnyard; the day Robert—known as Bobby back then—came to slaughter a steer at the dairy. Then there was the fight between Bobby and Henry at the county fair, the day Bobby learned how good he was at pugilism.

The rest of Ann's memory was a blur. There was her husband's opposition to Bobby and Hannah's courtship, compounded by stark religious differences. The Eagles family was Methodist; the Harris family was strict Anglican. Daniel Browett, who wanted to marry Bobby's sister, Elizabeth, was Quaker. Yet Hannah, Bobby, Elizabeth, and Daniel wanted a double marriage. It was almost more than the three families could endure. But it happened. First, in the Methodist chapel to satisfy Thomas Eagles. Second, in an Anglican church to satisfy Bobby and Elizabeth's parents. Then there were rifts in Bobby and Hannah's marriage caused by religion, or the lack of it. And other complications. Bobby's goal to become British heavyweight champion. Hannah's hatred of pugilism. Daniel and Elizabeth joining the United Brethren, becoming lay preachers. Tugs at Bobby and Hannah to join. Bobby's success in fighting. The contract with Squire Hastings. Yeoman status. A two hundred-acre farm. Promise of fame and fortune. One fight away from the championship. Wilford Woodruff. Mormonism. Conversion. Sacrifice. Emigration. Nauvoo. Help build a temple.

Ann's tired old head was swimming in near torture as she recalled the events of the past few years.

"Good morning to the Eagles family. Trust you all slept well."

It was Michael Heywood, the steward, making his rounds, pensively fingering the silk handkerchief that was wrapped around his neck, threaded through the shark vertebra bone.

Ann Eagles wiped her nose and gave him an evil eye.

Heywood's grin was warm. "Last day in Liverpool. We depart tomorrow mornin' at eight o'clock sharp."

Henry Eagles returned Heywood a mystified smile. "Oh, I'll bet you'll hate leaving Liverpool. I hear you sogers love it here."

Heywood bristled at the word *soger.* It was the worst term of reproach that could be applied to a sailor: a shirker, one who tries to get out of work. *Unfortunate fool probably doesn't know,* Heywood thought to himself. "What makes you say that?"

"I've been talking to a few of your sailors. They say it's a paradise; you know, the gin palaces, brothels, dance halls and the 'free and easies.' Did you go to the 'free and easies' last night, too?" Henry grinned, showing his missing teeth from his days as a pub brawler.

"If you mean the lewd shows, the answer is no," the steward said, tossing his head in disgust. "Many of our sailors do things like that, but it's not for me. I stayed on board all night. I don't even like the gin palaces. Regrettably, most of our sailors work like horses while at sea, and spend their money like asses ashore."

"I hear there're more than two thousand drinking dens," Henry said, letting his imagination run wild. "You're fibbing. I'll bet you could tell a story or two."

Ann grabbed her throat, and gestured to his. "Henry, that's enough."

Trying his best to remain polite, Heywood acknowledged that Liverpool's concentration of drinking places was the highest concentration anywhere in the world. Social reformers, however, had begun to build hostels, almshouses, and churches for visiting sailors, he said.

Robert cleared his voice, and stepped between Henry and the steward. "Hate to change the subject, but we're off to a meeting."

"A Mormon meetin', no doubt," Heywood replied. "Need help with directions?"

Robert waved him off. "No, thanks. I've been there two times already." He spoke of the large hall rented by Brigham Young and Willard Richards that had been used for church headquarters in Liverpool for the emigration effort, and as a Sunday meeting house for local members of the Church.

"Don't be late," Heywood added as he walked away. "A hundred Mormons. We'd hate to leave without you."

Ann Eagles sighed.

4

ANN EAGLES FELT UNCOMFORTABLE around Brigham Young. Especially when he looked her directly in the eye. His brown eyes seemed to penetrate her very soul, sensing all her fears.

"Your daughters want you to have this," the Apostle said to Ann, thrusting a book at her. The look on his face was serious and concerned. Brigham was broad and tall, with pale skin and thick brown hair. Ann guessed the year in England had taken a heavy toll on him. He stood with unmistakable authority, on squat, powerful legs.

Hannah and Nancy smiled at their mother.

Fighting the reflex to cough, Ann asked, "What is it?" Her old eyes tried to focus on the title.

"The Book of Mormon," Brigham said, his eyes dancing with delight.

"It's mine? My personal copy?"

"All yours," he confirmed, pointing. "We have boxes of them. Just off the press. All made possible by the generosity of John Benbow and Thomas Kington."

"Remember?" Nancy asked her mother. "They're the ones who organized the United Brethren congregation. Daniel supplied Brother Benbow with barrels when he operated the Hill Farm near Castle Frome."

"Brother Benbow donated two hundred and fifty pounds for the printing," Brigham explained, "and Brother Kington fifty pounds. Brother Benbow has already emigrated to Nauvoo."

Ann squinted as she tried to remember. She spoke slowly, and in obvious pain. "Didn't Brother Benbow lose the lease on his farm when he joined the Church?"

Nodding, Hannah continued. "Yes, he did. And so did we." Hannah's heart sank, remembering the day Squire Hastings had their belongings tossed out of their farm cottage. The squire had not taken kindly to Robert's conversion and retirement from pugilism.

Nancy brought a hand to her stomach. A thickening shroud of morning sickness settled over her. "You'll have to excuse me for a moment."

With a puzzled, concerned look, Hannah watched her sister wiggle through the crowded room and exit the door.

Brigham grasped Ann's hand, pointing to the Book of Mormon. "By the time you get to Nauvoo you'll have it read several times, and have your favorite verses marked."

Ann gave it a cursory glance, thumbing through it quickly.

"Sister Eagles, I feel impressed to give you a promise."

Ann looked up at the Apostle.

"If you will read the Bible and the Book of Mormon, every day, for at least fifteen or twenty minutes, you will be richly blessed. Combined with daily personal prayer, and application of gospel principles, you will be entitled to personal revelation. The Holy Ghost will prompt you in all the decisions you must make in your life. And if you will read the Book of Mormon daily, you will never lose your testimony of that book or of the Church."

For the first time since her arrival in Liverpool, Ann's eyes filled with light. She nodded. "I can do that."

Brigham gave her hand a tight squeeze and then released it. "God bless you. It's time to start our orientation meeting."

Hannah's mother swallowed with apparent uneasiness, the soreness in her throat slightly worse. "Thank you."

"Sit here by us," Elizabeth told Ann. "There's room for all your family." She pointed toward Daniel's mother, Martha, and his sister, Rebecca.

Nancy, arm in tow by James, did not find her way to the seats until after the song and prayer. To Hannah's eyes, she looked pale.

"Why isn't Elder Woodruff here?" Ann whispered to Hannah, barely audible.

"He's still in London, preaching." Pointing, she said, "But three of the Apostles are here. The large man seated next to Elder Young is Willard Richards, and next to him is John Taylor." Daniel and his six assistants also sat facing the audience.

Brigham Young spoke first, relating a brief personal history. Born in Vermont in 1801. Grew up in New York state, learning several trades: carpenter, joiner, painter, and glazier. Converted to the church by Samuel H. Smith, the Prophet Joseph Smith's brother. Became a close friend to the Prophet in 1832, after moving to Kirtland, Ohio. Ordained an Apostle in 1835. Mission to England, arriving in the spring of 1840.

Brigham's gestures radiated the repose of a confident man. His tone was stimulating as he spoke to the gathering. After citing scriptures and making opening remarks, he unfolded a piece of paper, saying it was a communication from the Prophet Joseph Smith.

"Brother Joseph writes: 'Let those who can, freely make a sacrifice of their time, their talents, and their property, for the prosperity of the kingdom; and for the love they have to the cause of truth, bid adieu to their homes and pleasant places of abode, and unite with us in the great work of the last days, and share in tribulation, that they may ultimately share in the glory and triumph'."

Brigham paused for a few seconds. "Gird up your loins, brothers and sisters. This will be a difficult trip. But we need you in Nauvoo. We have a temple to build. A temple that will provide the saving ordinances of the gospel, which will bring exaltation to your souls. The Savior, through the Prophet Joseph Smith, has revealed all those things. They will bring great blessings to you."

Brigham seemed to inflate with a devotion to the Prophet. Then he began to rattle off practical advice to the one hundred and nine Mormon *Echo* passengers, forming words rapidly, enunciating clearly.

"None of you can afford the price of a cabin so you are all going steerage," he said. "You've probably heard horror stories about the dark, rank, claustrophobic space between decks known as the steerage compartment. Some of you have already slept there."

Amen, Brother Brigham. Ann sneezed into her handkerchief, breaking the reverent silence that prevailed in the hall.

Brigham paused at the sound. He sent Ann a cheery smile, then continued in a very serious tone.

"We have inspected the steerage compartment on the *Echo* and find it suitable, a little better than most ships. It is up to you to keep it that way. You will comprise about fifty percent of the steerage passengers, so be leaders, not followers. Keep it clean and tidy. Brother Browett and his six assistants will have rules relative to baggage, food, taking care of slop buckets, and so on. If the steerage compartment starts smelling like a cesspool, you have no one to blame but yourselves. Many of you are going to get seasick. It is inevitable. I was seasick most of the time on my voyage over here. We are giving you a supply of lime for fumigation. Keep using it all the way to New Orleans. We don't want any of you to contact cholera or any other disease. I don't want to alarm you, but I have heard some vessels lose ten percent or more of their steerage passengers to various diseases. We can't stress this strongly enough—keep the steerage compartment clean."

Ann coughed, clutching her throat.

Brigham's voice hardened. "Now let me say a word or two about your food. The packet-line clerks we've been dealing with have recommended that you take aboard enough food to last six weeks. As you know, we've counseled you to pack enough for eight or nine weeks, just in case. If you don't have enough food, go buy some more. I hope you've included a good selection of the staples—sugar, molasses, rice, treacle, hard bread, raisins, cheese, potatoes, and oatmeal. If you can afford it, take a little dried beef. There will be live animals on board for slaughter, but they will be for the cabin passengers and crew only. We are sending some extra cooking grates with you. Were it not so, you would have to all use the galley and would practically starve to death waiting to use it. We have made certain the captain has approved of the cooking grates. We have secured some coal for them as well. Also, we advise you to take extra drinking water with you. The two tanks on board the *Echo* are enough for all the passengers, but it is not dispensed frequently enough to suit most passengers. Only three pints per day. If you have a little extra water you can even take an occasional spit bath."

Devoid of sleep the night before, Ann felt drowsiness settle in.

"I have instructed Brother Browett but will repeat to you: watch your food carefully. We have reports that unscrupulous sailors, sometimes even the captains and mates, will pilfer passenger food, and send it back on a tender and pocket the money for it. Don't worry about buying any of the guidebooks being sold by vendors. We've examined them and find them mostly filled with impractical instructions. Just follow what Brother Browett and his committee tell you."

Ann blinked, fighting the urge to sleep. She swallowed. The pain aroused her.

"I mentioned the sailors. Watch them. The crews of many of the packet ships are far from sympathizing with the lot of steerage passengers and rather frequently add to their woes. Some sailors try to force their intentions upon female passengers. And they might try to steal from you. Liquor among the sailors and other passengers will flow frequently. Drink will often promote outright sadism, so be careful."

Those remarks stung Daniel's sense of responsibility. He thought of the young single women in his company. His sister, Rebecca. Hannah's sister, Jane. Plus Hannah Stockton and Harriet Cheese. *God forbid anything to happen to them, or to any of the married women.*

Brigham invited Willard Richards to speak, the man who had been the

Prophet Joseph Smith's personal physician. As he stood, Ann reeled in surprise at the Apostle's height and width. For the benefit of the *Echo* passengers, he told of himself. Willard had been born in 1804 in Massachusetts, into a family of eleven children. Father served in the War of Independence. Baptized by Brigham Young, December 1836. Highly educated, former schoolteacher. Expert in botanical cures. Mission to England in 1839.

Willard's tone also was serious. "The ship will have a doctor. But few ship's doctors care to venture into the steerage compartment. They are there mainly to tend to cabin passengers. I'm glad to see Sister Browett in your company. She has been studying to become a midwife. She tells me she assisted another midwife in the delivery of three babies. She has studied Aristotle's book and the theory of botanical cures. I wish I were going with you, but that is impossible. I must stay here and help Elder Young. I repeat what he has said about the steerage compartment. Keep your quarters clean, and you will avoid the three diseases that sometimes run rampant on these packet ships—cholera, smallpox and typhus."

Cholera, smallpox, typhus. Startled, Ann blinked again.

"Typhus is a lice-borne disease, we know that. It afflicts the victim's skin and brain, causing dizziness, headaches and pain all over the body. It's better to prevent it than try to treat it. The ship's doctor probably wouldn't know how to treat those diseases, anyway.

"Theoretically, every emigrant who boards the *Echo* is required to have a medical examination by a government doctor. We can verify that all our Mormon passengers have complied. But we don't know about the other passengers. Sometimes the examination is cursory, if made at all."

Willard's remarks did nothing to brighten Ann's sour mood. Vivid negative images of the ocean voyage began to sweep over her. She plunged into a horrid gloom as she learned that more than five hundred vessels were counted as wrecked on the Atlantic route between Liverpool and the United States last year alone. Twenty vessels had been reported missing.

As Ann's lips pushed to a pout, Hannah touched her mother on the shoulder. "Isn't this exciting, Mama?"

Ann Eagles frowned at Hannah's words, a fever racking her body. She gave up the attempt to fight her drowsiness. Within minutes she fell into a troubled sleep, leaning against her daughter, dreaming of her voyage. *Black skies. Pouring rain. Hurricane force winds. Seasickness. Disease. Lack of sanitary facilities. Ship off course. Late arrival in New Orleans. Or no arrival at all.*

"Mama, wake up. It's time to go back to the ship. We've got shopping to do." Hannah held in her hand a written list of recommended supplies per person: hard biscuits, flour, oatmeal, rice, peas, sugar, beef, pork, and potatoes. The Brethren had issued a stern warning. Much of the meat sold near the quays would be either horsemeat or imported dried elephant meat, not beef or pork. Much of the flour and oatmeal would be dirty and infested.

Ann woke slowly. Her head throbbed. She coughed a painful cough, clutching her Book of Mormon.

"What did I miss?" she whispered. Out of the corner of her eye she could see Robert conferring with Brigham Young, Willard Richards, John Taylor, Daniel, and the other leaders of the Mormon company who had the responsibility to get her to Nauvoo.

"Elder Young spoke again," Hannah responded, helping her mother to her feet. "He compared us to the first Pilgrims. Their motivation was religious freedom. That was two hundred years ago. A lot of people are leaving Great Britain these days because of political upheaval and famine. We're an exception to that. We're leaving because we're heeding the call to Zion, to gather where the Church is headquartered, to strengthen the Church."

Hannah thought of another reason Robert and she were glad they were leaving England. Taxes. It seemed as though the British government was doing all it could to squeeze, abuse, and plunder its citizens. There were taxes of every imaginal kind. Taxes for living. Taxes for dying. Taxes for smoke going up a chimney. Taxes for light coming through a window. Taxes that stifled achievement. Excessive, confiscatory, tyrannical. In America, Hannah had heard, the tax burden was light. Especially in Nauvoo.

The Mormons poured out of the hall onto the street. Men, women, and children began their walk back to the *Echo*. A soapbox preacher stared at them.

"One of those ministers yelled at us the day we got here," Hannah told her mother. "Called us Latter-day *Satanists.*"

Her mother cringed. The anti-Mormon movement had reached Liverpool. Satan was busy everywhere, stirring up sentiment against the Savior's Church. "I'm not in the mood to be called names. What else did Elder Young say?" Ann sneezed into her handkerchief.

"Oh, lots more," James said, clutching a pale Nancy Eagles. "And Elder John Taylor congratulated us on heeding the call to Zion. He said we will find an inner peace in Nauvoo, a place where we can live a life devoted to the Savior. He wants us to set an example for unity and cooperation, and to keep our baptismal covenants. Once the temple is built there, we'll be able to make other covenants that will contribute to our exaltation. He talked about the temple for several minutes."

John Taylor had emigrated to Canada in 1832 and converted to the Mormon faith in 1836. He became an apostle two years later and accompanied Wilford Woodruff to England early in 1840.

Ann turned her gaze to Nancy. "Are you feeling well?"

"I'm fine," she fibbed. "I was listening all the time. Elder Taylor challenged us to replace human failings with Christian values of love, charity, humility, patience, and benevolence." She managed a faint smile. Listening to the talks by the Church authorities had heightened her desire to live in Nauvoo and assist with the efforts to build the temple.

A light gleamed in the eye of Jane, the youngest sister, who strongly resembled Hannah and Nancy. "He told us all to put off the natural man. We need to go to Nauvoo with the idea in mind to help build the temple, sustain the poor, and support our Church leaders."

"And a lot of practical advice, too," Hannah added. "He mentioned tent material. We have that. Remember? We may have to live in a tent until Robert can build us a house out of logs. There are so many new converts in Nauvoo that it has created a housing shortage."

Ann blew her nose.

"I liked the letter he read from another British convert, already in Nauvoo," Elias said.

Ann looked puzzled, and curious.

"It was from a Brother Moon. He says to remember that it takes five dollars to make an English pound, and there are a hundred cents in one American dollar. A month old pig sells for twenty-five cents in Nauvoo. A good cow will cost fourteen dollars. Flour is four dollars and fifty cents a barrel, and you get a hundred and ninety-six pounds in a barrel."

"How can you remember all that?"

"He's ruddy smart, like me," Henry said, patting himself on the chest. "Moon said in his letter that we'll be able to sell our potatoes for twenty cents a bushel, and beef and pork for three cents a pound."

Ann gasped at the report. Compared to England, Nauvoo sounded like heaven.

She blew her nose again. Such a hard decision.

5

ANN EAGLES HUDDLED BENEATH her wool blanket. She had reluctantly heeded the request that all steerage passengers disembark. Now she found herself standing in a line, wearing a double layer of clothing, her mood still sour, waiting for the packet-line agent to check her ticket. She did not like the fact that she was going to have to pay a New Orleans poll tax.

Robert stood at the head of the line with Daniel, and the other assistants, ready to count each Mormon passenger. More baggage was carted up the gangplank, thrust into the steerage compartment, and into the hold. Port medical practitioners appointed by the emigration office were inspecting both passengers and medicine chests. Their stamp was required before any passenger could board. They quickly rejected a pauper cripple, refusing the old man passage.

Other problems arose. An Irishman who had paid a small deposit for his family, pleaded poverty. His wife had an infant at her breast.

"I have not a farthing left to my name," the Irishman said, crying. Just as the authorities were booting the family off, Daniel quickly took up a collection from the Mormons. The Irish family remained.

A Scottish woman held a nine-year-old child to her breast, asking free passage for the child. She was laughed to scorn by the crew.

There was hustle-bustle everywhere. Passengers were dancing to violin music. In another area a bagpipe was playing. Some well-wishers were jovial. Others were crying, knowing they'd never see their departed loved ones again.

Straining, looking to the right and to the left, Ann forced out painful words through her sore throat. "I still don't see George or William. I guess they've forgotten about me already." Big tears rolled down her reddened cheeks. She made no attempt to dash them away.

To the west, where the *Echo* would sail, the skies were dark. Dockworkers were predicting rain and snow. The wind was from the north, biting.

Young Jane's faith was strong, evident in her words. "They will be here, Mama. They promised. They probably traveled all night on the train. They love you. We all love you."

"Don't dote on me. There are so many memories," Ann continued, dabbing at tears. "I don't know if I can do this."

Hannah took a decisive tone. Leaving the grasp of her children, she put her arm around her mother. "Sure you can, Mama. I know we're leaving part of our family behind, but you've got all of us."

"But I feel so rotten," Ann said, burying her head into Hannah's bosom. "The last place I want to die is on the Atlantic Ocean, aboard that ship." She cast a disparaging glance at the *Echo*. The ship strained even harder at her mooring lines, pushed by the wind, creaking, groaning.

Fighting her own nausea, Nancy interrupted. "Half the people who are getting on board have colds, Mama. I don't think anyone is going to die."

"Everyone's going to be seasick, too," Ann lamented. "Especially you." *You must be pregnant.*

Nancy turned, trying to hide her embarrassment.

Ignorant of his mother's concerns, the face of Elias remained lit with excitement. "I hear seasickness comes and goes. It comes the minute you get on the ship, and goes the minute you step off onto dry land again." He entertained no thought of turning around and going back to Apperley.

His remarks brought a rebuke from Nancy. "Not funny, Elias."

"Mother!"

Ann's face brightened. The voice was familiar. Two men approached the line of steerage passengers, weaving through crates, barrels, hogsheads, peddlers, and hundreds of people saying their final good-byes.

"Mother! We're here!"

"George! William!"

Hannah's oldest brothers embraced their mother.

"The train was late," George said. "Sorry. I'm glad we found you."

Ann collapsed into William's broad chest. Her voice was muffled, but the words shocked Hannah. "Take me home, please," she sobbed.

A flush of red crawled up Hannah's spine. "Mother, no…" Nancy, James, Elias, Jane, Henry, and Katherine reeled in disbelief.

Ann ignored her daughter. Her voice was raspy, but firm. "I'm sick. I'm homesick. I'm too old to go on this trip. Take me home, please."

This scene of confusion was interrupted by the appearance of the ship's captain, leaning from the main deck of the ship. He brought a seventeen-inch-long brass-speaking trumpet to his mouth. His name was inscribed just above its flared bell. His voice boomed. "Welcome to the *Echo*. My name is Captain Josiah Wood. I have just a few things to say, then you may board the ship for the trip to America."

Hannah momentarily looked up at the bearded, smartly uniformed man who was speaking. Though he was only a little taller than average, Captain Wood gave the impression of towering height. The shoulders beneath his blue jacket were wide and powerful. His face was gaunt with a heavy jaw, covered with a gray-flecked dark beard. His eyes were set deep in bony sockets. Hannah suspected that he had already briefed his cabin passengers, probably in the plush dining room over morning tea.

William's voice distracted Hannah's gaze. "Are you certain, Mother?"

The answer stabbed at Hannah.

"Yes, take me home." Ann tugged at William's coat. She took her first step away from the ship.

The captain's voice boomed again. "This sailing vessel was built in New York City six years ago, and has been across the Atlantic Ocean many, many

times and will get you across it this time, you can be assured. Each trip aston-
ishes even God Almighty with our crew's seafaring ability. We should run at
ten knots and with good winds we'll get you there in around six weeks—if we
don't have adverse weather. I'm glad we're sailing for the southern port of New
Orleans rather than New York because we have a better chance of avoiding the
icebergs. But until we get farther south in a couple of weeks the ocean water
will be dreadfully cold. Keep track of your children and each other. If someone were pitched overboard they would freeze to death in a short time, if they
didn't drown first. The water temperature is right at freezing."

"She must be serious," George said, rolling his eyes at Hannah in confusion. Shrugging, he followed William and his mother.

Hannah cast a concerned glance at Robert, who seemed unaware, his
gaze riveted on the captain. Placing her three children under Katherine's care,
Hannah waddled after her mother and two brothers. Nancy, Henry, Elias, and
Jane trailed after her.

Captain Wood's voice boomed behind them, very audible. "There is no
other body of water like the North Atlantic. It is unpredictable, violent and
treacherous, especially this time of year. We have recently heard of a ship
departing from Liverpool that was forced by foul weather to seek haven in a
Norwegian port. And that is north of here, opposite of where we want to go,
which is south."

Hannah cringed at the remarks, tears welling up. *I hope Mama's not listening. I don't have much chance of changing her mind as it is.*

Captain Wood wore a saucy grin. "We seamen speak of crossing the
Atlantic in terms of uphill and downhill. The uphill route is what we are taking, from Europe to America. That's because the prevailing winds are wester-
lies. We will encounter headwinds most of the way. Our ship will buck the
wind, so we will be tacking much of the time. It takes at least ten days longer
to sail from Europe to the United States than it does from the United States
to Europe."

Hannah could see her two brothers gesturing, talking with her mother in
front of the customhouse. Hurrying her pace, she poked at her sister, Nancy.

"Are you in a family way?"

Nancy blushed, the redness apparent. The captain's voice seemed distant, but she focused on his words, not on those of Hannah's.

Captain Wood searched the eyes of his steerage passengers. "If you've never sailed before this may be the most miserable six weeks of your life. Our crew is used to it. We won't get seasick. You will. We won't mind the pitching of the ship in the huge waves. You will. We won't mind that your berths are not heated. You will."

Hannah pulled on Nancy's arm. "I asked you a question."

"How did you know?"

"You were sick on the train, and again this morning. I've been through this four times, you know," Hannah said, poking at her stomach.

Nancy shrugged off her sister's concern. "You lived through morning sickness. I will too."

"But I wasn't about to get on a ship. Did you throw up this morning?"

"Just a little."

Hannah winced. The captain's voice was still discernable.

"I tell you all of this just to prepare you," Wood was saying. "If our voyage turns out to be more pleasant than the picture I've painted, very well. But at least I warned you of the worst that might happen. Once we get far enough south and far enough west, conditions will moderate. By the time we pass through the Caribbean the ocean will be calm, and the weather warm. You will be veterans of the sea and want to sign up as sailors."

Pausing to signal the end of his speech, Captain Wood yelled, "All aboard!"

With Daniel and his assistants looking on, the packet-line agent began the tedious job of checking tickets and calling the roll. Brigham Young and Willard Richards stepped on board, ready to accompany the *Echo* as she was tugged down the River Mersey by a powerful steamer. They would return on the steamer, continuing their mission for a few more months.

Squinting, Robert was baffled at the sight of the Eagles family huddled in the distance. He continued to help verify each Mormon passenger to the agent. Minutes later he could see the Eagles family breaking up into two groups. Head hanging down, Hannah led one group toward the ship.

"Where's your mother?" Robert asked, raking a curious gaze over his wife. Behind him, port officials began searching the ship for stowaways. Soon, one was found, concealed in a trunk. The search would continue for another twenty-four hours, until the *Echo* was released by the steamer.

A lump formed in Hannah's throat. Tears sprang to her eyes again, spilling down her reddened cheeks. "She's on her way home. She took Elias and Jane with her. George will be here in a few minutes with a carter to retrieve their baggage."

Robert gulped. *She didn't even say goodbye.*

The boatswain's call was distinct. "All hands up! Up anchor, ahoy!"

CHAPTER NOTES.

According to the Mormon Immigration Index, available from any Family History Center, Church of Jesus Christ of Latter-day Saints, the *Echo* departed Liverpool on February 11, 1840. The captain's last name was Wood. The author took the liberty to give him a first name: Josiah.

The Mormon passengers were: John Bailey, Richard Birch, Thomas and Dianah Bloxham and children, Caroline Braddock, Daniel and Elizabeth Browett, Martha Browett and daughter Rebecca, John and Mary Cheese and children, Peter Cook and children, John and Elizabeth Cox and child, Isaac and Ann Dunn, James and Hannah Dyson and children, Ann Eagles and children, Elias and Jane; Henry and Katherine Eagles, John and Alice Ellison, Elias English, John Field, Edward and Sarah Fielding and children, William Glover and child, Joseph and Eliza Halford and children, Robert and Hannah Harris and children, William and Eliza Jenkins, James Kershaw, Elizabeth Lambert, James and Ann Lavender, Giles Lloyd, James and Hannah Lord and children, Thomas and Elizabeth Margaret and children, John and Ann Newman and children, Edward and Mary Ockley and children, Henry and Ann Parker and children, James and Nancy Pulham, Levi and Harriet Roberts and children, James Robins, James Shelton, Mary Stockton and children, John and Alice Tagne, James Waters, Ralph Whitehead, Eli Whittle, David and Alice Wilding and children, and David Wilson and children.

6

CAPTAIN JOSIAH WOOD STRUTTED along the forecastle like a red rooster. While in Liverpool he had dined with Charles Dickens at the plush Adelphi Hotel. Dock engineer Jesse Hartley, in the throes of designing the soon-to-be-famous Albert Dock, had asked for his opinions. And he had sipped gin tonics with Samuel Cunard, who revealed his plans to organize a transatlantic steamship company.

A rare smile formed on Wood's face as he watched his passengers wave handkerchiefs and banners at family and friends standing at the quay. His Mormon passengers began singing hymns, which brought a pang of spiritual familiarity to his soul that stretched back to his youth. Through mystified eyes he watched two Mormon leaders, called Apostles—Brigham Young and Willard Richards—serpentine through steerage passengers, all taking their last visual sweep of Liverpool's docks and quays. Some were feeling their first regrets at leaving England. Captain Wood wondered if his Mormon passengers would be anything like the people he transported to New York in late 1839. They were "Old Lutherans," emigrating from Prussia in protest of the state church there. A thousand of them had moved overland to Liverpool where they boarded five ships, including the *Echo*. He later heard that some of them founded the community of Freistadt in Wisconsin, while others erected Trinity Old Lutheran Church in Buffalo, New York.

The *Echo* was being towed by steamship down the twenty-seven mile stretch of the River Mersey to the Irish Sea. The ship passed Birkenhead and its famous docks, with masts of vessels towering in the air, then New Brighton.

As instructed, the captain of the Mormons, Daniel Browett, along with Brigham Young and Willard Richards, joined the captain on the forecastle to hear his lecture to the crew. Not knowing he would be offending the three Mormons' sense of smell, Captain Wood lit a cigar and let it protrude between his crooked teeth as the ship passed respectable examples of Edwardian architecture along the bank. Soon the ship would pass Fort Perch Rock, a red sandstone coastal defense battery, armed with eighteen guns.

The captain was not in a particularly good mood. There were reports of the crew already arguing over space in their small living compartment, which they shared with coils of rigging, spare sails, old junk, and ship stores which had not yet been stowed away. Complaints were many. A large hawser had been coiled away on one seaman's chest. Personal hats and boots had all been fetched away and gone over to leeward. Blankets had been jammed under boxes. A sailor claimed that his Salem sea chest had been broken open, his accordion damaged, and his razor and strop stolen.

Wood's sour mood showed in his characteristic remarks to the crew. For effect, he held a braided leather bludgeon in his right hand. His hand was adorned with a small tattoo he described as "The Jerusalem Cross." He began to speak. "We're beginning another long voyage, my men. If we get along, we shall have a comfortable time. If we don't, then you have hell afloat. All you have to do is do your duty like men, and you'll fare well enough. If you don't, you'll fare hard enough. If we pull together, you'll find me a clever fellow. If we don't, you'll find me a bloody rascal."

Daniel shuddered at the captain's honesty.

The captain continued: "Many of you are new to the ship. Some of you have no experience. Like it or not, you'll learn to become sailors. If you obey orders, you'll be treated fairly. If not, you'll suffer for it. We not only have passengers aboard, but a full load of English crockery and textiles. We earn top freight rates if we reach New Orleans on time."

Captain Wood cracked the bludgeon against the bulwark.

For Daniel's benefit, and the crew's, the captain rehearsed the ship's rules. Fire will be lit on the ship's stove each morning at six. Every passenger not hindered by sickness shall get up no later than seven. The fire shall be put out at eight at night. All passengers to be in their bunks by ten. Passenger quarters to be swept out each morning before breakfast, and the sweepings to be thrown overboard. The deck in the passenger's quarters to be scraped weekly. Water to be distributed to the passengers each morning. Lamps to be lit in steerage after dark and burned until ten at night. Tobacco smoking not permitted below deck, nor the use of an open flame of hay or straw. Cooking utensils must be washed after use. Bedding must be brought up on deck once or twice a week to be aired out. Clothing may not be washed or hung up to dry below deck, but each week, as conditions permit, a day will be determined for general washing. Gunpowder forbidden. Cards or dice not allowed on board, they easily lead to quarrels. Games and entertainment are permitted as long as they contribute to the general good health of the passengers. Passengers must not speak to the man at the helm. It is taken for granted that every passenger is obligated to obey the orders of the captain.

Daniel wrote down the captain's rules, squinting at his memory. He was momentarily distracted by the discovery of another stowaway, found concealed in a barrel.

The captain struck his bludgeon against the bulwark again. "I've taken the liberty to have the mates search every sea chest and duffel bag in your quarters."

A combined gasp roared through the sailors.

Adams and Evans strolled through the stunned men, displaying a collection of pistols, bowie knives, gulleys, daggers, slingshots, and knuckle-dusters.

"Throw those things overboard," Captain Wood commanded.

Many of the sailors continued to gasp as a series of splashes rocked their ears.

The captain then issued an order for the seamen to form a single line and file past the ship's carpenter, nicknamed Chips, who stood at an anvil. With amazing dexterity, he knocked off the tip of the sailor's knife each man carried in his belt.

"We won't throw all knives overboard," the captain stated. "You would be helpless as a sailor without something to cut open stubborn knots. But without your tips, you'll be less dangerous when troubles arise between you. I warn you that our first mate has dealt with the roughest seamen in the world. If you choose to fight among yourselves, cut, gouge, bite each other, the first mate has my permission to beat you with billets of wood, his knotty fists, an iron belaying pin, a short length of rope, this bludgeon, or the Cat. Flowing blood has a way of correcting the wayward sailor."

As eight bells were struck, Captain Wood tipped his hat. "The first and second mates will now divide you into watches and give all you hearties your work assignments. You'll have port and starboard watches. Four hours on duty, four hours off. When you're off duty for the watch, that doesn't relieve you of work. You'll do any duty we assign you, any time of the day. In a few minutes I expect to see you heaving at the standing rigging, working the sails in the running rigging, climbing up the ratlines. If you have fear of heights, get over it. There will be no pity given greenhorns. You newcomers will soon learn to climb the weather side of the rigging and keep your eyes fastened on your work. No stealing. We gave a sailor twelve lashes last voyage for stealing poultry from the coop. Another got five lashes for dirty and unwashed clothes. The ship's surgeon can't save you from floggings, so don't try. Just behave. That's all I've got to say."

When the *Echo* and its steamer reached the Black Rock Lighthouse in the Liverpool Bay, Brigham Young and Willard Richards prepared to disembark. Brigham unbuttoned his heavy wool overcoat and reached inside his vest.

Brigham's brown eyes locked onto Daniel, standing on the deck with his bony ramshackle frame covered with a wool coat. "We saved you a surprise," Brigham said, handing him a letter. "It's from Elder Woodruff. There's one for Brother Harris, too."

Daniel's blue eyes watered. "I miss him." Elder Woodruff had not only taught and converted him, but also had called him to positions of Church leadership south of the River Severn in Gloucestershire. He served as district president, conference clerk, and missionary companion to the American.

"We miss him too," Brigham said, his voice a choking, reverent whisper. "But I suspect that by the end of the year we'll all be in Nauvoo together."

Daniel opened the letter and read the first few lines. He smiled. "I look forward to sharing this with my family."

"God bless you, Brother Browett."

Waving, shaking as many hands as they could, the two Apostles left the ship and boarded the steamer for the return trip to Liverpool. The *Echo* set her sails for the Irish Sea.

Within minutes Daniel and Robert prepared to share Wilford's letters with Elizabeth, Martha, Rebecca, and Hannah—and her children. Passengers were strung about the ship, some getting settled in their berths, some still enjoying the view of Liverpool Bay.

Daniel had his eyes locked on the Irish Sea, speckled with whitecaps rippling toward the ship before a crisp south-southeasterly. White sails of other ships flickered against the blue-gray water as coastal vessels picked their way through the channel leading to Liverpool. There were several. A rakish, two-masted Chesapeake Bay privateer. A British clipper weighted with porcelain and tea from China. A Black Ball line ship, wall-sided and flat-bottomed, with a sharp bow and straight keel, arriving from New York. A brig with an elaborately carved human figurehead—a woman with a flowing robe, stretching out rounded arms as if pointing the way to Liverpool. A British naval craft, battery fitted with ten cannonades, thirty-two pounders, and a pair of long thirty-twos. A sleek American schooner, the *Justina,* loaded with time-sensitive cargo. A Scottish ship, graced by the figurehead of a Highlander carrying his claymore sword. And ships carrying house flags of more shipping firms than Daniel could count. He made out a couple—Howland & Aspinwall, and A. A. Low & Bro.

Hannah's face was laced with a giddy wave of haughtiness as she contemplated the contents of the letters. "Didn't I tell you Elder Woodruff would find missionary work in London more difficult than in the Malverns?"

The letters revealed that after more than six months of missionary work in London, less than a hundred persons had been converted. Elder Wilford Woodruff had converted six hundred former members of the United Brethren in far less time than that, beginning that early day in March at the John Benbow farm. Daniel recalled an incident Wilford had shared with him in private. Satan came to Elder Woodruff during one of his first nights in London and tried to destroy him. Three mysterious angels clad in bright white saved him.

Robert gave his pregnant wife a grim sigh, recalling his pugilism match in London against Sam Gregory more than a year and a half ago. Gregory had slit Robert's nose open, but Robert rallied to win. "You've been right about London from the very beginning," he said.

"There're too many people living in one place," Hannah said, pressing an index finger into her husband's chest. "London reminded me of the story of the tower of Babel. The Lord ought to scatter them again."

Robert retreated backward, leaning against the bulwark. A spray of seawater licked him in the face. The *Echo* was picking up speed. "Careful, I don't want to fall overboard."

Hannah's dark vision of London began to blur. "I'm just glad you finally joined the Church and gave up pugilism. Otherwise we would be living in that evil city."

Elizabeth felt a pang of truth in Hannah's statement. She began to shiver. "My guess is that Elder Woodruff will be *glad* when he is able to return to Nauvoo. In a few months he'll be on a ship just like this one, headed home. By then, we'll be settled into a new house, one that we own, listening to the Prophet Joseph every Sunday, building the temple."

"Nauvoo. It still sounds so far away," said Hannah, leaning into her husband's chest. "It's going to be our heaven on earth."

Daniel held up a free hand, exposing a palm. "Elder Woodruff cautions us not to have an unrealistic expectation of Zion. The people there are just like us. They are mortals with everyday struggles to face." Inwardly, he was comparing his wife to Robert's. Hannah was pregnant with her fourth child. Elizabeth was still barren. *Why is the Lord withholding us the blessings of children?* he wondered.

"That may be so," Elizabeth said, her green eyes beaming. "But I'm going to dream about how *perfect* I expect it to be. I see a *nice* home with extra bedchambers for my children. A fertile farm. A temple. A city filled with members of the Church. Freedom to worship God as we see fit. *No persecution.*"

Robert laughed inwardly, thinking how Elizabeth resembled their mother, the way she overemphasized certain words when she spoke. From their father, they both inherited a long Roman nose, and sharp features. However, his hair was dark brown. Hers, blond.

"Shall I challenge the Prophet to a wrestling match when we get there?" he joked. "Elder Woodruff says he's never been thrown."

Hannah scoffed. "You've retired from fighting. Remember?" She turned her eyes to Daniel. "Are you going to keep a journal, like Elder Woodruff asks?"

"That's one of the important duties that I have as company leader," Daniel answered. "I've already started it."

DANIEL BROWETT DIARY BOOK ONE

WEDNESDAY Feb. 11, 1841 – I was set apart, by the laying on of hands, to take charge of the company of saints, and lead them to Nauvoo, by Apostles Brigham Young, Willard Richards, and John Taylor, at a council meeting held at 72 Burlington Street, Liverpool. Six assistants were set apart to be my counselors: John Cheese, David Wilding, James Lavender, William Jenkins, Robert Harris, and John Ellison. Passengers are arriving in Liverpool daily to make ready for the voyage. Many are from Herefordshire, Gloucestershire, and Worcestershire. Others are from Preston, and

Manchester. We are all destined for the colonies of the saints in the state of Illinois, and in the territory of Iowa. Passage has been secured on the Echo for two pounds seventeen shillings six demies for adults and nineteen shillings and three demies for children. Passengers provide their own provisions, bedding and cooking utensils. Their luggage goes free. In total, there will be more than 200 steerage passengers and I would guess around an additional 50 cabin passengers. Our ship, the Echo, has already arrived in Liverpool and is anchored near the customhouse. Stevedores are unloading its cargo from America. We have secured permission for the outgoing passengers to sleep on the ship even though it does not leave until next Tuesday.

My mother, Martha Browett, and my sister, Rebecca, have accompanied my wife and me. Parting from my relatives, especially my brothers, was very painful. Feelings of a peculiar nature arose in my bosom as we separated. My brother, Thomas, gave me a present of thirty shillings. His wife gave us her recipe for meat and potato pie.

THURSDAY Feb. 12 – Daily we are meeting more of the passengers who will join our company on the trip to America. Most of them are the industrious poor who are upon the point of starvation in this land, who have been working like slaves to procure a very scanty subsistence. By the kindness of the brethren they are enabled to escape from worse than Egyptian bondage and go to a country where they can by their industry obtain an inheritance and enjoy plenty for themselves and their children.

FRIDAY Feb. 13 – Some ships have been detained in Liverpool docks through fear of storms. We hear that several vessels have recently been sunk. Two came into the docks, which I saw that had lost their rigging, their masts broken down and otherwise shattered. Robert and Hannah met the Eagles family at the railway station today.

SUNDAY Feb. 15 – Elders Brigham Young, Willard Richards, and John Taylor gave us our final blessings and preached at the Sunday sacrament meeting. All passengers are to be ready to board at 8 o'clock Tuesday morning and all those that had not paid their full passage money or deposited two pounds towards their provisions would be put on shore, luggage and all. Those that had not done so were ordered to go immediately to 72 Burlington Street. There were several that were compelled to borrow. One brother was forced to pawn his clothing.

MONDAY Feb. 16 – We inspected the berths; they are on each side of the ship from one end to the other and one above the other; the first is about three feet from the floor and the second about six feet. Chests and bags are in the midway of the ship. Each one or family has cooking utensils consisting principally of tinware, cups, etc. Each passenger went to work and drove nails round his berth and hung up his cups, etc. Married couples are located in the center of the ship; single passengers are placed at the two extremities, the men at the bow and the women at the stern. We have placed curtains in many of the cabins and berths so as to ensure some privacy. The mate is surprised by the quantity of luggage put on the ship by the Mormons, saying the ship is sitting an inch deeper in the water than normal. Part of the duties of our presidency or six-man committee is to help load the luggage and personal belongings properly.

TUESDAY Feb. 17 – Passengers were loaded this morning. Hannah's mother, along with her younger brother and sister, returned to Apperley. Hannah and Nancy are much saddened. Elders Brigham Young and Willard Richards came on board, and remained with us overnight. About ten o'clock this morning a steamer tugged us out of port and down the River Mersey toward the Irish Sea. Many hundreds crowded around the dock to witness a shipload of sons and daughters of Zion depart from their native shore to the Promised Land. As we moved slowly out of port the saints aboard sang together: "Lovely native land, farewell / Glad I leave thee, glad I leave thee / Far in distant lands to dwell." The Apostles accompanied us about 15 miles to the black rock lighthouse then left on the steamer in good spirits. It was now all hustle and bustle on board for each passenger was trying to get settled on the ship. The captain anchored near the mouth of the river tonight, to give us one night on the ship to get used to it before we encounter the angry seas. The sailor appointed to look after the steerage passengers came down cursing. He told many that if they did not go to bed he would take them and put them in irons. I need to speak to the captain about the seamen's swearing habits.

WEDNESDAY Feb. 18 – We held our Morning Prayer meeting at 7 o'clock. Everyone's water allowance was issued this morning, three pints for each person for each day. A young man from steerage was caught smoking below deck. The sailors took him before the first mate. He was ordered to be taken to the poop deck and tied up by the hands to the mast. Captain weighed anchor about 10 o'clock and hoisted sail against a fair wind, moving away under the flag of liberty—the American stars and stripes, with a majesty seldom passed. The saints were all on deck and in good spirits. We sang a favorite hymn, "How Firm A Foundation," as we got underway. Everyone waved their hats and handkerchiefs as a last token of farewell as England shrank from our view.

THURSDAY February 19 – At 7 o'clock in the morning the bell sounded for all to arise. There is a strong headwind and it moves the ship to and fro. No fires on board, nothing cooked; those who can, eat biscuits and cold water. Most passengers are now seasick and confine themselves to their berths. Cabin companions are huddled together, one holding a basin. Many are on their hands and knees in evident misery. Some fear a watery grave. Captain Wood warns of the cold water; says not to let anyone go overboard. We hourly are giving administrations to the sick, anointing with oil, and giving blessings. Sister Nancy Pulham is very sick. We saw a number of sea creatures called porpoises. Daily prayer meetings, morning and evening. Captain put a sailor in chains for being drunk on duty.

CHAPTER NOTES

Daniel Browett's diary is fictitious. The author believes he kept one, based on the fact that he was a conference clerk in England, and that he was probably encouraged by Wilford Woodruff and the other Apostles to keep a diary or journal. However, an actual diary, at the date of this writing, has never been found.

The accounts in this novel, both in the narrative and in Daniel's fictitious diary, dealing with ocean travel, are taken from many sources. The author has compiled many actual events of other Mormon immigrant voyages into the fictional account of the *Echo*'s voyage. Even though the *Echo* is the actual name of the ship used by the Browett Company, no detailed information of the voyage was available.

According to Wilford Woodruff's journal, he wrote letters addressed to Daniel Browett and Robert Harris on January 27, 1841.

ROUTE OF THE *ECHO*

7

A RISING TREPIDATION SWEPT OVER Daniel. He stood on the fore-castle, gazing southwest, across the sea. As captain of the Mormons, he con-templed the task before him. In a small wooden ship driven by cloth sails, he must deliver one hundred and nine souls safely across the Atlantic Ocean to New Orleans, and from there by steamboat up the Mississippi to Nauvoo.

With his stomach not feeling particularly stalwart, he scanned the Irish Sea as the *Echo* tacked west. The seas were rolling high, their tops white with foam, the body of them a deep indigo blue, reflecting the bright rays of the cold February sun. Soon the ship would turn south into St. George's Channel, a body of water that separates Wales from Ireland. Next would come the Celtic Sea, where they would begin to lose sight of the British Isles. The treacherous North Atlantic awaited the *Echo,* a tiny spec in the veneer of water that covers seventy percent of the earth's surface.

Daniel had long ago learned that fear was an ally. But he had no idea of the true immensity of the oceans, the enemy Captain Wood must conquer for him. He did not know that the earth's oceans, for example, contain more than 330 million cubic miles of water. Or that the average depth is two miles, or more than 10,500 feet. That there are great oceanic trenches where depths exceed 34,000 feet, monstrous continental slopes dissected by submarine canyons. That the Mid-Oceanic Ridge is actually the greatest mountain range on earth.

There were other facts that Daniel probably did not know about the ocean. Mountains rise from the seabed floor, some of them forming islands. How surface currents are driven by the wind. How thermohaline currents move deep in the ocean. And he really did not know of the endless varieties of sea life—the home of great whales: Blue, Beluga, Humpback, Orca, and Sperm.

Immediately around the *Echo,* the surface temperature of the water hovered at only thirty-two degrees. A man overboard could die in less than an hour. Immediately to the north, ice covered the Labrador Sea, the Denmark Strait, and the Norwegian Sea. Great icebergs broke away constantly. Last night, as he gazed heavenward, Daniel wondered, *is planet earth the only member of the solar system to have an ocean?*

If the ocean were Daniel's *Enemy Number One,* the weather was *Enemy Number Two.* Sailors could be seen giving their oilcloth suits and stout boots another thick coating of grease and tar, preparing for the time they would have to fight biting winds, freezing rain, and snowstorms to keep the ship afloat. He had been constantly reminded that February was one of the worst months for crossing the Atlantic. Packet ships such as the *Echo,* loaded with cargo and passengers, sat low in the water, heavy, inviting angry seas to wash her fore and aft. Man-killing weather sometimes continued for two or three weeks without intermission. Late sunrises and early sunsets meant nearly sixteen hours of darkness every day at fifty-three degrees north latitude, the ship's current position. Not a pleasant thought.

There is another threat, Daniel thought. *The crew. Enemy Number Three.* He knew little about them. Mostly Yankees, four Italians, one Englishman, two Scotsmen, two Welchmen, one Irishman, three Frenchmen, one Dutchman, one Austrian, one German, two Spaniards, two native Indians from South America, one Negro, one Mulatto. And others of questionable descent. Some victims of a press gang, going through taverns, pubs, grog shops, and brothels, winding up on the *Echo.*

He leveled his gaze at them. An Italian darning winter stockings, his face looking as though it had barely survived the most obstinate assaults of the winter weather. The Dutchman lining his monkey jacket with an old flannel shirt. A Spaniard drinking a hot cup of tea, warming his hands, munching on a hard biscuit. The Scotsman standing near the pigsty, sheep pen, oxen pen, and the hencoop, tending to his animals and birds. The Negro assistant cook, standing at the galley, a kid of beef in his hand. One of the South American Indians, beaten with a rope so severely by the French captain of another ship that he still had a hard time lifting his hands to his head. The lone British sailor, dubbed "Lobster" by the other crewmembers, because of an old Navy overcoat he carried.

Who could be trusted? Who could not? Heywood had told him of the difficulty all ships had in hiring a good crew, trying to compete with princely wages offered by the shops and saloons of American ports. Too many crewmen were derelict crimps virtually kidnapped off waterfronts in exchange for an advance in pay. Many a seaman, newly returned from a voyage, would saunter into a bar or brothel and the next day awaken from his stupor to find himself on another ship. Some saloon operators purposefully doped the drinks of sailors, scooped up the drugged man, held him in the basement, and sold him to the highest bidder to become an imprisoned sailor.

Daniel thought of Brigham Young's warning. *Beware of certain sailors who have lustful eyes for the young women.*

Daniel cast a glance at his sister, Rebecca, huddled in the cold wind with Elizabeth and Martha, trying to enjoy the view of Ireland off the starboard bow. Despite the big Browett nose, a mark of French ancestry, and rather irregular front teeth, Rebecca had developed into one of the belles of Apperley during their last two years there. She was a tall blonde with a sulky demeanor and a lively personality. Her mouth, skin, and blue eyes were lovely; her thin figure so striking that it is no wonder she had already become an object of lust among the sailors of the ship.

She seemed so vulnerable.

The crushing burden of his responsibilities screamed at Daniel. He suddenly felt alone. He thought of his reccurring dream. He was alone in a canoe.

He was gently rowing across a river in a mist of great darkness. The waters cast him about until he came to a fork in the river. He had to choose which way to go. He kept choosing the right fork, and as he did so the mist became a little lighter but the waters rougher. His goal was to reach the light he could occasionally see through the mist. When he could see the light, it was bright, inviting, and peaceful. But every time he paddled hard to reach it, he woke up.

Daniel wondered if there would be any correlation between his old dream and his new voyage across the Atlantic.

At that very moment, in the dank interior of the ship, *Enemy Number One* was claiming its first victim in the form of seasickness. Her stomach felt it first, a faint queasiness, like a nest of rats moiling inside. Nancy Eagles Pulham, two months pregnant, rose from her berth, staggered toward the ladder with James at her side, and stopped suddenly in her tracks.

"I'm not going to make it topside," she said weakly. Her face was pallid and white. She was consciously aware of the stares of dozens of passengers.

James scanned the dark, gloomy confines of the steerage compartment until his eyes found a wooden bucket, sliding slowly to the port side, as the ship tilted.

Nancy's body, inner ear, and eyes were sending different signals to her brain, resulting in confusion and nausea. Her system was not adapting to its new surroundings, the movement of the ship on a fluid, rolling sea. Nancy's visual stimulus was misleading her brain, trying to tell her that the berths, cabin walls, and boxes scattered around the steerage compartment were stable when they were not. She should not have tried reading, but she did. She should not have gone below, but she did. She should not have tried sleeping, but she did.

She should have stayed on the main deck, facing forward, taking deep breaths of fresh air, locking her eyes on either the coast of Wales or the coast of Ireland, but she did not.

Nancy vomited.

James grimaced. "Lay back down. I'll tell Daniel you're sick."

There was a faint nod of the head. Her voice was weak but determined. "I'll be fine. Just get me to Nauvoo."

"I know you will, sweetheart. I'll get some help."

James rushed to the main deck, where he was greeted by strong winds that had puffed out every sail like a pigeon's breast. He looked at the sky. It was sullen, and gray. He let his gaze fall to the cold cauldron of seething seawater below, staring at the jagged masses of waves, which were leaping like gray-bearded demons in some kind of weird witch dance of the sea. Never resting, always threatening.

He dumped the contents of the bucket overboard, scanning the main deck. He climbed onto the poop deck. Aft, he saw the smoking compartment, located in front of the wheelhouse. A message was scribbled on the door.

Meeting in progress. Do not disturb.

James knocked.

David Wilding opened the door.

James peered inside, his forehead corrugated with worry lines. He saw his cousin, Daniel, with whom he had shared the secret of his wife's pregnancy. "Nancy is sick. She's throwing up. So are a few others."

From a velvet-cushioned bench, Daniel looked up. "I'm not surprised. I suspect that most of us will be that way sooner or later. Tell everyone to use the buckets. We don't want the compartment to smell like a pig swill."

James nodded his understanding.

"Find Elizabeth," Daniel added. "She can help."

James closed the door, and began a search for Daniel's wife. There was a prayer in his heart. *Please, God. Make my wife better. I don't want to face Nauvoo alone.*

Daniel returned to the business of his meeting, quickly reviewing instructions he wanted his assistants to enforce. Scrub quarters daily. Sprinkle quarters with lime every third day. Haul rubbish up daily and throw it overboard. Air out the bedding. Kill all the rats possible. Because of limited berth space, take turns sleeping. Settle disputes and arguments quickly. Handle complaints quickly and efficiently. Administer to the sick. Make certain everyone addresses one another with respect as "brother" and "sister." Tell everyone to allocate food conservatively in case the trip takes longer than expected. Watch children carefully. Keep them from the sides of the ship.

James found Elizabeth among a crowd of passengers preparing to listen to Captain Wood tell a sea story. He had just emerged from the opulent dining room where he had dined on beef stew and oven-baked bread. He was dressed as though he had just undergone an inspection from President William Henry Harrison of the United States, his clear blue eyes gleaming, and this time smoking a pipe.

James Pulham's voice sounded like dreaded thunder in Elizabeth's ears.

"Where is she?" she asked, her lips curling into a concerned grimace. Hannah had shared her suspicion that Nancy was suffering from early pregnancy sickness.

With James leading the way, she followed him to steerage.

Nancy lay on her berth, her image distorted and pale, like a ghost.

Elizabeth opened her satchel and stared at her collection of castor oil, paregoric, carbonate of soda, laudanum, an assortment of herbs, and composition tea. Several other Mormon passengers were seasick as well, moaning and groaning in their berths, some disgorging into buckets, and others sitting with their heads between their knees. Elizabeth was concerned most about Nancy, however.

A man blasphemed his way down the ladder until he reached steerage. He was short, middle aged, thinning brown hair, and wore thick glasses with wire rims. "I'm the doctor," he announced, still swearing. He smelled of grog. "I'm here to drag the sick out of bed and treat them."

Elizabeth felt her spine tense up. "With language like that, you're not welcome down here. I don't care if you *are* the ship's doctor."

The doctor took off his glasses and stared at the blonde-haired woman who dared talk back to him. "And who are you?" He swore again, with extreme vulgarity.

Daniel's wife poked a finger into the stunned doctor's chest. "Elizabeth Browett. And if you use the Savior's name in vain just once more, I'll *personally* throw you off this ship. If you stay, you *must* apologize. If not, leave and never come back."

There was a round of applause. The doctor narrowed his eyes for a few moments, drew his face into a smirk, cast a furtive glance at young Rebecca, and retreated up the ladder.

A ship's hand, lurking in the shadows, summoned below to help with stowage, began to laugh. He whispered into a passenger's ear. "Shiver me timbers. First time I've seen Old Sawbones scuppered like that. Took a woman ta put the ol' tub in his place."

There were more sharp words from Elizabeth. She screamed upward. "And tell that sailor who was down here *cursing* last night and this morning that we've had enough of him, too. *Got that?*"

More applause from nearly every berth.

Elizabeth turned her attention back to Nancy. "When did your morning sickness start?" she queried, mixing soda with water. "Try this first."

Nancy shook her head. Her voice was weak. "I'll just throw it up. It started a day or two before we left Apperley."

"I'm *not* taking no for an answer. *Down it.* Then you'll need some ginger and honey. It will help your digestion, and reduce your vomiting and cold sweating. Were you sick on the train?"

Nancy took the cup, drew it to her lips, and drank. "Yes," she moaned, waiting for a reaction. *What digestion? I haven't been eating.*

Hannah and Dianah Bloxham descended into the fetid compartment. Their children were still on the deck, watched by their fathers.

"I'm sorry you're sick again," Hannah said to Nancy. She thought of the day Nancy stepped off the train in Liverpool, feeling queasy even then. The memory invoked flashes of her mother. She wondered if her mother were settled back in Apperley, happy with her decision to remain in England. *Mother, how we miss you,* she thought. *Elias, Jane, George, and William, too.*

Nancy moved her eyes slowly upward. Then she made a rapid move, grabbed her bucket, and vomited out the soda water.

Elizabeth shook her head mournfully and mixed the ginger and honey.

The ocean held Captain Josiah Wood, a Bostonian, in an enduring spell. Part of the spell came from the fourfold mystery of its shoreline, surface, horizon, and timeless motion of the sea. A myriad of things fascinated him. The alien world below. The multitude of living things, swimming and darting, living and dying. The interplay of light and reflection between the sea and the sky. The track of sunlight on the water and the rosy color of the clouds. The unique sea smell. The crashing sound of breakers. The glitter of waves dancing under the sun and the moon. The feel of spindrift blowing across his face. The salty, bitter taste of the water. The slim grace of tall sailing ships. How ships disappeared in the ocean, first the hulls, and then the tall masts. Seamen's chanteys. The ocean as a cruel mistress, demanding masculine virtues of courage and strength. The challenge to determine the ship's position at all times.

The captain, in his own way, was a religious man. On clear nights during voyages, no matter how cold the wind and how rough the sea, the captain liked to spend some time alone near the wheelhouse or on deck. The broad dark ocean, the streaming pure air, the crowded stars arching overhead, had always made him feel what the Bible called the spirit of God hovering on the face of the waters. This religious awe, inspired by nights at sea, had always kept him as a believer, although he rarely spoke of this to other sailors, and sometimes his weaknesses gave way to sin. But on every voyage the Almighty was there for him, a presence actual, if disturbingly unpredictable. And it showed in the stories he told.

Joseph Harris, five, and the older Bloxham children—Charles, eight; Lucy, seven; Tommy, six—along with several other children, sat at the captain's feet. With their mothers below helping tend to Nancy, their fathers kept a watchful eye on their children.

"Four years ago March," Wood began, scanning his large crowd, "I was first mate on the ship *William Rhodes* bound for New York. We had fifty-three steerage passengers, nearly all Irish, and full cargo out of Liverpool. Strong squalls damaged some of our sails, but we were still running ten knots under all sail one evening and we struck a field of ice. An iceberg ripped the starboard side. A huge, ugly hole."

Joseph, Charles, Lucy, and Tommy drew a thick wool blanket around themselves, eyes wide open in awe.

Captain Wood stood erect, his chest heaving, his face carrying a smug smile. "We were off the Newfoundland Banks, and I knew we were going to sink. I knew if we sank, the water would freeze us to death in short order."

Joseph's jaw dropped several notches.

The captain paused, letting his words penetrate. Under thick eyebrows, he looked at the ocean. "Just as cold as that," he said, pointing. "You wouldn't last long if you fell overboard."

The children shuddered.

"The crew was ordered to reduce sail and to give up the royals and topgallants, and furl them. We rigged the pumps but we couldn't cope with the rush of water below. We cleared away the longboat, and the jollyboat in the stern was lowered. Both boats dropped astern on their painters. Several of our passengers perished as they made a mad rush for the boats. They drowned in that cold water. The ship sank at midnight, taking with her thirty persons."

His mouth still wide open, Joseph gasped.

A gush of wind swept through the deck. Unfettered, Captain Wood pulled his cap tightly over his head.

"But the good Lord was with us. We lashed together the two boats for awhile and our captain took the names of those who had been saved, then separated the boats and set a course northwest for Newfoundland and advised my boat to do the same. The weather was cold and the sea was rough. We rigged a drag with the oars to keep the longboat's head toward the sea and try to reduce the height of the waves. We talked about the necessity of lightening our load because we were taking in water. That would mean some of the passengers would have to get out of the boat and swim, but they would only last a few minutes in the frigid waters."

The captain paused. Locking his eyes with young Joseph, he smiled and then asked, "Do you know what happened next?"

Joseph shrank, burying his head into the blanket. Robert sat beside him. "Ask him what happened, Joseph."

The child's voice was soft, almost inaudible. "What happened next? Did you drown?"

Chuckles were heard among the crowd.

Captain Wood boomed a laugh. "No, lad. I didn't drown. I'm here to prove it. See, touch me. I'm still alive, aren't I?"

Timidly, Joseph reached out and touched Captain Wood on the hip. More chuckles.

"Young lad, you'll be pleased to know that the American ship *Patrick* spotted us and she took us in just in time. Our captain was picked up by a French lugger on the fishing grounds and carried into St. Pierre. Everyone in both boats was in a dreadful state of exhaustion, but we were well cared for in hospitals."

"Enjoy your voyage, folks," the captain said. He returned the pipe to his mouth and took a deep puff.

8

A DARK FEELING OF INSECURITY rose over Daniel. From the Celtic Sea, gateway to the Atlantic, he could no longer make out the English coast to his left, or the Irish coast to his right. How could a ship like the *Echo* navigate in the open ocean? Especially in bad weather, with no visibility?

He pulled Heywood aside. "How does the captain know where he's going?"

Heywood laughed, sensing the Mormon captain's fears. "It's time you met Neptune."

"Neptune?"

"Our navigator. His real name is Harvey Crump. The captain tagged him with the nickname. Greek god of the seas. By the way, the captain says to tell your wife he has reprimanded both the doctor and the sailor for their language in front of the Mormon passengers."

"Thank you."

Heywood found Neptune in a room with charts strewn across an oak table. An ornate mercury barometer, with a column made of mahogany and brass, and scales of ivory, was fastened to the wall. An odd-shaped box containing some kind of instrument lay on the floor. The captain's medicine chest, containing a collection of medicaments, lay poised on a shelf. A box of signal flags, enabling the captain to communicate with foreign skippers using an international code, lay just below the medicine chest.

Neptune was not overly handsome. Daniel judged him to be in his thirties. He had wisps of gray in his brown hair, probing blue eyes, an arrestingly deep voice, and the carefree smile of a sailor. He was finishing his duff, a sailor's pudding in a wooden bowl, and apple pie. When introduced, he stuck out a hand. "Tip me yer daddle."

Daniel looked perplexed.

"He's offering to shake hands," Heywood explained.

Smiling in relief, Daniel complied.

"Pleased ta meet cha, Captain Browett. I'd remember ya anywhere. Yer the one with the beautiful sister on board, in steerage. Right?"

Daniel shrugged off the comment.

"Ya best 'scuse me. One more bite of me clacker, please." Neptune thrust a final spoonful of apple pie into a mouth surrounded by a full beard.

"Captain Browett is responsible for more than a hundred of our passengers," the steward said. "I think we owe it to him to explain how we navigate the ship. He seems a little nervous about it."

The weary tension of Neptune's face dissolved into a warm, gentle smile. He wiped his mouth. "My pleasure, Cap'n Browett. Where to begin?"

Daniel was still bristling over Neptune's remark about Rebecca. "I'm the student. You're the teacher."

Although it was difficult, Neptune dropped his colloquial sea accent, and did his best to sound educated. "My job's ta always be able to find the ship's position on the ocean by observing the stars or the sun." Neptune reached for a printed booklet. "Ta do that, I need this here *Almanac*. It tells me where the sun, the moon, the planets, and the stars are going to be hour by hour, day by day, even years into the future. And I've got my precious *Waggoner.*"

Daniel thumbed through the *Almanac* and the *Waggoner,* a volume of sea charts, quickly. To his untrained eyes, both were a mumble of confusion.

"Second, I need an accurate chronometer. A way to tell accurate time."

"A clock?"

"Yep, a clock. I'll tell ya why in a few moments." Neptune rustled the papers on the table. Among them were maps that were more the flamboyant expression of a printer than a reliable, usable chart. Others provided information on depths, ocean-bottom contents, and coastal details. "Third, I need these charts. Using 'em, I can establish our position in latitude and longitude, or in reference ta landmasses. Like England, Ireland, the Caribbean Islands, the tip of Florida. And the delta of New Orleans, our destination."

Daniel scratched his head. He was not certain he understood even simple terms like latitude and longitude. He scanned the charts. A wind chart, indicating the directions of prevailing winds throughout the world. Tide charts, revealing that tides in the Atlantic are higher than those in the Pacific. Storm charts, revealing that the Atlantic is the stormiest sea in the world.

"Finally, I need an angle-measuring instrument. A sextant. I use it ta measure the angle of the sun or the North Star above a horizontal line of reference."

Daniel was lost. "A sextant?"

Neptune reached to the floor. He pulled an awkward looking instrument to his lap, coddled in a neat box. "This may look complex t'ya, but ta a trained navigator it's simple ta use. At noon each day, when the sun is at the highest point in the sky, I look through the eyepiece. My vision hits a fixed mirror that's only partially silvered, which enables me ta see the horizon that's beyond the mirror. Another mirror at the end of a moveable arm reflects the sun's image toward the fixed mirror."

Neptune handed the ebony-framed sextant to Daniel. As he braced himself with one hand against the roll of the ship, Daniel held it up, peered through it, and pulled a face.

"Ya won't see anything in here. But outside, when the mirrors are properly aligned, the sun would appear t'ya as if it rests perfectly on the horizon. The angle reading corresponds ta your latitude."

"And if there is no sun?"

"We use the North Star at night. It's a little more complicated. At the North Pole, which is ninety degrees latitude, Polaris, or the North Star, is directly overhead at an altitude of ninety degrees. At the equator, which is zero degrees latitude, Polaris is on the horizon with zero degrees latitude. Even early Arabs used the North Star. They used one or two fingers' width, a thumb and little finger on an outstretched arm, or an arrow held at arm's length. They'd sight the horizon at the lower end, and Polaris at the upper."

Daniel had just come from the deck. There were thick clouds in the sky. "And if you can't see the stars?"

"Good thinkin'," Neptune said. "Because of the weather, I'm navigatin' the ship using an old method called dead reckonin'. Sailors like Columbus used dead reckonin' all the time."

"Dead reckoning?" Daniel had never heard of the term.

"Very simple," Neptune said. "I find my position from a known point, Liverpool, and I measure out a course and distance from that point on the chart ya see on the table." Neptune pushed the chart toward Daniel.

Daniel noted the lines and pinpricks.

"From our startin' point, I measure out my course and the distance we have sailed from that point on my chart. I prick the chart with a pin to mark each new position. Each day's ending position is the starting point for the next day's course-and-distance measurement."

Daniel lowered his brows in deep thought, listening.

"In order for dead reckonin' to work," Neptune continued, "I need a way ta measure my course, and a way ta measure the distance sailed. I can measure the course with my magnetic compass. Sailors have used them since the twelfth century. I just do a time and speed calculation. I multiply the speed of the ship, in miles per hour, by the time ta get the distance we've traveled since the last measurement."

Still squinting, Daniel asked, "And how do you measure speed?"

"We can do it just like Columbus did. I have someone toss a piece of flotsam tied to a string over the side. I have two marks on the ship's rail a precise distance apart. We mark the time when the flotsam passes the forward mark, and when it passes the aft mark. We've been measuring ever' hour since we left Liverpool Bay."

Daniel puffed out his lower lip in disbelief.

"In fact, that's where the term 'knot' came from," Neptune said.

"What do you mean?"

"Remember I told ya the piece of wood or flotsam had a string tied to it? In the mid-sixteenth century, when English navigators began the practice, the length of line let out in a given number of seconds was measured ta determine how far the ship had traveled. Later, calculations were simplified by markin' off intervals in the line with knots. These were spaced so's that the number run out in the time of a sandglass equaled the number of nautical miles the ship ran in an hour. Hence the term, 'knots.' Speeds measured in knots by means of a log were logged, or recorded, in a logbook."

Daniel's eyes were wide open now. "Go back to Columbus. You mean to say he discovered America using that method?"

"Yep. When he departed Spain he merely sailed south to the Canary Islands. Sailors called it 'sailing down the latitude.' From there, Columbus sailed westward across the Atlantic. He covered more than four thousand miles in seventy days of relatively easy sailing. That means he averaged sixty miles a day. When the Pilgrims from your country sailed to America, they could barely average fifty miles a day."

Daniel slowly shook his head. "We're obviously not going to follow the same route as the Pilgrims."

"Naw, we're not. We're gonna use the same method Columbus used, but we'll certainly use the sextant along the way when we have the visibility. We're gonna sail southwest to a point near the Tropic of Cancer, then head due west from there. If the winds are really bad, we might strike out more south than southwest, then strike a course due west. Obviously, that'll take longer."

Daniel pulled a face. *Longer?*

"Let me tell you about latitude and longitude, and the need for an accurate clock."

Captain Browett nodded his agreement.

"Let's use Columbus as an example again," Neptune said. "He sailed south along a certain longitude, the imaginary lines that run north and south.

When he reached the latitude he needed, he turned his ships west. Latitude lines are the imaginary lines that run east and west."

Daniel's face screwed into a puzzle of concern. "But how did Columbus know his latitude?"

Neptune scoffed inwardly. He thought he had covered that with Daniel. "Remember latitude can be determined by the height of the sun at noon in conjunction with its declination, or by usin' the North Star at night."

"And longitude?"

"Dead reckonin' again. More accurately, it's 'deduced' reckonin'. Just like we're doin', mariners would throw a wood chip overboard. The time it took for the chip ta pass from stem to stern measured speed, and the ship's navigator set the ship's hour glass ta local time by the sun at noon."

Daniel scratched his head. "I don't get it."

"Several centuries ago the Greeks observed that longitude could be regarded as a function of time. By carryin' a clock on board, a sailor could find his longitude by readin' the clock's time when the sun was at its highest point, or noon. He'd convert the difference in time ta determine the ship's longitude ta the startin' longitude, usually homeport. Ever' four minutes of difference would indicate one degree of longitude."

"And it actually worked?"

"If'n the sailor had a reliable and accurate clock," Neptune said, running a hand through his dark beard. "And that was a problem. The most accurate clock back then was the pendulum clock. But even when gimbaled, it couldn't keep accurate time at sea. The British Longitude Act of 1714 promised a prize of 20,000 pounds ta anyone who could come up with a solution ta the longitude problem within half a degree."

"I suppose someone won the prize."

"One of your own, actually. An English clockmaker by the name of John Harrison. He eventually constructed a very precise clock that was stable against the movements of the sea. It was large, awkward, and heavy, mounted on springs in a gimbaled case. But it worked. He kept refinin' it. His fourth clock was truly a masterpiece, and small, just a little larger than a pocket watch. During the first months of sea it only lost nine seconds, well within the limits to win the prize. At first your British government only gave him half the money, insisting on additional tests. It took Harrison another forty years of designin', buildin', and refinin' sea clocks before he received the rest of his money, at age eighty. But only after intervention of your King."

"So you have an accurate clock on board the *Echo?*"

Neptune found the clock, covered by a chart. "We call it our chronometer. I use it with the sextant to determine our position. Of course I need my Almanac with tables of sunrises, sunsets, and the declination of the sun for the different dates. Since the time of Ptolemy in the second century, every seafarin' nation used their homeports as a startin' point for measurin' longitude. Several main places and cities became baseline references for longitude, like the Azores, the Canary Isles, Cape Verde, Rome, Copenhagen, Jerusalem, St. Petersburg, Pisa, Paris, and Philadelphia."

"Why was it so important to have a—what do you call it?—a baseline reference for longitude?"

"Stay with me. I'll have ta get even more technical. Unlike latitude, where the earth's axis of rotation determines two poles and a corresponding equatorial starting line, there's no logical startin' point for measurin' longitude. Since latitude is measured in degrees startin' from zero at the equator and endin' at the poles with ninety degrees, it was decided that longitude could be measured in somewhat similar fashion. Since the world revolves once every twenty-four hours, and there are 360 degrees to each rotation, then the world turns fifteen degrees every hour and one degree for every four minutes."

Daniel's head was swimming. He feigned understanding.

"Just as the equator is used ta separate the Northern and Southern Hemispheres, a zero degree meridian, and its extension, the 180-degree meridian, was needed to separate the Eastern and Western Hemispheres. Longitude is now measured both eastward and westward from the prime meridian, zero, to the 180-degee meridian. Because England was the world's greatest seafarin' power over the last two centuries, Greenwich, where the Royal Observatory was located, became the zero meridian. The publication of the first *British Nautical Almanac* in 1767 entrenched Greenwich as the prime meridian almost world-wide."

Heywood took a deep breath as he contemplated the Mormon captain. "Is all this clear, ya old Devil Dodger."

"Devil Dodger?"

"That's what sailors call preachers," Heywood explained, chuckling. To Heywood, it signaled that Neptune liked Daniel.

Daniel chuckled, too. "No. But I suppose I have more confidence that Neptune and the captain know how to get us to New Orleans."

"We might get blown off course," Heywood concluded, "but if we have some sunshine or clear evenin's now and then, the cap'n will always know exactly where we are."

Daniel put a hand to his mouth. *I certainly hope so.*

The ship's galley was placed under the fo'c'sle just aft of the foremast, a sort of bricked-in-kettle with barely enough room for the cook and his assistant to work. The sixty-eight gallon cauldron was made of copper, heavy riveted and divided down the middle into two chambers. This morning the two sections held the usual fare, salt beef on one side and beans on the other. As each sailor approached the galley, he was issued his chunk of salt beef, identified by a small wooden tag, marked with his mess's symbol. He carried his own bowl and spoon, on which his initials were scratched. No matter how the ship tumbled in the open sea, crewmembers ate every morsel.

It was just the opposite for the steerage passengers of the *Echo*. As the odor of salt beef and beans seeped from the cauldron, those who were seasick became worse.

"We may all be sick by nightfall," Elizabeth said, shaking her head while she braced for the next roll of the ship. "Not just Nancy and a few others."

"I'm afraid you're right," Daniel answered, watching his homeland slowly disappear to the east, where patchy fog loomed. Except when swirling stormy winds tore into its sails from a favorable direction, the *Echo* was slow, having a difficult time averaging ten knots like Captain Wood claimed, even under all sail. Despite her feeble sluggishness, the *Echo* carved through the icy water with a deliberate motion, controlled by a crew that deftly responded to the captain's orders. The crew quickly forgot Daniel's request not to use normal seaman's language. Robert determined he was going to keep his young children away from them as much as possible.

Hannah held onto the rail, ducking a spray of seawater, taking stock of the frightening skies that loomed to the south.

WEDNESDAY Feb. 18 – We held our morning prayer meeting at 7 o'clock. Captain weighed anchor about 10 o'clock and hoisted sail against a fair wind, moving away under the flag of liberty—the American stars and stripes, with a majesty seldom passed. The saints were all on deck and in good spirits. We sang a favorite hymn, "How Firm A Foundation," as we got underway. Everyone waved their hats and handkerchiefs as a last token of farewell as England shrank from our view.

THURSDAY Feb. 19 – At 7 o'clock in the morning the bell sounded for all to arise. There is a strong headwind and it moves the ship to and fro. No fires on board, nothing cooked; those who can, eat biscuits and cold water. Most passengers are now seasick and confine themselves to their berths. Cabin companions are huddled together, one holding a basin. Many are on their hands and knees in evident misery. Some fear a watery grave. Captain Wood warns of the cold water; says not to let anyone go overboard. We hourly are giving administrations to the sick, anointing with oil, and giving blessings. Sister Nancy Pulham is very sick. We saw a number of sea creatures called porpoises. Daily prayer meetings, morning and evening.

9

THE RATS HAD MOILED INSIDE Daniel's stomach during the night. He felt the same queasiness that afflicted so many others. He strolled on the poop deck under slate-gray skies with his wife, mother, and sister, hoping to clear his head and settle his stomach. He had not eaten. Like other passengers, the Browetts had brought aboard a selection of beef, pork, salted herring, cheese, peas, beans, prunes, potatoes, rice, rye bread, butter, as well as essentials such as salt, pepper, sugar, vinegar, tea, and sea biscuits. Nothing sounded good to him right now. Besides, the captain had imposed a no-fire restriction because of occasional high winds.

As Daniel, Elizabeth, Martha, and Rebecca strolled past the animal pens, they spotted Heywood, the steward, talking with a crewmember. He approached with a cheery face. "Brass monkey weather, don't cha think?"

Daniel nodded. He never felt so cold. Not even the day when he stood before Elizabeth's gruff old father and asked for her hand in marriage.

Heywood pointed to the other crewmembers. "This is Coop. Our ship's cooper. Makes all our casks. He's a valuable man. On pirate ships, the coop would always get one and a half shares of the loot taken."

Daniel slowly extended his hand. He spoke as though emerging from a fog. "I was a cooper. I suppose you have a real name."

"Jack Coffin, 'tis." Coop said, laughing, showing crooked teeth. The Yankee had dark brown hair, brown eyes, and a ruddy complexion. His grip was firm. His job was to break down every cask used for storage after it was emptied to save space, and reassemble it for the next trip. His largest cask, known as a tun, held 256 gallons, usually filled with wine or olive oil. Smaller casks were called pipes, 128 gallons; hogsheads, 64 gallons; and tierces, 42 gallons. Harness casks held salt beef and salt horsemeat. Drinking water was carried in water casks known as butts with a capacity of 126 gallons each.

"The crew changes just about every trip, Captain Browett," Heywood said, sounding wise beyond his years. "So we just get used ta calling certain crewmembers by what they do. We call the ship's carpenter Chips. Blacksmith's Blackie. Cook's Doc. Cook's helper is known as Soups. And ya met Neptune, our navigator."

The Hindu word for a particular type of sturdy Indian cotton cloth is dungri. Coop was dressed in undyed bell-bottom tan dungarees made from a discarded sail. Most sailors' work clothing and hammocks, Daniel discovered, were made of the cloth. The bell-bottoms enabled crewmembers to roll the legs above the knee when washing down the decks. In case a sailor was washed overboard, he could remove the bell-bottoms and use them as a life preserver by knotting the legs, then flipping the trousers over his head, belt first, in a scooping motion to catch air. Coop's heavy black Pea Coat, which he always wore in cold and foggy weather, was made from pilot cloth (p-cloth), a heavy, course, strong-twilled cloth.

Coop had wandering eyes, like every other sailor on board. They raked over Rebecca with an alert, searching look. He found her attractive, with her pink and white face alive with curiosity. Flowing strawberry blonde hair streamed from a yellow bonnet.

"My, aren't you the sweet little lass?"

Daniel shook off fiendish images in his mind as he placed himself between Coop and Rebecca. "She's my younger sister."

A scar under Coop's eye twitched as he contemplated Daniel. He suddenly tipped his well-varnished black tarpaulin hat, worn on the back of his head, and excused himself. "Gotta check my casks for leaks," he said, winking. Half a fathom of black ribbon trailed from his hat as he walked away.

Daniel had no time to feel relieved.

"Can ya remember what I taught ya yesterday?" Heywood asked.

Daniel groaned, and mentally shook himself. "About the ship and the sails, you mean?"

"Give it a try." Heywood's eyebrows arched upward in anticipation.

"Maybe another day. I'm not feeling that well." He turned his eyes to the restless sea. "I can't get used to the pitch and roll of the ship."

"More roll today than pitch, Cap'n Browett. "The more she rolls, the less she pitches. A little quiz is just what cha need. It'll take yer mind off yer seasickness."

Daniel took off his cap, ran his fingers through his own blonde hair, scratched his head, and gazed at the dark skies. Earlier, the ship had sailed through thick, patchy fog.

"I'll help you Daniel," Rebecca said, coloring as one of the Italians walked by whistling.

"What do you know about ships?" Martha asked her daughter, wringing her fingers. Her gray hair contrasted with that of her daughter's, as did her wrinkled skin, the sunspots on her hands, and her worn-out looking checkered blue bonnet.

Elizabeth floated up to Heywood in her mauve wool dress, a heavy black coat draped over her. "Give us a try," she dared, her green eyes flaring.

"Tell me how the ship is runnin' and what is happenin' to the sails and the wind," Heywood challenged, his eyes wide and shiny. He folded his arms.

Daniel gave his wife a blank stare. She returned it, baffled.

"It's not that hard, Cap'n Browett," Heywood said. "Take a guess."

Daniel made a skeptical face, chaffing at the word *captain*. "Running dead before it? The wind seems to be astern." He winced, waiting for a reaction.

Heywood gave a harsh laugh. "No, Cap'n Browett. Dead before it is the way you'd run into a gale when you're down to topsails. Look up, Cap'n

Browett. You too, ladies. It's not the best sailing position for a ship with all the canvas spread. Right now we're runnin' free with the wind on the port quarter. Runnin' that way, every sail draws to the limit and she clips along like a railway train."

"Port quarter?" Daniel groaned, and tugged at his chin. *Port means left, starboard right. The quarter—is that the direction between the beam and stern?*

Heywood considered his students' stupefied look, and chuckled.

"What do you mean, *running free?*" Elizabeth asked, her pretty face screwed into a mask of curiosity.

"Runnin' free means that wind is comin' from just enough to one side that it gets a good chance at every sail, and from near enough behind so it drives the ship smartly. Got that?"

Elizabeth nodded, pretending she understood.

"In that position, no sail blankets any other sail from the wind," Heywood added, turning back to Daniel. "And whose job is it to make certain every sail keeps drawin' full?"

Martha ventured a guess. "Captain Wood's?"

"No! No! No! The second mate. You've met him already. Adams is in charge of all the sails, all the masts and all the rigging. That's him dead above us, comin' down the mizzenmast. Because he's the second mate, he's earned the title of *Mister* to all the sailors."

Daniel, Elizabeth, Martha, and Rebecca cast their eyes upward, into a dizzying collection of masts and sails, and a spiderweb of cordage. It renewed Daniel's queasiness.

"The mate is up there to keep a better eye on every sail. He orders 'em trimmed whenever the weather leeches start shivering. The wind's hauled to the northeast so the mate will have to trim the sail if he wants things shipshape, should Captain Wood come on deck. See, up there? See the weather leeches?"

Strongly conscious of Heywood's presence, Rebecca locked her eyes in a steady upward stare.

"Tell me what weather leeches are, Miss Browett."

"I haven't a clue," Rebecca said, bracing for the next roll of the ship.

"That's a term used to describe the edges of the sails nearest the wind. Right now, they are on the port edge, or left."

Rebecca witnessed them shivering in the wind, as it shifted.

"With the sudden shift of the wind, you can see a sail here and there beginnin' to buckle," Heywood said. "Even greenhorns like yourselves can tell they are no longer filled, or drawing like they should be."

Adams swept into action. He jumped from above, landing near Rebecca. "Starboard main braces, men—make it lively!"

Rebecca retreated, regarding the young man who appeared to be no more than twenty-five years of age. He had a dark brown beard, and scars on his neck.

Adams turned, bowing. "Pleased to meet cha, missy." He gave Rebecca a prolonged stare, and then barked more orders.

Rebecca blushed darkly, retreating.

As the *Echo* sailors on the main deck leaped to haul on the brace, a combination of rope and tackle that held the starboard tip of the main yard in position, Adams ran forward and slacked off the port brace.

"Hear the yard holding that sail creak?" Heywood asked Rebecca.

She nodded.

"Now watch. It's swingin' slower now, hangin' more diagonally across the ship. The weather leech has been carried far enough forward. The mate is makin' certain that the tacks and sheets are properly reset."

Adams could be heard barking another order. "Now busy yourselves trimming the main topsails above the mast!"

Soon every sail, up to the royal at the top, was drawing full.

"A jolly good demonstration, as you English would say," Heywood said, his mouth curling in gratification. "I should tell you that the *Echo* is a square rigged ship, meaning she carries three masts and a full complement of square sails, plus a series of triangular sails between the foremast and the big pole sticking twenty feet out the front of the ship—called the bowsprit. We call those triangular sails jibs and staysails. Their purpose is to steady the ship in her course. In high winds, when it's impossible to carry any other canvas, these small sails are the only ones set."

Heywood's eyes darted from Rebecca, to Martha, and back to Daniel and Elizabeth. His smile curved up, self-satisfied and wise. "Now look up there, Captain Browett. Isn't that a beautiful sight, a sky-filling mass of canvas hung from the yards, between the masts, and between the foremast and the jib boom? How many sails would you guess?"

The wind was giving Daniel a headache, and he was tired, and still queasy. He shrugged a guess. "Eighteen?"

"Two score and one, Mr. Browett, two score and one. Some cut square, some triangular, set and spaced so cunningly that every square yard is drawing full. New passengers are always impressed. Top to bottom the sails are the royal, the topgallant, the upper and lower top sails, then there are the course sails. They're called the foresails and the mainsails, sometimes called cross-jacks. All together, our ship will spread nearly ten thousand square yards of canvas."

Daniel shrugged, becoming disinterested.

"You just witnessed Adam's slacking off a brace. Tell me, what are braces?"

"Ropes that control the tips of each yard?"

"Correct. And what is a yard?"

"Things that hold the sails."

"Correct again, Mr. Browett. And a halyard?"

Daniel's face drew a blank.

"They are used to raise and lower the yards. Brails, or buntlines, are used to haul the lower edges of each sail up to its yard for furling."

Daniel nodded.

"And leech lines?"

"Those are the iron-wire stays that hold each mast in place."

"Very good."

"And why do we construct the masts in three sections? We went over this yesterday."

"To make it easier for repairs. You can dismantle it in three separate pieces."

"And why do we rake each mast?"

A blank again. "You didn't mention that yesterday."

Heywood grinned. "Since wind pressure on the sails always tends to 'topple' the masts forward, we 'rake' it or slant it back with heavy wire cables from different parts of the mast, attaching the cables on the bulwarks."

Heywood grabbed a cable with one hand. "Like this one, here. There's a lot more that fails to meet the eye of the average passenger."

"I believe you."

"Well, that's all for today. I must tend to other duties. Shall we have another session tomorrow?"

Daniel held up a rigid palm. "I think I've had enough for a while."

After Heywood departed, Daniel vomited over the side.

Suddenly, the wind began howling like a demented demon.

Wiping his mouth, Daniel looked to the west. A shiver of dread crept along his spine. The sky was black there, at midday.

FRIDAY Feb. 20 – Headwind continues. We see to it every morning that the ship is cleaned thoroughly. Many more are seasick. The mate opened the New Testament at the 27th chapter of Acts and asked some of the passengers how they would like to be shipwrecked like the Apostle Paul! Brother Levi Roberts replied instantly: "It is very likely we shall be shipwrecked but the hull of this vessel has got to carry us safe to New Orleans!" The mate was then called away to hoist the royal sail. Because of the bad weather there is much murmuring among the passengers. Some want to go back to England and wait for better weather.

10

HANNAH FELT TRAPPED, like all steerage passengers. She feared that any second the angry sea would either break the *Echo*'s side or come over her top. That would release a raging torrent of freezing seawater into the hatchways, drowning not only her, but also her husband, her three small children, and everyone else. *I should have returned to Apperley with my mother. Please, God. Deliver us from this tempest. Do not let this storm harm my family or my unborn child.*

The *Echo* had left the Celtic Sea and was entering the broad, uninviting expanse of the North Atlantic.

A sailor's voice, screaming: "We're battening down the hatches!"

The hatch closed with a deafening thud. A puff of fetid air came out, smelling of cesspool, slopbuckets, soaked bedding, and a perpetually rotting hull. The sailor quickly slid the long slender iron battens through the metal loops on the side of the hatch. He flinched for a second, thinking of the poor souls trapped below, and then ran to attend to other emergency duties.

Hannah shuddered at the loss of light. A lone dim lantern swung wildly from the center of the compartment. Pots, pans, tins, and boxes seemed to fly past. Several inches of seawater sloshed about her feet. Women screamed. Children cried.

"Daniel says to lash the children to the berths," Robert said in a panic, throwing a powerful arm around his wife. "Us, too."

Normally adventurous and daring, Robert was frightened for the first time in his life. Ignoring their cries, he secured Joseph, Lizzy, and Willie into the berth with a rope. Then he did the same to Hannah, and to himself.

"Mama! Mama!" the children wailed.

Lord, please tell me I'm dreaming, Robert silently screamed.

Captain Wood was normally a flawless decision maker. He had known the *Echo* was in trouble from the moment black banks of freezing fog turned into gale force winds from the southwest, bringing strong slanting rain that struck his face and arms as though it were shot from a musket. With his passengers huddled below and out of the way, he turned his attention to his crew and the ship, determined to bring things under control.

"Hang onto that rope!" he yelled to a midshipman hanging in the rigging, clutching at the swaying yard.

The second yard main mast's lower topsail, although close reefed, was stretched almost to the breaking point. The *Echo* was plowing through the angry sea at a reckless speed, certain to destroy herself if the remaining sails were not quickly reefed.

"Lash the wheel!" the captain roared to the helmsman.

The February storm had approached with unprecedented speed. As soon as the watch had confirmed the gale, Captain Wood had struck a cry to deal with the emergency. He had ordered the helmsman to change course, which would take the pressure of the wind off the sails as much as possible. His crew was divided up and sent to the control center for each mast, and the captain began barking orders to each leader to spill the sails. The top-most sails were given up first because they were the farthest from the center of gravity, done by releasing the sheet lines. Once done, the clewlines, leechlines, and buntlines were brought into action, each of which raised a section of the sail up the yards.

As each sail was released it filled out like a balloon then—pop! It collapsed with the report of a small cannon, and sank away to a handful.

"Up you go!" the captain screamed, watching impatiently as crewmen scrambled up the icy rigging to furl the sails. Soon his seamen were hovering in the air like judgment angels, both hands free to work, several with one foot on the rigging and the other trailing behind.

Looking straight up into the maze of sails, all of them flapping in the wind, Captain Wood yelled, "Watch yourselves men! Don't let the main royal yard snap off!"

It was too late. It snapped, the cracking sound barely heard above the roar of the sea.

From his position on the deck, Captain Wood couldn't tell which of his seamen was plunging to his certain death in the freezing water. But knowing that the slightest change in wind direction could turn the *Echo* just one or two degrees either way, the captain had no time to mourn the loss of one sailor.

The entire ship with every one of its more than two hundred passengers was in peril.

"Wreckage from another ship dead ahead!" a sailor yelled at the top of his lungs as he retreated from the foremast.

As the captain rushed to the forecastle deck to get a better look, a rope suddenly snapped, cracking like a bowstring. It whipped by the captain's face, stinging his frozen cheek, knocking him down the stairs to the main deck again. Almost before he could react to the sting and before he could struggle to his feet, a sensation of vertigo swept over him. Captain Wood was pitched against the bulwark as another angry wave hit the ship, this one the largest yet. Clinging desperately to the bulwark, he watched helplessly as the *Echo* turned nearly on her side in the raging inferno, her masts almost horizontal. He knew that unless a miracle happened, he would have to issue an order to arm his seamen with axes and cut away the topmast. That would lower the ship's center of gravity and lessen resistance, reducing the risk of capsizing.

With her starboard keel out of the sea, the *Echo* slowly turned a full counter-clockwise circle in the swirling mass of milk-white boiling foam.

As the ship turned on her side, with all steerage passengers still trapped in an eerie darkness, Robert prayed that God would spare his family and all the passengers on the ship. He wondered if God had forgiven him for being so egotistical and full of pride, neglecting his family, pursuing the riches of the world, mistreating his wife, delaying his investigation and baptism into the Church, and for wanting to do bodily harm to an Apostle of the Lord.

Hannah screamed again, still caught in her chaotic panic.

"Hold on," Robert grunted. "It's not over yet!" He cringed, wondering if the ship would upright itself. He uttered another prayer, asking God to calm the storm, to protect his wife and children, and to let them reach Nauvoo in safety.

Hannah sobbed, drawing short labored breaths.

As the *Echo* righted herself, Captain Wood lay on his back for a moment, gasping for breath, taking stock. He picked himself up with a surge of adrenaline and, after a string of oaths, scanned his ship for damage. He cast his eyes upward, counting sailors and sails that needed to be closed.

"Man overboard! Man overboard!"

Captain Wood recoiled at the words. Still a bit fuzzy, he found Adams, the first mate. "How many men have we lost?"

Adams felt a rising uncertainty. "Just one, cap'n, that I know of. No one can see 'im,"

"Keep a sharp lookout, and get the rest of the sails reefed as quickly as possible. There's probably water in the holds, so tell Evans to get some men on the pumps."

"Aye, aye, sir!" Adams quickly scanned the ship for the first mate.

"What about the wreckage of the other ship?"

"Still on the starboard side, sir. We're watchin'. I got two men in the wheelhouse. We're steerin' away from it, now. The initial gust o' the storm hit us hard, but I don't think the waves will push us on our side again."

The captain wheeled, his eyes searching again. "Steward Heywood! Where are you?"

The door to the deckhouse opened, and the steward popped out. "Right here, sir!"

"Go check out the cabin passengers, and tend to any of their needs. And make certain the hatch stays battened down. There's still going to be some waves crashing overboard. I imagine it's chaos down there with our steerage passengers, but they'll survive. We'll open the hatch when the storm quiets down, whenever that is."

"Aye, aye, sir!"

Chaos was a mild word to describe the condition in steerage, thought Daniel, still grasping the true horror of the situation. Fear gripped everyone there. "Everyone stay in your berths," he yelled. "We don't know if the ship will turn on her side again."

Overturned trunks, boxes, tins, pans, bottles, and other unsecured objects danced on the floor between berths, clashing and cracking against each other in jumbled confusion. Still lashed to their berths, women and children screamed and cried. Some vomited. Grown men wept. Water seeped through the hatch door, trickling onto the floor. The lantern, still lit, swung wildly.

Daniel glanced at James and Nancy, in the next berth. Nancy's head was buried in her husband's chest. James was squeezing her tight. James returned Daniel's glance, pleading, as if to say, *This is making Nancy worse. Can't you do something?*

"Say your prayers," Daniel said in a voice audible to all. "Say your prayers."

11

THE FIRST LIGHT OF DAY appeared on the horizon Sunday morning. The storm had not let up. However, the mate had proved right in his prediction that the ship would not roll on her side again. One sail had been ripped to ribbons. Waves were still crashing over the deck, and a freezing rain was lashing the sea and the ship, coming down in windblown torrents.

Hearing reports that the pumps were not keeping up with the amount of water in the bottom of the ship, Captain Wood summoned his officers to his cabin below the wheelhouse. Choked with anguish, the captain gave an order to Evans, the first mate: "I want you to go to the captain of the Mormons— what's his name?"

As Evans drew near, the captain saw in his brown eyes a profound exhaustion. Evans stood erect, momentarily taking off his tarpaulin hat, revealing swirls of matted dark brown hair. "Mr. Browett, sir."

The captain spoke in hurried clips, the veins on his brow showing. "You go to Captain Browett. Tell him this. Tell him that if the God of the Mormons can do anything to save this ship and all the passengers, they had better be calling on that God to do so. We are sinking at the rate of a foot an hour. If the storm continues, we'll be at the bottom of the ocean before daylight."

Evans blinked his eyes, not previously knowing that the captain had assessed the situation so seriously. More water must have gushed into the ship's hold than anyone had imagined. Wave after wave still pounded the *Echo* in the dark, spraying seawater over her hull. He wheeled, placing the hat back on his head. "Yes, sir!"

The captain ran a meaty hand across his worried brow. "Heywood, you go with him. You seem to know Captain Browett quite well."

Heywood saluted briskly. "Yes, sir!"

Bounding out of the captain's quarters, Evans and Heywood dashed through the dining room, filled with fear-stricken cabin passengers, and through the saloon, where more cabin passengers huddled. Evans and Heywood exited through the door leading to the main deck, and opened the hatch in the driving rain.

A wave of relief swept over Daniel as he heard the hatch open, metal scraping on metal, and watched two figures illuminated by a lantern descend into the steerage compartment. A welcome gush of damp sea air rushed in. Daniel jumped out of his berth, balanced himself against a timber, and strode toward them, crouching. His dim eyes became cunningly alert.

"Cap'n Browett?" Evans called out.

"I'm here," Daniel answered, fatigued, but intensely awake, his pulse quickening. He focused his eyes on the two men. As if on queue, much of the shrieking, crying, and sobbing subsided.

Evans looked grim. "Message from the cap'n, sir. The ship has taken on much water. Pumps can't keep up with it. There's danger of sinkin'."

Daniel hesitated, shocked, not knowing how to answer. There was a pause. He studied the two men in the eerie reflection of the lanterns. "What do you mean, *sinking?*"

The hatch had been left open. Another gush of seawater poured into the compartment.

From a taunt, downturned mouth, Evans answered. "Cap'n says the ship is sinkin' a foot an hour. Water's still coming in. Waves are crashin' over the bow, over the sides, even over the wheelhouse. Cap'n fears we may end up at the bottom of the ocean."

Dizzy with the words he had just heard, Daniel made a quick reaction. "Let us bear a hand at the pumps. We have plenty of strong men."

Within seconds, Robert stood at Daniel's side, along with five, then ten, then twenty Mormon men.

Evans held up a free hand, exposing his palm. "Maybe later. Our crew's handlin' the pumps. It's the storm we fear. If'n it does not quiet, the pumps will not keep up."

Daniel gave Evans and Heywood a quizzical look. "I feel you came down here with a request of some kind. What is it?"

The look on Heywood's face intensified, his focus total. He took off his cap. He spoke slowly, emphasizing each word. "Captain Wood wants you to call on your Mormon God to save the ship."

Daniel took on a new countenance, as though he were emerging from a dream. With a tilt of his head, and in a low, firm baritone voice, Daniel made his answer, refusing to believe the preposterous thought that the ship would sink. "The God we believe in is the same God you believe in. He will not let us down. You go back and tell the captain that we are not going to the bottom of the ocean. I have a hundred and nine souls on board that embarked from Liverpool on a voyage to New Orleans, with a final destination being our Zion, a place called Nauvoo. We will, I repeat, we *will* arrive safely in the port of New Orleans. Our God, and your God, will protect us. We have been sending fervent prayers to him, and we will continue to do so."

The ship shuddered again, reacting to a giant wave. A trunk danced by the men, and several boxes.

Daniel took a deep breath. "Tell Captain Wood that this ship is in God's hands, and all will be well."

Heywood saluted smartly. He turned to Evans. "Let's give Cap'n Wood the report."

Evans saluted Daniel and his voice cracked. "Thank you, sir."

Another burst of seawater greeted the two men as they climbed the ladder out of steerage, nearly dousing the lantern.

Daniel watched the hatch close, his skin tingling. The sound of voices rose, deep within the compartment. Light from the single lantern spilled out, showing faces of faith.

"Everyone lash themselves in their berths again, except for my assistants."

Six men crowded around Daniel: Robert Harris. John Cheese. David Wilding. James Lavender. William Jenkins. John Ellison.

Daniel's gaze traced the outline of each man. He could hear his own heart racing. He was silent for a moment, and then spoke confidently. "Brethren, I want you to kneel with me in a special prayer. I want each of you to be mouth, saying a prayer with your own lips, asking the Lord to stay the storm, and calm the ship. Brother Wilding, you can be first, and we'll go around the circle, left to right. I'll be last. Pray like you've never prayed before. Remember, the object of prayer is not to change the will of God, but to secure for ourselves and everyone on this ship the blessings that God is already willing to grant. We just need to do a better job asking."

The steerage compartment fell into a reverent silence, except for the movement of loose items on the floor, the creaking of the ship, and the sound of waves crashing against the hull. One by one, the seven Mormon leaders begged their Heavenly Father to calm the storm and save the ship.

When Daniel finished his prayer, the men remained on their knees.

Robert sensed a glimmer of contentment in Daniel's eyes, and a feeling of peace. Within seconds, Robert could feel a change in the motion of the ship. Instead of pitching and rolling, she seemed to tremble, shudder, and then become almost dead still. The former hardheaded pugilist was awed, both by the profundity of faith of everyone in the company, and by the scope of the power of prayer.

Daniel rose to his feet. "Brethren. Spread the word. All is well."

A look of astonishment crossed the face of Captain Wood as he stepped out of his quarters. The *Echo* floated dead still. Two sails, still furled, hung limp.

"Look," Heywood exclaimed, his expression dazzled.

The captain followed Heywood's pointing finger. In every direction—north, south, east and west—the billows were still raging. But in the area immediately surrounding the ship, the waves were silent. Only a gentle ripple could be seen, like a breath of fresh air on a calm sea. The conclusion was simple. The Mormon God had done His job.

His eyes riveted on the eerie scene, Captain Wood gave an order to his first and second mates. His voice was crisp, his chaotic fears dissolved. "Continue with the pumps. Get the repairs made. Let's take advantage of the calm."

"Yes, sir!"

In the welcome light of morning, Captain Wood surveyed his three eighty-foot masts. They were solidly intact. Other than the royal main yard that had snapped and was being repaired, all others were in good shape. Ripped sails were being mended. Shaking his head in continued astonishment, absorbing the peculiar site of continued storms all around him, he sent Heywood to thank Captain Browett.

Minutes later, Heywood returned. "Cap'n Browett has a request, sir."

"Speak up, Heywood."

"He requests permission for religious services to be held on deck, sir. Sometime this afternoon, if it's all right with you. Today is Sunday, you know."

"You tell Captain Browett that he can have his religious services at any time, any day, on my ship."

"Yes, sir. I'll tell him that."

As Heywood turned to go, Captain Wood touched his shoulder. "Pass the word to the crew. They have my permission to attend Captain Browett's religious services."

"Yes, sir!" Heywood took a few steps, and then retreated. "One more request from Cap'n Browett, sir."

"What is that?"

"He wonders if there is a large barrel on board not being used that could be improvised in some way to hold enough water for a person to be immersed."

"Does he think all his Mormons need a bath today?"

"Sir, he's seeing to it below that everyone is cleaned up and taking spit baths as best they can. But, no, sir. The barrel is not to be used for a bathtub."

A puzzled look came over the captain. "Then what's it for?"

"There are already several people among the non-Mormons down in the steerage compartment who are requesting baptism. Mormons apparently baptize by immersion, like the Baptists."

"You tell Captain Browett he can have a large barrel for his baptisms. Two if he wishes. Have the ship's carpenter see to it."

"Aye, aye, sir!"

12

THE STATEMENT FROM JOHN COX shocked Robert and Daniel. They had just emerged from an early Sunday morning meeting, preparing for the sacrament service to be held on board. "Henry Eagles thinks we ought to return to Liverpool. In fact, he's adamant about it. He's stirring up some of the passengers."

"Oh, no," Robert exclaimed, shaking his head in disbelief, and rolling his blue-gray eyes.

Daniel grimaced. *What next?* He thought of Laman and Lemuel's murmurings in the Book of Mormon.

Robert sensed Daniel's concern. "Knowing Henry like I do, it doesn't surprise me. Doesn't he know he just witnessed a miracle? Seems to me he ought to be begging for baptism."

Daniel leveled his gaze at the calm ocean, storms still raging in the distance. "You have to remember," Daniel countered, "that miracles don't convert people. The Spirit converts them. Remember in the New Testament all the accounts of the Savior's miracles, and yet the Jews remained hard-hearted and sought to kill Jesus."

"I can't believe he's doing this," William Jenkins said over Daniel's shoulder.

Robert scoffed. "Henry's very insecure, despite his outward huffy personality. I know he wants to go to America. That's why he married a Mormon girl. He's fightin' demons all the time. He's so unpredictable."

"If you hear of anyone else taking up Henry's charge, let's nip it in the bud," Daniel said. "I've talked to the captain. He assured me he has made the Liverpool to New Orleans trip in bad winter weather several times. I know the Lord is with us. The worst of the weather is behind us now. But there will be other storms. Just not as bad. Satan does not want this Company of Mormons to reach Zion. Satan does not want a temple in Nauvoo. That's a fact."

The men nodded.

Daniel added, "Remember, I'm talking about faith in our meeting today. Perhaps that will help." In the meeting, Daniel had assigned his assistants topics for subsequent Sunday services: repentance, baptism, and gift of the Holy Ghost. After that, New Orleans would be only two weeks away, if they stayed on schedule.

"With Henry, it won't," Robert said.

Daniel's tone was firm. "It will with everyone else. We just can't let Henry poison anyone else."

Sabbath at sea was a day of "almost" rest for the *Echo* sailors. They could be seen washing down the decks early, keeping only one watch, and later dressing in their best white trousers and red-checkered shirts, changing the sails when necessary. It was a day for reading, talking, and mending clothes, the only time those privileges were allowed by Captain Wood. Doc was preparing his Sunday treat. The noon meal would be scouse, made by pounding biscuits into crumbs, adding it to salt beef cut in small pieces, a few potatoes, boiled up together and seasoned with pepper. Dessert would be duff pudding, a heavy, dark, clammy mixture of cooked flour and water, doused with molasses, and washed down with watered-down brandy or grog. It was looked upon as a luxury by the crew.

As Daniel meandered around the ship, gathering his thoughts, he wondered how many of the crew would attend the Mormon services. From the captain to the smallest boy, he had never been around a bunch of men who swore more, unless it were the rough crowds that pervaded the pugilistic matches in London. He had been there twice to watch Robert fight. Wilford Woodruff was in London now, preaching the gospel. Daniel wondered how the Church authority was faring.

To Daniel, the few shafts of sunlight that peeked through the clouds on this Sabbath morning seemed to close the curtain on the life-threatening weather that had plagued their trip so far. A pearl-gray murk veiled the surrounding skies, and medium breezes scattered the fog ahead of them. The sea had a nacreous light that belonged more to the day than to the darkness. To him, it was a sign that weather in the coming days would not be perfect, but it wouldn't sink the ship.

The *Echo* was sailing steadily southeastward in the North Atlantic below the fiftieth parallel. She was heeling no more than two strakes under her top-gallantsails. The sea had calmed, and so had the passengers.

The challenge to Daniel, however, was to convince Henry and those he may have influenced. Daniel had always been a man who had a deep sense of responsibility and a plow horse work ethic. Those emotions gripped him as he prepared to speak.

Peering at the crowd that had gathered on the poop deck for the meeting, Daniel saw men in caps, women in shawls, children in blankets, curious crewmembers in their duckcloth trousers, and several non-member passengers. Many were standing. Others, including the sick, were sitting on deck chairs, boxes, crates, and trunks that the steward had quickly assembled. Nancy Eagles arrived, looking pallid.

The singing was loud but reverent, the prayer full of thanksgiving.

His arms folded, a pleased look on his face, Captain Wood stood at the back of the crowd. He gave Daniel a nod of acknowledgement.

A big grin lit up Daniel's face. "Thank you, Captain Wood, for permission to hold this meeting."

Captain Wood smiled. He had his own Sabbath day service to conduct. A memorial for the lost sailor, and the auctioning off of his belongings.

"I wish to add that the captain has also given us permission to hold a prayer meeting every morning, here on this deck. It will be at seven o'clock. Everyone is invited."

The Mormon passengers expressed their delight with reverent nods.

Daniel scanned the crowd for Henry. He was not there, although Katherine could be seen sitting next to Hannah.

Standing with his back against the outer wall of the smoking compartment, Daniel preached his sermon on faith. He talked about the miracle of the calming of the storm, and the power of prayer. "You had tremendous faith to board this ship and sail out into the dark and perilous North Atlantic. I know you have faith that we will reach our destination, even though every day we must contend with the uncertainty of more storms. Even though I know that the worst is over, I know that this ship will yet encounter more storms.

"We may liken the storms we are witnessing to life itself. God puts storms in our path to strengthen us, to temper us, to make us stronger. So don't get your hopes up. The captain says we are already off course somewhat, and we may yet get farther off course before we reach our destination."

Daniel talked for forty minutes, quoting Paul in the Book of Romans, Ether in the Book of Mormon, citing verses from the Doctrine and Covenants, and things Wilford Woodruff had taught him about the principle of faith.

To conclude, Daniel said, "Brothers and sisters, this journey is sure to be a trial of our faith, individually and collectively. Life is a trial of our faith. Accepting the gospel is a trial of our faith. We have not seen America, but we know it is there. We have not seen New Orleans, but it is there. To have our spiritual eyes opened through faith necessitates a trial of our faith. Believing without seeing will result in greater seeing. This opening of our spiritual eyes is not granted to us by the Savior without effort on our part. It comes only as we are willing to exercise our faith and trust in the Lord when the path we must pursue is not fully illuminated. Faith is a gift of God, granted to us a little at a time, as a reward for personal righteousness. I thought of that the first night out. The night was full of blackness; I could not see any star, only storm.

I knew the captain had faith in his crew and in his instruments. Despite the storm the ship was set in a path toward New Orleans. Despite the storm we will follow that path and soon arrive at our destination.

"No matter how the wind may blow us, I promise in the name of the Lord we will arrive at our destination. But again I feel to warn each of you that this journey will be like our individual lives, it will not be without peril, not without danger, and not without affliction. Peril, danger, and affliction will be the trial of our faith, both on this trip and in our individual lives."

Robert stole a glance at his sick sister-in-law, Nancy. His face turned sad. *What Daniel has said is true. For Nancy and James, this journey is going to be a trial of their faith.*

In a happier note, six persons were baptized in the barrel.

Doc's assistant was a simple-hearted black man from Georgia who, in the past, constantly chided the crew about how badly they spent their Sabbaths. Touched by what Daniel had said, he was found later in the afternoon lecturing Heywood the steward while the lost sailor's personal belongings were auctioned off.

Sitting on the spars, the thirty-six-year-old black man, Jeremiah, spoke in a soft tone. "Are you sure o' dat?" he asked, learning that the missing man was a German.

"He spoke no language except English and German," Heywood said.

"I was mighty 'fraid he was a Finn. I been plenty civil to dat man all da voyage, cause I feared all Finns'r wizards. They 'specially have power over da winds and da storms. But he died in da storm, so I 'spect he had no power a-tall."

Heywood shook his head, stunned by Jeremiah's conclusion.

The black man continued, this time making sense in his deep southern drawl. "A man dies on da shore, his body remains wid 'is friends, da mourners go 'bout da streets. Ya follow 'is body to da grave, en a stone marks da spot. Da man is shot down in battle, and da mangled body remains an object, o'da evidence o' death. But at sea, one minute da man is near you. Ya hear 'is voice.

In an instant he's gone. Nothin' but a vacancy. You miss da form, da sound of his voice. All dese things makes death so mournful. Good t'ing. We be kinder ta each other for a while. I hope God won't be too hard on da poor fella. A sailor's life is but a mixture of good wid much evil, a little pleasure wid much pain."

Heywood fell silent, thinking about the lost sailor, hired in Liverpool. The men told him the German didn't know how to swim and was very heavily dressed. Now everything in the man's chest had been sold to the highest bidder and the chest itself was being taken aft for additional storage of ship's goods.

Rebecca Browett silently escaped from her berth in the section of steerage assigned to single passengers. Only the light of a dim lantern enabled her to find the ladder that led to the main deck. Once there, she tried to steady herself as the ship pitched and rolled. By memory she walked in the direction of the water closet. The one reserved for cabin passengers. *Far preferable to the chamber pots below,* she thought.

The man stood hidden behind the mizzenmast. Silence surrounded him. Only a few steps separated him from the water closet. He waited in the darkness. Moments later, he watched the girl emerge. He could hear the latch close.

"Rebecca."

The sound of her name startled her. Her pupils widened. She stood motionless, as though she were frozen solid. "Who's there?"

The form of a man approached. "Henry Eagles."

A measure of relief came over Rebecca. *At least it's not one of the sailors.* Nevertheless, she cringed. "What do you want?"

"I've always wanted to tell you something."

Rebecca's heartbeat steadied. "Oh?" She stepped toward the hatch, toward safety. She scanned the deck. *Where are the sailors on watch? In the cordage? On the bow?*

Henry took a step toward her. "I should have married you instead of

Katherine."

Rebecca gasped.

"You're much prettier. I kick myself everyday for making the wrong choice."

Rebecca could hear herself breathe. "I'm going below. Don't follow me or I'll scream."

"I just have a favor. Convince your brother to turn the ship back to Liverpool, will you? This ship will never get us to America alive."

Without comment, trembling as she went, Rebecca disappeared.

SATURDAY Feb. 21 – Wind continued ahead. Blows fresh rain. Captain says it is blowing us off course. He entertains us with stories of previous voyages and shipwrecks. Spray like snow drifting up hills. Sea dashed over side of the vessel. Sister Pulham is dreadfully affected with nauseous sickness, perhaps more so on account of her being with child. Not a morsel of food or drink will remain in her stomach. The moment she lifts her head she is sick almost to death. Met in council with my assistants. We are concerned about all the sickness. We give priesthood anointings and blessings daily. Towards six o'clock the wind ahead blows fresh and increases to a hurricane. The ship was heaving most tremendously. Tubs were rolling about, pans and kettles all of it in an uproar, women shrieking, children crying, all hastening to their berths. Wind continued all night. Captain ordered the hatches battened down; that caused the women and children to cry all the worse. Our prayers saved the ship.

SUNDAY Feb. 22 – We had a successful first sacrament meeting on board. The sermon seemed to help the feelings of those who are seasick. Many more are seasick. A few have recovered.

13

BEFORE PRACTICAL TIMEPIECES suitable for shipboard use were invented in the late eighteenth century, sailors kept track of time using the hourglass. The ship's bell reported the time to the captain, officers, and crew. Each time the sand ran out, the ship's boy would turn the glass over and ring an appropriate number of bells. Each watch was four hours in length. One bell was struck after the first half-hour. Two on the first hour. Two plus a third on the half-hour following the first hour. Two groups of two bells for the second hour, and so on until a total of eight bells were rung on the fourth hour to complete the watch. If there were no incidents to report, the call came: *eight bells and all is well.*

Henry Eagles awoke in a foul mood at two bells during the morning watch. Rats moiled in his stomach. His head throbbed. His back ached. He rubbed deep-set dark eyes, sunken with fatigue, recalling his nightmare: *Hurricane force winds. Driving rain. Icebergs. A sinking ship.*

Except for non-member passengers he didn't know, he was alone. Even his wife was gone. There were the usual creaks and groans of the ship, the slight sliding of a trunk, and the gentle swinging of the lantern.

He didn't have the technical name for it, and he didn't know it until he boarded the *Echo*, but half of Henry Eagles' split personality suffered from hydrophobia, the fear of water. And thalassophobia, fear of the sea. Kymophobia, fear of waves. Henry was in great phobic company. Queen Elizabeth I suffered from anthophobia, fear of roses. Napoleon suffered from ailurophobia, fear of cats. Fredrick the Great was so terrified of water that he could not wash himself; instead, servants cleaned him with dry towels.

Cupping a hand over his ear, Henry could hear a Mormon hymn. Rubbing his long black whiskers, he stared at the hatch, where cold, foggy, fishy-smelling air came drifting. In his gloom, he thought of the mistakes he had made in his recent life. *Feigning respect for a new religion. Marrying a Mormon woman. Securing passage on this ship.*

Henry wrinkled his nose, gritted his teeth, set his jaw, wrapped his wool blanket around his shoulders, and climbed bare-footed out of the steerage compartment. *Back to Liverpool. Back to Apperley. Back to the dairy. Back to the pubs. Back to Alex and Richie.*

Daniel was mid-sentence, talking about the importance of daily scripture study, when Henry barged into the morning prayer meeting like an angry ox, his wide shoulders thrown back, his chin tucked hard into his chest. He made a cursory glance at Rebecca, wondering if she had told her brother about last evening's conversation, then focused his dark eyes on Daniel.

"Mr. Browett. It's your responsibility to convince Captain Wood to turn this ship around and return to Liverpool."

All eyes swept to Henry. Without a cap, his thick, wild black hair hung loosely over his face. His broad chest heaved, expressing frustration and anger.

Daniel's jaw dropped. He was fresh shaved, wore a black overcoat over his brown tweed suit, and had his gray scarf wrapped around his neck. His reaction was conciliatory.

"Henry, I know we have passed through terrible storms, and had a bad experience. But, thanks to God, we survived. I've consulted with Captain Wood many times, even as recently as this morning. He's confident we can move forward, despite the weather."

Henry's dark eyes flared. "What do you mean, 'move forward?' We've all heard the captain say we've been blown way off course. If you're not man enough to approach him about turning around, someone else is going to have to do it for you. We would have been better off if we'd all died in Gloucestershire."

A scripture in the Book of Mormon came to Daniel's mind, a murmuring of Laman and Lemuel, speaking of their wives and children: *…and it would have been better that they had died before they came out of Jerusalem.*

A pained expression crossed Hannah's face, and she glared at her brother. When he met her glance, she hung her head in disappointment and shame. Her eyes met Katherine's. Both women were thinking the same things. *How can you talk like this to your company leader, in open rebellion?*

Trying hard not to show emotion in his face or voice, Daniel winced inwardly. "Henry, if you'd like, we could bring this to a vote. If the majority is in favor of turning around, I'll meet in council with the other brethren, and we'll discuss it. But we have to take into consideration all the other passengers as well. In my view, everyone wants to continue."

The fog in Henry's brain was permanent. "Not everyone."

"You are alone in this, Henry."

The two men regarded each other.

Henry's anger deepened. The veins in his neck expanded, and his muscles became tense. As he rolled his fists into balls, they appeared to be the size of nine-pound hammers. "By the time you get a vote and have another meeting, we could very well be manning the lifeboats. Get this ship turned around. Now!"

Detecting a foul spirit, Hannah's children began to cry.

Daniel exhaled slowly, turning a pleading glance toward Robert. "Henry, please calm down. There is an orderly way to handle this."

Robert rose to his feet.

"You're all a bunch of rum dogs. Turn this ship around!" Henry growled. His mind was fast fading into madness.

"We'll consider your request in our council." Daniel raised his arms, and held his palms up.

Henry drew a seething inhalation, clearly prepared to attack. He lunged at Daniel, grabbed the gray scarf, swung him around with a powerful left arm, and hit him square on the jaw with his right fist. Daniel tumbled to the deck, clutching his jaw.

Katherine jumped to her feet, screaming. "Henry! No! Please!"

Robert erupted. Quick as a cat, he leaped in front of Henry. "You're looking at trouble, Henry. One move, and I'll break your ribs again."

There was no ripple of concern within the former Methodist dairyman. In his current madness, he forgot that his brother-in-law had been within one professional fight of competing for the British heavyweight championship. And that Robert had pummeled him in revenge after Henry and two friends had ganged up on him in Apperley. He took a swing.

Anticipating the move, Robert ducked. Instinctively, he shot two right-hand punches to Henry's midsection followed by an uppercut to his jaw.

Henry's breath hissed and he fell forward, still swinging wildly. Robert finished him off with a right to the nose, bringing an instant gush of blood. Henry crashed to the deck, cursing.

Daniel fought the urge to laugh. *That's for me, and for Rebecca,* he thought.

Robert stood over his brother-in-law, peering down, simmering with rage. *You shouldn't have attacked Daniel. You crossed the line.* "If you get up, I'll hit you so hard you won't wake up until we get to New Orleans."

"You broke my nose!" Henry whined.

"Sorry, I missed. I was aiming for your ribs. If you'll apologize to Daniel, I'll apologize for breaking your nose."

Henry said nothing. Katherine kneeled at his side, holding a handkerchief. Henry took it and drew it to his nose.

"Take 'im away," Robert said, his face still twisted in anger.

Henry rose to his feet, hung his head, and walked toward steerage. At last glimpse, he was leaning his head over the bulwark, vomiting.

Rubbing his chin, Daniel pointed to Elizabeth. "Better go with Katherine and see what you can do to help him." He cast a quick glance at his sister.

Rebecca rolled her eyes. *Serves him right.*

Robert opened his eyes, and then closed them again. He rolled his dry tongue through his mouth, and over his lips. *What time is it?* he wondered. Hannah was curled up beside him, sleeping soundly.

Robert slid out of the berth, his head spinning. He didn't know if his stomach was upset because of his fight with Henry, or because of the four cups of apple cider he had taken just before bedtime. Until now, the rolling of the *Echo* had not bothered him. He was one of the few men who had not been seasick, and had been proud of it. That was until now. A special area of his brain, the vomiting center, was about to initiate the vomiting sequence. Without much effort on his part, his windpipe would close and the abdominal wall and diaphragm muscles would tighten suddenly and forcefully. That would eject food and fluid up the esophagus and out. Robert's target was the ocean, not anywhere in steerage, where he had helped clean it with lime the day before, or on the deck. He followed the dim light ebbing from a lantern that swung back and forth in perfect rhyme with the rolling of the *Echo*. Hurrying now, before his stomach erupted, he climbed out of the hold.

Reaching the top, Robert could hear voices along with the constant flapping of the sails and the creaking of the wooden ship. Most of the voices seemed to be coming from the area of the poop deck so Robert stumbled in the opposite direction. He wanted to empty his gut without anyone seeing him, and then disappear back into his berth. He groped to feel the rail. The previous night he had seen a sliver of a moon. Tonight thick clouds blocked out the dim light that might have shown up in the sky. Leaning over the rail into the invisible sea spray, he made a terrible involuntary groaning sound as his stomach rolled inside out.

The roar of the sea drowned the footsteps behind Robert.

Thud!

The powerful blow to the back of Robert's head came from nowhere. It was a deadening sound, wood meeting flesh. It was as though Satan himself had sucked the strength from his body. Robert legs were quickly paralyzed. He was conscious enough to feel the sensation of someone picking him upside down and throwing him over the rail. He fell face down, toward the icy cold Atlantic waters.

CHAPTER NOTES

The author thanks Bear Downing, www.yacht-volant.org/SailorTalk/seaterms, for information about how ships and sailors kept track of time, using the hourglass and the ship's bell. His research is used elsewhere in this novel.

14

HANNAH WENT FROM DEAD ASLEEP to full awake. She did it with such suddenness that she felt overwhelmed with a sense of fear, like a child awakening from a nightmare. She had no idea what had awakened her, but guessed it was some noise or movement. She had the sensation that someone had touched her. Immediately she knew that Robert was missing. Her children were asleep, not stirring. Sitting up, she held her breath and stared into the darkness.

Robert, where are you?

Sometimes Hannah was unable to trust her feelings, but right now there was no doubt. Something was wrong. Slowly rolling out of her berth and putting her coat on over her nightclothes, she waddled toward the ladder leading out of the hold.

A voice whispered in a muttered colloquy. "Where are you going?"

"Who's there?" Hannah said anxiously, feeling her unborn child kicking inside her womb.

"It's me." The voice belonged to Thomas Bloxham.

"Robert's missing," she whispered. "I'm worried."

In the dark, Hannah's brother-in-law reached to touch his chin, thinking. "He's probably on top visiting with the other men who can't sleep because of the storm. You stay here. You're in no condition to be climbing up the ladder in the dark. As soon as I find him I'll send him to you. I was just going up to the deck myself."

Deftly as a child, Thomas climbed the ladder. The stark cold of the morning air washed over him as he strode toward the nearest voices on the poop deck. He wiped a spray of seawater from his face. "Who's there?"

"It's me, Levi Roberts. We couldn't sleep. Is that you, Thomas?"

Thomas squinted. In the dark he could see the faint outlines of Levi and Daniel Browett, wrapped in their blankets, sitting. "Anyone here seen Brother Harris? He's not in his berth. Hannah's worried."

"Not us," answered Levi.

Daniel rocked to his feet, a wave of unexplainable concern sweeping over him. "There's another group on the forecastle deck," he said. "Let's ask."

Bounding down the steps onto the main deck, Daniel and Thomas crossed it, and climbed the steps onto the forecastle deck. Levi followed.

"Have you seen Brother Harris?" Daniel asked two men, his anxiety rising.

"No, why?" John Cox asked.

The voice of Thomas Bloxham sounded grave. "He's not below, and we can't find him on deck either."

John and William Jenkins rose to their feet.

"We'll help you look," William said, sounding concerned.

Daniel's reaction was quick. "Circle the ship. John, William, go left. We'll go to the right." Daniel took a few steps, cupping his hands over his mouth. "Robert!"

With each swell, the *Echo* was rising and falling, staggering the searching men, drenching them with spray. The dark waste of air and water did not reveal their lost comrade.

"Robert! Robert!"

Reaching the port side, Daniel continued to cup his hands and yell Robert's name. Suddenly, over the crash and slosh of the breakers Daniel thought he heard something.

"Quiet, Levi!"

Daniel cupped his hand over his ears.

"Help!"

Daniel turned to Levi and Thomas. "Where's that coming from?"

Thomas leaned over the rail, pointing. "Down there! I can't see him, but I hear something."

Levi yelled at the top of his voice. "Man overboard!"

Shoving Levi, Daniel yelled, "Go find the captain! Hand me a rope!"

"I still don't see him," Thomas said, horror stabbing his heart.

His eyes riveted on an unclear blur in the water below, Daniel said, "He's right there, I barely see him now. Quick! Lower me down."

Daniel tied the rope around his waist, and handed the end of the rope to Thomas. He perched tenuously on the rail as Captain Wood arrived, sprinting.

"Let me get some of my crew members to help," the captain said, eyes wide open, staring over the side.

Daniel shook his head. "Let's not wait for anything. Lower me, now!"

With those words, Daniel released his grip and pitched himself overboard. The rope cinched around his waist, and he steadily dangled toward the water. He focused his eyes, gasping as Robert disappeared under a gigantic wave, reappeared, and disappeared again. One arm was hooked onto a rope ladder.

"Throw down another rope!" Daniel yelled. "And lower me some more!" As his body struck the water, he shivered and nearly lost his breath.

"Help me," Robert pleaded, his voice slow and labored voice.

"I'm here," Daniel said. "Hang on."

A rope with a loop already formed struck Daniel on the back. Daniel was amazed how painfully slow his hands worked. He placed the loop around Robert. "Pull us up!"

Fueled by the power of more than twenty men, the bodies of Robert and Daniel were swept out of the frigid North Atlantic.

Captain Wood lost no time. Experience had taught him that he had less than a half-hour to correct a hypothermia victim's body temperature. Sometimes victims appeared to be clinically dead because of a marked depression of brain and cardiovascular function. At least the man who had been hanging onto the rope ladder was still conscious. "Pull all their clothing off, right now. Wrap them in wool blankets. Adams, fetch me the brandy and cayenne. Be quick about it."

"Yes, sir!"

As Robert's clothing was peeled away, blue skin was visible, illuminated by a lantern. Shaking uncontrollably, Robert moaned.

When the brandy and cayenne pepper arrived, Adams quickly made a paste in a wooden bowl. Captain Wood went to work on Robert first, applying the paste first to his neck, head, sides, and groin. Then the entire body. The captain did the same for Daniel.

Robert closed his eyes. His blood surged, and a welcome warmth spread through his body.

"Let's get 'em to my quarters," the captain said. "My cabin has a stove." He turned his eyes to Levi Roberts. "Just so you men know, one of the worst things that can be done now is to administer these men any kind of alcohol."

A faint smile crossed Levi's lips. "We Mormons don't use it anyway,"

Captain Wood hunched forward in his straight-backed chair, staring at the seven men that occupied his quarters. He narrowed his eyes, face drawn, brooding about the incident that nearly killed one of his passengers. Robert Harris had related in detail what had happened to him: waking, climbing out of steerage, seeking privacy because he was sick, almost losing consciousness when he was struck, and grabbing the rope ladder.

A crashing thunderstorm, with thick rain hissing down sideways from skies black at night, accentuated the gloom that he and the Mormon men felt. The rain pelted the captain's quarters. *Dat-dat-dat-dat-dat.*

Robert sat in the corner, wrapped in a blanket, suffering from a dull headache. Blood seeped from a wound at the back of his head, and a huge lump had formed. He sipped on a cup of warm herbal tea Elizabeth had prepared for him.

"I think it was Henry Eagles," the captain concluded, pulling on his beard in deep thought. He turned his eyes to Daniel. "From what you have told me, he certainly had the motivation. From what I understand, he's not even a member of your church. I'm told he's been trying to coax you to turn back to Liverpool."

The other men nodded in agreement.

"I'll have him put in chains."

Robert's face took on an unsettled look. "He'll never admit it. I didn't see him, so I can't say for certain that it was him who struck me."

John Cheese swallowed his astonishment, his voice sharp. "You needn't protect the bloke just because he is your brother-in-law. He should not go unpunished."

The captain's bushy eyebrows arched. "I'll interview your Mr. Henry Eagles, in the presence of this committee. Perhaps he'll confess. You have to understand, however, that this ship is under my command. It's my responsibility to deal with things like this."

Shrugging his shoulders in resignation, Robert said, "Fine. By the way, thank you, all of you, for rescuing me. Captain, your potion sure works."

"Amen to that," said Daniel.

"I'll have Adams fetch Mr. Eagles."

To Daniel's eyes, Captain Wood was clearly frustrated with Henry Eagles. The questioning had gone on for more than twenty minutes, with hostile expressions of denial. Now, the captain was livid with anger. He removed his hat, tossing it on the table in his quarters, revealing a wrinkled, wind-tanned brow and a receding hairline.

"I've got a mind to place you in chains, confession or not," the captain said, staring at Henry. "I have the authority to do that. Do you understand, Mr. Eagles?"

Henry sat slumped in a chair, perspiring, his eyes set in an evil qualm. His look was grim: a nasty face with hate scored on it. His nose was bent slightly to one side, victim of Robert's punch. "I didn't do it," Henry said. "And you can't prove that I did."

"You can't prove that you didn't," the captain said.

It seemed to the seven committee members that Henry had repeated those words a hundred times.

Robert rose to his feet, chewing on his lip.

Henry leaned back on his chair, unsure of what his old enemy would do. *I'll get even with Robert and Daniel if it's the last thing I do.*

"Henry," Robert snapped. "I know you don't like me. But I will promise you before each member of this committee that if you will just admit what you have done, I will not press charges. I will not let the captain put you in chains. If you'll openly confess, I'll openly forgive you. Even though you tried to kill me, I'll forgive you completely. Is that understood?"

Captain Wood reeled, narrowing his eyes at Robert. *Who gave you authority to say that?*

Henry's voice was firm. "I didn't do it."

After a glum pause, Robert said, "I promise to not press charges."

Henry screwed all the heavy features of his face into a mask of disagreement. In a gravelly voice he repeated, "I didn't do it!"

Robert returned a skeptical glance at his brother-in-law, and then turned to the captain. "Do you promise that if he will confess that you will not put him in chains or press charges of any kind?"

The captain uttered a noncommittal grunt.

"That a yes or a no?"

Captain Wood shrugged, and spread his hands. "Fine with me."

Henry moved restlessly in his chair. "I'm not going to confess just to make this little Mormon committee happy."

John Cheese cast a disdainful eye toward Robert. "Why are you so willing to let him off without being prosecuted?"

The atmosphere in the room turned thick with curiosity.

"I think I know the answer to that." Daniel said, his face dissolving into a warm, gentle smile. "A year ago Brother Harris would have torn Henry apart for hitting him on the back of the head, and tossing him overboard. My brother-in-law is a different person now. I think it's hard for him, but he's trying to turn the other cheek, like the Savior taught."

John folded his arms over his stomach. "Is that right?" he asked Robert.

With a tart grin, Robert merely shrugged his shoulders.

Daniel whispered into the captain's ear.

Tightly, sarcastically, Captain Wood said, "Mr. Eagles, you may go."

MONDAY Feb. 23 – Trouble with Henry Eagles this morning. He wants the ship to turn back because of the storms. One of the passengers, not in our company of saints, has been dangerously ill for several days. She died about two o'clock. Several of the ship's crew came to look at her, as it was the first that died on board. One of our own company sewed her up in a sheet. Buried her in the sea two hours later. We saw porpoises again, and several small birds. Captain said we made ten knots an hour today but slowed to five knots by evening as the wind came against us strong again.

TUESDAY Feb. 24 – During the night Brother Harris was seasick and leaning over the side fell or was pushed into the sea but he was able to catch himself on ropes. Hannah, thankfully, woke up suddenly and noticed him missing; we soon found him and pulled him to safety. He refused to press charges against Henry, who we know is the guilty person who threw Robert overboard.

WEDNESDAY Feb. 25 – Still off course, winds are stronger. Our committee fears it a consequence of someone actually trying to kill Brother Harris. I fear it was his brother-in-law but Brother Harris still refused to press charges. Towards six o'clock the wind ahead blows fresh and increases to a hurricane. The ship was heaving most tremendously. Tubs were rolling about, pans and kettles all of it in an uproar, women shrieking, children crying, all hastening to their berths. Wind continued all night. Most are still sick. At 10 at night an awful wave came over the hull and water came down the hatchway and alarmed all the people very much. Captain Wood confided in me that we might indeed sink. I told him that we would not sink, that God would protect us. The storm subsided somewhat.

15

HENRY SHRANK WHEN HE SAW Hannah strolling awkwardly toward him and his wife on the crowded main deck. She placed her bulging torso in front of her brother, shaking her fist.

"How could you do such a thing, Henry?" she said in a raging tantrum. "You almost murdered my husband."

Hannah's jaunty bluntness reduced Katherine to tears. She turned hastily to her husband. "It was you?"

Word had already spread like wildfire among the passengers that Robert had been rescued during the night. During their morning stroll, Henry had remained tight-lipped with his wife.

Henry turned on his heel and walked the opposite direction, passing a sailor carving a ship model from a bone.

Hannah overtook her brother, tears stinging her eyes. "I just want to know why," she demanded.

"It wasn't me," Henry said, his eyes narrowing. Pregnancy, besides making his sister an odd shape, had hollowed her cheeks and her eyes, and exaggerated her full mouth. "I told that to the captain, to the committee, and now to you. I didn't do it."

Hannah threw a distrusting glare at her brother. "You've been a poor liar since you were a child, Henry. I don't believe you."

Katherine turned her face away in embarrassment, the flush of humiliation staining her cheeks.

In a quick irritated gesture, Henry waved an arm fore and aft. "It could've been one of the crew members. Why don't you question them?"

Hannah ignored Henry's denial, biting her lip. "I just want to know why. Don't you have any feeling toward my children and me? Would you leave them fatherless? Who would care for me in America, a mother of three children?" Pointing at her midsection, she corrected herself. "Four."

"Did Bobby see me?" Henry asked, his cheeks flaming red, partly because of the blows he had sustained from Robert, and partly because of his swelling anger. "Can he positively identify me? No, he can't. I didn't do it, dear sister."

It infuriated Hannah further that her brother had just called her husband Bobby, as he had been known in his youth and before his baptism, instead of Robert. She continued her verbal attack and her ruffled manner, but she soon realized it was useless. Henry had never been the type of person to humble himself and admit to anything he had done wrong. She pointed out that this was a serious charge that could lead to prosecution, and that neither she nor Robert wanted him to face the prospect of being put in chains by the captain and his crew.

They bantered until Robert saw the incongruous scene of sister arguing against brother. He quickly strode to the middle of them and took Hannah by the arm, and whisked her away. As he floated by, he said to Katherine in a polite voice, "How's Sister Eagles this morning?"

Katherine stammered an answer. "Fine, Brother Harris."

Henry stood silent and rigid, his back arched like a soldier under inspection. His eyes were still unyielding.

Tugging on his wife's arm, Robert said, "Hannah, let it go. He's never going to admit to anything. And he's right. I can't identify him. I didn't see who it was. You don't want your own brother in chains, do you?"

Hannah's pink face sharpened. "No, of course not! I just want him to admit to it."

"He won't, so quit stirrin' it up."

Dropping her voice to express her contempt, she said, "But what if he tries it again? This is quite unnerving to me."

"What can we do? We can't follow him around."

"A lot of people on the ship feel the worsening storm is a result of Henry's act of attempted murder."

"I know, I've heard it, too."

"They're comparing it to Laman and Lemuel's disobedience."

"I know." Robert took her hand and held it to his face.

Hannah's eyes misted. "If Henry would just admit it perhaps the storms would go away and we would get favorable winds."

THURSDAY Feb. 26 – Winds unfavorable. Captain says we are off course to the southeast. At least the weather is slowly warming. Murmuring continues. I called the Saints on deck and chastened and reproved them sharply, reminding them that these are the trials and tribulations I spoke of, which brought them to repentance. One lady not of our company was thrown from her bed and her shoulder dislocated, which was tended by the doctor on board.

FRIDAY Feb. 27 – Winds still unfavorable. A crewmember caught neglecting his duty, having too much liquor. Got flogged 24 lashes.

SATURDAY Feb. 28 – We have decided to have a special sacrament meeting tomorrow and ask everyone to fast and pray for more favorable weather. I have assigned Brother Jenkins to talk about repentance. I hope Henry will listen. I don't know of anyone who needs to repent more than Henry Eagles. Captain says we are getting closer to Spain than America.

"No, I'm not going to the Mormon Sunday worship," Henry whispered in a tone laced with sarcasm and continued defiance. He turned his big-jawed face away from his wife in their berth.

He remained wrapped up in his blanket, his broken nose still in pain. He detested his loss of privacy. *A man can't even have a conversation with his wife without everyone listening. I want to go home.*

Katherine matched Henry's clipped tone perfectly, though whispering. "You'll appear all the more guilty if you miss the meeting. Besides, the topic is repentance."

"Why don't they pick a subject like brotherly love?" Henry snapped back. "Or turning the other cheek." He smiled inwardly at his cleverness.

Giving her husband a crabbed grin, Katherine slid out of the berth. "Stay here if you wish. I'm going."

Henry sighed. He knew Katherine was right, although he would never admit it verbally. His absence might be construed as an admission of guilt. *I'll deny it to my death.*

Only a few Mormons had acknowledged Henry's presence before the meeting began. Greetings had been with forced smiles, and contemptuous glares. Henry regarded the impassive silence with smugness. Now, William Jenkins was speaking. Henry stared out to sea, trying to ignore the sermon. He had nothing to repent of.

Soon, however, William's words began to hang over Henry like a dismal pall. Repentance: a change of mind, a fresh view about God, about oneself, and about the world. All are stained by sin, *some more than others.* All must be cleansed in order to enter the kingdom of heaven. Repentance is not optional for salvation, it is a commandment of God.

If I walk out now, I'll draw too much attention, Henry said to himself.

"Repentance means to change one's life in accordance to God's will, to stop doing what's wrong and start doing what's right. I hope all within sound of my voice can understand what I am saying."

Henry grimaced, feeling that all eyes were staring at him.

A scripture. The Savior's words rocked Henry. *If they would not repent they must suffer even as I.*

"There are two ways to pay for sin," William explained. "The first is to repent, confess, and give your sin to the Savior. The second, refuse to confess, refuse to repent, and suffer even as the Savior has suffered. We all know how he sweat great drops of blood in the Garden as he took on himself the sins of the world. If we repent, the atonement of Christ has claim upon us. If we don't, we will suffer even as He has suffered."

If there is life after death, I hope I am far away from Robert Harris.

"There are those who falsely suppose that Christ's suffering supplants suffering on our part, when we repent. In the proper process of repentance, we must feel remorse for our past sinful life. We must suffer in body and soul. We must feel the anguish associated with true repentance. One has not begun to repent until he has suffered intensely for his sins. One has got to go through a change in his system whereby he suffers. and then forgiveness is a possibility. If not, we, in the next life, suffer like Christ suffered, eternally."

Long before the closing song and prayer, Henry skulked away, his head hanging.

Four more were baptized in the barrel.

SUNDAY Feb. 29 – Morning winds unfavorable. I ordered our whole company on deck. Meeting commences with Brother Wilding singing a hymn, prayer, then another hymn by the congregation. Singing again, then breaking the bread and handing the cup. Brother Jenkins addressed the congregation about repentance. I think he was directing his remarks to Henry Eagles. All on their knees for a special prayer. Immediately afterward the winds became calm and favorable. We were able to sail southwest all night. Captain is overjoyed. So are we.

16

REBECCA BROWETT SLOWLY ASCENDED the creaky wooden ladder out of steerage, grateful that everyone appeared to be asleep. To her eyes, the main deck was deserted. For the past several nights, and despite her earlier encounter with Henry, she had grown accustomed to sneaking into the water closet located near the stairs leading to the forecastle deck. *No chamber pot for me.* Without looking up, she darted inside. It had given her a rush of adrenaline to think she could sneak around the ship in the middle of the night undetected.

Emerging from the head, the scene above the masts and tall sails seemed bizarre. Her jaw dropped as she began witnessing a celestial phenomenon that had amazed people for centuries. Flickering curtains of lights danced across the dark sky. It was the Italian scientist Galileo who first used the expression *Aurora Borealis,* Latin for red dawn of the north. Rebecca recalled the words of the steward earlier in the trip. *With luck you'll see the northern lights. No pencil can draw it, no colors can paint it, and no words can describe it in all its magnificence.*

Momentarily paralyzed by the sky as she stared upward, with the sound of the wind slapping the sails, Rebecca suddenly felt clammy. As if ignited by some unseen force, she began to sprint toward the hatch. It was too late. A beam of heat screamed from the top of her skull to the tips of her toes as the man's fist crashed down on the back of her neck. Everything went black as she collapsed to the deck.

The sudden wave of panic that rose in Daniel as he jerked awake in a cold sweat was a frenzy of unexplained fears. His initial instinct was for Elizabeth. She was sound asleep. *Rebecca!* Daniel's panic turned inward, his senses on overload. Without checking his sister's berth, he shot up the ladder.

"Rebecca! Rebecca!" As he topped the ladder, he stumbled, sprawling across the deck, still screaming his sister's name.

As he stood, he was greeted only by the rocking of the ship, the wind pushing the sails, and the sound of waves crashing against the hull.

"Rebecca!"

"What's wrong?"

Daniel wheeled to see Robert emerging from steerage.

"I don't know for sure. But I think something has happened to Rebecca." Daniel's spiritual reflex was his only compass.

"She's not in her berth?"

"I don't know."

A bewildered look crossed Robert's face as several more men emerged from below, asking questions. *You haven't even checked her berth?*

Daniel began issued orders, pointing in the dark. "Robert, you and Thomas search the poop deck. Levi and John, take the forecastle. Hurry!" *Where are you, Rebecca?*

They found her less than five minutes later, lying unconscious in the longboat, used for shore excursions and as a lifeboat. Some of her clothing had been torn away. She had been the victim of a cruel attack.

Daniel lifted her head slightly, looking for signs of life.

"Rebecca?"

He pressed an ear to her nose. She was breathing. Tears of relief came to Daniel's eye.

"I wonder who…?" Daniel's words trailed off. He thought of Henry. And he thought of every lustful sailor aboard the ship.

The Mormon men scanned the *Echo* in the darkness, even the mass of cordage.

The attacker had escaped without a sign.

Rebecca began to groan.

Thank God, she's alive, Daniel thought. He scooped her into his arms and carried her below.

Rebecca's morning headache was marked with blurred vision, partial paralysis in her right eye, a ringing in her ears, and a persistent throbbing pain. Luckily, Daniel's noisy appearance on the main deck had frightened the attacker away before anything more serious happened to her. Rebecca could remember nothing. She had not seen the man who attempted to molest her.

As the burden of Rebecca's sorrow sunk into his own mind, Daniel grimaced in the gloomy confines of steerage. He turned to Elizabeth, who was still examining her sister-in-law. "I'll talk to the captain about this right away. Spread the word among all the women, young and old. Keep yourselves out of harm's way. It goes without saying that many of the sailors are very worldly and can't be trusted." *And Henry.*

Daniel touched Rebecca on the arm. "I'll be back with the brethren soon to give you a priesthood blessing."

She nodded her approval, tears streaming down her cheeks.

Shaking, struggling to regain his composure, Daniel made his way to the captain's quarters. He drifted into troubled thoughts, filled with incoherent frightening scenes of what it must have been like for his sister to endure the cowardly attack in the dead of night, all alone, defenseless. He became angry with himself, that he had not been there to protect her, and he wondered if there were other dreadful things going on that he was unaware of. He felt as though he had let his sister down, and there was a possibility that he was letting others down.

Elizabeth knew her husband's thoughts. For an instant she compared his reaction to Rebecca's attack to the time in England when he found out that

John Benbow and Thomas Kington had joined the Mormon Church, abandoning the United Brethren faith they had created themselves. He initially saw their conversion as illogical, and it depressed him, even to the point of temporary sarcasm. But all it took was a simple powerful testimony from Elder Wilford Woodruff to convert her husband to the gospel. With every calling and responsibility he had been given, Daniel had proven that he was a man with a plow horse work ethic, a deep sense of purpose, who was highly disciplined, stable, dependable, and a high achiever.

Elizabeth knew he blamed himself for everything that went wrong.

The captain's reaction was immediate. "Whoever done this will be flogged and put in chains," he said, slamming a bottle of brandy down and pouring himself a drink. He was tormented with the knowledge that one of his sailors had breached a trust and molested one of the Mormon passengers. It made it all the worse that the passenger was Captain Browett's sister, the man who had saved his ship. A smoldering rage began to take shape in his chest.

"My sister was struck from behind. She has no idea who it was." Daniel went on to say he saw no one at all when he and his men searched the deck. He related everything about the attack he could think of.

"Captain Browett, we had a night watch. There was a handful of sailors on deck. Just because you didn't see them, I'm sure they saw you."

Daniel stared at the captain in disbelief. "Then it could be one of the sailors. Do you think there is a witness?"

Wood slammed his goblet to the table. "Possibly. I'll start by questioning every man who was on the watch. What about Mr. Eagles?"

Daniel grimaced and his eyes narrowed. "He threatened both Mr. Harris and me after the incident the other day."

"I'll question him, too."

"I hope you get the right man in chains."

17

EVERYTHING SEEMED NORMAL, hauntingly normal, to Daniel as he left the captain's quarters.

Everywhere, in the bright morning sunshine, sailors were doing their usual duties: hauling ropes, furling and reefing sails, swabbing decks, scouring decks with blocks of sandstone, and moving steerage and cabin passengers from one deck to another. Some were singing sailor songs such as *Blow the Man Down* as they would raise a topsail yard, or *Haul the Bowline* when a rope had to be tightened in short, quick motions. Sometimes a chantey was led by one of the sailors who had a knack for incorporating the idiosyncrasies of various crewmembers into the lyrics. Daniel knew it made the work of a sailor more tolerable. He tried to listen to the lyrics to determine if there was anything sung about a possible link to what had happened to Rebecca, but the lyrics were too hard to understand.

He peeked into the crew's quarters under the forecastle deck, where the off duty sailors were smoking their filthy clay pipes, loafing on their sea chests, and napping in their bunks. One or two were reading, one of them from the Bible. As the watch changed, sailors dressed in their rancid oilskins and unwashed bodies swarmed out of their quarters while others swarmed in. Several had quids of chewing tobacco staining their beards.

Daniel found it hard not to be judgmental. He knew that while the ship was in Liverpool all of the sailors had been paid, but that most of them had quickly frittered away their money on drink and women in the pleasure dens of the British port. He detested them for their lifestyle but knew that a blanket indictment was not fair, thinking of the single sailor he had seen reading the Bible, and of Michael Heywood, who seemed to have high moral values. Daniel knew that most packet officers, such as Adams, Evans, Neptune, and Captain Wood, had sprung from the ranks of ordinary seamen. The captain had told Daniel that packet sailors generally would not sail in any other trade, many of them openly declaring that their goal was to become a captain so that they could earn a lot of money. Whoever was going to be locked in chains certainly would have his career rudely interrupted and his life ruined. Whoever the guilty man was, it would serve him right, Daniel thought.

The ship seemed to be making up for lost time. During the entire voyage the sailors had been worked night and day. *Night is the time to try the nerves and make quick passages,* the captain had been overheard to say many times. Since being blown off course, the captain had made certain that every possible inch of canvas was flying, making hairbreadth decisions night and day. He was doing it with a daring that would have amounted to recklessness had Captain Wood not made them on the basis of unrelenting vigilance and profound knowledge. Daniel guess that the Captain was under extreme pressure to make up for the two weeks they were behind, and get to New Orleans as soon as he could, unload, then return to Liverpool with another cargo of freight and passengers. The loss of one sailor during the storm was probably keenly felt. Now a second sailor was going to be lost, this one to a flogging and to chains.

Unless the guilty man turned out to be a member of his own company. Henry Eagles.

As Captain Wood conferred with Adams, the second mate, poring over the night watch list and determining who should be questioned first, the first mate, Evans, burst through the door. "Captain! The sailors have spotted a vessel. She is flying the colors out of Tripoli."

"Tripoli?" the captain groaned. *What next?*

As he hurried outside, the captain took off his cap and ran a hand through his hair, thinking. If it were true, it was the first vessel anyone had spotted since they left the coast of England and Ireland. *But why did it have to be Tripoli?*

Adams followed, his face full of concern for the crisis concerning Rebecca and for the approaching ship.

Captain Wood's chin muscles twitched. "My telescope!"

Emerging from steerage with James Pulham and Robert, where they had given Rebecca her blessing and Nancy Eagles another blessing, Daniel took in the Captain's nervous concern. "What's out there, captain?"

Captain Wood peered through his brass and wood telescope as though he were in utter bewilderment. "A foreign vessel," he answered in a faltering voice. "She has a black hull. She's bearing down on us."

Daniel tensed up. "Where are we?"

"The winds and ocean currents have pushed the ship into the treacherous eddies south of Spain and Portugal, only about a hundred leagues from the tip of northern Africa. As you know, we've been imprisoned by factors we have no control over. We're around thirty-seven degrees latitude according to the sextant. We're tacking west now, but we've been spotted."

"What kind of vessel?" Daniel held a hand over a worried forehead and squinted in the direction the captain was looking. *Satan really doesn't want us to reach Nauvoo.*

"Tripoli. One of the nations of northern Africa. Looks like she's fitted with cannon."

"Is America at war against Tripoli?" James asked, drawn in by the drama of a congregating crew as they watched the vessel approach.

"We used to be. Ever heard of the Barbary Wars?" The captain could see that even at full sail the *Echo* was no match in speed for the approaching ship, which sat much higher in the water. His ship was already under as much canvas as possible. Wetting down the sails wouldn't gain much additional advantage.

"No, sir."

The captain's face was wrinkled with concern. He withdrew the telescope from his face. "The wars go back thirty or thirty-five years. The four Barbary States of North Africa—Tripoli, Tunis, Algiers and Morocco—plundered our seaborne commerce for years. Not just the United States, but all European nations suffered at their hands. Barbary pirates raided trading ships that passed through this area back and forth from the Mediterranean. They survived either by plundering or blackmail. Great sums of money were paid just to allow foreigners to trade in African ports and sail unmolested through Barbary waters. More and more they demanded tribute money and seized ships. Even held crews for ransom or sold them into slavery."

Daniel's eyes widened. "Is this a pirate ship?"

The captain pressed the telescope to his face again. "There's no skull and crossbones like the pirate ships of old, but we don't know her intentions. She's cutting a feather across the sea, barely a ripple. We'd never outrun her. I suspect there are still a lot of hard feelings among the Barbary nations. There's nothing we can do to protect ourselves. We're a passenger ship."

"Would they actually sink us?" Daniel asked, his pale face wrapped with concern.

"I don't think so, but it depends on who they are, and who the captain is. These people are Muslims, and there are factions of them that have a long history of hatred toward Christians dating back to the Crusades. They consider us infidels. You've heard of the Crusades haven't you?"

"Yes."

"In the seventeenth century, pirates that we now call the Barbary Corsairs worked under the protection of the Ottoman Empire. The Corsairs were commissioned to attack Christian shipping throughout the Mediterranean. Soon they became daring, even raiding the south coasts of Ireland and England. Not all the Barbary Corsairs were Muslim. Some were Jews and renegade Christians. Some were from Greece and the Balkans."

Daniel's background in history was limited. "But you *did* say the Barbary

Wars ended many years ago."

"America finally got tired of putting up with the seagoing terrorists."

"Terroritsts?"

"Yes," the captain said. "The rulers of the Barbary States tolerated the pirates for a cut of the loot. Most of the loot was pretty mundane stuff—food, clothing, pans, ships stores, and tools. And a little gold. The only way America and other nations could protect their citizens from pirate attacks was to pay a large sum of money—tribute money. Acts of piracy weren't exactly an extension of the Holy Wars. The pirates were bloodthirsty fanatics sanctioned by Islamic despots."

Daniel gulped.

"Our president believed their behavior threatened the future of the modern world. The pirates committed atrocious acts against many people."

Atrocious acts? The thought caused Daniel to shudder.

"They were experts at instilling terror against the modern world with cannons and scimitars. The Barbary nations first declared war against us in 1785, and goaded us into combat again in 1801 and 1815. Our first president, George Washington, wished back in his day that our new country had the power to reform them or crush them into non-existence. Our navy was built largely because of the pirate's hostage taking and escalating ransom demands that became politically unbearable."

The captain handed Daniel the telescope.

Holding the glass steady against his eye, Daniel could see the worrisome ship approaching. His pulse quickened. "So America declared war in return?"

"We sent naval squadrons into the Mediterranean," the captain said, speaking in hurried clips now. "Lots of bombardments on the coast. Even hand-to-hand combat. In three or four years the pirates were partly wiped out. The Barbary States cried 'uncle.' The War of 1812 between your nation and America didn't do the process any good. But afterward we sent two more naval squadrons back into the Mediterranean. By resolute force we brought the rulers of Barbary to terms. Tribute payments ended after the last official war, in 1815. But pirates kept preying on European and American ships until

France captured Algiers eleven years ago."

"That means we shouldn't be seeing pirate ships," Daniel said.

"Almost," the captain replied. "Nowadays acts of piracy have been reduced to just a few renegade ships. Perhaps like the one we're looking at out there. A few radical Muslims believe they must always be stirring up a war. Otherwise, the world would soon cease to fear them."

"You know your history very well, sir."

"All our captains know naval history very well," Captain Wood said tensely.

Daniel narrowed his eyes. "The word 'pirate' has always sounded so romantic, until now."

The captain snorted. "Strip away the romance, the creaking ship on a moonlit tropical sea, and the thunder of surf as they tote their chests of gold to a hiding place, and what do you have? Pirates are nothing more than thieves, and murderers as well."

"What can I do to help?"

"Ask your people to pray," the captain said. "I have faith in your God. Your prayers saved the ship once. Please do it again. I don't want to see that pirate ship get out their grappling hooks and start vapouring us."

"Vapouring?"

"A term to describe pirates when they start growling and chanting war cries, waving their weapons, and clashing their cutlasses. Pounding on the ship's rails. Trying to frighten their prey into submission."

A despairing vision came over Robert as he listened to the captain's conversation with Daniel, and as he watched the Tripoli vessel close the distance between it and the *Echo*. The captain continued to look through his telescope, leaning forward, silently glassing the approaching ship, searching for the color of her flag and evidences of the number of men, cannon, and weapons.

It struck Robert that perhaps God *was* going to punish the *Echo* passengers for their constant murmuring, for Henry's actions, and for the new crisis surrounding Rebecca's attack. And perhaps his own failing for retaliating against his brother-in-law. Robert had read in the Book of Mormon the story of Lehi's trip across the ocean, and the disobedience of Laman and Lamuel. In Robert's opinion, there was a chance that God had weighed the *Echo* in the balance and found it wanting.

Each second passed with nerve-wracking irony. The captain reported he could see sailors on the Tripoli vessel fully armed, waving guns and swords in the air. It appeared that the *Echo* was doomed unless God intervened.

His mood reaching the depth of dismalness, Robert's apocalyptic vision vanished as he saw Henry and Katherine join the kneeling passengers. He could see Henry standing defiantly for a few seconds, and then Katherine pulled him to his knees. Despite a reluctant disregard for his old enemy, Robert stood up and found his way to Henry, wading through dozens of people, tapping him on the head.

"Follow me, Henry," he said in an agitated voice.

Henry remained motionless, cursing beneath his breath. Robert reached for Henry's collar, giving it a powerful jerk. "I said follow me."

Under the curious glares of the passengers, Henry struggled to his feet. Robert pushed Henry toward the empty smoking compartment, at the rear of the poop deck. "Get in there, and be quick about it."

He shoved Henry through the door and closed it.

"Leave me alone! What do you want?" Henry whimpered, cowering on a padded bench in the far corner.

Robert gave Henry a cold unsympathetic stare, contemplating how frightened he appeared sitting there in the corner, his dark hair tousled, a wild look in his eyes, the veins in his neck sticking out. Robert gritted his teeth in frustration. "Henry, you know what you did, and I know what you did. We've got something serious going on out there. Everyone feels that the storms we've encountered and our being off course are a result of your constant murmuring, agitating other passengers to make them want to return to Liverpool, and your act of aggression against Daniel. And they feel that this ship coming toward us is the same thing. An act of punishment, if you will, from God."

Henry's face took on a hard, sullen, puzzled look. "This is stupid," he shot back. "You can't blame me just because some idiotic pirates are out there wanting to take advantage of a helpless immigrant ship."

Robert grabbed Henry by the front of his shirt, and put his face to his. Robert's voice was low, authoritative, and impatient. "Henry, for the sake of all of us, listen to me. I just want you to do one thing. Admit what you did. If you'll do that, I'll totally forgive you. I'll not hold it against you. I will not press charges. Just admit what you did."

Robert waited for an answer, hoping Henry would understand the peril they were in. Through the window, he could see the Tripoli vessel coming alongside.

Fear stabbed at Henry's bowels and his mouth dropped as he contemplated Robert's words. His voice trembled. "And you think if I did, this ship—this pirate ship or whatever it is—will go away, just like that?"

"It's full of armed sailors. And the ship is armed with cannon."

"I can see. Let go of me."

"They have a history of hating everyone from England and America. We're on an American vessel."

Henry uttered a low gloating laugh. "I know that. I'm not stupid."

Robert pointed a bony finger at Henry's face. His voice was stern. "They're going to board us, Henry."

Henry drew a deep breath. "You won't hurt me?"

"No, I promise."

Henry looked away, and his voice tone changed. His mind brought to remembrance the principles he had heard during the Sunday preaching. "Do you think it's true that the wicked must suffer for their own sins?"

"If they don't repent."

"Okay. I did it. I'm sorry." His eyes lit with fear, Henry looked up at his brother-in-law, who still held his shirt in a powerful grip.

Robert's eyes narrowed once more. "And Rebecca? Were you the one?"

"No! No!" Henry shook his head violently. "That was not me. I swear to God. You've got to believe me."

Robert contemplated his brother-in-law for a few moments, then glanced out the window again at the pirate ship. A feeling came over him. "Okay. I believe you about Rebecca. And I forgive you for what you did to me. Thanks for leveling with me." Robert released Henry and stepped toward the door.

Henry sank to his knees, muttering. "Please, God, let us live! Let us live!"

Relieved that his confrontation with Henry was over, and that he had obtained a confession, albeit forced, Robert said a silent prayer, begging God to accept Henry's confession and turn the Tripoli vessel away. He exited the room.

Captain Wood was addressing Daniel's concerns as Robert approached: "It's hard to predict what the pirates will do. There's no gold on board. Just used furniture. And a few tools for farmers. Maybe they'll take a look and leave."

"Maybe it's time to stand alongside the bulwark and show them just how many passengers there are on board," Robert suggested, joining Daniel and the captain shoulder to shoulder. "There're a lot more of us than there are of them."

The captain, who had been scanning every brightly dressed pirate on the foreign vessel with a measure of fear, suddenly changed his countenance. He summoned Adams to his side. "Mate, bring all the passengers and crewmembers over here, and be quick about it. Let's give them a show of strength. Unlock the chests. Brandish every weapon that we have."

"Aye, aye, sir!"

Daniel wondered if the captain regretted confiscating pistols and knives from the crew at the beginning of the voyage, and tossing them overboard.

Within seconds men were streaming to the starboard side of the ship, steerage passengers from the hold and from their praying positions on the deck, cabin passengers from the dining room and from their cabins, and deck hands from the riggings. Robert made a quick count and compared the count to the number of pirates as the Tripoli vessel closed within fifty yards. The *Echo* men outnumbered the pirates at least twenty to one. He suspected that every male passenger, like him, would defend his family with every ounce of vitality he possessed. Robert hoped the pirates could not detect the fear on every face of the men on board, and the fact that they had no weapons—except for some of the *Echo* crewmen. If the pirate ship used her cannon to sink the *Echo*, any supposed treasure would be lost to the bottom of the ocean, two miles down.

Henry emerged from the smoking compartment. Robert motioned at him. "Stand here, by me," he said.

Eight-year-old Charles Bloxham stood next to his father, erect, as though ready for battle.

Cannons aimed at the *Echo*, pirates brandishing muskets and pistols, the Tripoli vessel edged alongside the American ship.

"What do you want?" Captain Wood hollered at the top of his voice.

A man in a bright orange and black turban yelled back in a foreign tongue with a coarse, tough look, revealing large yellow teeth surrounded by a black beard.

Daniel turned to the captain with imploring eyes. "What did he say?"

"I don't know. I don't understand his tongue. He's speaking in Arabic. I don't suppose he understood my words, but I think he knows my meaning."

"What are you going to do?"

"Nothing right now. I think he's sizing us up. If he can comprehend that we're an American vessel full of poor English immigrants, he might reason we're not worth ransacking." The captain took off his cap and bowed toward the man wearing the yellow and black turban. "At least there's no vapouring going on."

The man bowed back, and laughed through his dark beard. He said something else to the captain, and then turned to his crew and yelled some commands, pointing at the *Echo*. In seconds the brightly dressed pirates were climbing the rigging, crawling out on the swaying yards, tugging on slippery ropes.

In minutes, the Tripoli vessel turned away.

MONDAY March 1 – We were spotted by a North African ship out of Tripoli, which came aside. The Lord heard our prayers and the foreigners did not board us. No one could understand what they were saying. They argued amongst themselves, then left. Captain feared they were remnants of the old Barbary pirates and he will report the incident to proper authorities. Winds stay favorable.

TUESDAY March 2 – Fine morning. Weather continues favorable. Sister Pulham is still deathly sick; her stomach seems to have changed its functions, nothing will pass through her. Her husband fears for her life. Mr. Henry Eagles seems more at ease, even talks to me.

WEDNESDAY March 3 – Rainy morning. Another vessel in sight. Captain says not to worry about other vessels anymore. Afternoon mild. Winds favorable. The captain and officers are kind and humane men. One of the sailors, an intelligent man, told me that he had been in the passenger line of shipping for years and never saw anything like the passengers on the *Echo*. The sailors wonder how a company of people who were many of them strangers to each other can bear and forbear in the manner they do. We have commenced teaching him the gospel.

18

DAYS LATER, WITH THE CRISIS of the pirate ship over, and the weather pleasant, Daniel leaned against the deckhouse, contemplating his responsibilities.

The *Echo* had just passed the Madeira Islands, and the captain reported that the ship's position was now near nineteen degrees west longitude and thirty degrees north. The bad news was that they were still four weeks away from New Orleans. The good news was that from here on the ship could make good time, with a heading almost due west. They would soon reach the Tropic of Cancer about the midpoint in the Atlantic Ocean, with the West Indies as their next target. The ocean and the weather seemed less of a threat now, in Daniel's view.

The sailors? That was another matter. Daniel accepted Robert's belief that Henry was not involved in Rebecca's attack. He refused to believe that any other passenger was the guilty party. That left one stirring conclusion: one of Captain Wood's men, still on the loose.

From his position near the mizzenmast, Daniel scanned merry groups of his Mormon steerage passengers on the three decks, elbow-to-elbow, thick as flies on a honey pot, mingling with the smartly dressed cabin passengers, telling stories, singing songs, and cracking jokes. Others were making use of the cooking grates, trying to make a tasty lunch out of things like oatmeal, rice, half-rotted potatoes, and rancid drinking water—all stored in barrels that had previously been used for wine, indigo, and tobacco. For a moment he listened to the older children comparing their individual tallies of the number of rats hunted, chased, and killed in various parts of the ship.

Michael Heywood, whose teeth gleamed under a broad smile, interrupted Daniel's deep thoughts. "Are we sailing with the wind at our quarter or close-hauled today, Captain Browett?"

Daniel bristled. There had been so much going on since his last "sailing test" that he didn't know if he were in the mood for another grilling or not. The incident with Henry, Robert's near death, seasickness, Rebecca's ordeal, the appearance of the pirate ship, had worn him out. He was looking forward to having a quiet day at sea.

"Wind at our quarter," he guessed.

"Wrong," Heywood exclaimed, shaking his finger at Daniel. "We're running close-hauled, which means beating the windward against the headwind. Today the wind is coming out of the southwest, almost the direction we want to go. The nearest a square-rigged ship like the *Echo* can come to sailing directly against the wind is sailing on the port tack, or the starboard tack. When the wind strikes the sail squarely it imparts a powerful drive both forward and sideways. The glancing force of the wind on a close-hauled sail imparts much less headway and leeway to a ship. We're running close-hauled today, not running as good as yesterday, but making some progress nevertheless."

Daniel shrugged his shoulders, feeling glad he wasn't a sailor.

"Fair weather is the time to send down tackle from aloft and repair it. Notice all the sailors working today?"

Adams approached, pointing at a sailor. "What's this daydreamin' all about, sonny? Here with you, on the jump, and coil down this gantline! Make it snappy! Have it ready to run free when we send down the main royal!"

The young sailor set himself briskly at task to arrange the rope in a neat coil.

Adams yelled at nother sailor, who was in the dizzying heights of the masts. "Aloft there on the main top gall'nt yard! Overhaul the starboard bunt-line and leechline, and put a light stop on 'em."

"Aye, aye, sir!"

The mate now roared to a group of sailors scattered among the upper sails of the main mast, who were spinning out their jobs too long. "Lively up there men! Lower one of those sails down for repairs!"

Adams then turned his attention to sailors on the fife rail, which contained two wheels and connecting shafts, part of the pump system used to keep water out of the hold. "I wanna know if those pumps are working properly! See to it!"

Daniel noted that yet another sailor was performing as blacksmith of sorts, using a hot fire to make new hooks and rings for the blocks. Still another, one of the ship's carpenters, was making a new yard to repair one that had been destroyed in the storm.

Others yet were weaving rope yarn into mats for securing and protecting jury spars, and another was working with the dexterity of an embroiderer to work collars of hemp lace around the shrouds to keep them in place.

Daniel felt a sudden chill. *Which man attacked my sister? Are other young women of my company still in danger?*

Both Daniel and Elizabeth had spent a lot of time earlier in the day with Rebecca trying to assess her emotional damage. Physically, she nursed a tender lump on the back of her head, complained of aches throughout her body, did not sleep well during the night, and had no appetite.

"Why would someone want to harm me that way?" Rebecca said in disbelief. "I feel so humiliated, so confused, so ashamed."

"Shame is what your *attacker* ought to feel, not you," said Elizabeth. "Please don't blame yourself. You can't control the actions of another person."

Rebecca stole a glance at Daniel. "I know I shouldn't have been on the main deck during the night. I'm sorry I failed you. You must think I'm terribly stupid."

"Nonsense, Rebecca," Daniel shot back. "It's important that you don't blame yourself."

"You still can't remember anything?" Elizabeth asked. She feared Rebecca might have serious repercussions in the future: continued feelings of guilt, bad dreams, mood swings, confusion, sadness, vengeance, degradation. She might even refuse to go back on deck for even a breath of fresh air.

Rebecca opened up. "Just looking up into the sky at the lights, then the feeling that someone was coming after me. I never saw who it was. Next thing I knew I was lying in my berth with that terrible headache. I wonder what that awful man did to me while I was unconscious."

"Nothing," Elizabeth said emphatically. "Absolutely nothing. Your clothing was a little tousled, but that's all. Luckily, Daniel scared the man away. You have nothing to be embarrassed of, nothing at all."

A tear came to Rebecca's eye. "But what about next time? I don't feel safe. That man is still out there, somewhere. And what about the other girls? And other women?"

Daniel looked gloomy. *I've failed my own sister. This can't happen again.*

THURSDAY March 4 – Still no apprehension of the guilty party who accosted my sister. I fear she will be emotionally scarred for a while. I feel she harbors an inner anger not only toward the guilty sailor, whoever he is, but also toward all men in general. Quite calm at night. Music and dancing on board. Brother Harris played the violin.

19

Tirley, Gloucestershire, England

WILFORD WOODRUFF WAS IN a relaxed happy mood. With his most engaging smile, he strode into the parlor of a two-story home in Tirley, two miles west of Apperley, with Elders Willard Richards and Thomas Kington. He warmed his hands over a crackling fire in the hearth, lit by John Davis. John's new wife, Mary Ann Weston Davis, began warming up a lamb stew in an iron pot.

Wilford had reason to be in a good mood. While laboring in London, he had received a letter in mid-February from his wife, relaying instructions from Joseph Smith that members of the Twelve should return to Nauvoo. Leaving London, he had returned to the Malvern Hills to begin saying goodbye to friends there. On this day he and Thomas Kington had given talks at the Gadfield Elm chapel, visited members in Corse Lawn, and now in Tirley. He had plans to attend a final conference in Manchester in early April then depart for America with Brigham Young and the other Apostles as soon after that as possible. Wilford felt his work in England was about done.

John bent over and kissed his wife while she stirred the stew, causing her to blush. She hesitated, then smiled at Wilford, saying, "I remember so vividly the first time I met you, Elder Woodruff."

The words surprised and impressed Wilford. With almost boyish gratification he said, "If you'll refresh my memory I can probably recall the moment myself." Feeling the warmth of the fire, he began unbuttoning his overcoat.

Mary Ann grinned at the now-famous missionary's bright, clean-shaven face, with his broad chin, neatly groomed brown hair, his bushy eyebrows, and his deep-set eyes. "You came to call on Brother and Sister William Jenkins. I was living there doing my apprenticeship as a dressmaker. It was about a year ago. You were waiting for Brother Jenkins to come home and you were siting by the fire and soon you commenced singing. I can still remember the words: *Shall I for fear of feeble man, the spirits course in me restrain.* I think you have a beautiful voice, by the way."

"You do have a vivid memory, Sister Davis," Wilford said, his jolly reminiscent smile widening. He gave Mary Ann a pleased look. "I remember the occasion as well. You told me at the time that you often traveled with your father as a young girl to purchase and sell houses and land. And I remember that you came to the Malvern Hills area to serve an apprenticeship as a dressmaker."

Mary Ann had since become an expert milliner, learning how to make fashionable Victorian clothing for wealthy women in the area.

She asked her husband to stir the stew while she cut a loaf of bread into neat, even slices. "What I remember more than the song was the feeling I had, Elder Woodruff. While you were singing I looked at you and you seemed so peaceful and happy. I knew then you were a good man and that the message you carried as a missionary was true, even though I yet had not heard you preach."

"You have an extraordinary young wife, Brother Davis," Elder Woodruff said, his mouth watering at the sight of the bread being cut, and the smell of the stew as it heated up. "You have been married only a few months?"

"Yes," John said, anxiously stirring the stew as the fire grew. He did not want to serve his guests scorched stew. "We were married on December twenty-third. My mother's clergyman from the Church of England performed the service."

"On Joseph Smith's birthday. Well, congratulations to the both of you."

"Thank you," they said in unison. John kissed Mary Ann on the cheek again. This time she did not blush.

Wilford's tone turned serious. "So many of the members of the Church have departed for America that we are reorganizing the Church in this area. Brother Kington and I have a request, an assignment for you. We would like to ask you if the remaining church members in this area could use your love-ly home as a meeting place for awhile. We have called Brother Edward Phillips to serve as your leader. If you approve, he will come each Sunday and conduct services. He has had experience in two other conferences of the church, so he is well qualified."

Mary Ann's face beamed with pride. She glanced at John, and they exchanged happy nods.

"We would be honored," John said.

"Thank you very much," Wilford said, searching John's face. "Brother Davis, you worked with Brother Daniel Browett, didn't you, in a cooper shop?"

"Good memory again, Elder Woodruff. I still work there." John replied. "I think about Brother Browett and his company sailing toward America every day. I hope their voyage is going well."

"They should be reaching New Orleans about now," Wilford said as his stomach growled. "It's been more than three weeks since they left Liverpool, hasn't it? It took only twenty-three days for our ship to sail from New York to Liverpool. Unless they've encountered bad weather, their voyage should be about over."

John motioned for everyone to sit at the table. He asked Brother Kington to bless the food.

After the blessing, Willard Richards asked John, "How are your parents doing? As I recall your mother was upset when you joined the Church." He took a spoonful of steamy stew, and blew on it before he carefully placed it in his mouth.

"She still is, maybe even worse now. She gets quit stirred up about it."

John did not particularly like talking about her. It was an embarrassing subject. Of all his friends who had joined the church, none of the parents objected like his own restless, impatient, domineering mother. It seemed to John that his mother had spent her entire life expending most of her energy trying to preserve her power over his father, over him and his brothers and sisters, and even over Mary Ann. He had been baptized without obtaining her permission, which made her angry when she found out about it, and she was not happy when he married a Mormon girl. Ever since childhood, John had realized that his mother was not a person of a rational mind. She felt she was a hundred percent right on all issues all the time, and was out to prove it. Her dominant personality even carried over to her beliefs about religion.

Wilford swallowed his first bite, and asked for a slice of bread. "You were baptized last spring, weren't you?"

John's eyes sparkled, and he spread his hands. "Yes, May, after I heard you preach in Dymock. Brother and Sister John and Jane Smith were in that meeting."

Thomas Kington was helping himself to another bowl of stew. He paused, cleared his throat, and said in a matter-of-fact tone, "The Smiths are going to Nauvoo with me on a voyage scheduled May tenth."

"Brother Kington is taking with him quite a few of the members from the Malvern Hills branches," Wilford said, reaching for a second slice of bread. "Who are some of them?"

Thomas held up both hands and began folding his fingers one at a time. "Brother James Barnes and his wife, Brother and Sister Clift, the Collett family, the Hill family, Caroline Moore. There will be many others when they make their final decision. I have secured passage from the port of Bristol on a ship called the *Harmony*."

Because Kington had spent a lot of time setting up a branch in Bristol, he had kept his eyes and ears open for ships sailing to America. The *Harmony* was scheduled to leave the fifth of May, destined for Quebec, Canada.

Although the ship did not have many passenger berths, the shipping company had agreed with Kington to build enough for the Mormon passengers. The *Harmony* was a small, square-rigged ship of 429 tons built in Whitby, North Yorkshire, in 1809.

Elder Woodruff swallowed then locked eyes with John, then Mary Ann. One eyebrow went up. "Have you two thought about going to Nauvoo?"

With an easy, knowing grin, John made his reply. "Yes, oh definitely yes. We're still praying about when we should do it, but we want to go. I would like to resolve things with my mother first. I need to work things out with Daniel's two younger brothers on taking over the cooper shop…things like that."

John reached over and took his wife by the hand. "We think we would be very happy living in Nauvoo. When do you leave for America, Elder Woodruff?"

Wilford sat to one side of his chair. "Elder Young has us booked on the ship *Rochester* out of Liverpool on April tenth, just a few days after our final conference in Manchester. Before that I've got to do all I can to keep reorganizing the branches here, down south in Monmouth and Bristol, then on up to Birmingham and then the Potteries."

"We are very sorry to hear about your daughter's death," Mary Ann said, giving the Apostle an affectionate look. "It must be difficult to have a loved one pass away when you are so far away."

"It is, thank you. But I'll soon be home with my beloved Phoebe. We'll be fine."

Wilford's bad dream had come true. His daughter had died last July, and the shock and sadness was behind him. He had managed to overcome his grief through his testimony of the gospel, the plan of salvation, and plunging himself into his Father in Heaven's work.

After dinner and as his guests were leaving, John asked Elder Woodruff, "One final question before you go. How's the Church doing in London?"

Wilford stared in the air for a few seconds, snorted to himself in frustration, then said, "Quite different than here in this part of England. We didn't have our first baptisms until late November. But by the time we had our February conference there on the fourteenth we counted a hundred and six members. We certainly stirred Satan up there. The old devil does not want to let go of people's lives. But when we face difficulty well we are rewarded with greater strength. Greatness of character can come only from the rigors of the experience in which it is forged."

"We have certainly found that to be true, Elder Woodruff," Mary Ann said, nodding in agreement.

Wilford added, "As I do the Lord's work I remember what the Prophet Joseph Smith told me—that it has been the plan of Satan to hamper this work and distress the Savior's servants from the beginning, to keep us from bringing souls to Christ. Satan seeks to extend his power in the world in opposition to the kingdom of God. We do not stand unopposed. Let that be a voice of warning to you, Brother and Sister Davis. Be careful! But don't let fear keep you from moving the work forward."

"Thanks for the advice, Elder Woodruff," John said as Wilford, Willard, and Thomas opened the door to leave.

As he watched the three men walk down the lane, John again thought about his resentful mother. If there was anyone he was afraid of, it was her. He hoped she would not find out that their home would be a meeting place. It was his nature to avoid conflict. It seemed to be the nature of his mother to create it.

20

THROUGH THE THIN WOODEN SLABS that divided the berths it sounded like crying. Daniel was used to hearing Nancy Pulham's weak sobs, from early morning until late at night. This time it was a man crying. It was James. Daniel dressed quickly and tapped gently on Pulham's berth. Very few other steerage passengers were stirring at this early morning hour.

"James?"

No answer. The sounds ceased.

"James. Is everything all right? What is it?

A sad muffled voice finally answered. "I'll be right out, Brother Browett."

James ran his hand across Nancy's cold forehead. "I won't be long."

"I'm going to be fine, won't I?" Nancy answered in her weak and tender tones. "I've been dreaming of Nauvoo, and all the Saints there. I've seen our little home, made of American logs."

"I have too," James replied, tears welling up.

"I want to give you this child. And many others."

"I know. I love you." He bent over and kissed Nancy on the forehead.

The two quilts hung over the berth to make a door parted, and James emerged. His eyes were red, and his nose was wet. James reached into his pocket for a handkerchief, and quickly wiped his eyes and nose. He pointed to the steps with his freehand. Daniel followed.

As soon as they were topside, standing next to the bulwark opposite the foremast, James took a deep breath, and bit his lower lip. "Brother Browett, Daniel, will you please give my wife another blessing?"

He gazed into Daniel's eyes for a second or two and then turned away to face the ocean. He wiped his eyes again, feeling guilty about asking Daniel to give his wife yet another blessing.

Since the *Echo* had left Liverpool, she had already received five priesthood blessings.

James turned back to face Daniel. "I can't understand why she is failing so. I have faith that she will be healed, but she's getting weaker every day. She still can't keep anything down. Her hands and feet are always cold. Her lips are turning blue."

James had held his wife in his arms all during the previous night, saddened by her withered body. She felt nothing like the woman he had married. Her chest was almost flat, and her face was drawn in. Her skin didn't bounce back when lightly pinched and released. He guessed she weighed no more than six stones. Every time she tried to eat something, she threw it up. Her frail body was dehydrated. Elizabeth had tried every remedy she could think of. Eating frequent small meals. Fluids immediately before and after meals, but not during. Eating bland food. Avoiding strong odors. Not lying down after eating. Getting up slowly. Elizabeth now guessed that Nancy needed mineral supplements, but none were available.

"I know," Daniel said, giving his friend a sad look. He had also done his best to exercise his faith, day in and day out, so that Nancy could be healed. Now he had the feeling that there was a good chance she might die after all.

"Go below and get your scriptures, Brother Pulham."

James gave Daniel a blank, frustrated look. His wife needed a blessing, not a sermon.

Daniel returned James a determined look, and motioned to the stairs leading to the steerage compartment. "I'll wait here. Go on, get your scriptures."

As James disappeared back down the gloomy hole that comprised the steerage compartment, Daniel stared out to the open sea, lit dimly by a sun that was barely rising over the eastern horizon. The *Echo* was plowing through deep-blue swells at a sedate ten knots. The captain had told him they were nearing the West Indies, but New Orleans was still several days away. Daniel wished they were only a day or two out. Maybe Nancy could hold out that long.

Chips strolled past. As the ship's carpenter, he was placing oakum between the seams of the planks. Daniel had seen him earlier checking the hull for leaks, wading through stagnant bilge water in the hold. Vapors from the water were strong enough, in Chips' words, to "poison the devil."

A tear clouded Daniel's eye as James returned. They walked to the captain's quarters and secured some privacy. The captain was in the dining room with a few of the early morning risers among the cabin passengers.

Daniel cleared his throat and reached deep inside his own soul. What he was about to tell James was a breach of his own security, and had it not been for the fact that Elder Woodruff had pointed out these few scriptures and commented on them in a teaching moment, Daniel would never have believed this way. The principle was contrary to Daniel's way of thinking, but it was a true principle and it was time to share it with James. "Open your Doctrine and Covenants to section forty-two."

A gentle sea breeze fluttered the pages as James found the section.

Daniel said, "I have a question, Cousin James. As we read the words out of this book, whose words will we be reading?"

"Joseph Smith's?" James asked in a mild voice.

"Yes, but no." Daniel said patiently. "Joseph Smith wrote the words down on paper, but they are a direct revelation from…"

"The Savior Jesus Christ."

Daniel tried his best not to sound smug or self-righteous. "Correct. This is a revelation given *through* the Prophet Joseph Smith. It is Jesus Christ speaking. The first verse says: *Hearken, O ye elders of my church, who have assembled yourselves together in my name, even Jesus Christ the Son of the living God.*"

James followed along. He quickly examined the language in following verses. No doubt, it was the Savior speaking. James looked at verse two: *Again, I say unto you, hearken and hear and obey the law which I shall give unto you...*

"Elder Woodruff taught me that section forty-two has become known as the 'Law of the Lord to his Church.' It contains instructions for missionary work, the Savior's law of teaching, the law of consecration, laws governing clothing and work, and the laws concerning death and the law of administering to the sick. That's the part we need to read and talk about."

He asked James to read verses forty-three through forty-eight, then deliberately asked: "What does the Savior tell us to do when someone is sick?"

James paused for a few seconds while he looked through the verses again. "Nourish the person with herbs and mild food, just as Elizabeth has been doing. She's an angel."

"Yes, the Savior instructs that there is a place for the skillful administration of herbs, the medicines found in nature. And?" Daniel hesitated, waiting for James to review the verses once again.

Daniel paraphrased the verse in his mind: *Two or more elders of the church should lay their hands upon the head of the sick person and administer to them...*

James read the verse. Daniel gave James a warm smile. "Correct. One elder anoints the head of the sick with oil that has been consecrated and dedicated for the healing of the sick, then two or more elders lay their hands upon the head of the sick person and seal the anointing and give the person a blessing as dictated by the spirit."

James nodded his head up and down in agreement, and said in a sad voice, "And we have done that several times for my wife, yet she continues to get worse."

Daniel swallowed hard, and his eyes began to moisten. They had come to the part that he needed to teach his cousin. Yet it made Daniel feel uncomfortable, even guilty, that he had to be the one to point this out to James. He bit his lip, paused for a few seconds, and then said in a soft voice, "Does verse forty-four say that all the sick will be healed?"

James looked down, pondered the words, and read it again. He began to cry.

Daniel paused for a few seconds, then read the words to James: ...*and if they die they shall die unto me, and if they live they shall live unto me. Thou shalt live together in love, insomuch that thou shalt weep for the loss of them that die, and more especially for those that have not hope in a glorious resurrection.*

James momentarily glanced at Daniel. "My wife is going to die, isn't she Daniel?"

Daniel shuddered, wondering if James were taking all this in correctly. "I don't know for certain, James, but we need to be prepared either way. Sometimes there are miraculous healings performed by the power of the priesthood, but sometimes..." Daniel reached out and touched James on the shoulder. "But sometimes..." He couldn't finish the sentence.

James wrinkled his face and then turned away, facing the open sea. He tried to absorb the possibility of his wife not recovering. He felt it pointless to argue; yet he was hurt by the reality of it. A few days ago the sea was a monster. Today it was placid, warm and inviting. Still, it was no place for a burial. He quivered at the thought of Nancy's body sinking into the bottomless ocean. James hung his head and spoke in words barely audible to Daniel. "I understand. But it is hard, so hard. We have talked so many times about how wonderful our lives are going to be when we get to Nauvoo and live among the main body of the saints."

James wept again.

Daniel waited for several seconds before continuing. He wiped more tears from his eyes and put his arm around his cousin. "There is a certain joy in these passages of scripture, James. If your sweet Nancy does pass away, certainly she will someday have a glorious resurrection. What the Savior is teaching us here is that some who die have no hope of a glorious resurrection. What that means is, of course, that everyone, everyone who ever lives on earth will be resurrected as a gift from the Savior through his atoning sacrifice. Everyone will get his physical body back again. But some will be resurrected with a telestial body and be given a telestial glory, far short of a glorious resurrection. The Savior is teaching us that someone like your wonderful wife, Nancy, has fol-

lowed the Savior's teachings and has been baptized and kept the commandments. She has hope of a glorious resurrection in the Celestial Kingdom,
James."

James tearfully acknowledged that Daniel was right, nodding his head.

Daniel took away his arm, opened his book again and read. "Finally, let's
read verse forty-six. *And it shall come to pass that those that die in me shall not
taste of death for it shall be sweet unto them.*"

Through still misted eyes, James asked, "Does that mean even though
my wife may die physically, she will not die spiritually?"

Daniel closed his book and tried to hide his own insecurity concerning
the possibility that Nancy might actually die. He said, "Correct. The Savior
means that if we keep his commandments and his doctrines and enter into the
Celestial Kingdom, it will be sweet to that person because he or she will be in
the presence of God our Eternal Father and the Savior, to live forever."

"I understand, Brother Browett."

Daniel added, "And someday, when you pass on, you will be reunited
with your wife. I feel that is true."

James managed a brief smile, his voice trailing off. "Thank you…"

"Another thing that is hard to understand is how and why so many
young people die. Why do some people live a long life and yet others pass
away in their youth?'

"I admit that troubles me, Brother Browett."

Daniel bit his lip again and carefully formed his thoughts. "I hope these
words will help you. We labor in this life according to divine appointment.
Some of us live a great length of time; we have had a child die already on this
trip. When the Prophet Joseph Smith was in the jail at Liberty, Missouri, he
was told by the Lord: *Thy days are known, and thy years shall not be numbered
less; therefore, fear not what man can do, for God shall be with you forever and
ever.*

"When it appears a loved one is about to die, we exercise our faith that
the person will live, just as we are doing in the case of Nancy. But those
prayers and our faith are always subject to the overriding will of the Lord. If

He wills to take one of his daughters from this life to the next, then His will prevails."

James swallowed hard.

"The principle that men are appointed to die does not necessarily mean that each individual has a predestined moment in his life when death is to occur. And it does not mean that God will intervene to prevent accidents, carelessness, or wicked choices that bring sorrow and death. The Savior has indicated that death for many of his children is on a flexible time schedule. *For there is a time appointed for every man, according as his works shall be.*"

Daniel had more he could have said. But he knew the principles he wanted his cousin to learn had been taught. "I know it is still hard."

"Yes, it is…"

Seeing Robert and Thomas Bloxham walking toward them, Daniel made one final comment. "I don't know if your wife will live or die, but I will get more of the brethren, and we will give her another blessing."

"Thank you, thank you very much."

FRIDAY March 5 – Ship on course. Wind brisk. Ship going between 8 and 9 knots an hour. Warm day. Thunder at night, lightning flashed, rain poured down in torrents. Robert and I, assisted by James, gave Nancy another blessing.

SATURDAY March 6 – Wind blows ahead. Blows fresh rain. This morning a child of Mr. and Mrs. Boardman died, a fine little boy only three years old. This afternoon we committed his little body to the deep. I pray we won't have to do the same for Nancy.

CHAPTER NOTES:

The incident in the home of John Davis and Mary Ann Weston Davis is true, based on an autobiography included in *Women's Voices* (Deseret Book, 1982). According to his journal, Wilford Woodruff visited the Davis home on the date indicated.

21

ROMAN, GREEK, AND OTHER Mediterranean seafarers of ancient times held to the custom of mounting a sacred idol in the stern of their ships. The Latin word for idol is *puppis. Puppin* became *poupe* by the time the word made it into Italian, French, and Middle English. When Daniel learned of this, he thought it was ironic that Mormons worshipping the true God, Jesus Christ, were meeting on the poop deck, named after forbidden idols.

On this Sunday, the slow, rocking movement of the *Echo* combined with the Mormon preacher's soft voice was putting Captain Wood in a doze, when a tap and a whisper roused him.

"Sleepy, captain?" Daniel asked, a calm smile on his face.

"No, I'm sorry," the captain said, clearly embarrassed, yawning, making a helpless gesture. "I promised you I would listen to the sermon today. I'll stay awake."

Captain Wood would not have agreed to attend the Sunday Mormon services on the poop deck on this Sabbath day had it not been for what seemed to him a strange chain of events with the Mormon passengers. The calming of the storm. Keeping pirates at bay. The conversion of several non-Mormon passengers. Their baptism in a water-filled half barrel. The death of a three-year-old non-Mormon boy named Boardman. And the unusually interesting sermon delivered by Captain Browett of the Mormons.

Captain Wood was used to stormy weather, heavy seas, seasickness of passengers, and even the occasional deaths of passengers. What he wasn't used to was Mormons. Daniel's Browett's sermon at the Boardman boy's funeral service had intrigued him. The boy had died two days ago of dehydration. He suspected that it was something about Captain Browett's strange religion that was responsible for the intrigue.

And he felt responsible for the attack on Captain Browett's sister. He believed it was definitely not Henry Eagles, but likely a member of his own crew. Feelings of guilt had swept over him the past several days since the incident, but his investigation held no conclusive evidence.

Yawning again, stretching his facial muscles, rolling his tongue over his teeth and through his mouth, Captain Wood sat erect in his chair and surveyed the scene again. The bright faces of the well dressed Mormon audience. The wide-eyed curious non-Mormon guests, several of his crewmembers dressed in their summer whites. Steward Michael Heywood sitting next to Captain Browett. Daniel's sister, Rebecca, under the protective care of Elizabeth. The odd character Henry Eagles. Then there was the deathly sick Mormon woman, Nancy Pulham. Despite her grave illness, not being able to keep food in her stomach, looking frailer every day, there she was wrapped in a blanket, held in the arms of her husband. Captain Wood had expected her to die any time, but she appeared to be bravely hanging on.

With an uncertainty in his mind about why another Mormon named Wilding was giving the Sunday sermon instead of Captain Browett, the captain settled back into his chair and tried to focus on what the preacher was saying. *Are all Mormon men ministers? Is that why some of them refer to one another as "elder?" Why don't Captain Browett, Wilding, and the other Mormon leaders wear ministerial collars? They dress so differently than the preachers and reverends I've known in New York where I lived, and in the many ports throughout the world where I've visited.*

"The doctrine of Jesus Christ and his Father," Wilding was saying, "is to have faith and believe on His name, repent of our sins, then be baptized by immersion for the remission of sins and receive the Gift of the Holy Ghost."

To Captain Wood's ears, the opening remarks out of preacher Wilding's mouth brought a familiarity of doctrine he had heard in other sermons in his youth. Yet, as he thought about it deeper, he wondered why Wilding had mentioned the doctrine of Christ and the Father. *Weren't they the same person? Baptism by immersion? And what was the Gift of the Holy Ghost?* A skeptical curiosity came over him, and he concentrated on Wilding's next sentences.

"When the Prophet Joseph Smith was translating the Book of Mormon, he came to passages of scripture about baptism. He and his scribe, Oliver Cowdery, went into the woods to inquire of the Lord relative to the necessity of baptism. Perhaps it was Second Nephi chapter thirty-one they were translating at the time."

Captain Wood made a face. It was not the first time he had heard of the Book of the Mormon, but it was the first time in his life that he had actually wondered about it. Questions came to his mind: *Is this the Golden Bible I've heard about? What is Second Nephi? Who is Oliver Cowdery?*

"As they prayed, John the Baptist appeared and informed them that he had been sent to them under the direction of the Apostles, Peter, James, and John. John the Baptist laid his hands upon the heads of Joseph and Oliver and conferred upon them the Aaronic Priesthood, using the words that now constitute Doctrine and Covenants section thirteen, which has been canonized as scripture."

The captain of the *Echo* threw his head back in deep thought, fidgeting in his chair. Wilding's comments hit him like a hurricane bursting against the ship's topsail. *John the Baptist? He appeared and gave Joe Smith and his friend the what priesthood? Is this Mormon claim plausible, believable, or provable? And scripture called the Doctrine and Covenants?*

Brother Wilding continued.

"Following this event, Joseph and Oliver had the right to function as priests themselves and they had the keys or power of presidency in the Aaronic Priesthood, now once again restored to the earth. These keys gave Joseph and Oliver the right of administration or control, the right to ordain others, and also the right to direct how and when those other priesthood holders would be allowed to use their priesthood. Most importantly, they now had the authority to baptize. With that authority, with that priesthood, Joseph and Oliver baptized each other by immersion in the Susquehanna River. They were baptized by immersion, complete immersion, following the ancient pattern. Baptism is symbolic of the death, burial—immersion in water—and resurrection—raising out of the water, of the Savior Jesus Christ."

The captain blinked in deep thought. He had never considered the symbolic nature of the baptismal ordinance, but it made sense to him. For a brief moment he pictured himself standing in the water with Daniel Browett.

"We learn in the Doctrine and Covenants, section twenty, verse thirty-seven, much more about what the Lord expects of baptismal candidates. First, candidates are to be humble before God—no bargaining and nothing held back, but willing to do whatever God requires. Second, baptism is performed when the candidate truly manifests a desire to be baptized. Third, baptism is performed when the candidate has a broken heart and a contrite spirit—in other words, remorse for sin and proper repentance. Fourth, when he can testify to the Church that he has repented, or that he has begun the repentance process. Fifth, when he is willing to take upon himself the name of Christ. And sixth, when he has a determination to serve Christ for the rest of his life and bear the fruits of membership in His Church."

Thinking of the thirty-seven years he had spent on the earth—the misdeeds of his youth, the adventurous years of being a young sailor, the swank hotels, the sumptuous food, the dazzling women, the bars, the taverns, the liquor—the captain hunched his shoulders, and shrank at the thought of him sitting in front of some Mormon preacher, confessing all his sins. It gave him pause if that's what it would take to become a Mormon, and never go back to the lifestyle of a sailor.

"Baptism has always been practiced whenever the gospel of Jesus Christ has been on the earth and has been taught by men holding the holy priesthood who could administer the ordinances. I believe Adam was baptized. I believe all the Old Testament prophets and Church leaders practiced baptism.

We know from the Book of Mormon that baptism was practiced long before the coming of Christ."

Captain Wood squinted one eye and tried to recall what he had read in the Old Testament. He could not think of a passage that said Adam was baptized.

"Baptism is not optional if one wishes the fullness of salvation. Jesus said a person must be born of water and of the spirit—we are all familiar with that scripture from John chapter three verses three through five. When the Savior sent the twelve Apostles forth to teach the gospel he told them that whosoever believed and was baptized would be saved. He also taught that whosoever did not believe would be damned."

His pulse quickening, his face flushed with a personal, private awareness that he had never been baptized into any church, Captain Wood shuddered at the word "salvation" and its connection to baptism. *What was a fullness of salvation?* Captain Wood sighed at the term, confessing to himself that he didn't know. He had always believed that because he read the Bible once in awhile he would go to heaven. Now it sounded like there were additional requirements, and he was uncomfortable.

"Baptism by immersion in water has several purposes. It is for the remission of sins. It is for membership in the Church, the true Church of God, as restored in the latter days. It is for entrance into the Celestial Kingdom. Heaven, or the Kingdom of God is divided into three parts. Celestial, where God our Father dwells; Terrestrial, and Telestial. And finally, baptism is also the doorway to personal sanctification when it is followed by the reception of the Holy Ghost."

Those phrases struck Captain Wood as odd, and he tried to recall if he had ever heard the words *celestial, terrestrial, and telestial.* Were they Bible words? What did this Mormon mean by "true church?" Weren't all churches "true" as long as they were Christian churches?

To Captain Wood, Wilding was speaking with an easy calm, his face inspiring and incredulous.

"In latter-day revelation we learn that the Lord has set the age of eight years as the time when a person begins to become accountable and can be baptized. I believe this has always been the correct age both in Old Testament and Book of Mormon times."

The captain bit his lip, folded his hands over his stomach, and wondered: *Where did this Mormon get an idea like that? Baptism at eight years of age?*

"Baptism is a most sacred ordinance. It is an ordinance which a person, can remember throughout life as a reminder of the personal commitment to Jesus Christ, to serve Him, and to keep His commandments. Its symbolism is beautiful. Its consequences are so desirable. To you in this audience who are not yet baptized, I testify in the name of Jesus Christ that what I have told you today is true. There are authorized representatives holding the proper priesthood who can baptize you into the Kingdom of God."

Captain Wood stared at a cloud-flecked sky and the bright sun that was drenching the *Echo* as it slid along the sea, his mouth becoming a slash of tight lips, his eyes narrowing, his teeth grinding, and his mind gripped in deep thought. The Mormon preacher went off on other related baptismal doctrines, and the captain lost an awareness of time. The captain's previous life seemed to stretch out before him, and he thought again of his years as a seaman, his wife and family back in New York, his worldliness, his twenty-thousand-dollar-a-year income, his rank, the *Echo*, the ports, the cargo. Would he trade it for the life of a Mormon? What if he actually submitted to baptism and changed his life? Spent time with his wife and family? Went to church every Sunday? Even moved to Nauvoo? Strangely enough, he felt good as he entertained those thoughts.

Perched on the edge of his chair, slowly coming out of his trance, Captain Wood wiped his brow and watched as Daniel Browett and the other Mormon elders surrounded the sick woman, Nancy Pulham, and said a prayer over her with their hands laid on her head. He rose to his feet, thought of a few orders he needed to give, and shook himself back to reality. Then he wondered why the Mormons were making such a fuss over the Pulham woman. Unless they had some kind of supernatural power, in his opinion the woman would die before the *Echo* reached New Orleans anyway.

Later, Captain Wood heard that five more persons had been baptized in the barrel.

SUNDAY March 7 – Ship in its proper course. After breakfast church assembles for preaching. Brother Wilding gave a powerful sermon on baptism. Afterward several came forth and requested baptism. Sister Pulham attended Church in her weakened condition; we gave her another blessing. Captain Wood listened to the sermon today. Heavy squall in the evening. A child, not of our company, died of scarlet fever. The girl's body was committed to the deep.

MONDAY March 8 – Fine morning wind southeast, continues all day. Sister Pulham continues very sick and is getting weaker. She wishes very much for a little porter or ale. The captain found some in the lower hold. We were in hopes when she got the porter that she would retain strength until we got to land but it was ordained otherwise. Her poor body has shrunk to a mere skeleton.

22

THE CRYING WOKE DANIEL. It came from Pulham's berth. Instantly, Daniel knew Nancy was gone. He guessed the time to be five thirty in the morning.

Daniel shook himself. The Spirit had told him during the blessing that she would not live. Even though he had tried to deny those feelings, he knew of its surety.

In a low whisper, Daniel woke Elizabeth. "It's over."

Elizabeth rubbed her eyes, finding them welled up with tears. "Does Hannah know?"

"No. No one does. James is still in the berth with Nancy. I think he'll come out in a minute."

Elizabeth sat up quickly, noticing the sobbing from the adjoining berth. She knew the inevitable was going to happen sooner or later. Maybe sooner was better. Nancy had suffered so much. Last night she had been so weak and incoherent she could barely carry on a conversation. The thought of Nancy's passing brought a grim reality check to Elizabeth. Lady Luck seemed to have deserted her good friend; life didn't seem to be a barrel of fun right now. She had a hard time understanding why Nancy could not have pulled herself out of her sickness; had it been herself, she would have done just that, pulled herself out. She thought about the day ahead, the funeral service that Daniel would have to conduct, the people who would need cheering up, and the consoling that would have to be done.

Daniel pulled on his clothing, worrying about what he was going to say to James, then later to Hannah. He worried, too, about how Henry would take the death of his sister; Henry was difficult to predict. It depended on which personality Henry was wearing today. On the one hand he seemed to have the ability to accept things and be cordial about them; or on the other hand this might cause him to erupt again and blame the Church, Elder Woodruff, Daniel, or others for Nancy's death. Daniel cringed at the thought, because whenever Henry acted up, it brought feelings to himself of bitterness and resentment, and those feelings made him uncomfortable. As leader of the company, he knew he was not supposed to feel that way.

A few minutes passed as Daniel and Elizabeth dressed, still speaking in whispers, worrying, wondering, and contemplating. Suddenly, although slowly and deliberately, the privacy doorway quilts to James and Nancy's berth parted and James emerged, fatigued, eyes red, sweating, and looking like his body ached everywhere. He exchanged looks with Daniel and Elizabeth, and then hung his head. Daniel walked to him and gathered him in his arms.

"Do you want me to tell Hannah and Henry?" Daniel asked.

James nodded his head.

"I'm sorry, James," Daniel said, knowing that a gloom would soon be spreading over the entire ship.

Despite the many priesthood blessings, despite the prayers, despite Elizabeth's efforts, despite the efforts of the ship's doctor, Nancy was gone, and Daniel still felt somewhat responsible for her death because of his position as the company leader.

"I know," James managed to say, the human touch of Daniel's hug dissolving a brief bitterness he felt over the passing of his beloved wife. "But at least her suffering is over."

For a few moments Daniel did his best to console his friend, trying to get rid of the guilt he harbored over Nancy's death, expressing his sorrow, his empathy, and his sensitivity. Then he began the task of informing the others, notifying the captain, preparing the body, announcing the time of the burial service, and other details. Amid this, he still felt a certain frustration that God had chosen to take Nancy rather than let her be healed. He believed in the little sermon he had given James from the scriptures in the Doctrine and Covenants, but deep down inside he had privately hoped that it would have been the will of God to let her live.

Hours later, staring at Nancy's linen-wrapped body as it lay on on the main deck near the foremast on a table borrowed from the captain's quarters on the main deck near the foremast, Hannah knew the white sepulcher would forever remain etched in her memory. The news that Nancy had passed away had not shocked her, for she had expected it. But the reality of it all jolted her severely, and made her dizzy with grief. As when her father had died, she became despondent, and in the past three hours she went through the same alternating periods of crying and being strong. She even helped wrap the body. But she didn't know if she could bear to watch Nancy's body buried in the sea. There were no flowers to place on the body, or to throw in the ocean. There was no way to find this spot ever again. No tombstone. Nothing but an endless expanse of blue water.

Hannah shuddered, thinking of Captain Wood's most recent story about Ferdinand Magellan, who sailed the seas in 1521. Curious as to the ocean's depth, he spliced together six pieces of rope and then lowered his improvised sounding line to a depth of 2,500 feet without reaching bottom. His conclusion: the ocean was immeasurably deep. Hannah's morbid conclusion: *Nancy's body will sink forever in a watery grave.*

As Hannah waited for Daniel to begin his remarks at the burial ceremony, she placed her head on Robert's shoulder and cried again. She thought of what to say in a letter to her mother in Apperley, England. She would have to post it in New Orleans. She wondered how long it would take to reach her mother. Would it have been better for her mother to be here, or worse? Perhaps her mother would have known what to do to save Nancy. But

Elizabeth and the captain had done everything humanly possible, and Daniel and Robert had done everything spiritually possible—giving several blessings, asking all to exercise their faith and helping James understand the possibility of death. Hannah grieved for James as much as she did for her sister. He looked so alone. Now he had to go to Nauvoo a widower. She hoped that someday, after an appropriate time of mourning, James would be able to find another wife. No one would ever replace Nancy, in her mind, but James deserved the best. He had treated her sister superbly in every way.

As Daniel stood to begin his remarks, he surveyed the large crowd that had gathered on the poop deck, bathed in the bright, late-morning sunshine, to pay their final respects to Nancy Eagles Pulham. A brisk breeze tumbled through the Caribbean, filling the sails, flapping the American flag, and making the waters slightly choppy.

James still looked numb but impressionable, seeming to observe and remember everything that was going on during this traumatic day. His last conversation with Nancy. The consoling words from his friends. The vast expanse of the ocean that would soon swallow up his wife. And the dreams that were shattered by Nancy's death.

Daniel glanced at Nancy's brother, Henry, and found him subdued but unemotional. All through the morning Henry had been mostly silent, a little judgmental a times, but tolerable. He had given a warm hug to Hannah, talked to her briefly, but seemed a little distant, perhaps confused by death itself. Captain Wood had proven a gentleman, standing near Daniel in his starchy whites, chin high, his face rigid, ready to assist in whatever way he could. Same with Michael Heywood, newly baptized.

Daniel gathered his thoughts. James had requested that he talk about the "glorious resurrection." In truth, Daniel had known that would be the topic of his funeral sermon before James asked, and had been searching the scriptures for several days. In his opinion, Nancy had suffered nearly as much as the Savior. She deserved a glorious resurrection.

He began: "By far the greatest example of meeting death with sweetness amidst pain and agony—as Sister Pulham has endured these past many days—is the Savior, our Lord Jesus Christ. He approached His final moments on earth, even though He was suffering greatly during His crucifixion, with a great peace and calmness."

James began nodding. Tears streamed down his cheeks.

Danieal continued. "Jesus did not fear death for He knew it was a prelude to a triumph over the grave. Those of you who have received a testimony of the truthfulness of the restored gospel know death to be part of the plan of a wise, all-knowing God. You look forward to reunion with loved ones in the spirit world and to embrace family and friends in the flesh following the resurrection. Brother Pulham, I know you have that strength in your personal testimony."

James nodded again.

"I testify to you that at the moment of death, Brother Pulham, the anticipated reunion may begin as evidenced in the accounts of those who have been greeted by angels. Elder Woodruff taught me that the Prophet Joseph Smith has written about the death of his brother, Alvin: *He was one of the soberest of men, and when he died the angel of the Lord visited him in his last moments.* Brother Pulham, an angel of the Lord ministered to your sweet wife in her final moments."

Daniel paused to exchanges glances with James, who managed a brief smile, acknowledging that Daniel spoke the truth.

"Above all men, Brother Pulham, you will miss Sister Pulham the most. You will mourn her death. We mourn with you."

James looked up, acknowledging Daniel.

"And with you, Sister Harris," Daniel said, "and you, Brother Eagles. You lost a beloved sister."

Hannah looked up. Henry did not.

"But we have learned that all the mourning traditions of our people do little to comfort us. Comfort comes in the knowledge of the plan of salvation. Death was sweet unto your wife and sister. She is now at rest. There is nothing dreadful or terrible in it. Angels escorted her to the society that exists in the spirit world. Sister Harris, Brother Eagles—she has been reunited with your father, who passed just four years ago. In that society, they await the passing of your mother, and when she passes in a few years, they will be there to greet her."

Daniel opened his Book of Mormon. The deck was so silent that most people could hear him turn the pages. "Alma, in the Book of Mormon, said: *Behold it has been made known unto me by an angel, that the spirits of all men, as soon as they are departed from this mortal body, yea, the spirits of all men, whether they be good or evil, are taken home to that God who gave them life.*"

Clearing his throat, Daniel said, "The evil doers, however, eventually will be resurrected unto a lesser glory than those who have kept the commandments, such as Sister Pulham, and her resurrection shall be sweet because she will be resurrected into a higher glory, even that of the Celestial Kingdom."

Daniel stole an awkward glance at Henry Eagles, who seemed to hang his head in stunned silence. He wondered if Henry had ever actually read the Book of Mormon, or even the Bible for that matter. He knew Henry's parents read passages to him in family gatherings, based on what Hannah had told him. He wondered if God would judge Henry as an evildoer. If so, he wondered if Henry would be consigned to a lesser kingdom than his sister and his father. The thoughts of that troubled him, and Daniel knew they were troubling Henry right now.

"Brother Pulham, it is my prayer and hope that you will live your life in accordance to the principles of the gospel, work for your salvation and exhalation, that you may be joined one day with your wonderful wife in the Celestial Kingdom, that portion of heaven where God our Father will give us life eternal, even eternal lives…"

To conclude, Daniel dedicated this spot in the Atlantic Ocean—wherever it was—as the final resting-place of the remains of Sister Nancy Eagles Pulham.

Hannah refused to watch as Nancy's wrapped body was placed on a large plank. A hymn was sung as the ship's sails were furled. The *Echo* stopped, dead in the water. Another hymn was sung as Daniel and his assistants raised the inward end of the plank so that Nancy's body slipped almost silently into the ocean. Stones placed inside the wrappings caused her body to quickly sink into its watery grave. To where it sank, no one knew. Fifteen thousand feet, straight down.

TUESDAY March 9 – All the Saints attended a funeral on deck for Sister Pulham. Brother Pulham asked me to preach the sermon, using the sweet resurrection as my text. Afterward she was buried at sea. Breezy all day, wind changes toward evening, wind ahead continues all night.

WEDNESDAY March 10 – Fine morning wind, calm towards 11 o'clock. Becalmed some uneasiness respecting the fires in the cooking grates. The captain has manifested the greatest sympathy for the death of Sister Pulham. He oftentimes attends our prayer meetings which we hold each morning and each evening.

THURSDAY March 11 – Calm wind, ahead foggy. Showers all afternoon, wind changes favorable southwest all night.

23

A FIT OF DEPRESSION SWEPT OVER Daniel in the days following Nancy's funeral. He worried about everything. How Hannah was accepting the death of her sister. How James would cope without his wife. The fact that a crazed sailor was still on the loose. That Rebecca was still suffering from anxieties. The deteriorating quality of everyone's food. A lack of fresh fruit and vegetables. The length of time it was taking to get to New Orleans. How to find steamboat passage up the Mississippi. And on it went.

Daniel's mood affected Elizabeth, and she saw in him the old weakness of trying to help others without helping himself. She knew it gave him a feeling of self-satisfaction and productiveness, but it was wearing on him, and her, too. Everyone else's needs were cluttering his mind.

But it was Elizabeth who saw the need to reach out to the children on board, who seemed to be sinking into certain restlessness. Oh, they had their stick horses, homemade dolls and jigsaw puzzles all right, but after nearly a month on board ship playing with just those few toys, the children were becoming bored. Hannah, at one point, had asked the children to write letters to God. Among the most clever were these:

Dear God. I wish there was no such thing as sin.

Dear God. I am English. What are you?

Dear God. You made a lot of religions. Do you get mixed up sometimes?

Dear God. I would like to live nine hundred years like Methuselah.

Dear God. I didn't think purple went with orange until I saw the sunset you made last night.

An idea struck Elizabeth—why not organize some games for children? Use the games to pry Daniel out of his pensive mood. And help Rebecca continue her climb to recovery.

At first, with steward Heywood's help, she tried simple games such as "London Bridge" and "Here We Go 'Round the Mulberry Bush," followed by noughts and crosses (which Heywood said the Americans called "tic tack toe"), and then games of draught.

But it wasn't until Elizabeth thought about giving the children and their parents special family prizes for just plain silly little things that Daniel seemed to snap out of his low mood and begin to smile, and forget about the drab day when Nancy was committed to the deep. Elizabeth first thought of it as she watched little Mary and Sarah Lords, the only set of twins. Why not give a little prize for being the only twins? That started a chain of festive events.

Under a canopy of bright blue skies, a light breeze, and warm sunshine, Elizabeth, Daniel, Rebecca, and Michael Heywood summoned the parents to participate with the children.

"Let's see now," she said, surveying her cast, "which of your families have at least five children on board? Let's see your hands, and we'll give each of you a prize." Elizabeth grinned and watched as three sets of families responded, feeling a special warmth as she saw her sister's family among them.

An energetic hand shot up from seven-year-old Lucy Bloxham, fair skinned, blonde hair done in pigtails, bright blue eyes, and freckled face. "Mine does!"

Her eight-year-old brother, Charles Robert Bloxham, shot his hand skyward, too. Missing his two front teeth, six-year-old Tommy Bloxham followed suit, his hand reaching high, as did the other two Bloxham children, Emma, four, and Johnny, two.

Their mother, Dianah, pulled her husband, Thomas, toward Elizabeth to

watch each child claim a piece of hard tack, smiling, but thinking about Isaac, their baby, who had died in Deerhurst, England, a few days after her baptism. Had he lived, they would have had six children on board, not five. Dianah stole a glance at her husband and wondered if Thomas still thought there was a connection between her being baptized just a few days prior to the baby's birth and his dying, and if that were the reason why he had stiffened his neck and not joined the Church himself. He never talked about it. All she could do is wonder.

"So does mine!" said ten-year-old Agnes Stockton, the youngest of Mary Stockton, a widow. Elizabeth recognized the Stockton children: Edward, the oldest at twenty; then Hannah; John; Ruth; and Agnes.

And me!" screamed little James Wilding, son of David and Alice Wilding.

Elizabeth's eyes brightened with an idea, and she burst out laughing. "Brother and Sister Wilding, you not only get a prize for having five children, but also the prize for having the most children named after our Church leaders."

The Wildings laughed with delight. Their youngest was seven-month-old David William Patten Wilding and another, a three-year-old boy, was named Heber C. Kimball Wilding—both named for Apostles. The other Wilding children were George, twelve; Elizabeth Ann, nine; and James, five.

"I suppose when you have *another* son you'll name him Joseph Smith Wilding," Elizabeth commented.

That caused everyone on deck to laugh.

But oddly enough, and quite suddenly, Elizabeth felt depressed but hid it well, wrinkling her face only for a few seconds. Five children, four children, three, two, one—and none for her.

There was no woman in the world who wanted to give her husband children more than Elizabeth Harris Browett. Even since her blessing at the hands of Wilford Woodruff, Brigham Young and Willard Richards, Elizabeth had failed to become pregnant. The blessing occurred in England, at a Church party at the home of Thomas Kington. When she said her prayers night and

morning she pleaded with the Lord to become a "mother in Zion."

Fighting back her tears, she said, "And how about families with four children?"

"Mine! Mine!" screamed five-year-old Alice Cook. Widower Peter Cook came forward and was recognized for his four children—starting with seventeen-year-old Edward, then Nancy, Alice, and one-year-old Seth.

"Me, too!" said eight-year-old George Halford, causing Joseph and Eliza Halford to accept a little prize from Elizabeth for their four children, George, Sarah, Catherine, and Elizabeth.

So on it went. Families with three children: John and Mary Cheese (Harriet, John and William), Edward and Sarah Fielding, Robert and Hannah Harris (Joseph, Elizabeth and William), Thomas and Elizabeth Margaret; families with two children: James and Hannah Lord (Mary and Sarah); and parents with one child: John and Elizabeth Cox (Ann), James and Hannah Dyson (Samuel), and Henry and Ann Parker (John).

When the day was over, after a day of entertaining the children, eating a fine cooked meal of boiled potatoes, dried beef, and fresh bread, with Daniel successfully pulled out of his own depression, Elizabeth Browett could not get the portraits out of her mind of child after child marching forward to claim their simple little prizes of hard tack.

Daniel had no idea that she cried herself to sleep that night, feeling sorry for herself that she had not yet given her husband a child.

FRIDAY March 12 – Royal mast up foremost topsail, 9 knots per hour. Two of the company chosen to superintend the fire. Wind continues favorable all night. Misting rain.

SATURDAY March 13 – One child's foot scalded. Some of the regular passengers murmuring respecting the price of provisions being charged too high. Provisions for the church members may run short because of the delay. Captain says we are several days behind schedule.

SUNDAY March 14 – Brother John Cheese preached at sacrament meeting, to be valiant in the gospel — "to be valiant is to be courageous, brave, and bold in the testimony of Jesus Christ, to never let go of one's testimony, to endure to the end…it is to be fully committed to the doctrines of the Kingdom and the cause of Zion…those not willing to give all their heart, might, mind and strength in the service of God will not be numbered in the worlds to come with those who do." Weather continues fine. Heavy rain at night again.

CHAPTER NOTES

The information about the children of the voyage is accurate, taken from the Mormon Immigration Index, and from Family Group Records. The "Dear God" letters are from the book, *Children's Letters to God,* Workman Publishing, 1991, compiled by Stuart Hample and Eric Marshall.

24

EDWARD PHILLIPS' EYES CLOUDED with concern.

From a corner in the parlor of John and Mary Ann Davis' small stone cottage in Tirley, warmed by red coals from the hearth, Edward glanced out the window to see a gathering crowd of ruffians.

At first there were only three men, then five, then nine, then a thick crowd of more than a dozen men was visible—shouting, gesturing, jostling in the center of the narrow road in front of the cottage. He paced back and forth on the planked floor, heels clicking, trying his best to deliver a Sunday sermon to his small Mormon congregation, doing his best to ignore the obvious— trouble was brewing outside.

The weather had lapsed into light rain and fog; a pearl-gray murk veiled other mobbers standing in the trees, covering themselves with umbrellas.

What could he do? He calculated his choices.

He could ignore the gathering mob and hope it would dissolve itself if not provoked. If they stormed the house, he could escape by going up the stairs to the second floor and disappearing down the outside stairs at the back of the house. He knew they were after the Mormon preachers, not their congregations. As the mob became larger and more vocal, that appeared to be the only option.

The meeting had started without any hint of trouble. Edward had commented to his congregation of eleven persons prior to the opening song and prayer that he believed Elder Woodruff had been led by the Spirit to the United Brethren, and testified "it seemed to me that we had come to a precipice within the United Brethren, seeking further light and knowledge, and we could go no further until Elder Woodruff placed a bridge over the precipice, and we went on with glad hearts rejoicing."

The comment had caused John Davis to tell twenty-seven-year-old Edward that, "A good way to bring back the feelings of the Spirit is when we recall our own personal conversions." John was in a jovial mood. He was happily married, had taken over Daniel Browett's cooper shop, had been a member of the Church for several months, and his home had been selected as a meetinghouse for the few Mormons in the Tirley area. He often thought of Daniel and Elizabeth—and his other Mormon friends who were on their way to Nauvoo—and hoped someday to emigrate to America himself and find his personal Zion.

Edward had agreed, saying that he could remember clearly the day he first heard Elder Woodruff preach at Ridgeway Crossing back on March fifteenth, a year ago, then again a day or two later at Benbow's Hill Farm. "My mother told me that day that I should come home a baptized member of the Church, so I obeyed my mother and got baptized that day. My sister, Susannah, got baptized right after that."

"It didn't take you long to become a leader in our Church after that," Mary Ann had told Edward. Edward had nodded in agreement, smiling, and thinking back to the time he was ordained a priest just a few days after his baptism and put in charge of the Ashfield and Corcutt branches, with George Brooks as his assistant. Once he was ordained an elder by Wilford Woodruff he began to assume responsibilities in the Gloucestershire area with another member, John Gailey.

Edward had prepared all week for his Sunday sermon at the Davis home, and had begun by explaining what was meant when members of the Church testified that they believed they were members of the "true church" of God:

"When we bear our testimonies it is common to hear that we believe we are members of the only true and living church on the face of the earth. That is a phrase taken from the scriptures and we hear it often. I want to teach you today that the gospel is not just *the* particular system used by Latter-day Saints to enter God's kingdom, it is the *only* way anyone enters God's kingdom. Although there is truth in other churches and many, or most, believers and members of those churches are good people, *only one church* possesses the fullness of the gospel and its priesthood keys. And that is the Church of Jesus Christ of Latter-day Saints. Worthy people of other faiths will have to experience a conversion at some point, whether in this life or the next, to the doctrines and principles of Christ as taught by prophets of old and prophets of the latter day before they can enter into the highest degree of heaven, the Celestial Kingdom. Without that conversion they may dwell in heaven, but it will be in either the Terrestrial or Telestial Kingdom and they will not have a fullness of glory or full exaltation. There is no other way."

It was at this point that the men in the crowd outside began to yell insults at the Mormon sacrament meeting attendees. John, Mary Ann, Hannah Simmons, and the other members of Edward's small congregation turned their necks to look out the window.

Mary Ann's normal cheery look faded abruptly. "Who would they be?" she asked in a fretful tone.

Edward looked out the window for an uncomfortable five or ten seconds. It was at this point that he began to contemplate his options. His face sobered as he looked into the frightened faces of his congregation.

Eyebrows raised, eyes looking sideways at the other members of the church in his home, John pulled up the corners of his mouth into a fake smile. "Ignore them, dear," he said to his wife. "Go on with your talk, Brother Phillips." He disguised the fact that he recognized some of the mob as ruffians who frequented taverns in Tirley and Apperley. Two of them were old friends of Henry Eagles—Richie and Alex—men he regarded as apostate Methodists.

Edward began again, but he knew the crowd out there meant trouble. He knew that as their numbers swelled, their courage would increase also. "Just as a living plant is connected to its roots, so the Church is a 'living' church because it is connected directly to Jesus Christ, the source of light and truth, by continuing revelation and by the direct bestowal of priesthood authority."

Blonk!

Something hit the house. Whatever it was bounced harmlessly away, but it missed the window by only a foot.

John's face turned grave, his lower lip thrust out, but he knew that if the people inside his house showed any visible fear, it would only encourage the mob. He gestured to Edward to keep talking, but an air of uneasiness was settling into the room. No one moved.

With a worried shrug, Edward cleared a lump in his throat to continue. "Latter-day Saints have direct and living links with God in the chain of priesthood authority from Jesus Christ to Peter, James and John, to Joseph Smith…and eventually to each priesthood holder. Each priesthood holder in the Church can trace his line of authority to the Savior that way."

The crowd of ruffians walked closer. Now their voices could be heard: "You Mormons in there! Go home! Or we'll come in there and drag you out!"

A wave of fear swept over Mary Ann as she glanced through the window again.

Knowing that his words would not obscure what was taking place outside, Edward raised his voice: "When the communication of direct revelation is cut off, the church dies, just as a girdled tree dies when cut off from its roots. A Christmas tree may appear to be alive, but it is a dead tree, because it is no longer in touch with its roots. In the same way, a church may appear healthy but in truth it is dead or dying if continuing direct revelation does not exist. A living church is one still connected to God, its source, through living Apostles and Prophets who both hold the keys to the priesthood and receive direct divine guidance."

Smash!

A window shattered, scattering glass throughout the parlor. Mary Ann and Hannah screamed.

Richie and Alex, faces reddened, unkempt wild hair spilling down over their foreheads, veins in their necks standing out like ropes, led a charge toward the door.

The yard was suddenly full of warty, red-faced ugly men, yelling, bellowing, waving arms, shaking fists, beating their breasts, jumping, surging, running, and cursing.

It was a frightening specter to the small congregation inside the Davis home.

The noise swelled to a general mad roar as the men neared the door.

"Get Phillips!" a bloodthirsty voice screamed. "Get their preacher!"

Under Edward's startled glance, John was swift to react. "Quick! Let's get Brother Phillips upstairs and he can get away down the stairs at the back of the house."

Pounding could be heard against the planked front door, which had been locked.

John glanced out the window to see a mass of men peering back at him with angry, devilish eyes. He rushed toward the door to brace it against the onslaught. He was knocked backward as the door was torn off its hinges and the first of many maniacal men stormed into the house.

"Stop! You have no business being in my house," John yelled at the mob.

Almost before John could finish his sentence, Richie drew his right hand back, cocked it, and slammed a fist into John's uncovered jawbone. Blood quickly coming to his mouth, the force of the blow knocked John off his feet. As he hit the floor a powerful kick slammed into his stomach and another to his ribs.

More men were streaming into the house now, throwing the other Mormon men onto the floor and beating on them, also.

Bloody faced, clutching at his stomach, feeling the punishment of endless kicks, catching glances of other men withering on the floor, John heard Alex say, "This is what you get for letting a Mormon preacher into your house! Let this be a warning!"

The convulsive, panicky mob peered up the stairs.

"Where's the preacher?" Alex screamed frantically. "Find him, quick! He's gone up the stairs!

The last thing John remembered was the mobbers trampling past him up the stairs. He opened his mouth, groaned, felt his vision become blurred, and passed out.

A brawny man led a surge of mobbers up the stairs.

"Where's Phillips?" Richie demanded of the women when the attackers found them.

Mary Ann, Susannah, and the other women covered their faces and screamed, melting to their knees, not daring to look at the attackers.

Alex pointed to the back door. "Phillips is not here! He's escaped down the back stairs!"

"After him!" Richie screamed, stumbling toward the door, then darting down the stairs with a few mobbers following him.

"I can't see him," Alex yelled. "I'll go out the front door!"

He stormed back down the stairs. When he came to John's motionless body, Alex thrust another powerful foot into it. The body rolled over with the blow.

Alex ran outside into a murky gloom, blinking, yelling, "Where is he? Where's Phillips?"

25

AT SEVEN BELLS IN THE FORENOON watch, Neptune and other sailors gathered on the poop deck. They had the sextant with which they were going to make their noon observations of the sun in order to calculate the ship's latitude. When the sun was observed to be at the Zenith, Neptune called out, "There he goes!"

Heywood, acting as timekeeper, signaled for the bosun to turn the half-hour glass and ring eight bells, resetting the shipboard time for the day. Latitude was determined to be twenty-five degrees sixteen minutes south, just above the Tropic of Cancer. Course was southwest.

Afterward, as the *Echo* almost silently carved through clear blue water with lazy clouds drifting overhead, the afternoon watch found Daniel and James having a conversation with Captain Wood on the forecastle deck.

Daniel had taken James with him to talk about the gospel with the captain. He thought it would help take James' mind off the loss of his wife. They found the captain, dressed in summer whites, plunged in passion about his life at sea, sipping on button ale, a beverage made of ale mixed with butter sugar and cinnamon.

To build a relationship of trust with the captain, Daniel and James showed an interest in shipbuilding. Their interest was not contrived—they wanted to know how ships were constructed, what kinds of materials were used and how long they lasted. They were impressed that the *Echo* had withstood three weeks of intense Atlantic storms without any discernable damage except for a ripped sail or two that the crew quickly repaired.

It was a good moment for Captain Wood, who had asserted several times that he did not normally spend much time with steerage passengers, but was making an exception because he firmly believed Captain Browett had saved the ship by praying to the Mormon God.

When he found out that Daniel and James were carpenters, he immediately tried to sway them to join the shipbuilding industry.

The captain said, "Forget Nauvoo, your Mormon city. Go to New York and build ships like this one. They need men like you and you'll make a good wage."

He told them that many of the emigrants who crossed the Atlantic seaboard aboard packet ships later found work in the shipbuilding trade—often in yards where the packets were built, mostly in New York along Manhattan's East River.

There, more than a dozen yards kept carpenters, joiners, and caulkers on the job from sunup until dark earning more than a dollar a day.

Daniel gave the captain a warm smile that reflected an appreciation of the offer. "I'm certain we will stay in Nauvoo when we get there, Captain Wood, but we're curious about how ships are constructed. I've had dreams about Noah's Ark. I'd like to have been there to help Noah build it."

Captain Wood returned the smile. He was impressed that Daniel always referred to something in the scriptures to make a point. "Well, I'm not a ship builder, but I can tell you what I know."

The captain cleared his throat. "The *Echo* was built in 1834 by a New York City firm by the name of C. Bergh and Company. Probably the largest company in New York is the Brown and Bell who built the *Britannia, Rochester, Siddons,* and the *North America."*

With the sun blaring out of the clouds, James held one hand over his eyes and asked, "Is the *Echo* considered a large ship?"

The captain smiled again, this time tremendously, and gesturing broadly with his arms as he eyes spanned the ship. "One of the largest. It's registered at six hundred sixty eight tons, just a little larger than the *Britannia* and *North America,* but the *Rochester,* for example, is seven hundred and fourteen tons."

James whistled. "That means there's a lot of wood in this vessel, isn't there? It looks to be mainly oak and pine."

The captain nodded and gestured again, his eyes brightening, even glowing. "Whenever possible American builders use the best hardwoods but a lot of ships in Maine and into Canada are built of spruce, hackmatack, and pine. They are known to us as 'soft wood' vessels. This ship is framed in white oak but pitch pine has been used for the outside planking and inside lining. The keel and keelsons, as you've seen, are fashioned from massive pitch pine logs. And those masts and spars you see above us are cut from tall, straight pine that grow in our American forests. The foremast and mainmast are nearly ninety feet high and nearly forty inches in diameter at the base. The mizzenmast is no slouch. It's eighty feet high and thirty-four inches in diameter."

Daniel tried to imagine what America was going to look like. He knew that it was big and that the forests were immense. He gazed to the west, where he thought New Orleans lay, and to the north, in the direction of New York and the Atlantic seaboard. "I suppose most of the work takes place out of doors?"

"Correct, Captain Browett," Wood said, standing erect, blinking, smiling broadly. "Exposure to the weather helps season the wood. First, the keel is set out on blocks, and then the keel timbers are joined and scarfed together with big fastening bolts. The stem and stern posts are raised upright along with their supporting knee and angle pieces. After that the ribs or frames are attached. Then they build things they call knees and beams which support the decks. It's easy to see how the planking is attached to the ribs—they use what they call toenails or trunnels, which are wooden pegs made of oak. The workers pound them into holes made by augers."

James gasped at the captain's words.

"They use both steam and horse-powered derricks to place timbers into position. Timbers that comprise the keel and the ship's frame. One by one, the gigantic horseshoe-shaped ribs are hoisted upright and fitted onto the keel. Once they are up, the keelson is bolted along the hull's centerline, sandwiching the frames tightly against the keel. Then come the planks."

"Why do we see different thickness of the planking?" Daniel asked.

"You do have a keen eye for detail," Captain Wood said, pointing to the deck. "The heaviest planks are called 'wales.' They brace the ship front to back and wherever there will be severe strain on the ship. When bolts are used, they are usually made from copper. Sometimes iron bolts are used above the ballast loadlines. To waterproof the vessel where the berths and cargo are located, the builders use felt and copper sheathing. That also helps prevent the attachment of retarding marine undergrowth, like barnacles. Our deckhouses are planked with white pine on white oak framing."

"We see painters working just about all the time now that the weather is good," James said. He was looking at two of the crewmen with paint buckets and brushes, draped over the side of the ship.

"Dry rot is the number one enemy of a ship like this," Captain Wood said. "The shipworm is the number two enemy—little critters we call the toredo. We work to prolong the life of the vessel by constantly painting her. Once in a while the owners pull her out of the water and re-copper the bottom."

Daniel's response was one of astonishment. "Sounds like a lot of work not only to build a ship like this but to keep her in good sailing condition."

"Precisely. So if in your group you have carpenters and others that need good paying jobs, the shipbuilding industry on the east coast of America is in constant need of joiners, mast and spar makers, trunnel makers, sail makers, ironmongers, rope makers, tinsmiths, coppersmiths, block makers, caulkers, pump makers, ship chandlers, painters. You name it."

Daniel felt the captain was making a sincere compliment, but did not understand the passion of the Mormon people to gather to Zion. "We have people that could build some fine ships for your country, Captain Wood. But we're going to Illinois to help build a city called Nauvoo."

The captain shook his head indulgently, and grinned. "Yours is a peculiar people, Captain Browett. I've never seen a large group of passengers so well behaved. You are to be congratulated. I'm curious as to why so many Mormons are leaving England. I've heard that several vessels have been full of Mormons last year and that many more are booked this year. Are Mormons something like Methodists or Anglicans or Catholics?"

"Yes, sir," Daniel answered, "We are all Christians. We accept Jesus Christ as our Savior. But the real name of our Church is the Church of Jesus Christ of Latter-day Saints. It is the Savior's Church. It is not the Mormon Church. We get our nickname because we have a book—translated from an ancient record—called the Book of Mormon. Our Prophet, a man named Joseph Smith, translated it. We are called 'Mormons' but this is not our Church, it is the Savior's Church, so the Savior has instructed us to call it by his name."

"So that's how you are different from the Methodists, or I should say the Protestants? And the Catholics? Because you have a Book of Mormon?"

"That's part of it. We are a restored church, not a reformed church."

Captain Wood thought of all the talks he had heard—the Sunday services and the funeral for Nancy—but he didn't understand totally what Daniel meant. "What do you mean, restored?"

"We believe that after the death of the Savior and all of the Apostles that the world gradually fell into what we call an apostasy, meaning that ordinances were changed and corruption crept into the Church. The reformers, like Martin Luther, sought to correct that corruption, but eventually that effort, by Martin Luther and many others, came to be called the Protestant movement. The reformers were protesting—protesting the way the original Church had changed. We believe the Savior knew this was going to happen. There are scriptures that teach us that and tell us that the Apostles such as Paul knew it as well."

The captain scratched his chin through a thick beard. He wasn't certain he wanted to spend more time learning about the Mormons, but his interest was pricked. "Go on," he replied, in an inviting tone.

"So the world fell into spiritual darkness for hundreds of years until the time came for the Savior to organize his true church on the earth again. This pattern of having the gospel on the earth, followed by an apostasy, is seen in the Bible if you study it carefully. The pattern is simple to follow—first there is a prophet, like Adam, or Noah, or Moses, then there is a falling away, then a restoration through another prophet. The prophet the Lord used in these, the latter days, is a man by the name of Joseph Smith."

"Joe Smith, the Mormon Prophet. You mentioned him in your sermons. Fine sermons, by the way."

"Thank you, captain. Yes, sir. That's him. In 1820, in answer to his prayers, the Savior, and his father, the Eternal Father, both appeared to Joseph Smith and told him to join no church. That began a process, which we will tell you about, called the restoration of the gospel. As part of the restoration, so we could have an understanding of the fullness of the gospel, the Prophet Joseph Smith was given an ancient record to translate. That record, a history of a people that lived on the American continent from about six hundred years before Christ until four hundred years after his death, is what I hold in my hands—the Book of Mormon. The Savior sent John the Baptist to restore the Aaronic Priesthood—note that I am using the word 'restore'—and later he sent his Apostles, Peter, James and John, to restore the higher or Melchizedek Priesthood. Then in 1830 the Savior instructed Joseph Smith to organize, or restore, His Church on the earth."

Shaking his head up and down to acknowledge he understood, the captain said, "So all of you in your company are Mormons, people who believe this restoration?"

"Yes. We believe that God restored his Church on the earth again."

"How did so many of you in England become Mormons?"

Daniel turned to James. "You know the answer to that question as well as I do, Brother Pulham. You tell the captain."

James cleared his throat. "I'll do the best I can, captain. As soon as the Church was organized, Joseph Smith, just like the Savior did when he ministered personally on the earth, began training and sending out lay missionaries, volunteers who were willing to make personal sacrifices and preach the restored gospel to the world. They travel without purse or scrip. Some of those missionaries came to England, members of the Quorum of the Twelve Apostles...an organization that was restored to the earth...so there are Apostles living on the earth again. They came among us and told us about the restoration and the Book of Mormon. Many of us who joined wanted to emigrate to America and live with the other members—called Saints—in Nauvoo, Illinois, where Joseph Smith lives. That, sir, is where we are going."

The captain smiled again. "There's no ship building industry in Illinois."

"But we will help build a temple," James said.

"A temple? For what?"

MONDAY March 15 – A vessel in sight. Wind changes at night to southwest.

TUESDAY March 16 – Rainy morning, wind continues favorable. One lad is partly scalded. Everyone is anxious to reach New Orleans.

WEDNESDAY March 17 – Showery, no wind, calm. Gallant mast up, sky sail mast. Captain told us about ships, we told him about the gospel; we will continue to teach him.

THURSDAY March 18 – Flattering winds. Sailors begging to paint the ship, calm towards the evening. Sailors caught three small sharks, giving one to me to share with some of the steerage passengers. The flesh of a shark is considered a luxury. Larger sharks have a strong smell but the small ones, cut into small slices like beef, broiled with salt and pepper, eat very well. It resembled codfish in taste and made a fine meal.

26

IT WAS A DARK AFTERNOON in England, with low black clouds threatening rain. A dank north wind off the Malvern Hills whistled past the stone cottage where John Davis lay in a near coma, his breathing shallow, and his lungs burning with pain. With sad filmed eyes, Mary Ann kneeled beside him in an upstairs bedroom, sponging his head with a sodden white handkerchief,

John had reached a point where he ate or drank precious little. He had a swollen jaw, a missing tooth, and a swelled, puffy lip. The doctor had told Mary Ann that John had several broken ribs and, worst of all, internal injuries, causing a hot fever. He was bleeding from his lungs. However, aside from a few minutes during the assault, John had remained conscious throughout the painful ordeal. He constantly asked about the others who were injured by the mob. Mary Ann had assured him they were fine. Indeed they were, compared to John. John was the only one confined to bed by doctor's orders. The doctor had also told Mary Ann not to let anyone disturb him. No visitors. Stress would cause the lung to bleed worse. The sight of her husband lying in the bed slumped Mary Ann, who had gloomed around the house for days since the beating.

A knock downstairs. Mary Ann quickly descended the steep narrow stairs to the parlor and opened the door. Mary Ann cringed when she saw her mother-in-law standing there in a black chiffon carriage dress. As they locked eyes, Mary Ann gave Charlotte Edmunds Davis a mutinous stare. In return, the older woman glared back with narrowing steel-gray eyes.

"Aren't you going to invite me in?" Mrs. Davis said, impertinent.

Mary Ann didn't know how to respond. *No one, absolutely no one,* should visit John, according to the doctor. However, this woman was John's mother. Under normal circumstances, Mary Ann felt that a mother should be welcomed, even invited to assist in the healing process. But John's mother had been so extremely vocal about her opposition to John being baptized into the Church that Mary Ann feared she would say something that would upset her husband and make things worse, not better. Trembling, she said, "The doctor told me that John should have no visitors. I'm sorry."

The fifty-five-year-old iron-nerved woman pushed Mary Ann out of the way, stepped inside and planted her legs apart. "Nonsense! I'm his mother!"

Defiantly, Mrs. Davis pulled her dress up slightly and bounded up the stairs. The only thing Mary Ann could do was follow, uttering feeble protests.

John knew it was his mother from the voice downstairs. "Hello, mother," John said in a shaky voice as Mrs. Davis barged into his bedchamber. He made a weak gesture with one hand. Her presence, a haunting burden, gave him pangs of anxiety because of his mother's open hatred of Mormons.

As Mrs. Davis' eyes fell on her son, she opened her mouth in horror. Her own sources had told her of the beating, that the mob had gotten carried away. They were supposed to have beaten up Mr. Phillips, the part-time Mormon minister. But here lay her own son. The injuries to his mouth and face shocked her. John's pale complexion and gaunt look told her that there was more to his injuries than she could outwardly see. But first things first. She had come to speak her mind. She could inquire about his health later.

"This business with your church has got to stop, John," she scowled. "It's an illegal church. We're making every effort to have Parliament make a declaration. Your Mormon missionaries will be barred from coming here."

In a slow, pained voice, grateful that his jaw was only badly bruised, not broken, John replied, "Oh, mother, please. We've been over this before. This is my church now, please let it be."

Mary Ann interrupted, her voice full of despair. "Don't make him talk, please, Mrs. Davis. The bleeding in his lungs may start again."

Ignoring her daughter-in-law like she was not even there, the mad woman continued without taking a breath, talking rapidly to her son. "If you don't renounce your religion there will be other incidents. It's for your own safety. If your wife wants to continue with Mormonism then let her. Send her to America with the other Mormons who have run away. I'll find you a new wife, one that's not a Mormon."

Swelling with emotion, John's eyes widened. He rolled over on his side. He could hardly believe his ears. *My own mother! Part of the anti-Mormon movement.*

"Mother," John paused to cough, moaning in pain. "Did you tell someone that we were having a meeting in our house last Sunday?"

"John," Mrs. Davis said in an unapologetic voice, "you shouldn't have Mormon preachers in your home."

John attempted to rise.

"John, no! Stay down!" Mary Ann placed a hand on his shoulder. She turned to face her adversarial mother-in-law, sobbing. "Can't you see what you're doing? Please leave. Right now!"

John coughed. He tasted blood. "Mother! I asked you a question!"

"John, listen to me," Mrs. Davis warned. "There will be other incidents. You will be in danger. Quit this church and come to your senses."

With those words of finality, the woman turned and left.

With another audible groan, John rose to his feet, ignoring his wife's protests. "Mother! I asked you a question." He followed down the stairs.

"John! Please!" Mary Ann followed, trying to hang onto his arm.

John used all his strength to tear his arm away from Mary Ann's grip. "Mother! Come back here!"

The door opened and slammed shut.

Four steps from the bottom, John fell. Withering on the floor, he was quickly encompassed in the arms of his wife. He fainted in pain.

27

THE FIRST LOG BOOKS USED ON SHIPS were literally just that—comprised of shingles cut from logs. The shingles were formed into a book by drilling holes in one edge and were bound together by weaving leather through the holes.

At four bells during the morning watch, Captain Wood was basking in the sunshine near his quarters, writing in his paper logbook, when he saw Robert Harris strolling along with his son Joseph. During his years on the seas between England and the United States, Captain Wood had met merchants, politicians, dukes, duchesses, authors, admirals, generals, engineers, senators, detectives, actors, and actresses. But he had never met a bonafide challenger for the British heavyweight championship. The captain motioned for Robert to approach.

"I hear you were a fighter back in England," Captain Wood said, giving Robert's fluid motion and sculptured torso an appraising look. He ignored other passengers as they strode past them, swinging their arms, looking pre-occupied, and virtuous. Others leaned against the bulwark, sniffing the sea air, and gazing at the clear blue waters of the Caribbean Sea.

Robert's face reddened. "Yes, sir. I was."

"Folks tell me you could have been champion."

A shrug. "Maybe, maybe not." Robert turned his attention to his boy. "Careful, Joseph. Don't get too near the rail. Some of the sailors report they've seen sharks."

"Your modesty impresses me," the captain said. "I hear you were one fight away from challenging for the title."

"Yes, but perhaps I would have lost."

"Or perhaps you would have won. My guess is that if you would have stayed in England you would be the champion by now, and quite rich and famous." The captain's tone was slightly cynical.

Robert spread his arms in a graceful, resigned gesture. "That doesn't matter now. I have a new life, and I'm happy."

"I don't understand," the captain said, smiling transparently, obviously baffled. "You gave it all up just to become a Mormon? Why?"

Ironic, Robert thought. "That's the message of my talk today at our church services. Brother Browett has asked me to tell my story. You're welcome to attend again."

Captain Wood scanned Robert's infectious grin, a curiosity swelling within his soul. "Thank you, I will."

At the spacious poop deck they found Daniel in a position beneath the mizzenmast, preparing for the meeting.

More than a hundred passengers were clamoring for seats under the shade of a huge canopy that had been erected with the assistance of the crew.

A hymn was sung.

As Dianah Bloxham offered an opening prayer, Captain Wood's thoughts remained on Robert. *Why is a man like him mixed in with hundreds of poor, common British steerage passengers who paid a pitiful low fare for passage across the ocean?*

Uneasiness lined Robert's face as he began to talk. It showed in his blue-gray eyes, the twitch in his jaw, and the wringing of his hands. Captain Wood suspected Robert would have been more comfortable in a boxing ring than in front of a large crowd. He was not a professional preacher.

"A few months before my marriage I became obsessed with pugilism, and soon it consumed my life," Robert began, beads of sweat forming on his forehead. "I wanted to become the British heavyweight champion. I was willing to sacrifice anything to reach that goal. I didn't realize it at the time but looking back I think I was willing to sacrifice even my wife and children. I thought the money I would make after I was champion would bring happiness to myself and to my family."

Captain Wood rolled his eyes. *Money* is *happiness, silly man.*

Robert paused, and cleared his throat.

"Then the most wonderful miracle happened. Elder Wilford Woodruff was sent on a mission to England. He began teaching the gospel of Jesus Christ throughout the Malvern Hills. My best friend, Brother Daniel Browett, was converted, as was his wife—and my sister—Sister Elizabeth Browett. They were converted by the power of the Spirit. Elder Woodruff was the person the Lord used to bring that power, that Spirit, to the Malvern Hills. My wife attended a meeting where the restored gospel was taught. She, too, was converted by the Spirit. They had a powerful testimony that the true Church was once again restored to the earth, that the Book of Mormon is the word of God as is the Bible, that the priesthood had been restored. They wanted me to have that same testimony."

A testimony? The captain drew a face, wondering what the term meant.

"But I was too proud to listen. I was too caught up in the ways of the world. I wanted power, money, and the honors of men. Fortunately for me, my wonderful wife, Hannah, and my sister, Elizabeth, had a plan. You might call it a trick, even. They invited Elder Woodruff to my home knowing that sooner or later I would come home and find a missionary meeting going on in my own house. It was a risk on her part. Yes, I was mad, very mad, as she feared I would be. I went in the house to throw the American missionary out. I thought I could do it with one arm tied behind my back. But I couldn't do it. I did not understand the Spirit that was in my home that Elder Woodruff brought there. I was confused. I thought I needed help. I went back to my brother's pub and brought several of my friends back to my house. I told them to wait outside and I would give the sign to rush in, grab Elder Woodruff, and take him out and rotten egg him. Again, I couldn't do it. I could not raise my arm to give the sign."

Captain Wood gave Robert a perplexed look. What kind of power, unseen, could prevent a sure-fire future boxing champion from raising his arm? All his life he had believed in power that you could see, feel, and touch. He couldn't see the wind but he could feel it. It was a power that he learned to use, whether it was against him or with him. But this power—the power of some unseen spirit—was something new to him.

Robert began to relax now. His words flowed. "I knew I had to listen to the message. I told my friends to leave. From then on the miracle of conversion happened in my life. The Spirit told me everything that Elder Woodruff was teaching was true. It was a very personal experience, hard to explain. It changed my life. I was baptized shortly thereafter."

With a heavy sigh, Captain Wood contemplated what his life would be like if he were to have a spiritual "rebirth." It would probably mean that he would give up his seafaring life, and the thoughts of that troubled him, so in love with ships, oceans, and his position was he. He gnawed on his lower lip, and wondered about his wife in New York City whom he seldom saw, and his four-year-old daughter who had asked him why he had missed her last birthday party.

Robert's amazing and inspiring tale continued. "Since my baptism I have come to learn that the power I was feeling that night came from the Holy Ghost. That power can come upon anyone before baptism and it is the convincing witness that the gospel is true. It gave me a testimony of Jesus Christ and of his work and the work of his servants, like Elder Woodruff, upon the earth. After my baptism, I received the official Gift of the Holy Ghost, conferred by the laying on of hands by proper priesthood authority. I have learned that the gospel is full of symbolism—that the hand is a symbol of power and authority, that the extended hand is a symbol of friendship, confidence, and trust. I learned that the laying on of hands represents the placing of God's hand upon the head of the one being blessed."

Captain Wood's face turned serious.

"When God the Father and his Son, Jesus Christ, appeared to Joseph Smith in 1820," Robert continued, "a great truth about the godhead was restored to the earth. The Father and the Son are two different beings, two distinct personages, each with a body of flesh and bones. I have learned that the Holy Ghost is likewise a distinct personage or spirit, but not possessing a body of flesh and bones. The Holy Ghost has a special mission. I felt the power of that special mission. By the power of the Holy Ghost I was converted to the gospel.

"I have learned that the Holy Ghost will not dwell in unclean tabernacles nor strive with people unless they keep their minds as well as their bodies clean, and are diligent before the Lord. The Holy Ghost does not strive with God's children but rather comes to teach, to comfort, and edify only as we prepare ourselves to receive his companionship. When hands were laid on my head, the wording was—'receive ye the Holy Ghost.' That is, a directive was given to me to live the commandments so that I would have the right to have the Holy Ghost teach, comfort, and edify me.

"On the other hand, I have learned that all men, me included, are endowed with what we call the 'light of Christ' and that light will labor and strive with people to bring them to the additional light that comes from this member of the Godhead. I believe with all my heart that Thomas Kington and John Benbow were full of the light of Christ when they organized the United Brethren congregation. The light of Christ touched the lives of each member. It prepared them for the further light and knowledge of the fullness of the gospel. When Elder Woodruff preached the gospel, the Holy Ghost manifested the truthfulness of it to each one. As I understand it, every member of the United Brethren, around six hundred souls, accepted baptism into the Church. All except one."

Robert paused and turned his gaze to Captain Wood. Robert's eyes appeared shining and enormous to the captain. To Robert, the captain appeared slightly stunned, returning only an abstracted glare.

"I have learned that the Holy Ghost enlightens our minds when we study the scriptures. By that enlightenment I have gained a testimony of the Book

of Mormon. Now, when I read the scriptures under the direction and influence of the Holy Ghost it is like hearing the voice of the Lord. To read under
the direction of the Spirit is to hear that voice.

"I have learned that I have stood in the light, accepted the light, and the
gospel is now my life. I have been baptized and placed my life in the door that
leads to salvation. But I know that I must work hard and endure to the end.
Just because I once stood in the light doesn't mean Satan is going to let me
stay there. He will seek to reclaim me. I know that seekers of salvation must
regard the quest as a journey rather than an event. Baptism alone will not get
me to the presence of God after death. I must advance grace to grace, continue to have faith, combine it with good works, keep the commandments all the
days of my life, repent quickly when I make mistakes, serve God in whatever
capacity he may wish, stay active in the Church, and endure to the end.

"To those who have not yet been baptized I can only pray that you will
feel the power of the Spirit and gain the same testimony I have gained. Give
up your pride. Be humble. Accept the restored gospel of Jesus Christ, for it is
the true gospel restored to the earth once again."

After the meeting, Captain Wood walked away in a subdued mood. Robert
found him an hour later. They found a spot on the main deck to talk. Below
them, sailors were lashed about the waist and ankles, suspended upside down,
caulking outermost seams with oakum.

"Can you understand why I'm on this ship now?" Robert asked.

"I think so," the captain answered. "But you have done something that
I couldn't do." He thought of the upside-down sailors, caulking the "devil
seams." He had never done that, either. They seemed caught between the devil
and the deep blue sea. If the ship rolled just right, they were dunked momentarily. No one liked being caught between the devil seam and the deep blue
sea.

"Nonsense," Robert said. "If the Spirit testified to you about the truthfulness of the gospel, you could do it."

"No. You're a better man than I. I couldn't give up my life as a sea captain."

Robert grimaced at the captain's conclusion. In an eerie way, Captain Wood sounded just like Robert's brother, John. John had refused to listen to Elder Woodruff. He was still in Apperley, managing his pub, the Ferret's Folly. *John's folly. The captain's folly. Failure to embrace the truthfulness of the gospel.*

FRIDAY March 19 – Hot sun, little breeze. A child fell down the hatch and broke her arm.

SATURDAY March 20 – Hot morning, more than any hot summer's day in England. The captain caused a canopy to be erected to shade us from the sun.

SUNDAY March 21 – Fine morning, no wind, dead calm. Ship steering south-southeast. Sacrament meeting on deck. Brother Robert Harris told of his conversion and taught us about the power of the Holy Ghost. Several more came forward and requested baptism. Captain attended the meeting.

MONDAY March 22 – Wind changes northeast, little breeze. Fine night.

28

DESPITE HIS STUBBORN FAILURE to embrace Mormonism, Captain Wood remained a clever, cordial man, in every way different than men Daniel and Robert had previously met in their lives. The captain had a countenance that was open and hearty. He made bright jokes, including bold pleasantries about the trip, the passengers, the ship, and America. He expressed a deep regard for the members of the Mormon company, and made himself available for conversation and help. Daniel found this convenient as he began to worry about securing passage on a steamboat for the trip up the Mississippi River. Arrival at New Orleans was only days away. Because his company was one of the first to leave England, the Brethren in Liverpool had told him precious little except that steamboats were the only way to get to Nauvoo from New Orleans, unless a man were to walk or ride a horse or a mule.

Captain Wood had been to New Orleans twice, and had passed on what he had learned. One day the captain boasted to Daniel that America was so large that he doubted if it would ever get all settled. But he added that the westward migration of pioneer settlers and the rapid growth of agriculture, commerce, and industry in the Middle West was responsible for the development of inland waterways.

"I was once asked to become a steamboat captain," Wood said, "but I can't see myself strapped to a side-wheeler, confined to wherever a river wants to take you."

The captain knew a few pertinent things about steamboating. The first steamboat in America was Robert Fulton's *Clermont*. It began hauling passengers and freight on the Hudson River between Albany and New York in 1807. A big side-wheeler called the *New Orleans* was built in Pittsburgh in 1811, and pioneered steamboat traffic on the Mississippi.

Captain Wood talked to Daniel and his assistants from a chair on the poop deck. He shifted his weight, crossed and uncrossed his ankles, and chewed on an unlit clay pipe. "Actually the first steamer that descended the Mississippi was the *Pennsylvania,* and I know a story about her. She came down the Ohio from Pittsburgh, and made such a noise that in the minds of all the simple-hearted people they thought an earthquake was happening. Some fled to the hills, others crowded the river shore and in their alarm fell-down upon their knees and prayed to be delivered from the roaring demon coming down the river."

The captain laughed heartily at his story.

Daniel laughed with him, inwardly admitting that he liked people who laughed from their belly and their diaphragm, not from face muscles. Daniel fancied that the captain loved telling horror stories about vessels whether they were ocean going or river going. "How do I go about getting passage to Nauvoo?" he asked before the captain thought of another tale.

"Best I can tell you, Mr. Browett," Captain Wood said, "is that there will be a few steamboat company offices in New Orleans, and you'll just have to walk in and tell them what you have. Any of them will be more than happy to do business with you. A hundred and nine passengers plus baggage is big business to them."

Daniel wondered in silence for a few moments. Everyone in the company was anxious to get to Nauvoo as quickly as possible. Securing property and farms and building some type of home or shelter was on everyone's mind, and they were already two weeks behind schedule because of the fierce Atlantic storms they had encountered.

"How long do you think it will take to transfer off the *Echo* and get our things onto a steamboat?" he asked. "Just a few hours?"

That remark gave Captain Wood a good laugh. "How about a few days? Loading and unloading a ship like this takes a lot of hard work and patience. You might even have to wait a few days to find the right steamboat."

Daniel's face was a picture of concern. "Except for the sails, do steamboats look something like this ship?"

That question caused the captain to laugh again. "No, Captain Browett, not at all. But I suppose that's not a bad guess when I stop to think about it. The first steamboats built in our country actually looked a lot like seagoing vessels with their deep hulls and rounded keels. A few of them tried using sails to take advantage of favorable winds. But we found out that the deep-hulled riverboats sat too low in the water, and sometimes our rivers get shallow, especially in the late summer. Gradually steamboats were redesigned, and the boat you will go up the Mississippi on will look totally different than the *Echo*. It will have a shallow hull, and its steering wheel will be at the front of the boat in a pilot house, perched thirty or forty feet above the main deck. Here on the *Echo*, the steering wheel is aft, by my cabin."

Daniel cocked his head thoughtfully. "Then I guess the Americans don't use flat steamboats to haul cargo out into the ocean?"

"I can remember when the first steamboats were built of wood, tin, shingles, canvas and twine," the captain said, his weathered face still carrying a smile. "They looked like a bride of Babylon. If one of them, or even one of today's steamboats, tried to haul cargo from New Orleans to the tip of Florida, the ocean would take one playful slap at it and people would be picking up kindling on the beach for the next ten years. No, Captain Browett, steamboats are riverboats. We think someday that steam could power an ocean vessel, but not for now."

"Do you think I can get all of our Mormon passengers on just one steamboat?"

"Oh, yes," Captain Wood said with a respectful grin. "But prepare to be just as shocked as you were when you saw the steerage accommodations on our ship. Unless you can afford to book cabin passage, you'll be considered as deck passengers. All the cabin passengers will go first class on the upper deck, while all the deck passengers will be crammed onto the main deck with the cargo, livestock, and the deckhands. Depending on the size of your steamboat, expect to see two- or three- or four-hundred passengers on the main deck with you."

"Well, Captain Wood," Daniel said in an plaintive voice, "we've endured steerage on the *Echo*, and I guess we can endure whatever challenges await us as deck passengers on some strange steamboat going up the Mississippi River from New Orleans. How long do you think it will take us to reach Nauvoo?"

"I don't know for certain because I have never been up the river myself, but I would guess about two weeks total."

Daniel cringed. The *Echo* was already two weeks behind schedule. He was anxious to get his Mormon company to Nauvoo.

TUESDAY March 23 – Wind blows fresh from west-northwest. Towards night wind brisk. Mizzen sail hoisted. Sailors busy.

WEDNESDAY March 24 – Wind brisk, ship going between 8 and 9 knots per hour. Hot day. Heavy rain at night.

29

SAILORS ON THE ECHO LIVED in crowded conditions. Near the end of long voyages, tempers ultimately flared. Captain Wood wisely kept weapons such as pistols and cutlasses under lock and key. However, every sailor kept a knife as part of his kit, examined at the beginning of the voyage to make certain that the point was broken off so that it was less of a weapon.

Several of the sailors had been ordered to tar the ropes. One, a Spanish sailor, was forced by a French sailor to put his hands into the barrel of tar and stir the contents. When he was asked to remove his hands and wipe them on his own chest, the Spaniard erupted. He grabbed a tar brush and rammed it into the Frenchman's face. Soon they were standing face-to-face. One of the Spaniard's threats was cultivated with the statement, "I don't like th' cut o' yur jib."

The French sailor locked his eyes on the nose of the Spaniard. "Now yer showing yer true colors."

"Yer nothin' but bilge. If I had my barker, I'd blast your guts," the other said, referring to his pistol that had been confiscated.

"If I had me bilbow, I'd cut you in two," countered the Frenchman again, referring to his sword with a fine tempered blade.

Henry Eagles watched the rising confrontation with no idea what the two statements meant. The ship's rigging and, more specifically, her jibs often determined nationalities of ships of the sea. A Spanish ship would typically have a small jib if she carried any at all. A large French ship likely would have two jibs. English ships would fly only a single jib. The jib was the first part of the ship to arrive at any given place. A man's nose, like a jib, is the first part to similarly arrive. Thus the phrase implies the first impression one sailor had of another. Early warships carried flags from many nations to deceive or elude another ship. Civilized warfare required each ship to hoist her true national ensign before firing the first shot. A ship tricked in this manner was said to have been bamboozled.

A third sailor stepped between the Spaniard and the Frenchman, risking his life as the two men were brandishing their stubby knives. "Pipe down, and get back to work. The captain's apt to find a blunderbuss and fill ya both with buckshot."

The bosun's whistle was called a pipe because of its long narrow shape. On old Roman rowing galleys, the pipe was used to call the stroke. Because of its shrill tune, the pipe generally could be heard above the hubbub of deck activity.

Henry knew that "pipe down" was a warning to stand back.

The Spaniard was too hot-blooded to heed the warning. He shoved the third sailor out of the way and lunged at his adversary. The two men locked each other's wrists in powerful grips, keeping the blunt knives at bay. As they spun in circles, they found themselves crashing into a dark-haired Englishman, a head taller than either of them. Henry Eagles.

Motivated by an instinct bordering on fear that the knives might injure him, and just as Adams, the second mate, arrived, Henry lashed out as though he were in a pub fight at the Ferret's Folly in his home hamlet of Apperley. His balled-up fist caught the Spaniard on the ear. Another found its mark squarely on the Frenchman's nose, drawing blood.

The sight of Adams brought the fight to an end. Adams stared at his two sailors with narrow eyes. "I see the wind taken out of yer sails by the Englishman. That's good. Now carry on. When we get to New Orleans, you'll have access to your weapons. If ye wish ta fight, no quarter asked, no quarter given, that'll be yer pleasure. But if ye do, that'll end yer contract of employment on this ship. Now get outta here before I run ya through the gantlet and let every man take a swipe at ya."

Adams referred to an oft-used battle maneuver by sailing ships. By passing close to her adversary on the weather side, a ship could blanket the wind from the opponent. This would cause the opponent to loose headway and maneuverability, reducing her ability to fight.

With the Spaniard and the Frenchman glaring at each other now, Adams made another forceful statement. "Mind yer P's and Q's, or I'll have ya chained."

At waterfront taverns, until sailors got their advance pay for their next voyage, tavern keepers had a scorecard where they would place a mark for each pint ("P") and quart ("Q") that the sailor ordered. It was up to the tavern keeper to be mindful that no pints or quarts had been left off the customer list. And it was up to the sailor to ensure that the tavern keeper made no extra marks.

A scorecard filled up guaranteed that the sailor would become "three sheets to the wind." A square-rigged vessel like the *Echo* had three sheets to control her primary sails. The mainsheet was used to control the fore-and-aft mainsail. The windward sheet and the leeward sheet were used to control the foresail. If all three sheets where cast to the wind or let go, it would cause the ship to stagger on a course, like a drunken sailor.

Adams glared at the two men, wondering if either of them was the man who had attacked Rebecca Browett. Adams won the glaring contest as they surrendered their knives. The Frenchman retreated first. The Spaniard went the opposite way.

"Thank ya Englishman," Adams said. "I was ready ta toss 'em overboard and let the sharks have 'em."

Henry rubbed his right fist, still stinging from the blows he had inflicted. He pulled one corner of his mouth into a tart smile. "Anytime."

If anyone would have asked him, Henry Eagles would have said that he didn't know when the exact time was that he began to think about abandoning the Mormon company when the ship reached New Orleans. It may have been the first time he struck up a conversation with some of the gentile passengers. Whenever it was, the idea solidified in his mind when he was embarrassed in front of everyone after he attacked Daniel and Bobby roughed him up for it. Ever since he admitted to Bobby that it was he who hit Bobby over the head and tossed him overboard, he felt uncertain of himself, forlorn, and out of place. Everyone avoided him.

Even now, he stood alone at the rail, overlooking the blue seas surrounding the islands of the West Indies, reflecting on the trip and the decision he must make. He was anxious to arrive in New Orleans, and hoped that it would take a day or two or three before Daniel secured passage on a steamboat up the Mississippi to Nauvoo. That way, he could scout the city he had been told so much about—the original French Quarter, the American sector, and the Fauberg Marigny—and make a decision. He had heard nothing that would particularly dissuade him. The climate was tropical and he wouldn't have to put up with cold, snowy winters. It was a bustling seaport with a sensual if not hedonistic atmosphere, and the thought of that excited him. When a crewmember told him the French referred to New Orleans as the "Isle d'Orleans," because of the rivers, lakes, and swamps surrounding the city, he became intrigued. Henry liked the sound of the French word, and repeated it over and over again. He was anxious to mingle with the people there, a mixture of river boatsmen, soldiers, former pirates, Creoles, and Anglo-Saxons, all of whom were giving the city a reputation of a community filled with drinkers and carousers. If the *Echo* crewmembers were correct, New Orleans' population had been growing faster than any other American city, and was either the third or fourth largest in the country. Henry's mind entertained thoughts of working on a steamboat, operating a restaurant or bar, becoming a cotton merchant, or, if nothing else, operating a dairy and selling milk to the city's bulging population. At the worst, he could become a bricklayer, like his Grandfather Eagles.

Henry glared at Robert's children as they counted flying fish in a contest with the Bloxham children to see which child could count the most by seeing them first. Henry resented Robert, and knew he always would. The only times Henry had gotten the best of Robert, Henry had to have the help of Alex and Richie the first time, and the assistance of stealth and a wooden club the second time. Robert was the only man to have ever whipped him, and he knew he would undoubtedly lose again, if he were to try, even though his adversary was not in training now. It would not be enjoyable living in the shadow of Robert Harris all his life in Nauvoo. New Orleans would be a better alternative.

Henry spat in the ocean, and then he hung his head. He wondered what Katherine would say. Day by day she seemed to enjoy being a Mormon more and more. She might choose the Mormons over him.

It seemed to Henry, after five weeks on the *Echo*, that Katherine was also growing quite distant from him, that she felt some shame in the way he had acted, although up to this point she had not said much about it at all. She spoke less, their intimacy wasn't the same, and she spent more time with the other Mormon women than with him. Right now she was with Dianah Bloxham, helping tend her youngest children. Henry oftentimes thought about how it would be to have children of his own. When he did, he had mixed emotions. Children would be a burden, a millstone around his neck, especially in New Orleans.

When Katherine came walking toward him an hour later Henry decided to talk to her about staying in New Orleans. That is, if he could swear her to secrecy first. He didn't relish bringing up the topic, so he made idle conversation with her first, talking about the weather and complimenting her on her skin tone, which had turned from pale white to a nice bronze tan.

"This trip has been worse on us than we supposed," he began.

"Oh, I don't know," Katherine said, brushing her dark brown hair aside. "It's so pleasant now I've almost forgotten the bad days. And you need to keep quiet about what you think happened to your sister's body."

"I'm just curious, that's all," Henry said in a huff. He had speculated in front of Hannah that perhaps Nancy's body had resurfaced somewhere, and became a prey for fish. Or that she was rotting in the bottom of the ocean. Or perhaps she had sunk so deep the corpse would never decompose. And he constantly asked how the resurrection would compensate for all these possibilities. His remarks had not only offended Hannah, but everyone else on board.

"Keep your curiosity to yourself from now on," Katherine warned.

Henry changed the subject. "I wonder how we British let the French explore this part of America first?" he asked in a halfhearted manner.

"I guess it doesn't matter, does it? It's all part of America now. I heard the Americans were smart to buy it from the French. The Louisiana Purchase, that's what they called it."

Watching for Katherine's reaction, Henry said, "They say New Orleans is quite European in its makeup. We might be better off settling there instead of Nauvoo."

Katherine was swift to make a verbal response, surprising Henry with her knowledge. "They're European all right, but Irish, German, and French. Hardly any English, is what I've heard. But you can stay there if you want. I'm going to Nauvoo."

A helpless vexation came over Henry. Unless his wife stayed with him, he would be all alone in New Orleans, and he didn't like the thoughts of that at all. Her quick reaction so took him by surprise that he had to think about what to say next. Maybe he loved her after all. His mind seemed confused. Over all the months they had been married, he could still remember how he felt on their wedding night and the days and weeks following. Sometimes he admitted to himself that being married was good, but he had never told her.

Returning his thoughts to the port of New Orleans, Henry said, "Don't say anything to anyone. It's just something I've thought about."

"There's one thing you don't understand, Henry," Katherine said, feeling a note of sadness that Henry had no clue about the feelings of the other members of the Mormon company. "Brother Harris has totally forgiven you for what you did. So has everyone else. They've tried to reach out to you since, but you're so proud you reject everyone. It's time to get over it, Brother Eagles."

With that final note of sarcasm, Katherine walked away.

Henry's somber mood brightened when he finally found a gentile passenger who had also noised about that he was thinking of settling in New Orleans, rather than in the frontier country west of St. Louis. Richard Hargraves, a grizzled thirty-seven-year-old former saddler whose wife had died a year earlier in Sheffield, was traveling with his only son, sixteen-year-old Dickey.

"Why go up the Mississippi when the land of opportunity is right in New Orleans?" Hargraves began to say whenever Henry talked with him. "Maybe we can go into business together."

"What kind of business?" Henry asked with a growing suspicion. He didn't mind Hargraves making suggestions, but he reserved the right to make all final decisions. That's a point he would clear up with his new friend at a later date.

Recalling what one of the crewmembers had told him, a former resident of the port city, Hargraves—medium height, dark brown hair, mischievous brown eyes and a sharp nose—was quick to respond. "How about a gambling house? We would get rich quick. Or anything in the hospitality industry. We could own a restaurant or a pub."

Pausing to think for a minute, Henry said, "What would we use for money?"

"We could pool our money together."

Not wishing to divulge how much money he had in his possession, Henry simply said, "How much do you have? Enough to start a business?"

"More than three hundred pounds. And you?"

Henry did a quick calculation. Fifty-four pounds of his own. Thirty pounds that his mother had given him. And fifteen pounds that his wife's family had given Katherine on their departure. "I've got about the same," Henry said, not uncomfortable that he had lied.

"Splendid," said the former saddler. "Let's start looking for a way to invest our money as soon as we get there."

Henry nodded. He would have to work fast. After arrival, he knew he would have only three or four days until he and Katherine would be scheduled to leave on a steamboat for Nauvoo.

THURSDAY March 25 – Ship on her course. Sister Harris and a Mrs. Walmsley, not of our company, may give birth any day.

FRIDAY March 26 – Weather fine but ship heaving, a few sick. Mrs. Walmsley had her infant this morning; but the infant died about 5 o'clock. Little Joseph Harris celebrated his fifth birthday today.

SATURDAY March 27 – Fine morning. Several rainbows; ship in sight northeast. Squally about 11 o'clock. The Walmsley child was committed to the deep.

SUNDAY March 28 – Fine day, wind blows fresh from the previous night about 12 o'clock. This being Easter Sunday we had special services on deck for all passengers, even many of the nonmember passengers attended. John Cheese gave a talk on the resurrection.

30

CONSTANTLY REFERRING TO HER Aristotle book, Elizabeth tried to remain calm. Four other wives, all trying to be "assistant midwives," surrounded her. Little beads of sweat dotted her forehead. It was hard to believe that she was actually functioning as the official midwife for the first time. And it was harder to believe that Hannah's time had come.

Labor pains had started about two hours before dawn, and now the sun was barely up and the baby's head was showing. Elizabeth was surprised how quickly her sister-in-law dilated. "Push! Push harder, Hannah!"

Elizabeth reached for a clean sheet to catch the baby.

"I still say it's going to be a girl," Sister Wilding chattered. "You need to even up your family, Hannah. Two girls and two boys."

Pushing as hard as she could, Hannah paused to catch her breath. "Right now I don't care if it is a boy or a girl." She forced a smile as she pushed again.

Wiping her brow again, Elizabeth said, "Once more and I *think* we'll know." She chuckled to herself. Steward Heywood had told her that on warships women in labor had to find privacy on the gun deck between two of the guns. If the labor became particularly difficult, the captain would call for a full broadside to be fired during a contraction. The broadside was usually powerful enough to move the entire ship a foot or so sideways, giving the woman an extra push. *Fire the broadside.* She almost said it out loud to Hannah.

Robert paced back and forth on the deck. He peered down the hatch and yelled. "I don't hear a baby crying yet. How much longer?" His oaken constitution was wilting some. He was not a man of great patience.

Trying to keep his brother-in-law's mind occupied, Daniel asked: "I can't remember. How long was Hannah in labor with Joseph?" The five-year-old boy, and Robert's other two children, were being jointly tended by a host of Church members while Hannah was in labor.

Uneasiness crossed Robert's face. "Seems like all night and all day. Probably close to twenty hours. Liz and William came a lot quicker. Actually, if the baby is born in the next few minutes it will probably be the quickest one. But it still seems like a long time."

An answer came from below. "Any minute now."

Even though he was used to the fetid gloom of the lower decks, the stale, over-breathed air, the crowded, unwashed bodies, and the miasma of latrines, Robert worried about the birth that was about to happen. Even in the best of conditions back in England, there was a high mortality rate. He had confidence in Elizabeth but it was her first experience as midwife. What if something went wrong? What if the baby didn't breath properly? What if Hannah went into convulsions? What if a clot of blood formed, loosened, and worked its way into Hannah's brain? Every birth risked not only the health of the mother, but her very life as well.

"Relax," Daniel said. "Everything will be fine."

In many ways, Daniel wished the shoe were on the other foot. He would like to be the nervous father, pacing back and forth on the deck while Hannah tended to Elizabeth, assisting his own son or daughter into life on earth. It was still perplexing to him why he and Elizabeth had not been blessed with a child. But so far, nothing. Not even a miscarriage.

"I'm not nervous," Robert said ruefully. "I just don't like waiting."

When Hannah first told him seven months ago that she was pregnant, he hoped for a girl. But now that they were on their way to Nauvoo he hoped for a boy. There would be lots of work to do on an American farm. Americans did not have farm servants, at least in the north where they were going. There were no black slaves in Nauvoo. There would be just him and his own family. Daniel and he could help each other. Joseph could become a good helper in just a few years. But looking more long term, Robert could see a house full of boys. In a way, he wished Hannah could have waited until they were actually on American soil to give birth. But he reckoned the ship was close enough to New Orleans to say this next child was a native American. He glanced at the red, white, and blue American flag flapping in the breeze, stood erect and attentive, and suddenly felt a surge of new pride swell through him.

"Four children," Daniel said. "And none for me."

"Maybe your luck will change when we get to Nauvoo."

"I hope so, especially for Elizabeth's sake."

The cry of a newborn baby pierced their conversation.

"It's a boy!" a loud voice declared.

MONDAY March 29 – Fine day, ship at 9 knots an hour. Sister Harris gave birth to her baby this day.

TUESDAY March 30 – At break of day came in sight of Guadeloupe, bearing south, southwest. There was a general rejoicing at once more beholding land. Sailing along its northern side we could distinguish trees, windmills, sugar boilers, etc. Saw many flying fish and birds. Later, Antigua to the south-southwest of us just visible at a great distance.

Levi Roberts came looking for Robert and Hannah. He found them in their berth, which was lit by two candles, tending the new child. Hannah had just nursed the baby boy, and was now holding him as he slept.

"How's he doing?" Levi asked.

"Eats like a horse already," Robert said in a proud tone, pulling the blanket apart so that Levi could see the child's face. In the recesses of his mind Robert thought of the day the Reverend Spencer Hobhouse came hobbling to

his home in Apperley alleging that the two oldest Harris children, Joseph and
Lizzy, were doomed to hell because they had not been officially christened in
the Anglican Church. He laughed inwardly as he gazed upon his new child.
No infant baptism. The boy would be baptized at age eight, the age of
accountability, in the Lord's way. By full authority of the priesthood, by total
immersion.

"The captain wants to see both of you," Levi said, reaching out to touch
the baby with one finger. "Baby's are sure soft, aren't they?"

"Why?" Robert asked.

"He didn't say, but I'll bet it's about the baby. Watch the upper deck. It's
been raining, but it's nice and balmy right now."

Bearing the bundled-up baby in a basket, with Daniel and Elizabeth and
Thomas and Dianah pacing behind, Robert and Hannah entered Captain
Wood's quarters. Outside, a jocund chorus of passenger noise was cut off as
the door closed.

Hanging his thumbs in his deep blue jacket lapels, the captain appeared
to be in the best mood since the departure from Liverpool. After seating
Hannah in his private chair, Captain Wood welcomed them and said with a
charming grin, "This is the best behaved group of passengers I have ever had
on the *Echo*. I would like to have our ship remembered. If you will name your
new child 'Echo,' after the ship, I will give you a certificate for him. This certificate will enable him to travel free of charge on any water all his life."

Smiling at the captain and feeling a bit flustered, Hannah rocked her
newborn son with a gentle motion. "Echo?"

"I'd think of this ship every time I called his name," Robert admitted to
the captain. "That's a nice gesture, Captain Wood. But I think my wife has
another idea about the baby's name."

"Captain," Hannah said, regarding the captain in a quizzical manner, "I
have my mind set to call the child Thomas Eagles Harris after my father. And
not meaning any disrespect to you or your crew, I think that if we all survive
this voyage and land in America alive, neither I nor any of my children will
ever want to try it again."

With that, Hannah bundled up her baby and left.

CHAPTER NOTES

According to the Robert Harris family history, the incident regarding the birth of Thomas Eagles Harris is true. Captain Wood wanted Hannah to name the child after the ship, and offered a lifetime of free passage.

31

REBECCA'S PHYSICAL CONDITION took a sudden turn for the worse. Although Rebecca seemed to have healed inwardly from her night-time attack, Elizabeth was puzzled by the fact that Rebecca now lay in her berth complaining of swelling legs, swelling gums, a loss of strength, and a loss of appetite.

Elizabeth summoned Captain Wood for his opinion.

With Daniel and Martha looking on in curious speculation, the captain made a quick pronouncement. "Scurvy."

Elizabeth's voice cracked. "Scurvy? Are you sure?" She thought it was related to Rebecca's mental anguish over the attack.

"Spongy gums?" Captain Wood asked.

Rebecca nodded yes.

"Loose teeth? Stiff joints?"

Again, yes.

The captain addressed Elizabeth. "What's been her diet?"

Elizabeth shrugged, her face lined with guilt. "I haven't paid that much attention."

Martha answered. "Probably not as good as it should be. My daughter's always been fond of meats. She doesn't like things like potatoes and carrots."

The captain sighed. "We don't have many cases of scurvy anymore. Scurvy is caused by a diet heavily laden with salt provisions, the free use of grease and fat, want of cleanliness, and laziness in our eating habits. Ever heard of the term *limey*, as applied to British sailors?"

Daniel scratched his chin in thought. "Yes. I've heard the crew call your British sailor that."

"Years ago, when captains learned that a lack of fresh fruits and vegetables caused scurvy, British vessels began carrying a supply of limes. The Dutch had been doing it for years, and their sailors never contracted scurvy."

"So Rebecca needs some limes?" Elizabeth queried, making mental notes. She was grateful that Brigham Young and the Brethren had counseled them to buy extra food. Non-Mormon passengers were eating "ropey water," mixing hardtack with slimy water.

"Oranges, grapefruits, lemons, limes, whatever," the captain added. "Even fresh vegetables would help, like raw onions, raw potatoes. I don't know what your own supply is, but the ship's supply is gone. We're two weeks behind schedule, so we're down to horsemeat. We should have been in New Orleans by now. But a few weeks without those foods doesn't make much difference. Miss Browett must have been deficient in her diet even before she got on this ship."

Martha nodded in agreement, giving Rebecca a mournful stare.

"So what can we do?" Elizabeth asked.

"We are farther south in our course than we would have been had we not encountered the terrible storms at the beginning of our voyage. We can easily hail a vessel sailing from the Caribbean Islands to New York with fresh provisions."

"You would do that?" Daniel questioned, impressed with the captain's charitable offer.

"For you, Captain Browett, I would do anything."

Daniel flashed a friendly smile. "I can fill the baptism barrel with water."

Captain Wood laughed. "I'll instruct the crew to hail a ship."

Henry and Richard Hargraves turned their gaze on the small island of Guadeloupe in the Caribbean Sea. Adams, the mate, came walking by with Chips the ship's carpenter, and Blackie the ship's blacksmith.

"We've altered our course," Henry said, pointing to the island settled by the French following its discovery by Columbus. Columbus found the island inhabited by the Karib Indians, known for man-eating warriors who had rid the island of its original inhabitants, the Arawaks.

"Aye, 'tis a simple explanation," Adams said. "See there? Off in the distance? Another ship, coming from the island. We've been instructed to hail her down. Gonna purchase some of her fresh provisions. Captain Browett's sister has scurvy."

Henry shuddered. "What if it's another pirate ship?"

Adams laughed. "Nary a chance, mate. Not in these parts anymore."

Henry could make out a tiny spec in the Caribbean, the approaching ship.

"Sometimes the cap'n makes a stop at one of the islands," Adams said, looking a little riled. "Not this time. We're off schedule as it is. But I could sure use some monkey's blood."

Henry's dark eyes widened in disbelief at the term, "monkey's blood."

Adam's laughed again. "Tis what we call the red rum we get on the islands. Ah, the pretty native women. They smuggle it on board. Coconut milk's been replaced with rum. You just find the hole and suck it out."

"Can't we petition the captain to change his mind?" Hargraves asked.

"Believe me, mate, we've tried," Adams said. "We've tried. But all the crew would want some of their pay. Cap'n's not prepared to pay us 'til we reach New Orleans. Salt beef's all gone. We're down to horsemeat. Been in casks for two years, that horsemeat."

"Then you're working off your dead horse," Henry said with a chuckle.

Chips nodded. "Oh, for monkey's blood, bananas, and pineapples."

"I'd almost admit to being the guilty man who attacked Cap'n Browett's sister for a chance to be marooned on Guadeloupe," Blackie stated, gazing at the far off island. The term marooned dated back to the time of Sir Francis

Drake. Spain had captured Indians called Ci-maroon on the Darien coast of Panama, and took them to the West Indies as slave labor. The Indians were subsequently deserted by their masters and left to starve. Sir Francis found them and returned the Indians to their home, gleaning valuable intelligence from them in return.

Henry chaffed at Blackie's remark. For a brief moment he entertained the thought of reporting it to Daniel. Maybe it was Blackie.

Adams laughed coarsely. "Believe me, mate. Everything that's in Guadeloupe is in New Orleans. Including rum. Ya just don't have to hide it in a coconut."

Hargraves licked his lips.

And hour later, an ordinary looking hermaphrodite brig hove-to for the *Echo*. Adams ordered the crew to boom end the studdingsails and back the topsail.

"Brig, ahoy!" Captain Wood cried. "Pray, where are you from?"

"From Curacoa and Guadeloupe, bound for New York," a sailor answered.

"Have you any fresh provisions to spare?"

"Aye, aye," the sailor reported.

In an instant the longboat was lowered and the captain and four hands sprang in. The longboat danced across the clear blue water and pulled along side the brig. In a half-hour the men returned with a boatload of fruits and vegetables.

Soon everyone on board the *Echo* was feasting on oranges, grapefruits, tamarinds, lemons, and limes.

On the captain's instructions, Elizabeth pounded a raw potato into a mortar and gave the thick juice to Rebecca. The strong earthy taste and smell of the extract produced an immediate shuddering from her head to the tips of her toes. She complained of an acute pain throughout her body.

"It's taking hold," the captain declared. "Give her a spoonful every hour. By the time we arrive in New Orleans she'll be back to normal."

WEDNESDAY March 31 – Early in the morning another ship to the north of us. Fine morning. Sailors beginning to paint the outside of the ship.

THURSDAY April 1 – Fine breeze, ship at 9 knots an hour.

FRIDAY April 2 – About 8 o'clock as the first mate came to the men to give orders about painting the ship, one of the men struck at him three times, the mate having threatened the previous night to split his skull for having pulled the sheet off him. The captain came with handcuffs to confine the offender, but the man fetched a sword and said he was determined to support his authority and any of the men resisting him he would split him in two. Then the offender went down to his place refusing to come up. The captain asked for help. Myself and all six of our committee volunteered. We went in to get him but he gave himself up. The captain put him in handcuffs and ordered to the long boat where he will stay the remainder of the trip.

SATURDAY April 3 – Fine morning, squally later. Crew members having hard words at night.

SUNDAY April 4 – Sacrament meeting on deck in the warm breeze. Brother John Ellison preached about fasting: "Every Sabbath day is a day of fasting…this has no reference to abstaining from food…when the Lord says 'that thy fasting may be perfect' He means we should abstain from the things of the world, including the good things of the world…Sunday is a day to refrain from worldly activities regardless of how wholesome they may be. To justify participating in worldly activities on the Sabbath because they are good activities is to have an imperfect fast…it is the same as eating food in the middle of your fast on Fast Sunday…"

32

RAIN HAD BEEN FALLING all morning in Tirley. Water trickling off the steep thatched roof of the Davis home blurred Mary Ann's vision through the small windows of the upstairs bedchamber as she stared at them through misted eyes. Mary Ann Weston Davis was holding her husband in her arms. Sitting on the edge of their bed, she pulled another blanket over them. Life was ebbing away. She watched him slowly open and close his eyes as he ran a dry tongue over his fevered lips. Outside, there was a whistle of wind, a rumble of thunder, and a whoosh of raindrops against the window.

Mary Ann felt as though her heart was being torn from her body. Even with an understanding of the gospel of Jesus Christ, the physical loss of her companion was going to be hard. She had envisioned a long life together, of both her and John dying of old age in Nauvoo or somewhere in America. She wanted to watch her husband grow old, get gray hair, have an expanded waistline, and not only be a father to a dozen children but grandfather to perhaps a hundred. She wanted to laugh with him, cry with him, and experience trials and tribulations with him.

She knew John did not fear death, and she knew why. In the hearts of the righteous there is no fear of dying. In his weakened condition he had told her that he had wanted to live as long as the Lord would permit. But he had confided to her that he knew he was going to depart from earth life, and that he had a peaceful feeling about it. He felt that way despite the anointment and blessing given to him by Edward Phillips. John had told her several times that it should not be expected that people, even members of the Church, would be relieved from every illness or injury that comes upon them. After all, he had said, "Christ did not heal every sick or infirmed soul in Israel, even within the household of faith."

Mary Ann thought about life in the spirit world. Her husband would soon be there. Surely it was a place where there was no sin, pain, disease, decay, aging, corruption, or evil of any sort. No mobbers. It would be a wonderful place, but not the final destination in the eternal scheme of things. She knew that death was a temporary separation of the body and the spirit. John would be resurrected someday. She would follow him in death at a future time. They would live together as resurrected beings in the Celestial Kingdom. That was their goal.

Today was April sixth. Elder Woodruff had taught the English saints many times that the Church was organized on this day in 1830 because on that date in history the Savior had been born. Mary Ann wondered if there was any significance in the fact that John was going to die today. He could have passed on yesterday, or waited until tomorrow.

John had repeatedly told her to forgive his mother. No! Not in this world or the world to come! Surely as the sun comes up in the morning her mother-in-law was responsible for John's injuries and therefore would be responsible for his death. It was the same as murder. No one, not even the Savior, would expect her to forgive Mrs. Davis for murder, would they? She thought of his beaten bleeding body the day the mobbers stormed their home. The doctor had reason to believe John would have lived had he not fallen the day he chased his mother down the stairs and fell, re-injuring his internal organs and causing the bleeding to start again. Had Hannah Simmons not come by a short time later, Mary Ann doubted she could have gotten John back up the stairs and into his bed.

Mary Ann had not seen her mother-in-law since that dreadful day. Surely she knew her son was in critical condition and was about to die. Mary Ann thought about John's funeral. She wondered what she would say to Mrs. Davis. If not at the funeral, somewhere, sometime, she would give that evil woman a piece of her mind.

Still sitting at the edge of the bed with John in her arms and the rain still pouring off the roof, she could sense that John was breathing very shallow now. She peered into his eyes as they opened and closed again. He clutched at Mary Ann, saying something too soft, too weak, and too incoherent. He stopped speaking and Mary Ann's heart ached with a realization of what was to come. John drew a deep breath, and his body went limp as his spirit left him. She held him tightly and just sat in the room for a long time, tears trickling down her face. She felt so alone, her husband gone. She recalled Shakespeare.

Now cracks a noble heart. Good night, sweet prince; And flights of angels sing thee to thy rest!

CHAPTER NOTES.

The mobbing of John and Mary Ann's home in Tirley, and John's subsequent death, is based on a true incident. Mary Ann Weston's autobiography does not specifically state that John's mother was Anglican, but it states that they were married by a clergyman from the Church of England. The author has taken the liberty to portray the Davises as Anglican in this novel.

33

"LOOK AT ALL THE DOLPHINS, Charles," Joseph said as he pulled himself to a sitting position on the bulwark overlooking the stern. "See? Four, five, six. No, seven!" One leg was dangling on the outside of the bulwark, the other on the inside.

Except for occasional fish sightings, including sharks, the Caribbean Sea was an expanse of crinkling blue water. Earlier in the day a sailor high in the mast had spotted a whale in the distance. An hour later another whale came close to the ship, then disappeared. Now it was a school of dolphins, trailing the *Echo*.

"And eight," said Charles Bloxham. After two weeks of being in the warm sun every day, the skin was peeling under his locks of yellow hair, around his blue eyes, on his ruddy red cheeks, and especially on his freckled nose. A tall boy, he pulled himself to the tips of his toes.

"Where?" Joseph asked. He was equally sunburned as well. At five years old, he had been hard pressed during the entire trip to keep up with his eight-year-old first cousin. Both had celebrated birthdays a few days earlier.

His eyes darting to a shadowy figure underneath them, beyond the vision of the younger cousin, Charles pointed. "By the rudder, underneath the stern, see?"

A male adult passenger, a tubby man with a scarlet face standing at the stern with two other men, confirmed the sighting to Joseph.

Leaning, Joseph said, "I don't see."

A chilly, concerned look came over Charles. "Careful, don't lean too much."

Joseph ignored his cousin. "I wanna see the other one."

"Joseph!"

A pang of alarm swept over Charles as the *Echo* suddenly lurched, responding to a larger swell in the sea, causing Joseph to lose his grip and fall, plunging toward the water.

"Mister!" Charles yelled at the tubby man. "Get my Papa!"

With those words, the young boy leaped into the water. By the time Charles hit the water, Joseph was already thirty yards behind him, floundering.

The chubby man yelled at the top of his lungs: "Man overboard!"

The cry of distress instantly brought other passengers to the stern.

"Who is your Papa?" the man screamed at Charles.

Swimming as fast as he could, the man's voice was barely audible to Charles. He turned his body in the water to answer. "Thomas Bloxham!"

"Who's overboard?" an elderly lady with visible chin hairs inquired of the chubby man.

"Two young boys!" The man said, pointing. Screaming the name of Thomas Bloxham, he scanned the area for a life buoy.

When Thomas heard his name, he was sunning with his wife and other children near the skylight in front of the mizzenmast. He quickly responded to the chubby man's panicked voice, and squirmed through a pack of curious onlookers.

"Two boys overboard!" the chubby man repeated, still pointing. "Are you Thomas Bloxham?"

"Yes!"

"I think it's your boy!"

As Dianah screamed, Thomas jumped feet-first into the water and began to swim. At the top of the swells he could see Charles swimming away from him.

"Charles! Charles!" Thomas had heard so many sailors' stories about sharks he feared for the lives of both the boys, and his own.

Charles continued his swimming.

Daniel, Robert, and scores of other Mormon men arrived at Dianah's side at the stern. She spoke in short, clipped, excited sentences. "It's Charles. He's in the water. Thomas jumped in. He's trying to reach Charles. Charles is swimming toward Joseph."

Startled, Robert said, "Joseph?"

As Robert swallowed his astonishment, Henry jumped into the water.

"Yes, Joseph!" Dianah said with a fear-stricken look, her voice shrill.

Robert jumped into the water.

Daniel took a step toward the bulwark, but a heavy hand grabbed his shoulder. "That's enough men in the water," said Captain Wood, who had just arrived. "I've already given the order to lower a rescue boat, and sailors are aloft spilling the sails so that we don't get any farther away."

Glancing skyward, Daniel could see sailors scurrying up the riggings, some of them already doing their job. The ship slowed and minutes later it was dead in the water. The longboat was rowing toward the swimmers and the two boys whose lives were in peril.

In the Caribbean Sea, Robert kept pace with Henry but could not pass him. Atop a swell, he saw that Thomas had caught up with Charles, but he could not see Joseph. Robert put his face in the water and swam, surprised by the warm temperature of the water compared to the time he had been pitched overboard by Henry.

"Joseph! Joseph!"

Robert and Henry reached Thomas and Charles.

"Where's Joseph?" Robert screamed, out of breath, eyes wide open, and red from the seawater.

"That direction," Charles said, pointing east. "But I don't see him anymore."

From the top of another swell, the searchers scanned the sea. Nothing.

"Joseph!" Robert yelled.

Without a word, Charles suddenly dove under water. It wasn't until another swell came by that the searchers saw him again. He had Joseph. But the young boy appeared lifeless.

"Joseph!"

Robert, Thomas, and Henry swam toward the boys as the rescue boat approached. In seconds, Charles and Joseph were pulled aboard. Heywood and Adams were two of six men in the boat.

Robert stared in disbelief at his lifeless son, shocked and heartbroken. Through tear-clouded eyes he asked, "Will my son be all right?"

Joseph's limp body remained motionless. No breathing.

Heywood reacted quickly, laying the boy on his stomach and pushing on his back. "He's taken in a lot of water, but we have gotten to him in time."

Adams said, "Most of us sailors know this procedure. I would be surprised if the boy doesn't start throwing up water and breathing again."

Heywood's pushing motions were firm, equally spaced apart. From Joseph's lungs, water came gushing out of the boy's mouth. He began to cough.

"Joseph!" Robert yelled, wiping at his own tears. He exchanged quick glances with Thomas and Henry, and then returned his eyes to his son who began breathing again. As soon as Joseph fully regained consciousness and on cue from Heywood, Robert took his son in his arms.

Smoothing Joseph's hair and rubbing a hand across his sunburned cheek, tears still in his eyes, Robert reached out with a free arm and drew Charles to him. "Thank you, Charles. You're the one who found him. And you are a hero for jumping in after him."

"No, Uncle Robert. We shouldn't have been playing where we were. It's my fault. I set a bad example."

Robert sent a hand through the boy's wet, thick, blonde hair. "Nonsense, Charles. If anyone is to blame, it's me. I should have been with him."

"Me, too, Robert," said Thomas. "I should have been there."

"It was just an accident," Henry said, a rare concerned look crossing his face. "It's no one's fault. It was an accident, so don't blame yourselves."

Robert reached out a right hand. "Thanks for what you did, Henry. You jumped in before I did. I appreciate your concern."

For an instant, Robert recalled his wedding day, six years earlier, in the hamlet of Apperley. After several months of hate-filled confrontations with Henry, his brother-in-law unexpectedly had made a gesture of friendship. "Hope you have a nice honeymoon. You'd make a good dairyman. Maybe you ought to think about it. You could work at the dairy instead of at your father's butcher shop. You'd be welcome."

"What was that all about?" Robert asked Hannah, his new bride.

"Oh, that's the other Henry. There's two of him, you know. This one can be quite pleasant when he wants to be."

In the longboat, Henry accepted Robert's hand with a slight shrug. "No problem."

MONDAY April 5 – My nephew Joseph Harris fell overboard, looking at fish. Another nephew, Charles Bloxham, 8, jumped in after him. So did his father, Thomas, and both Robert and Henry. It was a terrible moment, but he was rescued. We credit Charles with saving Joseph.

TUESDAY April 6 – Joseph is doing fine. Today we celebrated the anniversary of the founding of the Church. It is the Savior's birthday. The festivities commenced with an assembly on the forecastle and the firing of six musket rounds. A pageant was performed with the presidency and twelve young men robed in white. Twelve young women then appeared in light-colored dresses carrying scrolls inscribed amid ribbons and white rosettes. Twelve older men followed them, each carrying a Bible and a Book of Mormon. The Saints received the sacrament of the Lord's Supper. We celebrated for three hours with songs, recitations, speeches and dancing. We are now close to Jamaica; we can see very fine coffee plantations. Ship in her course. The mate caught a fish called a barracuda that resembles a pike. About noon we saw a whale blowing water; could not tell its size. Toward evening squalls.

WEDNESDAY April 7 – Captain spoke with the Julius of Plymouth America from Rio de Janeiro bound for New Orleans. Cargo coffee. The captain and a mate caught two albatrosses and let them loose on deck and the children were excited. Toward five o'clock in the evening trees sighted northwest, an island called Grand Cayman and a turtle fishery; saw two other ships ahead. One of the boys on board, not of our company, was a very bad boy and they were obliged to tie him up to the ship's mast for a few hours. During the evening we found that a rat had given birth in a shoe.

THURSDAY April 8 – Fine morning. Some harsh words passing between two of the passengers. Winds favorable. Sunset in red, the clouds on the south brightly speckled. Very hot; lightning at night. At 2 in the morning we were much alarmed by a crash and on awaking we were told that lightning had struck and the masts and sails were blown over.

FRIDAY April 9 – All day we were getting in the sails, broken spars, etc. We were drifting away with the current. Great uneasiness among the passengers. We are anxious to arrive. We managed to get four sails set and we sailed 3 knots per hour. Saw several dolphins, the most beautiful fish I ever saw. Passing the Island of Cuba and Port Anthony at night. We saw many tortoises and more whales playing about.

34

ABOARD THE *ECHO*, THE CAT-O'-NINE TAILS was simply known as The Cat. It was a whip with nine separate twisted hemp cord tails, each eighteen inches long, knotted near the end, on a single wooden handle. The long leather thongs were studded with iron, which left deep wounds across the back. Its only use was to flog sailors. Its origin dated back to Egypt, where domestic cats were sacred and said to have nine lives. Egyptians believed that good passed from the whip to the victim if the scourging utilized a cat hide. Although its use had been banned by law, the captain kept one around anyway. He had no aversion to using it on vermin.

When Heywood found Daniel, Daniel was eating his lunch. To the west, he could see a collection of vessels sailing to and from New Orleans. A New Bedford whaling ship. A U.S. frigate armed with big guns. A clipper returning from her Cape Horn run to San Francisco. A merchant ship loaded with cotton, destination New York. And an overcrowded slaver brig, built for speed, dashing toward port.

"The cap'n wants to see you in the smoking compartment," Heywood said, a stern look on his face.

Daniel hesitated, chewing his food.

"As soon as possible, Captain Browett." There was a sense of urgency in the steward's voice.

Two things struck Daniel as he entered the smoking compartment. First was The Cat. It was out of the bag, fondled by Captain Wood. The second was a sailor, sitting on a chair, shackled in chains. He had not been flogged or hazed, yet he was bleeding from cuts on his head and mouth. He was a stocky rawboned little fellow, only about five foot six with a fair complexion and dark hair, and with an elongated face severely pitted with smallpox scars. Gold earrings hung from both ears. His shirt had been ripped off and Daniel could see that his body was covered with tattoos, including his name tattooed on his right arm, John Poole, and the date, Oct. 17, 1838. The sailor was giving off a corrupt unwashed smell in the close little room.

"This is the man who attacked your sister," Captain Wood declared, his features set in an icy mask. "Would you like to hear his confession?"

Daniel bristled. He lowered his face for a moment in thought, trying to understand the broad sweep of emotions that came over him. Relief that a man had been caught. That the guilty party was not Henry. And that the women on board were somewhat safer now.

"No," Daniel said, "I'll take your word for it." His eyes flitted again to the sailor named Poole, but the sailor groaned and looked away.

"Would you like to bring your sister in so that she could hear his apology?" the captain pressed.

Daniel thought for a few seconds. While there would be a certain value in doing just that, he guessed Rebecca would be quite uncomfortable standing in front of her attacker.

"Not necessary," Daniel replied. "We can always do that later, if we change our minds."

The captain caressed The Cat. "Would you like to participate in the flogging?"

"No thanks."

He had heard of floggings with The Cat. Once the victim was over the barrel, tied hand and foot, face down to expose his back, the bosun would let The Cat out of the bag and begin his task. As the victim's back began to bleed, the nine tails would tend to stick together. The bosun would use his fingers to comb The Cat between strokes, to keep the tails separated.

"Very well, Captain Browett. This man will be flogged and held in chains in the cargo hold until we get to New Orleans."

Daniel cringed. There was no light and no air in the cargo hold. John Poole was paying a steep price for his indiscretion. The sailor would be experiencing a true hell. He didn't wait to ask if Poole would be hanged in New Orleans or put in jail. He went out to talk to Rebecca and his mother, to tell them the attacker had been caught. He wondered how often this kind of thing happened on immigrant ships.

Too often, he was certain.

SATURDAY April 10 – My sister cried when she learned that the man who attacked her had been caught. I pray we shall have no more such incidents. Entered the Gulf of Mexico. Mate caught a dolphin.

SUNDAY April 11 – Since we expect arrival in New Orleans soon, this may be the last sacrament meeting aboard the *Echo*. I preached the sermon on the virtues of an unpaid ministry in the true Church of Christ. I took for my theme the scripture that states, "…let them labor with their own hands that there be no idolatry among them" (D&C 52:39). I advised the saints that it has ever been the practice among the true servants of Jesus Christ to provide for themselves. In the Lord's church there is no paid ministry.

MONDAY April 12 – Hoisted a foretopsail, we went delightfully. An anchor chain was brought out. Preparations are being made for anchoring. The remainder of our provisions, which are not many owing to the long voyage, are being divided. Brisk wind toward evening. The man who molested my sister is still in chains, treated very poorly. I wonder if he will still be alive when we reach port.

TUESDAY April 13 – Cool morning. At six this morning two steamers came out to take us in tow to New Orleans. They threw their large cables and made fast to our ship. Passed the bar about noon. Captain said oftentimes ships are stuck at the sand-bar due to negligence of drunken steamer captains. At two o'clock the government offi-cer came on board calling the names of the seamen. He took the seaman who molest-ed my sister in chains. A skiff bearing a health inspector later came alongside. The inspector is looking for any cases of smallpox, cholera, or typhus. If he finds any, the sick person or person will be taken to a hospital in New Orleans. So far he has found none. If so, we would stand in danger of having the whole ship quarantined for up to 30 days. He told the captain there is already an outbreak of cholera in the city. We went up the Mississippi in grand style. Passed Fort Jackson about ten o'clock at night. Along the way, little boats came alongside with local people selling fresh bread. It was so expensive we bought but little. It was a welcome taste after weeks of hard sea biscuits.

35

MARY ANN WESTON DAVIS threw herself into the arms of Edward Phillips, sobbing. She withdrew, clutching his hand, unable to talk, trying to comprehend what her mother-in-law had just told her. She stared into the dreary, overcast sky. Standing at her husband's grave in the Tirley churchyard in a thickening drizzle, her coat pulled close, her breath smoking in the damp, frigid air, Mary Ann was confused and frustrated. Mrs. Davis had just contested John's will. It was a will John and Mary Ann had worked out together. An attorney had written it. All it said was that Mary Ann was entitled to her husband's estate, which was very little. The most valuable items in the estate were the pieces of furniture he had hand crafted in the Browett Cooper and Furniture Shop. The furniture was all Mary Ann had to remember her husband by.

The funeral had gone reasonably well even though Mary Ann had relented to Mrs. Davis' wishes that it be held in the Tirley parish church, conducted by the parish priest. The tradeoff had been that Edward Phillips be permitted to be one of the speakers. Otherwise, Mary Ann was going to insist that the services be held in the Mormon Gadfield Elm chapel. Mary Ann's mother-in-law and the priest were shocked at the attendance. Mormons more than filled the church; several people had to stand outside. The reverend had never had so many people throng to the building, not on any Sunday he could recall. Neither Edward nor Mary Ann saw Richie or Alex at the funeral, but they did recognize three other men who had been part of the mob.

Then came the reading of the will in the parish burial ground outside the church. Mary Ann had resolved to tell Mrs. Davis that she had forgiven her. In the days following John's passing, she had come to that conclusion as the result of her personal prayers. She had felt it was something she had to do. From then on, it would be Mrs. Davis' problem. But John's mother, with her own attorney ensconced firmly at her side, announced that she was contesting the will. She wanted John's homemade furniture for herself. Mary Ann had not gotten the words out about forgiveness.

Feeling terribly alone, tears streaming down her face, she said in a strained voice, "Oh, Brother Phillips, what am I to do? What am I to do?"

A new rush to judgment broke over Mary Ann. Part of her wanted to confront Mrs. Davis and accuse her of murder and theft, and part of her still wanted to forgive the woman. The feelings gave rise to one of terrible insecurity, not knowing how to handle the situation. Mary Ann gave her mother-in-law a skeptical, suspicious, spiteful glance as she clung to Edward Phillips. Mrs. Davis returned the glance with one of her own, filled with insensitivity and hatred.

"Let's not make a scene here," Edward advised, slowly leading her away. "All Mrs. Davis has done is protest the will. It's not a done thing. We just need to talk to your lawyer again and my guess is he will get it resolved and you will have the furniture."

As far as Edward was concerned, Mary Ann had a legal right to not only make a will but to lay claim to virtually all the personal and real property of her deceased husband. English law permitted men over the age of fourteen and women over the age of twelve to make a will; married women could make a will with their husband's consent. Edward knew that an English will was a sort of religious document intended to ease the testator's soul of any earthly burdens, and to prepare him for the hereafter. John and Mary Ann had followed tradition. Wills were made close to death and followed a standard format, opening with the testator committing his soul to god and affirming that he is "of sound mind." Edward entertained the thought that perhaps Mrs. Davis and her lawyer were going to contend in court that John was not of sound mind when he made the will, that the injuries to his head made him irrational.

Edward also knew that a personal estate had to be divided into three parts: one third for the widow, one third for the children, and the remaining third to be disposed of according to the "testator's wishes." There were no children. John Davis, the testator, had willed his property to Mary Ann. It was pure and simple. But he also suspected what Mrs. Davis' motives were. If the testator made no provision for the disposition of the remaining part, it went automatically to the Church of England. Mrs. Davis knew she had no legal right to her son's estate but if she could get at least a portion of it declared the property of the church, her minister would merely turn around and give it to her. After all, Edward was thinking, the reverend was probably just as much guilty of hiring the ruffians as Mrs. Davis. And if a judge declared John not of "sound mind," the church, and thus Mrs. Davis, would get the entire estate.

Stepping inside the lonely Davis home, Edward, Hannah Simmons, and Mary Ann wiped their feet on the entry rug and put two logs on the fire, which had nearly gone out while they were at the funeral. Edward had seldom felt any lower, but he suppressed any emotion in his voice. He had a ministerial position in the Church of Jesus Christ of Latter-day Saints, and had a genuine concern for Mary Ann's well being.

"I feel strongly that you should still go to Nauvoo, Mary Ann," Edward said. "Even without John, there's a new life for you there. I think you should gather with the Saints. Those are my honest feelings."

Nodding her head in approval as the logs began blazing in the arched hearth, Mary Ann threw herself onto the sofa, despondent, and replied, "What about my parents? If they find out they will try to stop me. They're not mean like John's mother, but they don't understand the gospel. They don't understand me, either. They want me to go home to Gloucester and give up my membership in the Church."

Her father and mother had visited Mary Ann twice since John's death, but did not attend the funeral. They did not want to be in the company of any Mormons. Pausing for several seconds, contemplating the alternatives and wiping away more tears, she added, "If I went, when would I go?"

Edward rubbed his eyes with his hand, trying to disguise his own tears, and sat in an empty chair. "There are ships leaving regularly as you know. The next one is scheduled to leave on April the twenty-first with Elder Woodruff functioning as the company leader. But that might rush things a bit."

Mary Ann nodded.

Edward was thinking of the pending legal battle between Mary Ann and Mrs. Davis. Mary Ann's concern about her own parents wasn't nearly as big an issue. He paused for a moment until Mary Ann looked at him. "Follow your heart, Sister Davis. If your heart tells you to gather to Zion, then go. Once you became of age, and especially after you got married, you separated yourself from your parents. You have your own life to live."

There was an awkward moment of silence as Mary Ann thought about her father and mother. Thinking it wise to change the subject back to a happier thought, Hannah said, "What about the ship that Thomas Kington is going on? Maybe you could be ready by then."

"That's the *Harmony,*" Edward replied, "scheduled to leave in early May. I think that's what you ought to do. Can you be ready by then? Both Sister Simmons and I will help you in every way we can. My sister and her husband will be on that ship—I'll ask them to watch over you."

"Oh, you mean Hyrum and Susannah Green?" Mary Ann asked, breaking her stupor. "I like them very much."

Edward gave Mary Ann a warm smile, trying to preserve a happy sense that the young widow would be moving toward a new life and a new adventure. "You'll be in good hands, Mary Ann."

A pleased but still-concerned-look came over Mary Ann. Her eyes red, her face still gaunt, she gave Edward a warm glance. "Please help me get the furniture John made for me."

"I will. I promise."

36

NEW ORLEANS IS LOCATED on a sharp bend of the Mississippi River just more than a hundred miles from the Gulf of Mexico. Founded in 1718 and named after the Duc d'Orleans, it superseded Biloxi, Mississippi, as the French capital of the colonial empire of Louisiana. In the mid-eighteenth century it developed into both a social center of culture and a rough river town. It was nearly destroyed by fires in 1788 and 1794. When a nearby plantation owner succeeded in producing sugar from cane the year of the second fire, prosperity followed. Louisiana was transferred from Spain to France in 1800, and became part of the United States in 1803, after the Louisiana Purchase. By the time the first steamboat, the *New Orleans,* came downriver to the city, it had become the state capital upon Louisiana's admission to the Union. River traffic increased after 1820, and by the time the *Echo* was towed up the Mississippi toward New Orleans in the spring of 1840, the city was the nation's fourth largest, enjoying an era of peaceful prosperity.

When a steamer latched onto the *Echo* near the mouth of the Mississippi, the ship joined a collection of other ships, canoes, keelboats, flatboat barges, ferryboats, covered skiffs, and pirogues hollowed from the trunks of large trees. All were skinny-dipping past an accumulation of silt bars that had formed at the mouth of the river. Because of the large delta, the sea never entered the river to flood the area. That's why the *Echo's* English immigrant passengers could see homes built right up to the levee. The river had a swampy, dank smell, different than the fresh seawater smell of the Caribbean.

When the *Echo* came near the wharves, Henry was astonished that so massive was the demand for loading and unloading areas that the wharves and docks extended for five miles. Ships flying flags from Denmark, Spain, Brazil, England, and every part of the world crowded the docks, competing for room with steamboats, barges, and flatboats. The *Echo* had settled into one of the wharves at La Fourche Packet Landing that extended back toward the levee some two hundred feet. Soon an officer from the Custom House was aboard, talking with the captain, and then declaring that passengers were free to disembark.

Henry, Richard Hargraves, and Richard's son Dicky, were overwhelmed by the sight of hogsheads and barrels filled with refined sugar, rum, coffee, molasses, flour, pork, lard, grain, cottonseed oil, and other products—all waiting to be loaded onto the *Echo* and other ships.

"Where's your wife?" Hargraves asked Henry as they walked down the gangplank, eyes open wide, gawking.

"We can do without her," Henry said, sticking out his chest, wearing his Sunday suit. His clothing made him feel like an important businessman, not a dairyman. No longer did his hands smell like the cowbarn. Today he was ready to rid himself of Robert Harris and the whole lot of Mormons.

Hargraves shrugged in indifference as they stepped through sacks of Domingo coffee, sides of leather, boxes of cordials, cocoa, and bananas being unloaded by stevedores from the Danish schooner *Christeanstandt.*

Henry gazed with astonishment at the magnificent New Orleans levee, from one horn of the crescent to the other. The levee was covered with active people of all nations and colors. Boxes, bales, bags, hogsheads, pipes, barrels, tropical fruits, kegs of goods, wares, and merchandise from all ends of the earth. Thousands of bales of cotton, tierces of sugar and molasses. Flour, pork, lard, cottonseed oil, grain, lead, furs. And mountains of imported coffee.

"This is the place for a businessman," the elder Hargraves exclaimed.

"Where to first?" Henry asked. "Shall we sample some Creole food, or go to a pub and start asking questions?"

Intoxicated from the scent of the wharves and the city, Hargraves answered, "Better start calling it a bar or saloon, you're in America now. I'm drooling for some New Orleans whiskey."

Watching Henry disappear into the jungle of longshoremen, roustabouts, teamsters, and cotton yardmen, surrounded by the stacks of cargo being loaded and unloaded, Daniel Browett turned to the others in the Mormon company who were disembarking. "Where do you suppose Henry is off to?"

"Katherine told me that Henry wants to explore New Orleans on his own," Hannah said. "Someone told him the United States mint is here. Maybe he's off to see it."

"Where's Katherine?" Daniel asked, sensing a deep concern.

"Right behind me. She's going to see the market with me."

Daniel gave the women a disconcerted look.

"It's okay, Brother Browett," Hannah said, holding her newborn baby in her arms, wrapped in a small off-white blanket. "She can help us tend all the children."

"Who's that with Henry?" Robert asked Katherine. Since Henry's help with the rescue, Robert had a slightly higher regard for his brother-in-law.

"A new friend, Richard Hargraves, and his son. They're from Sheffield."

Descending the plank, Daniel turned to the collection of men, women, and children that were stepping with glee onto dry land for the first time in two full months. He issued an emotional warning: "Remember, don't get lost. The captain says that because of the way the river winds around the city it is at first confusing to visitors—it almost seems there is no north-south-east-west. Some streets begin at one end of the city, and end up perpendicular to where they started. That's west, the way to the city. And don't lose your money."

Hopefully, he thought, everyone had their money stashed away in some secure spot on the vessel or carefully sewn into undershirts or inner pockets. It would be a disaster for anyone to lose what little they had before they arrived in Nauvoo.

When most of the group had reached the banquettes at the edge of the wharves, and stepped onto the uneven cobblestones that made up Decatur Street by the French Market, Daniel bought a copy of the *New Orleans Daily Crescent.* The captain had told him just before he stepped off the ship that there were eight newspapers in the city, and that he ought to check out the shipping company advertisements. He had advised Daniel to use the power of negotiation because of the number of Mormon passengers he had in his company.

Daniel quickly shuffled through the pages.

"Here's one," he said, displaying an ad for the *Lady of New Orleans.* "Says it will leave next Tuesday, the twentieth of April, bound for St. Louis, Cairo, Hickman, Memphis, Helena, Napoleon, and all intermediate landings."

"But it doesn't say *Nauvoo,"* a puzzled Elizabeth Browett said, exchanging a concerned glance with Hannah.

The comment caused Daniel to laugh. "You forget. Remember the captain said we would probably have to change steamboats at St. Louis and arrange passage for the upper Mississippi River." Pointing, Daniel scanned competing ads for steamboats named the *Vicksburg* and the *Missouri Clipper.*

"Let's check these out, brethren," Daniel told his assistants. "We don't have much time." He scanned a sky where the April sun was approaching the western horizon. "You ladies have fun, but be careful and stay together."

Daniel folded the paper under his arm and led his assistants though a collection of black, white, and mulatto stevedores toward Orleans Street, where he started reading business signs. Wagon after wagon passed by, creaking under the weight of cabbages, carrots, yams, and red and shiny tomatoes. Their drivers shouted and beat their horses.

Elizabeth turned her attention to the French Market. How different from the markets in London or Liverpool, she thought. Until they had started up the river channel, no one in the Mormon company had ever seen a

Negro other than the ship's cook. Here, among the hundred stalls called the Place d'Armes, old Negro women with bright striped tignons on their heads and with baskets on their arms were buying a little of this and a little of that. A Negro man passed by, whistling a tune of clear notes, bearing on his head a flat basket filled with pink roses. Another bore a basket full of purple figs. Three Negro women strode by selling *calas,* coarse rice fritters fried in hot fat. *"Bels calas, bels calas, tout chauds,"* they chanted. A Choctaw Indian squaw, wrapped in a blanket, was selling red and green baskets, her two mostly naked children crouched near a pillar of crumbling masonry. Other squaws sold herbs, roots, and file—pounded dried sassafras leaves for making gumbo.

Tucked in between fruit and vegetable stalls were coffeehouses, filled with men discussing the affairs of the day. Elizabeth could hear a mixture of languages—the rapid trilling of French, the soft slur of Italian, the romantic evenness of Spanish, and the easy droning of Negro voices. It all seemed strange but delightful. She approached two nuns, wearing dull blue dresses and stiff white headdresses, buying a bunch of bananas.

"Let's get some *bananas* for the children," Elizabeth suggested to Hannah, pulling out her English coins that the merchant gladly accepted. "It's been so long since we've had fresh bananas."

Another Negro man came by, bearing on his back some twenty or more red fish, each one strung through its mouth with a bit of green palmetto leaf. Elizabeth and Hannah and the others followed him to a fish stall where the man threw his shuddering burden on the flagstone floor.

"Lookee at the fish, Mama!" Lizzy yelled out, giggling, pointing, and looking up at her mother "They're going all plop plop!"

Joseph ran toward baskets filled with blue and green crabs. A few had escaped the baskets and were being chased by a boy in a dirty white apron with a pair of tongs in his hands. "Can I have one?" Joseph asked as he chased one still on the loose.

"Get away from that!" Hannah shrieked. "He'll pinch your fingers!"

Responding to Joseph's mother, Charles pulled Joseph away, then watched in horror as his six-year-old brother, Tommy, ran after another crab.

Thomas swooped Tommy up in his arms.

"Not so fast, son," Thomas said. "Look over here. Thomas pointed to thousands of fish hanging on hooks, others piled in baskets, red and blue in their iridescent coloring.

Next they came to the meat stalls. "Robert ought to be here," Dianah said, looking at the slabs of bloody beef and pork, and disemboweled rabbits hanging upside down.

"What's that noise?" Charles asked, casting his eyes upward.

"Parrots," his mother, Dianah, answered, gazing at the rows of cages hanging from the upper windows.

Charles stood motionless, his sunburned face lifted up. "Let's take one to Nauvoo!"

"We'll see," Dianah said, knowing that every shilling needed to be saved to start their new life there. She strolled toward the flower market where hundreds of potted plants and their smells were a welcome relief from the fishy and meaty smells left behind. Negro men with flowers tucked behind their ears or in their hats tried to sell them roses, ferns and little trees filled with blood-red peppers. An old beggar woman with wild white hair reclined on the stone floor, leaning back against a pillar, her crutch beside her. Someone had given her a bunch of grapes that she was eating one at a time, spitting out the seeds in the direction of a white rooster, its feet tied together with a bit of red rag.

"A day or two ago I would have paid good money for that rooster," said Thomas Bloxham. "But I think today we ought to try some food along the market here somewhere."

"They were selling oyster patties back there," Dianah said.

"No thanks. I'm not that hungry."

Daniel discovered that there were at least two steamboats in New Orleans scheduled to depart for St. Louis by Tuesday, so he divided his committee into two groups. He led the first group into the *Kennet Packet Service* office where they found an overweight balding man transferring figures from one ledger to another with a quill pen.

"I need steamboat passage to Nauvoo," Daniel said, feeling a rush of excitement.

"Is that on the Mississippi?" the man muttered without looking up.

"It's the Mormon settlement in Illinois."

"There are no steamboats that go there non-stop from New Orleans, Englishman," the agent said in a frosty tone. "You'll have to book one to St. Louis, and catch another boat from there." For a brief moment he looked up, disclosing puffy, glaring eyes.

"How much is the fare from New Orleans to St. Louis?"

"Thirty dollars. Distance of twelve hundred miles."

Daniel blinked. He quickly calculated that thirty dollars meant six pounds. He pulled a face. "Sir, that must be for cabin passage. How much is deck passage?"

Looking even more disinterested, the agent took a drink of warm grog out of a dark brown bottle. He licked his lips, liking the taste of the watered-down rum. "Five dollars. Distance is still the same."

"Do you have a group discount?" David Wilding alertly asked.

"How many passengers?"

"One hundred and eight," Daniel said, remembering the loss of Nancy Eagles.

The agent sat upright, eyes wide open. He cleared his throat. "I can book you right now for four dollars each," he replied, pulling out a contract for the Missouri Clipper.

"Some other representatives of our group are checking out another boat. We need to talk to them first."

The agent's chin stiffened. "You won't want to book on the other steamboat going to St. Louis on Tuesday."

"Why not?"

"Too dangerous. Ours is the best boat on the river, built only two years ago. We have the number one safety record on the river."

Daniel gave the agent a hard look. "We'll be right back."

"Suit yourself, but take this with you," the agent said, handing Daniel a newspaper clipping. "There are a lot of steamboat accidents. This will tell you about them. Don't wait too long. We might be booked full by the time you get back."

The Mormon men dodged a steady stream of horse-drawn omnibuses as they crossed the street in front of the Kennet office. In a few short minutes they saw the other group—Robert, James, John Lavender, and William Jenkins walking toward them.

Daniel waved, yelling. "Over here, Brother Harris!"

With a burst of confidence, Robert reported his findings. "A steamboat called the *Lady of New Orleans* leaves Tuesday for St Louis. The agent told us to be sure we book on her because the other steamboats in port are too dangerous." He pulled a newspaper clipping from his vest. "The *Lady* has the best safety record on the river."

Daniel drew his face into a smirk. "Let's see that." He scanned Robert's clipping, comparing it to his. It was exactly the same clipping. He laughed. "Fierce competition around here, I'd say. What's their price?"

"Three dollars for deck passage, children under fourteen half price, children under four go free," John Lavender said. "But they need deckhand help. They'll give a dollar off for up to twenty men to be wooders."

"Wooders?"

"All we have to do is help load wood onto the boat twice a day," Robert said.

Daniel was intrigued. "Let's go see. Twenty dollars is a lot of money."

"And luggage?" Robert asked.

"Each adult is allowed a hundred pounds," John replied. Twenty-five cents per hundred weight over that."

"Sounds good," Daniel said, ruffling the paper in his hands.

"What do your clippings say?" John asked.

"Same as yours." He glanced through the first three accounts of steamboat disasters. Pulling a face, he wadded up the clippings and threw them away. "Our people are frightened enough without reading this rubbish."

A HISTORY OF STEAMBOAT DISASTERS

The Washington. This deplorable accident happened on the Ohio River on the 9th day of June 1816. The cause was a disarrangement of the safety valve, which had become immovable in consequence of the accidental slipping of the weight to the lower extremity of the lever. The Washington had been anchored off Point Harmar on the Ohio River. The end of the cylinder was suddenly blown off and a column of scalding water was thrown among the crowd, inflicting frightful injuries on nearly all the boat's crew, killing many on the spot. The captain, mate and several others were blown overboard. The deck was strewn with mangled and writhing human beings, uttering scream and groans. Several of the wounded, under the influence of their maddening torments, had torn off their clothes, to which the entire skin of their limbs or bodies adhered; the eyes of others had been put out and their faces were changed to an undistinguishable mass of flesh by the scalding water. Total of eight dead.

The Constitution. The boiler exploded while the steamer was ascending the Mississippi River on the 4th day of May 1817, killing or wounding thirty persons, eleven of whom perished instantly. Others perished when the excited passengers threw themselves into the current. One unfortunate wretch was boiled alive, the skin having separated from his body; the poor man retained consciousness for several hours before he died. Another passenger was found lying aft of the wheel with an arm and leg blown off. Captain Bezeau and his lady, with some others, were fortunate enough to escape unhurt.

The Tennessee. On a dark night, the 8th of February 1823, in the midst of a tremendous snowstorm, the steamer Tennessee was ploughing her way up the turbulent Mississippi near Natchez under a full press of steam when she struck a snag and immediately commenced filling with water. Some supposed the boat had run into the bank but the fatal truth was soon known. A hole as large as a common door was torn in the hull and she was going down. The yawl and long boat were lowered and nearly two hundred passengers crowded into them and they made for shore, but the boats could not return in time to save any others. A few jumped into the river and swam ashore, others pulled off the cabin doors and floated on them. One passenger swam out with a small bag in his mouth containing $3,000 in gold. No less than sixty lives lost in all.

37

AS HENRY EAGLES WALKED ALONG Decatur and Chartres Streets with Mr. Hargraves and his son—a teenage boy with penetrating green eyes, dark hair, and a gaunt face—he felt so anxious that he soon began to get a headache. Often that would happen when he felt stress and it was unusual stress this time. He had a big decision to make. Whether or not to settle in New Orleans, or stay with Katherine and the Mormons and go to Nauvoo. The endless string of bars, flophouses, restaurants, theatres, operas, gambling, and red light houses only confused Henry and made his headache worse. The St. Charles and the St. Louis, both opulent hotels, each took up a whole city block, and seemed to Henry to be an entire small city by themselves. Hundreds of white-gowned ladies and rich gentlemen strode in and out of the hotels. He was amazed that it cost half a pound or two dollars and fifty cents for one night's lodging. He came to the financial district and read signs for the big banks along Royal and Iberville Streets: Union Bank, the Bank of Orleans, the Bank of Louisiana, the Canal Bank, the Citizen's Bank, and the Louisiana Planter's Bank.

"Wretched place to build a city," Henry said to an Irish worker after he followed the Hargraveses along some of the drainage canals and levees.

"Aye, 'tis so," the man replied, his voice raspy. "We get so much rain here that our burial vaults pop right out of the ground. But we have the grandest celebration called Mardi Gras. You missed it. This year we had hundreds of people masked as Bedouins. Big parade. And eleven balls held on a single night. Buy you a drink?"

Over drinks of brandy and whiskey at a nearby saloon, Thomas McLeod proved nothing more than an alcoholic Irish immigrant who was employed as a canal digger, and complained about the Creole majority in the city who treated the Irish as second-class citizens. Henry did get out of him the fact that a few of the Irish had succeeded in business and had become wealthy.

Discovering that it was too late to do much about business on an early Friday evening, Henry taunted McLeod into telling him where the best entertainment might be.

The drinks caused McLeod's voice to slur. "Friday nights is when the boatsmen fight. Cock fights is good down behin' the Union Hotel. Or how's about a fight between a bulldog and an alligator? Only a dollar admission, jus' down the street. Tomorrow there might be another fight between a black bull and a grizzly bear. And there's a feller from New York who has a big dog. Twenty-three pounds of 'im. Who the man sez can kill sixty full-size rats in only five minutes. Thas also a dollar for a reserved seat, or jus' fifty cents general admission."

Even for Henry, the Irishman's taste for entertainment was a little too vulgar, especially when he talked about the ladies in the houses of ill repute. But the fights between the boatsmen intrigued him. After he paid for the drinks he talked Hargraves and his son into following him past a succession of barrelhouses and bordellos. Feeling a little braver with the liquor in him, Henry said, "I'm a pretty good fighter myself."

"You fancy yourself going up against the boatsmen?" Hargraves asked in surprise. "You're a fair sized feller all right."

Henry was about to say that he'd never been beat but knew Hargraves was wiser. The story of Henry being whipped by Robert on board the *Echo* had passed through all the passengers, Mormon and non-Mormon. When they arrived at the alley named by the Irishman, the first fight was about to start. Parting their way through the onlookers, Henry and the two Hargraveses could see two half-drunk, naked-to-the-waist, flatboat bullies circling each other in a ring formed by their fellows. They were leaping in the air, cracking their heels together, and shouting war cries.

"I'm a pizen wolf from Bitter Creek and this is my night to howl!" screamed a mulatto, flexing his arm muscles.

"I kin wrassle a buffalo and chew the ear off a grizzly!" the second said, speaking in a French accent.

"I'm a roaring rip-snorter and chock full of fight!" the mulatto countered.

"Ah'z raised with alligators and weaned on panther's milk!"

"I'm the child of a snapping turtle!"

Dropping his jaw in disbelief, Henry whispered a question to one of the boatmen, a Spaniard with ruffled dark hair, a full beard, and a wild look in his eye. "Why are they jabbering and not fighting?"

"You English? You talk like English," the Spaniard said in his own accent, but displaying a remarkable command of the English language. "A fracas between two flatboat bullies is a fearsome thing to see, English. They're red turkey feather men and they're just working up their torments. The fight'll start any second."

"What's a red turkey feather man?"

The Spaniard smiled a crooked smile revealing yellowed teeth. "The man on the crew who wears a red turkey feather in his cap is the toughest man on the crew, and wears the feather until someone whups 'im. These two are from different boats. We'll see who's the toughest."

Suddenly the mulatto charged the Frenchman and the fighting began. It was combination fistfight-wrestling match with no rules. Henry saw a fair amount of eye gouging and groin kicking. In about eight minutes it was all over and the winner, the malatto, furiously claimed he was going to yank out the tongue of the Frenchman, and would have done it except the Frenchman's fellow boatmen rushed to save the man. All around Henry, boatmen who watched the fight exchanged money. Some of them cursed, and some yelled in delight.

The Spaniard scanned Henry, noting the Sunday suit. "You're no boatman, English. Just here for a good time?"

"You might say that," Henry answered with watchful regard. "I just arrived a few hours ago."

"Clean from England, eh? Did your boat have a red feather man?"

Both Hargraves and his son chortled in laughter. The elderly Hargraves said, "Yes, but the red turkey feather man is not here."

The remark clearly irritated Henry.

Hargraves fixed his gray eyes on Henry. "Mr. Eagles, you ought to get Mr. Harris and bring him here. You could have a humdinger of a fight."

The Spaniard arrived at the obvious conclusion. "So, Mr. Eagles. You have an enemy. Am I right?"

Henry gave the Spaniard an incredulous, icy stare.

"You hate this man, I can tell," said the Spaniard. "I am right, *si?*"

Henry's eyes pooled with waves of abhorrence.

The Spaniard's tone hardened. "If you hate this man but don't want to fight him, get some *gris-gris*." The words that fell out of the Spaniard's mouth were neither French nor Spanish.

"What's *gris-gris?*" Hargraves asked, his face twisting in curiosity.

"Voodoo magic," the Spaniard said in a low voice, making a waving gesture with one hand, and narrowing his dark eyes. "Leave a bag of *gris-gris* on the doorstep of your enemy, and you can work incalculable harm on that person."

The older Hargraves laughed heartily, the liquor taking effect. "That's what you need, Henry Eagles!" Staggering and slapping Henry on the back, he added, "Ask the man where you get this *gris-gris.*"

The Spaniard didn't wait for Henry to ask. "From Doctor John. He's better than Maria Laveau. Cheaper, too. Go up that way." He pointed farther west, up a darkened alley.

Few men, even locals, knew the true history of Doctor John. Enslaved by the Spanish, taken to Cuba. Freed by his master for his loyal service. Became a sailor, a world traveler. Eventually came to New Orleans to find work at the port. Drawing from his life in Africa, he developed "magical" powers of influence over people who would pay for his skills. Became a property owner. Owned a house filled with Voodoo accouterments—skulls, reptiles, snakes. Even embalmed scorpions. Several wives and mistresses. Father of nearly fifty children. Owned slaves himself.

Forty minutes later, long after the sun had disappeared over the city, Henry staggered up the alley. As he approached a square of bricks at the upper end of a shed, Henry almost wished he had told the Spaniard that he wasn't interested in any *gris-gris*. But in a way the idea of meeting a Voodoo witch doctor that was supposed to also be a mind reader and a dabbler in astrology intrigued him. The Spaniard said Doctor John had a remedy guaranteed to provide "blanket protection" against all harm: shells and pebbles, soaked for three days in an evil-smelling oil rendered from snakes and lizards, wrapped in a hank of human hair. But the most celebrated magical effect that one could buy from Doctor John—who was described to be a huge coal-black Negro with a tattooed face—was the *gris-gris*. A little leather bag filled with powdered brick, yellow ochre, cayenne pepper, and mixed lightly with nail pairings, hair, and bits of reptile skin. The only way one's enemy could counter the charm was to procure a counter charm from another Voodoo sorcerer.

Henry fancied that Robert Harris wouldn't know enough to do that, so his fate would be sealed.

When Henry walked into the square he experienced a strange feeling that made the hairs on the arms and the back of his neck stand straight out. In the center of the dark square a fire burned, as did four sconces with lighted dips, placed in the four corners. The only other light came from two pyres.

The voice was deep and guttural. "Come up to da table in da center."

Henry's better judgment screamed at him to return to the ship immediately. But his better judgment was vetoed by curiosity and a brain obscured by a night of drinking. He took a step toward the table, but could not make out the form of a man. He paused, turning to see if Mr. Hargraves and his son would follow. Henry imagined that the younger Hargraves was scared out of his wits. As for himself, Henry felt like he had to urinate.

When Henry got to the table, an oblong wooden thing about eight feet by four feet, he saw the form of a black cat standing motionless there. It had one white paw. He reached out to touch it. It didn't move. It was a stuffed cat. Shocked, Henry turned his attention to a cypress sapling, about four feet in height, sitting on the table, planted in a firkin. Towering above the sapling he could make out the form of a huge black doll, its dress variegated by some kinds of cabalistic signs and emblems. Around its neck hung a snake-vertebrae necklace, and from the necklace hung an alligator's fang encased in silver.

The form of a man appeared, barely visible. It was Doctor John, sitting astride a cylinder made of thick cypress staves hooped with brass and headed by a sheepskin. A Negress squatted beside him, holding two large buzzard leg-bones, ready to beat an accompaniment on the sides of the cylinder upon Doctor John's command.

The deep, guttural voice asked, "Wha' you all need?"

Henry felt every muscle in his body tighten. For several seconds he was unable to speak. *"Gris-gris,"* he finally managed to say. "Just a bag of *gris-gris.*"

From the corner of his terrified eye Henry could see a third man, a young Negro, holding a long calabash, made from a foot-long gourd filled with pebbles. He shook it a couple of times. It emitted an eerie rattle.

Suddenly Doctor John jumped to his feet, reached into a hidden receptacle behind the large black doll, and drew out an immense snake that he brandished aloft wildly. Doctor John talked to the snake in an unrecognizable tongue, and the snake, in some odd way, seemed to acknowledge the dominion the Voodoo man asserted over it. Thrusting the snake into Henry's face, Doctor John repeated the words over and over again, "Voodoo Magnian."

Henry recoiled in fear, and sweat dripped from his brow.

Doctor John forced an evil laugh, and talked to the snake. "Wha' we gonna do wi' dis Englishman? Shall we all sell 'im some *gris-gris?*"

Henry wondered if Richard Hargraves and his son were shaking as badly as he was.

Thrusting the snake back into the receptacle, Doctor John returned with a small leather bag that he claimed contained the *gris-gris*. "Wih deh be anyt'ing else?" he asked as though Henry were a regular merchant. "For deh price, I predict da future, read yo' mind, cast da spells, an' remove da curses."

No answer.

"You all seek tu drive someone crazy? Ah's got an egg from da black hen. Write da name on da egg, toss da egg over da roof of yo' victim. After dat, he plum crazy, man."

Henry shook his head, no. He wanted some of the seashells and pebbles soaked in snake oil, but he couldn't get out the words. Fumbling, he paid Doctor John the required amount. As he turned to go, Doctor John again sat astride his drum.

Henry, Richard and Dickey walked out of the square to a monotonous *"ra-ta-ta-ra-ta-ta-ta,"* thankful to be alive.

FRIDAY April 16 – Arrival at New Orleans. Cast anchor at one o'clock in the afternoon. It was a long process and we were all impatient. It was interesting to watch, however. As we pivoted around a corner of the dock, a dozen or so crewmen at the capstan took up the first hawser (big rope), and they started pulling ship to the dock. Two skiffs—one at the bow and one at the stern—carried additional hawsers for completing the maneuver. As soon as the ship was fastened many more and myself went on shore. All of us felt a little like being released from a prison, and we longed to tread firm land once more. The market was open and the fruit and vegetables of all description were laid out in excellent order. There were people of all colors speaking every language under heaven, almost. There were many slaves working on the streets chained together, both men and women. We saw many slaves held in pens, awaiting sale. We were astonished at the great number of cigars that were strewn about the sidewalks, some only half-used. We scouted for a steamboat and found two possibilities. We are now discussing which one to take. A number of men came on board. At night as there were many strangers on board, we agreed amongst ourselves two men to watch at each hatchway for two hours in their turn.

Anguishing over every word, Hannah sat at her berth with pen and paper writing a letter to her mother in far away Apperley, Gloucestershire, England. She wrote with great care, slowly, recalling words that she had formed in her mind for days, knowing that she must write to her mother once the *Echo* reached New Orleans. In a way, she resented the fact that she had to write, feeling inadequate to express her feelings over her sister's death. She had pleaded with Robert, Elizabeth, Daniel—even Katherine and Henry—to help her, but they politely told Hannah that it was her sole responsibility. Writing the letter made Hannah think of Nancy again. How she fell ill almost at the first rocking of the ship. How she could not keep any food down. How she slowly lost weight, dehydrated, and finally passed away. Although Hannah had turned away when Nancy's body was commended to the deep, the thought of it haunted her somewhat. If only she could have lasted until they reached Nauvoo. At least there would have been a gravesite to visit with an appropriate marker. Perhaps one could be arranged anyway.

My Dearest Mother,

I take pen in hand whilst in the port of New Orleans and it is my sad duty to inform you that my dearest sister and your loving daughter Nancy has passed from this life, and is living with her eternal Father in Heaven. Oh! How my heart breaks to think of her passing, dear Mother! She passed away early in the morning, March ninth. You surely did not know that she was in a motherly way as we boarded our ship in Liverpool—she was experiencing sickness every morning from nearly the time we left our homes in the hamlet of Apperley. Even without the constant heaving motion of the dreadful ship she would have continued to vomit daily every morning. She was beset with an awful seasickness and no food or drink would stay in her system.

My husband and Brother Browett and many others of the priesthood brethren gave her many blessings, anointing her head with oil, administrating unto her that she might recover, but it was not the will of the Lord and she has gone to her rest. She passed from this life on the eighth of March in the evening;. Her poor body was wasted away and it was a blessing when her spirit departed. Brother Browett conducted a proper funeral for a Latter-day Saint, and talked about the glorious resurrection in the Celestial Kingdom of God on high. I am sick to have to inform you of this bad news. Her remains were buried in the depths of the Caribbean Sea. The sea was very beautiful at that place.

My baby was born March 29 just before we arrived in New Orleans, and I have named the boy Thomas Eagles Harris after my father. Elizabeth, my sister-in-law, has turned out to be an excellent midwife. She assisted to deliver the baby. He is a healthy baby and the children are doing well; Joseph, Lizzy, and Willie liked being on the ship after a few days.

We have safely arrived in the Port of New Orleans where I will post this letter. We will remain on ship for a couple of days while arrangements are made to secure a packet steamboat and transfer our baggage. We now face a two-week trip on another vessel that will take us up the wide Mississippi River to our final destination where the saints of the Church are settled: Nauvoo, Illinois. I hesitate to give you more bad news. My brother Henry has acted in a most distasteful way with my husband and tried to do his body harm and knocked him to the sea on a dark night just a few days voyage out of Liverpool in a storm. Brother Browett found Robert clinging to a rope ladder and he was pulled to safety. Robert, bless him, says he has forgiven my brother. I hope Henry will be better behaved from this time on. The storms blew our ship off course to the south; we even saw a pirate ship as we skirted Portugal and got near the northern tip of the African continent. The pirates were from Tripoli but seeing we were nothing more than poor emigrants they did not bother us.

We so look forward to our final destination. Our dreams are still to settle with the saints in Nauvoo and we are told it is a beautiful city in the American wilderness and I am most anxious to arrive at that place. It is as though Nauvoo is our spiritual beacon because that is where we will find the Prophet Joseph Smith and the leadership of the Church. Mother, many ships will follow us. The British floodgate to America has been opened. How I hope that you will change your mind and emigrate. I do miss you so! And all my family I miss with all my heart. Please bring Elias and Jane and come to Nauvoo! It is my fondest wish that you can be instrumental in preaching the gospel to my brothers George and William and their families, then all of you come together!

I am so very curious. Did you marry Brother

Samuel Roberts? Robert would like to know, and Brother Levi Roberts would like to know. It would be so wonderful if you and he would come to America!

Please give my affection to my brothers and sisters. It is very expensive to post a letter from America to England so I don't know how often I will be able to write a letter. Our money will be used to buy a farm in Nauvoo and build us a home. My paper reminds me to conclude, please remember me to my friends and the saints that are still there.

Your affectionate and loving daughter,
Hannah Maria Eagles Harris

38

HENRY AND THE TWO HARGRAVES plopped themselves onto three barstools. The New Orleans bar on Canal Street on this late afternoon was smoky, dark, and packed with a broad assortment of wild characters. Henry was so depressed he couldn't speak.

Bit by bit Henry had learned that it was going to take far more money than he actually had to get into any kind of business in New Orleans. The "haves" who controlled shipping, steamboating, restaurants, operas, gambling, and prostitution were not going to let the "have-nots" in by the front door or the back door. He had tried to talk himself into the Banks' Arcade on Magazine Street near Gravier, a three-story building with a barroom, because a few sources had told him that's where the power mongers congregated. Now Henry feared that his misrepresentation might cause some criminal types to rob him. Even when he had lied about how much money he had, the businessmen they had talked to seem disinterested.

The depression was evident in Henry's riled voice as he spoke to Hargraves. "I hate the thought of living with the Mormons in Nauvoo."

"Don't blame you one bit, old top," the elder Hargraves answered, looking drained. "I'm staying in New Orleans even if I have to be a canal digger like our Irish friend from yesterday."

The remark caught the attention of a man at the next table of the crowd-ed smoke-filled barroom. "Just say the word and I can get all three of you jobs in no time," the man said in an Irish accent.

Henry and Richard whirled to face the Irishman.

"A steamboat nearly killed me," the man said, pulling his stool nearer. "I swear to never board another, and I'd advise you the same. Name's John O'Neil." As he thrust out his hand he went on to say that he was a work fore-man for one of the companies digging canals, and said he had been in New Orleans for more than four years.

Henry bristled, taking an immediate defensive stand. "What's wrong with steamboats? We just crossed the Atlantic. It took two months and we were nearly sunk several times. What could be worse?"

Signaling for an old black man to pour them new drinks, O'Neil, a short, fair-complexioned man with a square face and heavy hair graying at the sides, took out a tobacco pouch and rolled him a smoke.

Henry smiled mischievously.

"Had it in my mind to go into Missouri and settle," the Irishman said, lighting the smoke. "It was on a Sunday morning the sixth of May, I clearly remember. Our steamboat was the *Ben Sherrod*. There were lots of little chil-dren on board. They would run to the guards."

"The guards?" Henry asked in bewilderment.

"Extensions of the deck. On both sides. Beyond the paddle boxes, which gives greater width for storage. The children would run to the guards in excite-ment to see the next boat, or the water, or something. It was a beautiful day. I never suspected anything to go wrong during the trip."

O'Neil puffed on his tobacco and coughed.

"So what went ruddy wrong?" Henry asked, leaning forward on the table, his curiosity piqued.

O'Neil raised his thick eyebrows and squinted through the smoke. "Another steamboat shoved off about the same time, that's what went wrong. There's an old joke floating around New Orleans that goes, 'Know when the first steamboat race was?' The answer is, 'The first time two steamboats shoved off about the same time.' Steamboat captains are plumb crazy, especially if you get a few drinks in 'em. The build of the *Ben* was heavy, her timbers being of the largest size. But it being late in the season and but a few large steamers being in port in consequence of the severity of the times, the *Ben* got an undue number of passengers plus she had heavy freight on board, including several horses and carriages on the forecastle."

Hargraves leveled the Irishman with a cold stare. "My dear fellow, you mean the captain took to racing even under that load?"

The Irishman rubbed one eye and continued. "Not 'til two nights later when the steamboat *Prairie,* on her way to St. Louis, bore hard on the *Ben.* We had to stop at Fort Adams so the *Prairie* passed us. That vexed some of the passengers for fear the Prairie would get to Natchez before we did. This was the subject of conversation for two or three hours. The captain began assurin' everyone that we could beat her anyhow. So while we were at Fort Adams the captain gave orders to his crew to keep up the fires to the full extent. It was a little past eleven at night when we left Fort Adams. The crew began passing around a bottle of whiskey while the captain went to bed with his clothes on. As the *Ben* passed above Fort Adams toward the mouth of the Homochitta, the wood piled up in the front of the furnaces caught afire several times but was put out by the drunken hands. I know you boys have never seen a western steamboat, but the boilers are entirely above the first deck."

"We've seen several at the wharves just this morning," said the younger Hargraves, sipping on pure brandy.

O'Neil's face hardened. "I'm afraid you're a little young for drinkin' son."

"Not too young to drink, and not to young to work," the youth said in a sneer. "And not too young to smoke, neither. Care to share your tobacco?"

The Irishman ignored the boy's answer by taking a long drag on his smoke and shaking his head, intent on finishing his story. "As our boat was booming along through the water close in to the shore—sometimes the steamboats go real close to the shore to avoid the currents—a Negro slave along the beach called out to the fireman that the wood was on fire. The drunken fireman told him to go to hell and mind his own business. The slave hollered back, 'Oh massa, if you don't take care, you'll be in hell before I will."

The Irishman's audience of three laughed a good belly laugh, and poured more drinks.

"So there we were, going as fast as the boilers would paddle the wheels, the boat quivering and quaking in all her length at every revolution. The steam heated so fast that it continued to escape through the safety valve, sending a message that the drunken crew failed to understand. Finally, as we rounded the bar that makes off from the Homochitta, compelling the *Ben* to be in the middle of the river, the fire was discovered. It was about one o'clock in the morning. A passenger tried to seize a bucket and plunge it overboard for water, but it was chained short, and couldn't be used. As the captain was awakened, the flames burst out of control. When he saw the fire he panicked and screamed 'fire' to all he could. No sooner were the words out of his mouth than the shrieks of mothers and babies resounded through the boat. Men were aroused from their dreaming cots to experience the hot air of the approaching fire."

Henry gasped.

"The pilot headed toward shore but he scarcely got underway that direction when the tiller ropes were burned asunder. We were still two miles from shore and the vessel then took a sheer, and we spun around twice until she struck off across the river. The flames had now extended fore and aft. At the first alarm several deck passengers jumped into a yawl that hung suspended by the davits. About twenty people were thus launched into the angry waters and all of them drowned, I guess, because we never heard about them any more. The flames began to engulf the whole boat and hundreds leaped from the burning wreck into the waters. Mothers were seen standing on the guards praying for help. The horses were panicking too, trying to jump off but they were all tied up."

Henry exchanged a worried glance with Richard Hargraves.

The Irishman continued. "Never, were I to live until the memory should forget all else that comes to the senses, will I erase that hour of horror and alarm from my mind. I was swimming to the shore with all my might, trying to help a mother and her child. My strength soon failed me. The mother asked me to save her child and she sank from sight. I was lucky to save the child and myself. The *Ben* had swung off the bar and was floating down river. In every direction heads dotted the surface of the river. While I sat dripping and overcome on the beach, the *Columbus* came in sight and began picking up survivors. About that time the cylinders on the *Ben* blew up and the country was lighted up all around."

There was a silence at the table.

"How often does a steamboat blow up?" Henry asked, his face registering a terrible fear, but doing his best to hide his insecurity.

"Not all that often, but often enough that I wouldn't get on one if I wuz you," he answered. "Here's the problem as I see it."

The Irishman's eyes narrowed.

"Every steamboat has a safety valve on its engines, with a weight on it to indicate how many pounds of pressure of steam is building up. In their greedy desire to make better time, to earn more money to deliver cargo faster, all the steamboat engineers have discovered that by simply placing a little heavier weight on the safety valve arm, a bigger head of steam can be built up. That leads to the danger of blowing the boilers. Riverboats are clumsily constructed, have a stroke six times the diameter of the cylinder, make a very slow stroke, a great condensation of steam. Everything else about them is bad, too. Think about the risks: Snags are everywhere on the river, especially this time of year. Even lots of ice when you get beyond St. Louis. Some boats just plain catch on fire. Others strike rocks, ground themselves on sand bars, and, worst of all—the boiler explosions. Even if they don't blow up, it's plumb torture to ride on 'em unless you got the money to ride cabin class. If you're a deck passenger, pity, pity, pity."

Henry sat in stunned amazement.

"Most riverboat officers consider deck passengers as literally worthless once you've paid your fare. Some captains don't even stop if a deck passenger falls overboard. If they need to lighten the load for any reason, captains will put you off anywhere, no matter where you're paid to. Were you a cabin passenger or steerage passenger on the ship from England?"

With a spasm crossing his face from everything the Irishman was telling him, Henry finally gestured with open palms and said, "Steerage." Suddenly, steamboats sounded worse than the *Echo*.

The Irishman's grin showed a mouth of crooked teeth. "That means your people will book you as a deck passenger going up the river. And that means you'll have to share space on the main deck with the animals, the freight, and the deckhands. You'll be lucky to find any kind of resting-place on the piles of boxes, barrels, and bales that will be on board. And what'll you eat? Not on the upper deck in the dining room. You'll likely starve to death before you get to your destination. There's no tables, no utensils, no nothing, mate. I've been a deck passenger. It reminded me of a horse stable, nothing more. No saloon. No separation of quarters according to the sexes. No gilt, no plush, no glitter. All you'll see is the grimy, splintered planking on the deck and a bucket to scoop water from the river for the only aid to sanitation. Stay in New Orleans, mate. Stay in New Orleans."

Henry blinked at the Irishman in stupefied soberness at the conclusion. He was more determined than ever to stay in New Orleans. He reached into his pocket and took out the *gris-gris* he had purchased yesterday. *Tonight, Robert goes to his berth. I'll hide this somewhere. The Voodoo magic will begin its evil work.*

39

DANIEL STEPPED OFF THE MAIN DECK of the *Lady of New Orleans*. He strode a few paces away. Then he turned back to contemplate the steamboat that he and his five assistants had just contracted to take the *Echo*'s Mormon passengers to St. Louis, the first leg of their journey to Nauvoo.

The *Lady* was much different than Daniel had imagined a steamboat to be. He had guessed a steamboat to be a vessel with fine lines, an elegant finish, and the capability to race up the river with a fair amount of speed. The *Lady* seemed to be designed more for carrying freight than for transporting people. She sat awkwardly in the water with her twenty-eight-foot wide all-wooden body, designed to handle the incoming and outgoing of freight right at water level.

"The steamboat ain't nothing more than an engine on a raft, with thousands of dollars worth of jigsaw work around it," a local had told Daniel. "And flimsy construction at that."

There were three decks: main, boiler, and hurricane. There was an additional small deck rising above the hurricane called the "Texas," because it was annexed to the upper part of the boat. The piling of deck upon deck gave the *Lady* a bulky, top-heavy appearance that was partially mitigated by her length, which was a hundred and twenty-five feet. Her overall width did not count the "guards," extensions of the main deck beyond the line of the hull at the sides, adding greatly to the deck space. The guards provided additional room for freight and fuel and served as passageways between parts of the boat.

"Think that engine can power us up the river?" Robert asked Daniel.

A deck hand's explanation of the engine and boilers had confused Daniel, as did the sight of them. The engine seemed to be a mass of unorganized machinery. It was a menagerie of valves, valve gears, cylinders, rods, levers, gauges, and iron bars. Everything had been designed, he was told, as a low-cost solution to supply enough power to pull the steamboat up the river with its long, slow stroke of about twenty revolutions per minute, turning a single, large wooden paddle wheel. The engine received its power from six boilers placed lengthwise side-by-side across the forepart of the main deck, where they counterbalanced the weight of the engines and wheels aft. Each boiler was about forty inches in diameter and thirty-five feet long. A huge furnace, used to heat the water to provide steam for the boilers, was built up with firebrick and encased with sheet iron. The smoke and gas returning through the flues to the furnace end of the boilers were exhausted through twin chimneys rising on each side, affording the pilot an uninterrupted forward view from the pilothouse.

"I hope so," Daniel answered. "We don't have a choice, do we?"

The boiler, or second deck, carried the main cabin and its staterooms. Meals for first-class passengers were served in the main cabin, which was also used for dancing and social events. The main cabin ran fore and aft, continuous and unobstructed. It was divided by a midship gangway, which led into a forward cabin and a ladies' cabin. Kitchens and washrooms were adjacent to the wheelhouses.

On the roof of the Texas deck was the pilothouse, from which the boat was navigated. The elevated room, with windows on all sides, gave the pilot an uninterrupted view of the river. It contained a large wheel for steering the rudder and controls for operating the engines. A novel feature of this particular steamboat was a steam calliope, on which tunes were played when approaching a river town. A steam whistle and a large bell on the top deck were used for signaling.

"Just think," Robert said, still tracing the lines of the steamboat. The box-like structure appeared to him more practical than aesthetic. "The earnings from the fight I missed, the one with Ben Caunt, would have paid cabin passage on this rickety steamboat for just about our whole company."

"Don't tell me you're still thinking about the money you gave up to join the Church and come to America?" Daniel said, making a skeptical face.

Robert laughed and gave his shoulders a nonchalant shrug. "No regrets. Just get me to Nauvoo, safe and sound."

Together, Daniel and Robert peered north, up the Mississippi. North, where an endless flow of migrants and adventurers were pushing up the rivers, overland, crossing plains and mountains, bound for new lands, new homes, and opportunities waiting for them in the rich provinces of the vast interior basin of North America. They had seen the broadest collection of human beings any place on earth, natives of all sorts, and foreigners: men of business and men of pleasure. Parlor men and backwoodsmen. Farm hunters and fame hunters. Hunters of every sort—heiress hunters, gold hunters, buffalo hunters, bee hunters, happiness hunters, truth hunters, and still hunters after those hunters. Fine ladies in slippers and moccasined squaws. Northern speculators and Eastern philosophers. English, Irish, German, Scotch, Danes, Swedes. Santa Fe traders in striped blankets. Broadway bucks in cravats of cloth of gold. Fine-looking Kentucky boatmen. Japanese-looking Mississippi cotton planters. Quakers in full drab. United States soldiers in full regimentals. Slaves, black, mulatto, quadroon. Deacons and blacklegs. Hard-shell Baptists, Catholics, Lutherans, Presbyterians.

And Mormons, on the way to their Zion.

Standing on the deck of the *Echo* with all the Mormon passengers and speaking in a loud voice, Daniel clamored for attention: "Brothers and Sisters, I have just returned from the ticket office here in New Orleans. We will depart Tuesday morning for St. Louis on the steamer *Lady of New Orleans,* the first leg of our trip to Nauvoo."

A round of cheers. The men threw their hats in the air.

Protecting her newborn baby, now nearly three weeks old, Hannah smiled broadly and joined in the cheering. She was proud of Daniel and her husband and all the rest of Daniel's assistants. It flashed through her mind that they had done a good job in the face of adversity. The hurricane-force winds early in the trip. The ship being blown off course. Dealing with Henry over his attack on her husband. Rebecca's attack. The narrow brush with death when the Barbary pirates overtook the *Echo*. The death of Nancy, and almost losing her own son. Daniel and his presidency were to be commended. So was Captain Wood. He was a good man and Hannah would miss him but she, along with everyone else, was looking forward to disembarkment and getting up the Mississippi to Nauvoo.

Under a canopy of white puffy clouds, Daniel continued. "Elder Woodruff assured me in London that a letter has been sent to Nauvoo. When we finally arrive there the Prophet Joseph and the saints should be expecting us. I think that many of our old friends from England will be on the Nauvoo docks to greet us. I know we all look forward to seeing old friends such as John and Jane Benbow. The Benbows left last September on the ship *North America* with Elder Turley, and should be well settled in Nauvoo by now."

Gently rocking her baby in her arms, Hannah thought of other Malvern Hills friends that had already traveled to America on the *North America* and who would be firmly settled in Nauvoo by now: Robert and Elizabeth Cole Holmes. William and Ann Cole. William and Mary Jenkins Parson. John and Grace Ann Parry. Robert and Elizabeth Clift. Joseph and Eliza Crook Halford. And William and Mary Rowberry Jenkins. Hannah hoped that some of those friends would help the *Echo* passengers get established in their new home.

As she thought of the Jenkins, Hannah also thought of Mary Ann Weston, who had lived as a seamstress with the Jenkins family back in Gloucestershire before her marriage to John Davis. She hoped that Mary Ann and John were doing well and would be leaving England soon. She knew Daniel was anxious to see John again and both Elizabeth and she were looking forward to renewing their friendship with Mary Ann.

"The agent told me that the trip to St. Louis will take about a week," Daniel continued. "He further tells me we should have no problem arranging for passage on another steamboat that will take us from St. Louis to Nauvoo. We expect to be in St. Louis for only a day or two—at the most three—while our baggage is transferred again."

Reaching for Robert with her free hand, Hannah pulled him close and squeezed his hand. She looked at her other three children and smiled proudly. Joseph was looking more and more like his father every day: rich brown hair and brown eyes, husky and well-coordinated. He would become a good helper on their small farm in Nauvoo. Lizzy had just turned three on April first and was a free-spirited talker, just like her Auntie Elizabeth. Willie was now a year and a half. He had been a favorite crowd pleaser on the ship with his cute little smile and meandering ways.

Hannah leaned over and whispered, "Listen to Uncle Daniel, Willie. He's telling us about the rest of our trip."

Warm sunlight broke through the clouds, brightening Daniel's face. "From St. Louis we should be on the river no more than four or five days, then we will arrive in Zion, Nauvoo. I know you can hardly wait to get there. I know you dream about Nauvoo day and night."

Standing near Robert and Hannah, where she could help with the children, Elizabeth gave Daniel an affectionate grin. He knew that she dreamed about Nauvoo more than just about anyone. She wondered how Nauvoo would measure up to her ideals. In reality, the city might be much different than the utopia she envisioned. She hoped for a city of pure holiness, but deep inside knew that it would be less than perfect because people were not perfect. Compared to most places in the world, however, it would be a heaven on earth to her and Daniel. Certainly, there would be far less evil there than in worldly cities such as London, Gloucester, and Liverpool.

Throw New Orleans in the mix, too, Elizabeth thought..

"I truly hope Nauvoo will be all that you expect," Daniel continued. "I want to caution you that the inheritance you seek in Zion has less to do with land we will actually own and more to do with a place where we can live together and worship in the manner we please. America has a great Constitution that guarantees freedom of religion. Despite that, members of the Church in America have been driven out of Ohio and out of Missouri. At one time Zion was in Kirtland. Another time, Missouri. Now it is Nauvoo."

Henry Eagles bitterly grimaced. If enemies of Mormonism drove Church members out of Ohio and Missouri, how safe were they in Nauvoo? Just another reason, in his mind, to stay in New Orleans. He still could not feel anything but uncomfortable around Robert and Daniel. The trip on the *Echo* had been a nightmare as far as he was concerned. It wouldn't be much better in Nauvoo if he had to live in the shadow of his relatives. If he and Katherine went to another American settlement, away from Nauvoo, he could get rid of those feelings. If she wouldn't go with him there were plenty of other women in America who needed husbands. In the very least, Henry calculated he could start out in New Orleans by peddling produce in the French Market.

"Yes, we will build homes in Nauvoo," Daniel said. "Yes, we will own building lots. Yes, we will own farms. But more important we will live in a community of saints where we can organize into units and be ministered to by the Prophet Joseph Smith and members of the Quorum of the Twelve. Zion is built one member at a time. Zion is built one stake at a time. It doesn't matter where Zion is, whether it is in Ohio or Missouri or Illinois. It is not limited to one city or land; it is wherever the saints gather, because Zion means the 'pure in heart'."

Ignoring the Zion part of the talk, the thought of owning a farm intrigued Henry. He could buy himself a few cows and have an American version of the Nightingale Dairy, only he would call it the Eagles Dairy. The advantage of staying the course and going all the way to Nauvoo was that the saints had been told that they could buy land on credit from the Church. That way he could invest what money he had into cows and a barn instead of land. He could pay for the land later, or not at all. He could feign continued poverty. Who would dare look at his books? He could sell milk to the "pure in heart" and make a profit. Henry liked Daniel's little talk. Maybe Henry Eagles would be a big success in Nauvoo. He put his hand in his pocket and drew out his English money, looked at it, then put it away. Henry looked over the crowd in the direction of the docks where the riverboats were moored, and thought again of the Irishman's warnings. Nauvoo on the one hand, and a dairy, sounded good to Henry. But on the other hand, it appeared the only way to get to Nauvoo was on a steamboat. The thought frightened him.

Daniel's voice, clear and loud, carried to every Mormon passenger. "Elder Woodruff told me that the reason Zion did not flourish in Missouri was because of the unrighteousness of the saints which caused the Lord to chasten them. I pray that we may be instrumental in building a Zion city in Nauvoo and be righteous, obedient to the counsels of the Lord, that Zion may flourish in Nauvoo. The great Prophet Isaiah envisioned the latter-day glory of Israel, gathered to her restored Zion, when he proclaimed: *Enlarge the place of thy tent, and let them stretch forth the curtains of thine habitations: spare not, lengthen thy cords, and strengthen thy stakes.* So in keeping with that symbolism, the Church is now being organized into stakes wherever there are sufficient saints to gather.

"We have responded to a great yearning in our hearts to gather to Zion. We will be gathered with our own families into a stake in Nauvoo. Established stakes in the latter days will be rallying points and gathering centers for the remnants of scattered Israel. If we drive our stake securely into the ground we will be secure. Zion is the tent and the stakes of Zion are the binding pegs that support her."

Stakes seemed a funny word to Henry the more he thought about it. It was a stretch of the imagination to use that word to describe a unit of the Mormon Church. Why couldn't Joe Smith use the more traditional and less confusing "parish" system? Why did the Mormons have to be so different? If he actually ended up in Nauvoo, he hoped there would be other churches there as well. He had only three more days to make a final decision about whether or not to stay in New Orleans. Maybe someday he could talk Katherine into resigning from the Mormon organization and attending either some kind of Protestant church or, better yet, none at all.

Concluding his thoughts, Daniel said, "If we are righteous the Lord will fight our battles. He will help us fight wickedness. The Lord has helped the Prophet Joseph Smith secure a land for our inheritance. There will be a temple of the Lord built in Nauvoo. We will help build that temple. We will help build the city, a place where you can live in peace and fulfill your dreams. Nauvoo was established only two years ago so it is a new city, a new place, a new Zion. It awaits you. It awaits me. God bless us that we may arrive there in due time, meet the Prophet, meet our old friends, and work to establish our new homes."

SATURDAY April 17 – A heavy rain, thunder and lightning. No fire on board, no breakfast; at nine o'clock all the heads of families went to the customhouse to get permits signed. About noon the customhouse office came to inspect the luggage; rain coming down in torrents. Our women collected the water for washing clothes. The rain subsided and many went into the city to make purchases. It was reported the steward had the cook taken up to sell him, New Orleans in Louisiana being one of the chief slave states. We have been able to make a contract with a steamer to carry our company to St. Louis for two dollars and fifty cents each, including baggage, but we have to do the work of the wooders. It will take a couple of days to load our baggage from the ship Echo. Distance is some 1,200 miles. The Mississippi steamer is a strange looking boat with a shallow hull, wide beam, several tiers, and has tall, twin stacks with ornamental crowns. New Orleans is a fine place but all thought of religion is neglected. A couple of the women are already homesick in this strange land and broke down and wept like children. Weather warmer this afternoon. Great number of flies this time of year.

On awakening Sunday morning, it was Hannah who found the curious leather bag under Robert's berth as she rummaged on the floor, gathering up items strewn by her children.

"What's this?" she asked Joseph, thinking it might be something he had found during their second trip to the French Market. Putting it to her nose she pulled a face and said, "phew!"

On her way to Sunday services she threw it overboard, watching it land on the water and float there. It did not sink.

40

DON'T MISS THE SLAVE DANCES at Congo Square, Irishman O'Neil had said. Henry didn't want to attend the Mormon Sunday services on board the ship anyway, so here he was, eyes gawking around. As Henry watched a police official give a signal and the slaves move to the center of the square, he thought about Katherine and her expression of frustration with him as he left the ship.

"Not once have you taken me with you," she had said in a wailing voice.

In fairness to her, Henry thought, she wouldn't like to see half-naked Negroes dancing and cavorting about, the same as she wouldn't want to visit Doctor John the Voodoo man, or sit in a bar listening to steamboat wreck stories.

"Danzes Bamboula! Badoum! Badoum!" the male slaves shouted as they leaped into the air with bits of tin and bells and ribbon tied to their ankles. They slithered to the steady drumming of a Negro who beat two huge beef bones upon the head of a cask, out of which had been fashioned a sort of drum. The Negro women swayed their bodies from side to side and chanted an ancient song as monotonous as a dirge. Beyond them were the children, jumping and dancing, trying to imitate their elders. Soon the entire square became a solid mass of black bodies stamping and swaying to the rhythmic beat of the bones upon the cask.

Drinking whatever was set before him, Henry Eagles became drunk and lost in the new world of New Orleans.

SUNDAY April 18 – Held our last sacrament meeting on board the ship. We gave time for those who wished to bear their testimonies. Many tears were shed. All are thankful that we have safely arrived. Many expressed sorrow over Sister Nancy Pulham's death.

Captain Wood tried not to alarm Daniel. But he had to tell him that a member of his crew had spotted steerage passenger Henry Eagles about six o'clock in the morning. Eagles was crawling almost naked along the wharves near the New Orleans Custom House. He had been found almost unconscious, a huge knot on his skull, and bleeding slightly from several superficial wounds.

"He's lucky his throat ain't cut," the captain said as Daniel examined Henry. "We've got two more missing, a Mr. Hargraves and his son. Who knows if they'll be found or not. We've already notified the police. Someone must have robbed Mr. Eagles. There's nothing on him, not even his clothes."

Horrified, Daniel asked, "What do you think happened?"

The captain's voice reflected deep concern. "Some of my crew report that Mr. Eagles has been going into the French Quarter looking for a business deal of some sort or another, bragging that he has money to invest. Someone must have taken him seriously. Could be anyone—the roughneck Irish, the wild French or Italians, Voodoo blacks or Creoles. Believe me, you'll never know unless Mr. Eagles can remember anything. Even then, I doubt he could identify anyone. Any money he may have had hidden on him is gone."

As Elizabeth came running up, Daniel stared at Henry's mutilated body wrapped in a quilt, barely breathing. "Brother Eagles, can you hear me?"

Henry moved only slightly, but he acknowledged Daniel's voice.

A knot formed in Daniel's stomach. He looked at Elizabeth. "Better get Hannah and Katherine."

An iciness raked Elizabeth's flesh. "What shall I tell them?"

"Tell Hannah that her brother is hurt badly. Leave it up to Hannah to tell Katherine."

MONDAY April 19 – Most all post a letter to England to families and friends left behind. It takes much money, more than many can command. It seemed rather strange yesterday to see the people of New Orleans holding their market day on Sunday. There are people here who are French, Spanish, Italian, German, Anglo-Saxon, Indian and African. The population they say is at 100,000. Many wealthy people along Bourbon and Royal Streets, but most are living in poverty in rude shacks on the outskirts of the city. Wharves stretch for miles along the riverbank. We are praying for Henry Eagles. He was attacked and robbed, beaten most severely.

Captain Wood stood on the sunny wing of the *Echo* bridge scanning his Mormon passengers for the last time as they prepared to disembark.

The captain was in a jovial mood. He wondered if he would ever get the opportunity to bring another company of Mormons from Great Britain to America. He had never been around a more pleasantly puzzling people. He could see Daniel and his assistants approaching, probably to say their final good-byes. He had already complimented Daniel many, many times about the overall good behavior of the Mormon company, and had apologized profusely, time and time again, over the misbehavior of the seaman who had attacked Captain Browett's sister. It had clearly embarrassed Captain Wood.

The incident, or incidents, with Henry Eagles—who was being carried out of the steerage compartment on a stretcher—was practically the only serious blemish on the otherwise perfect behavior of the Mormon group. At least that was true when compared with the other non-Mormon passengers on this voyage, and all the previous voyages he had ever captained. He wondered if Daniel were going to ask him again if he would be baptized. He admired his tenacity.

Taking off his cap and placing it under his arm, Captain Wood extended his right hand to the approaching men. "The pleasure has been all mine, gentlemen. Thank you for your business." He stood erect, as though he were going to be inspected by an admiral. In fact, he held the Mormons in higher esteem that most admirals he had ever known. He especially admired the seven men who stood before him.

Matching the captain's courtesy, Daniel and his six assistants placed their caps under their left arms and shook hands with the man they had grown to respect. "We want to thank you for your patience and your diligence, Captain Wood," Daniel said.

Captain Wood smiled broadly through his thick beard and took a bow. "You are most welcome and good luck on your steamship journey up the Mississippi. I trust you will not have to endure any seasickness this time."

Locking eyes with Daniel, he added, "Are you certain you don't want to get back on the *Echo* and go to New York with me? Most certainly I can get you and a lot of your men good jobs in the shipbuilding industry. Sources tell me that Nauvoo is just a wretched settlement made up of log and mud cabins and knee-deep muddy streets, and filled with poverty stricken people."

Daniel's voice was wrought with conviction. "No, Sir, Captain Wood, we are not tempted to do that in the least. You've been listening to rumors from just a handful of dissatisfied immigrants. We think we are going to find a beautiful city on the banks of the Mississippi. In fact, in all seriousness, we invite you to come with us. What do you say?"

Tossing his head back with another hearty laugh, the captain hissed through his teeth. "And give up my commission? You have your lives. I have mine."

Placing an arm around the burly captain, Daniel said, "We have time to baptize you before we leave." He pointed to the river. "There's plenty of water down there."

"I must admit, Captain Browett, your doctrines make a lot of sense."

"I feel in my heart, Captain Wood, that you believe everything we have taught you. I just want you to know that the gospel is true. Joseph Smith is a Prophet of God. I think you know that, too."

"You've been very persuasive."

"*Then Agrippa said unto Paul, almost thou persuadest me to be a*

Christian."

"What?" The captain looked surprised but thoughtful.

"Remember the story in Acts? King Agrippa and Paul."

The captain ran his finger through his thick beard, scratching his chin, and held his head at an attentive tilt. "Yes, I think I do. But remember I'm already Christian. I just don't act like it sometimes. But I do read my Bible once in a while. I might even read the Book of Mormon you gave me."

"Last chance, Captain Wood. We have some white clothing that will fit you."

Captain Wood deflected the offer. "Some day I might write you a letter. To Daniel Browett, Nauvoo, Illinois."

Daniel looked at the captain with an affection he normally held in reserve for his best friends. "I'll look forward to it. We will still have some white clothing waiting for you."

"Goodbye Captain Browett."

The captain saluted.

"Goodbye my friend."

Daniel returned the salute.

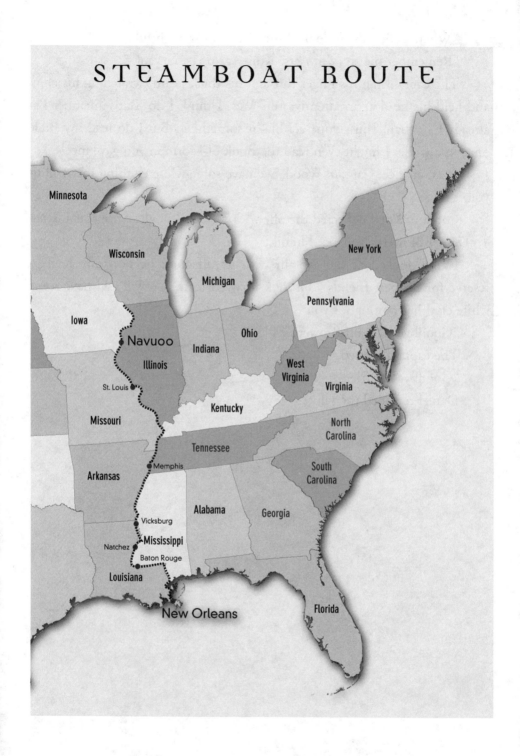

41

THE FIREMAN KNEW, WITHOUT AN express order, to begin burning resin and pitch pine at three o'clock. That caused columns of coal-black smoke to rise out of the smokestack, a sign that the *Lady of New Orleans* was going to leave within an hour. Another sign was that its flag was flying at jackstaff.

Daniel stared at the black smoke as he watched the last few people board the ramshackle steamboat. His one hundred and eight people were already scattered all around the main deck of the *Lady of New Orleans,* mixed in with the countless freight barrels, hogsheads, and baggage strewn from the port to the starboard guards.

When the main, hurricane, and boiler decks were filled with passengers, the last bells began to clang.

"All that ain't goin' better get to shore!" a deckhand yelled.

Daniel watched as the stage planks were hauled in and a crew of twenty-five swarthy Negro roustabouts quickly massed together on the forecastle and began singing. Tall columns of steam burst from the escape pipes, guns were fired from the shore, a brass band roared out "Hail Columbia," and cabin passengers waved American flags from the upper deck.

Making certain Henry was as comfortable as possible on a makeshift bed atop boxes of freight, using overcoats for a mattress, Katherine gently patted his forehead with a wet cloth as the first "boom!" from a cannon was heard, part of the traditional sendoff as steamers departed the New Orleans wharves.

Henry awoke with a start. "Where am I?" he said, with widening eyes, and shivers of pain thundering through his beaten body.

"We're finally leaving New Orleans, Henry," Katherine said, withdrawing the wet cloth.

Making a painful groan as he sat up, Henry looked at the crowded decks, the half-naked crews of perspiring Negroes, the wharves full of festive citizens from New Orleans, and listened to another roar of the cannon. Whistles screamed. Pistons slammed in a metallic chorus. Paddles slapped the water in a mechanical cadence.

"Am I on a steamboat?" Henry asked, his body stiffening.

Listening to the conversation with keen interest because of Henry's injuries, Hannah took a step toward her brother. "Welcome back to the world, Henry," she said, holding her new baby in her arms. "We're on a steamboat called the *Lady of New Orleans.* Another steamboat has just shoved off as well, the *Missouri Clipper.* It must be a tradition or something, but it looks like we're going to race her to St. Louis."

Henry brought his body very erect and his eyes opened wide as saucers. "Everybody off! Everybody off! The boilers are going to blow! Everybody off!" Groaning, Henry jumped off the boxes that had made up his bed, and continued to yell in a delirious voice, "Everybody off! This steamer is not safe!"

Hannah stepped out of Henry's way to protect her baby. She turned to Robert. "He's out of his mind. Can you restrain him?"

Robert had no time to think about Hannah's request as Henry began to stagger toward the edge of the deck, pushing aside other passengers and limping as he ran. "I'm getting off! Everybody follow me!"

Not far behind, Robert grabbed Henry by his shirt collar and jerked him off his feet. "Henry, don't jump into the water. You might drown!"

Henry continued to yell. "Let go of me! The *gris-gris!* Where is it? Did you place it in my berth? Let go...."

Henry Eagles fainted into Robert's arms.

Captain Andrew Lloyd was a man of few genuine friends. He had a monstrous quaking belly owing to his liking of whiskey and rich foods, earning him the nickname of "Two Ton Andrew," although no one called him that to his face. When drunk, he greeted newcomers with bone-crushing handshakes and tooth-shattering backslaps. He smothered his crew with fast talk and wild stories. He was bold, innovative, and blessed with an instinct for unscrupulous business dealings.

Possibly from long years of peering out to the Mississippi River, the captain's eyes were permanently marked with what looked like laugh lines. Strangers mistook him for a genial man, but Captain Lloyd was certainly not. Intense brown eyes, a broad nose, and a hard face covered by a reddish-brown beard, the man demanded total allegiance to his every wish and command.

"Full steam, Caruthers," Captain Lloyd said to his pilot as the *Lady of New Orleans* veered away from the dock. "Shave those boats as close as you'd peel an apple."

Neither Caruthers nor Lloyd paid any attention to the fists stretched into the air and the volleys of red-hot profanity from keelboat pilots as they were pushed out of the way.

Four river inspectors crowded the pilothouse. All wore polished silk hats, elaborate shirts, diamond breastpins, goatskin gloves, and patent-leather boots.

"How did you run Deterhan's Point coming down, captain?" one inspector asked.

"Tell him, Caruthers," Captain Lloyd said with a commanding nod. Then he cast his eyes on the turbid Mississippi, laced with sand and silt.

Pilot Benjamin Caruthers was a stark man, squarely built, but had a colorless translucence about him. His eyes hung disembodied in space. He made no gestures as he spoke. "The water's getting higher and higher with all the runoff from up north, so I had to run it a little different this time. I started out about seventy yards from the Cypress grove on the false point. I held on the cabin under the point 'till I raised the reef—quarter less twain—then straightened out for the middle bar until I got well abreast of the wreck of the *Sumpter,* then got my stern clean around and headed for the low place above the point. We came through a booming about nine and a half."

"Ain't it a square crossing going up?" another inspector inquired.

The captain answered for Caruthers, his disposition intensified and his focus total. "That's right, but the upper bar's working down fast. We need to make good time going up the river this trip." His cargo included kegs of gunpowder and one hundred thousand dollars in specie, consigned to the Exchange Bank of St. Louis. He would make a tidy bonus if he delivered on time. He lit a cigar and cast his eyes up the river.

A third inspector gave an approving nod.

Captain Lloyd not only knew by heart the names of all the towns and islands and bends on the Mississippi between New Orleans and St. Louis, but he also knew nearly every snag, wood pile, and deep embankment that ornamented the route. Just as a man could follow the hallway of his own home in pitch black darkness, Captain Lloyd and his pilot could follow the twisting, meandering Mississippi, with its millions of trifling variations of shapes, with their eyes open or shut.

"I judge the upper bar is making up a little at Bayou Iberville," the inspector said. "On the way down we had quarter twain with the lower lead and mark twain with the other."

The captain was blowing out steady puffs of cigar smoke. "Might be up to mark three by now."

"Lot of snags this year," the inspector added.

"I hear you."

"The *Missouri Clipper* is straight away behind you at full steam."

The captain scoffed. "We'll beat her to St. Louis. I've got two hundred dollars bet on it. Our machinery is well oiled, the piston rods were just overhauled, and we're loaded no more than the *Clipper.*"

"I heard you had some trouble with the larboard boiler on the way down," another inspector said.

"Fixed that, too," the captain growled.

"But you have to stop at Point Coupee and take in some sugar and molasses, don't you?"

"The *Missouri Clipper* likely will have to stop somewhere, too. If not, we'll push hard and beat her to St. Louis anyway." Captain Lloyd motioned to his mate. "Open one of the kegs of whiskey. Let's do some early celebrating." He reached for the steam valve and released it. A shriek filled the air.

Caruthers rang the bell for full steam.

42

DANIEL STOOD ON THE BOW of the *Lady*, scanning the Mississippi River, his new enemy. As he listened to the shriek of the steam valve and the clang of the bell, he felt another rising trepidation sweep over him. It was similar to the feeling that came over him as he contemplated the huge Atlantic Ocean: deliver his Mormon company of a hundred and eight souls safely up the river to Nauvoo.

The riverboat was following the Mississippi's meandering course in a northwest direction toward Baton Rogue. From there she would steam north toward Natchez, Vicksburg, and Memphis.

As Daniel gazed at the immensity of the river, he had no idea of the Mississippi's origin. The river is born twelve hundred miles north, in Minnesota, a land of glacial lakes and ponds, and beautiful conifer forests. There, the river is less than ten feet across. Picking up creeks and drainages as it meanders south, it rapidly swells in immensity. It becomes a good-sized river by the time it reaches Minneapolis. It forms the border between Minnesota and Wisconsin, and Wisconsin and Iowa. Formidable now, it picks up other rivers such as the Chippewa, Black, Upper Iowa, and the Wisconsin. Wider and wider it becomes, passing settlements such as Dubuque, Davenport, Keokuk, and Quincy on its way to St. Louis. Near there, the muddy waters of

Missouri, this time of year swelled with spring runoff, invade the Mississippi. Water overflows the banks in many places, making riverboat travel dangerous. A bird's eye view of the merger reveals that the mighty Mississippi appears to be two different rivers flowing in the same bed. Along one bank, its waters are still clear. On the other, waters are a murky, reddish brown. Eventually, they become opaque with the silt the tributary has robbed from the upper plains states. Not even the clear waters of the next major tributary, the Ohio River, which carries an even larger volume of water that the Missouri, can remove the indelible stain that the Big Muddy has given to the Mississippi. It has now become what many describe as the river with the spirit and muscle of God, but at times having Satan's own sinews. The divider and uniter of the North American continent.

Below the mouth of the Ohio, the river passes by the swampy mouth of the Arkansas Red and collects water from the Red River. In great bends, it winds its way through the wide, fertile lands where cotton is king. After passing Baton Rouge, it enters rich bottomland where cotton, rice, and sugarcane are grown. And after passing the levees of New Orleans, it shatters into innumerable capillaries and dumps into the Gulf, ending a 2,552-mile journey.

Daniel quickly determined that there were no large, uninviting ocean swells to threaten the steamboat, only occasional snags. The scenery was peaceful, even beautiful. The *Lady* steamed past woods, fertile fields, swamps, marshes, and shallow basins choked with lush vegetation. Daniel saw countless bayous, streams, creeks, and ponds that made the countryside a watery patchwork. For the first few miles, fresh and salt waters mixed in tidal estuaries and ponds, producing endless brackish marshes where he saw thousands of waterfowl and wading birds. The ponds were blanketed with countless thousands of water-hyacinth plants, surrounded by stands of cypress, tupelo-gum, and willow trees. Wildly twisted oak trees, some with twenty-foot girths, stood majestically. Their branches stretched out into vast moss-draped tents, mingling their leaves with other trees, standing guard over the water. Green tree frogs and cricket frogs were everywhere. And wildlife—bears, panthers, flying squirrels, armadillos, muskrats, alligators, wood ducks, pelicans, white-tailed deer, foxes, snakes, and skunks. The farther north the steamboat went, the more stands of pine and hardwood trees Daniel would see, lining the edges of the river and the bayous. Wildflowers thrived everywhere. Orchids in particular impressed Daniel. Chirping sparrows and red-cockaded woodpeckers nested in the trees with hundreds of other species. Waters teemed with fish and turtles.

The river was full of traffic. The *Lady* passed keelboats propelled by men half-horse and half-alligator in their endurance as they worked upstream. Daniel quickly determined that the keelboat men had a much easier job coming down the river; they had only to keep in the current and, rarely, to push the boat off a sandbar. They were free to drink and play cards, and fish and rollick and shoot and sing and dance juba. American passengers told Daniel that the settlers along the river regarded the keel men as a torment and a terror. With the force of a tornado they would roar through a peaceful settlement, drunk and pleasure-seeking, bent on fighting and finding women. Even religious camp meetings were never safe from their assault.

A leathery faced man dressed in animal skins stood near Daniel as he moved to the starboard side. Contemplating Daniel's fascination with the river, he began a conversation.

"Yer not from these parts, are ya stranger?"

Daniel looked into the man's searching brown eyes, set deep in their sockets. "No, sir. I'm from England. There's more than a hundred of us on board."

The man shifted a pint of whiskey from his right to his left hand, and offered Daniel a handshake. "Name's Donald Miller. English immigrants, eh? Ya'll talk funny. Where ya headin'?"

"Way up north. Nauvoo, Illinois. I'm Daniel Browett."

"Mormon?"

For a brief moment, Daniel's thoughts swirled into darkness. "How did you know?"

The man laughed. "I'm Missourian myself, from St. Louee. Trapper by trade. Most of us up in that country are familiar with Mormons. Most folks up there hate Mormons. You all kin relax, I'm not one of 'em. I'm friendly."

Daniel let out his breath. He had heard of the Missourians.

Miller let his arm sweep out toward the river. "Ain't nobody but Uncle Sam could afford such as river as the Mississip'."

Daniel sensed the half-drunk Missouri trapper was somewhat of a character.

"I lived along the Mississip' for years. Every evenin' before supper I lowered my tin bucket and drank that thick brown fluid 'til every drop vanished. Keeps my health a-going good. No need to filter it. It scours out your bowels. Stand in the sun five minutes and you'll find the water coming out of ya at ever' pore, beautifully filtered. Yer stomach will be converted into a sand bag, and ya can hear the gravel rattle as ya walk."

Daniel gasped. The water looked muddy.

"Now's the time to try some," Miller said, grabbing a bucket. "Good water in your system might prevent an onset of cholera. If the cholera don't kill ya, the doctor's favorite dose will, that's fer sure. Twenty grains of calomel, laudanum, camphor, and brandy. I'll get ya some of our wonderful Mississip' water."

"No. That's fine. I believe you." Daniel waved him off.

Ignoring Daniel's gestures, Miller set his pint down and reached over the edge of the riverboat. He dipped the five-gallon wooden bucket into the river. The strength of the current and the weight of the rapidly filling bucket, combined with Miller's sense of balance, pulled the trapper into the river. A stream of oaths came out of the man's mouth as he splashed his arms and legs.

"Help that man!" Daniel yelled, pointing to the floundering Missourian.

The pleas caught the immediate attention of Thomas Bloxham and Robert Harris, tending to their wives and children at the same edge of the boat, twenty or thirty feet away. As Miller swept past, Thomas and Robert reached out and pulled the man to safety.

Miller stood to dry himself. "An ordinary man would've drowned. I'm quite the excellent swimmer, ya see."

Daniel laughed. "The two men who helped you are my friends."

"More Englishmen?" He quickly scanned Robert and Thomas. "What'd I do with my bottle? I'll share with ya, by cracky."

"No thanks," Daniel said, holding up a palm. "But I'll try the river water now. Where's the bucket?"

Miller cast his eyes down the river. "Gone. But no matter. There's plenty a buckets." He spied one, and reached.

Daniel beat him to it. Holding onto Robert, he dipped it into the river, withdrew it, and took the first drink.

"Scours out your bowels, don't it?" Miller said, his eyes dancing.

Daniel nodded and laughed again.

The trapper continued his chattering. "I once traveled down the river in a steamer with a man, a mare, and a two-year-old colt. A sudden careen of the boat sent the man and his colt into the river, just like what happened ta me. As he rose puffin' and blowin', he caught holt of the tail of the colt, not having a doubt that the natural instinct of the animal would take 'im to shore. The old mare took a direct line to shore, but the frightened colt didn't follow and swam downstream. I sez to him, let go of the colt and hang onto the mare. The man sez back to me, it's mighty fine, you telling me to leave go of the colt. But to a man that can't swim, this ain't exactly the time for changing horses."

Miller laughed a lusty laugh.

Eight-year-old Charles Bloxham stood with his jaw wide open.

Seeing the boy's bewilderment, Miller began again. "Saw the biggest alligator of my life just now, while I wuz in the water."

Both Charles and his cousin Joseph gasped. All they had seen were birds—robins, crested flycatchers, redwing blackbirds, yellow-bellied sapsuckers, purple martins. And thousands of ducks and geese.

"I had a mighty impulse to destroy 'im, but it seemed to me that killing 'im with me bare hands would be too good fer 'im. The alligator boat will get 'im."

"An alligator boat?" Charles exclaimed.

"To dredge out alligators with. They're so thick as to be troublesome in these parts. I betcha I ain't got none in jolly old England, now have ya?"

Charles gave his father an absent look.

"Dang gummed things are everywhere, 'specially where the river's wide and shoal, like Plum Point and Stack Island, places we call alligator beds. Hard to read, alligator water. Ya can tell a wind reef straight off by the look of it, and a sand reef, that's easy. But an alligator reef doesn't show up worth anything. When ya do see it, the devils have swapped around so's, nine times in ten ya can't tell where the water is. They's so thick sometimes, they just scoop 'em up."

"What do they do with them?" Thomas asked.

"Take 'em to New Orleans. Make shoes out of their hides. Best durn shoes in the world. Last five years. Don't absorb water."

"You boys stay away from the sides of the boat," Robert warned.

"Good advice," Miller added. "Don't be dinner for a gator."

Thomas was curious. "What else is in that river water?"

"Next is a true story," Miller said, finding his bottle. "On the way down I wuz fishing over the side. Catfish loves frogs. We stopped at Vicksburg to take on wood, so's I went to the swamp to find me some frogs. It was fruitless. I wuz about to give up when I saw a big ole water moccasin trying to swallow a frog. I tried ta pull the frog away, but the snake held onto its meal. I poured some whiskey down the snake's mouth and he slipped away, sort of giddy like. That was one frog. I needed more. As I wuz a looking fer more frogs, I felt a tap on my boot. The snake was back with another frog in its mouth, looking fer a drink."

Miller spurted another lusty laugh.

Robert laughed with him.

"Water moccasin?" Thomas asked.

"Or cottonmouth. Pit viper kind of a snake. Big ones are six feet long, dark olive blackish color. Deadly venomous. Lurks around in the water. Might be on yonder branches, hanging over the water. Eats anything."

Dianah's skin turned green. "Thomas. Get those children away from the side of the boat."

When the *Lady of New Orleans* ran low of wood and pulled alongside the banks of the river near Donaldsonville, it was cold, dark, and raining hard. By lanterns and candlelight, Robert, Daniel, Thomas Bloxham, and seventeen other Mormon men, after being roused from their sleep by the mate, walked a plank that had been thrown out. The plank led up a nearly perpendicular bank, about twenty feet high. There they found a woodpile, offered for sale by a farmer who had been clearing his land. Each man placed four or five pieces of cottonwood and cypress on his shoulder and trudged warily along the narrow plank, taking in a total of six cords. Between the bank and the plank was a space of about fifteen feet, covered with mud so soft that many of the billets sank out of sight.

"Throw some blocks of wood in that mud!" the second mate yelled. "Make a path! Hurry! Time's a wastin'!"

The extra noise made by the wood crew did not awaken many of the children of the deck passengers on board, who had been put to sleep anywhere possible, on barrels, crates, and boxes. Within minutes, lightning flashed, a thunderclap shook the area, and the skies poured down rain.

TUESDAY April 20 – Several of the sailors wept when we took final leave of the Echo, in fact all of us had very solemn feelings. Three of the sailors promised to get baptized. We had a nice farewell talk with the captain. Perhaps he will be baptized some day. All luggage and passengers were on board the steamship about 2 o'clock. Departed New Orleans on the *Lady of New Orleans*. Great paddles whip and churn the water. The steam engine makes a colossal breathing sound. Mate says our steamboat is 167 feet long and 25 feet wide, and rated at 220 tons. Great deal of thunder but the country all up the river looked very fruitful. About 10 o'clock the mate came around to order our berths. We have iron rails for bedsteads; some will sleep in hammocks, others will be forced to sit up all night having no place. Some berths are very near the boilers and sometimes the people nearly suffocate with steam and in a few minutes the boat would take a turn and the wind would blow cool breezes in.

WEDNESDAY April 21 – Cool day, some rain. Passed Natchez. Took on wood two times. The American passengers are a mixture of backwoodsmen, farm hunters, buffalo hunters, Indian squaws, traders, US soldiers, Quakers, etc. Henry has regained consciousness. He looks to be recovering.

CHAPTER NOTES

In the 1840s, the water of the Mississippi was of remarkable purity. Ships leaving New Orleans for Liverpool filled their casks with the water, which had the reputation of keeping longer at sea than any other water known to seafaring men.

43

WILFORD WOODRUFF HAD HIS HOPES up for a more pleasant trip across the Atlantic the second time around. He was on the *Rochester*, watching it being towed down the River Mersey on a misty April morning. After fifteen months in England, he was on his way back to Nauvoo. His missionary labors harvested many souls into the gospel net. He had served in the Potteries, in London, and in the three-county area of Gloucestershire, Herefordshire, and Worcestershire, where he had converted six hundred former members of the United Brethren in just a few months.

"Well, here's where we find out if we've acquired our sea legs again," he told his berth mates, Elders Brigham Young, Willard Richards, Orson Pratt, John Taylor, Heber C. Kimball, and George A. Smith.

With a mournful shake of his head, Brigham Young said, "I don't want to get seasick again. If I do, just throw me overboard." He recalled his first trip, when his body had become so weakened from the effects of ague and seasickness combined.

"We have to expect it, I guess. It's still the stormy time of the year," Wilford laughed. "We'll ask the Lord to send a whale and have it spit you up on the shores of New York. You'll probably beat us there by three weeks."

That remark brought a chorus of laughs from the rest of the Brethren.

After a few minutes the conversation turned to a more serious tone when Brigham asked the group, "A year or two from now, when we look back, I wonder how many saints from the British Isles will have heeded the call to gather to Zion and settle in Nauvoo?"

"I think up until now a thousand saints," answered John Taylor, "according to records I've been keeping." The others quickly agreed.

Knowing that the *Echo* passengers were already in Nauvoo or getting close, Wilford thought about his missionary efforts among the United Brethren. He wondered about a man named Phillip Helot, a former lay preacher with the United Brethren, and the only lay preacher that had not joined the Church. Someday he hoped to find out if Mr. Helot tried to "resurrect" the United Brethren congregation, joined another church such as the Methodist or Baptist, or became a recluse. He also wondered if there had been some issues in Helot's personal life that kept him from feeling the Spirit.

Reaching into his satchel, Orson Pratt pulled out his journal and began writing:

It was with a heart full of thanksgiving and gratitude to God, my Heavenly Father, that I reflected upon His dealings with me and my brethren of the Twelve during the past year of my life, which was spent in England. It truly seemed a miracle to look upon the contrast between our landing and departing from Liverpool. We landed in the spring of 1840, as strangers in a strange land and penniless, but through the mercy of God we have gained many friends, established churches in almost every noted town and city in the kingdom of Great Britain, baptized between seven and eight thousand, printed 5,000 Books of Mormon, 3,000 Hymn Books, 2,500 volumes of the Millennial Star, *and 50,000 tracts, and emigrated to Zion 1,000 souls, established a permanent shipping agency, which will be a great blessing to the saints, and have left sown in the hearts of many thousands the seeds of eternal truth, which will bring forth fruit to the honor and glory of God, and yet we have lacked nothing to eat, drink or wear; in all these things I acknowledge the hand of God.*

44

AMONGST ROUSTABOUTS AND crewmembers, Captain Andrew Lloyd had the reputation of being the most prolific curser and therefore the most feared man on the Mississippi. His mastery of invective had a phenomenal breadth and versatility. In five minutes, it was said, he could shrivel any man without repeating a single oath. He seemed always in a fight, trying to cut a rival's time, or bankrupting his opposition. He liked to crowd other boats, but he didn't like to be crowded. He was known to drop a tub of lard into the boilers for an unexpected spurt of power, sending the gauges beyond maximum. He was known not only to fire rifle shots at opposing riverboats, but also to fire his cannon across the bow of another, for no reason than to irk the competitor and put on a show for the gallery. He sometimes refused to take freight on if he didn't like the shipper or the consignee. He was once sued for declining freight. A judgment in the Circuit Court went against him. Lloyd carried the case to the Supreme Court, but the verdict was sustained. Lloyd had to pay $3,000 in damages.

He had a favorite saying: "What's the use of being a steamboat captain if you can't tell people to go to hell?"

With the *Missouri Clipper* not far behind, the *Lady of New Orleans* approached Baton Rouge in a dark rainstorm with her furnaces roaring. The hungry monster needed fuel.

"Lively, men, lively!" cried the mate. All twenty-five Negro deckhands, stripped to their waists, joined by the twenty Mormon wooders, poured onto a muddy bank and attacked a pile of wood.

Load by load, pyramids of wood were carried to the Lady.

"Lively, men!"

A cry came from Captain Lloyd, standing on the hurricane deck. "Here she comes, round the point!" As to compel impossibility, the captain rang the starting bell. "We've got enough wood. We'll not be passed again, by thunder!" The two steamboats had passed one another three or four times in a contest of gamesmanship, picking up cargo, and stopping for wood.

The *Clipper* was belching smoke from both stacks.

The captain roared. "Tumble it in! Rush it! Damn the rest!"

The mate looked helplessly at his captain. *Is there enough wood to make it to the next stop?*

Again, the starting bell rang. With the *Clipper* hard on astern, an order was heard. "All hands aboard!"

Lines were let go. Planks were shoved in.

"Fireman, feed the furnace!" Barrels of combustibles were thrown into the flames at the captain's command.

"She's coming alongside!" someone screamed.

With a fear that the *Clipper* would crush the *Lady* to the bank, the captain reached for his rifle. He fired three warning shots into the air and screamed a stream of oaths. Narrowly missing her target, the *Clipper* steamed by.

The captain was thinking of Natchez, the city on the high bluffs, known for its crime and profligacy. He would overtake the *Clipper* before Natchez.

Daniel Browett cringed. He sensed that he had put his Mormon passengers on the wrong boat.

While Captain Lloyd dined in elegance on the upper deck, trapper Donald Miller was entertaining the Mormons as Hannah, Elizabeth, and Dianah prepared a lunch of dried horsemeat, corn pones, and water. A dark rainstorm was pelting the riverboat. Visibility was less than fifty yards.

"Why's a steamboat a 'she'?" Miller asked the women, constantly sipping on his pint. Plantations lined both sides of the river.

"I've often wondered," Hannah said. "But it hasn't been one of my top priorities to find out."

"Lucky fer you I'm here on this steamboat with ya," Miller said, glassy-eyed and laughing. "It's 'cuz no two of 'em act alike."

Hannah raised her brows while Miller tilted his head back and laughed, letting his belly bounce.

"And 'cuz they need a little touchin' up with paint now and then, to look just right." He roared again.

Elizabeth and Dianah broke out into laughter.

Miller was not finished. "Oh, tis true. One time a man built a freak steamboat so homely and awkward-looking that everyone referred to it as 'it'."

Dianah chuckled. "That's all?"

Miller took another swig. "Ah hah! Got one more. 'Cause it takes a smart man to manage her."

Daniel scoffed. "Does that describe Captain Lloyd?"

"Dunno. I suppose he's a smart one, but from what I've heard, he's a corker."

Daniel folded his arms. "Time for a blessing on the food. Robert?"

"Where are Joseph and Charles?" Robert asked.

"Getting water," Dianah said. "Go ahead. They'll be right back."

Robert blessed the food.

"Let me give a blessin'," Miller said, his eye twinkling.

Daniel shrugged a shoulder.

Miller hung his head. "And ta add what these Mormons have said, Oh Lord, bless the poor. Give to ever' poor family a barrel of pork. A barrel of flour. A barrel of sugar. A barrel of salt. A barrel of pepper."

Daniel arched an eyebrow in disbelief.

Miller hesitated. "Oh, hell no, Lord. That's too much pepper."

Daniel opened his eyes in shock. He was about to reprimand Miller, who was enjoying a good belly laugh, when he received another shock. Little Joseph Harris came running toward their makeshift table, two barrels of molasses. The boy's face had terror written on it.

"Father! Mother! Charles fell into the water."

Everyone jerked to his feet.

"Where?" Daniel asked, already taking quick strides in the direction that Joseph had come.

Joseph pointed to the rear of the boat. "He was trying to get a bucket of water. When the bucket filled up he lost his balance."

Robert was the first to arrive at Hannah's side as she ran aft to the point where Charles was last seen. Visibility was near zero. The sun had set an hour ago and rain continued to fall from a black sky.

"What is it?" Robert asked his wife.

"Joseph said Charles fell in!"

"When? How long ago, Joseph?" Robert inquired, his eyes peering into the vast, muddy Mississippi. He could see nothing. There was no sign of Charles, who had proved himself to be a good swimmer when he rescued Joseph in the Caribbean.

"Just a minute ago." Joseph had tears in his eyes.

Thomas arrived. "What is it?"

Robert regarded his brother-in-law with tenderness and alarm. "It's Charles. Joseph said he fell into the water trying to get his bucket filled."

Thomas dropped his jaw in disbelief and stared at the mighty river.

"Man overboard!" Robert yelled. "Thomas, tell the captain to stop the boat."

The instruction served another purpose. Robert knew it was suicide to jump into the icy water, unless the *Lady of New Orleans* turned around quickly. There were no lifeboats.

Thomas took a few hurried, panicked steps toward the pilothouse, worming his way through a gathering crowd. He saw Daniel. "My son is overboard. Stop the boat! Ring the bell!"

"Where are you going?" Daniel asked as he watched Thomas turn around and go the opposite way.

"Into the water after my boy."

Daniel grabbed Thomas by the arm. "Don't do it, Thomas. Let's get this boat stopped."

Arriving at the pilothouse, Daniel barked a quick order. "Stop the boat! We've lost a boy! It's this man's son," he said, pointing to Thomas.

Caruthers, a small, bald, mustached man smoking a stubby pipe, took a severe look on his much-wrinkled and weathered face. "Not without the captain's orders," he said flatly.

Thomas reached out and jerked the small man to his chest. "Stop this boat!"

"Not without the captain's orders," Caruthers repeated. The pilot clearly feared the captain more than the man who had lost his son.

"Where's the captain?" Thomas growled, knowing that the *Lady of New Orleans* was steadily chugging farther up the river while the currents were sweeping his son downstream.

"Don't know."

Daniel pulled Thomas away from the pilot. "We've got to find him quick!"

After a quick frantic search, yelling his name, they found the captain coming out of the dining room with the mate.

"What can I do for you?" Captain Andrew Lloyd asked, wiping steak grease off his lips and reddish-brown beard. He bulged in the middle, and from there his body tapered downward and upward. His eyes were dark and glazed.

"My boy fell overboard," Thomas barked out. "Stop this boat! Ring the bell!"

Captain Lloyd paused to consider the large Englishman. He narrowed his eyes. "Sorry. Our policy is never turn around or stop the boat."

Thomas's reaction was immediate. He pulled the captain to his face with his powerful arms. The captain smelled of whiskey. "Change your policy. My son is in the water!"

The mate was a husky man with a broad, flat, Slavic face. He stepped between Thomas and the captain. "Take your hands off the captain, or I'll have you thrown off the boat."

"That's where I'm going if this boat is not stopped," Thomas said, his face reddened with anger and frustration.

Captain Lloyd laughed. "You wouldn't last long. The water's freezin' with spring runoff from up the country."

Thomas gritted his teeth.

"Perhaps the *Missouri Clipper* will pick your boy up," the mate said, trying to sound consoling. "She's not far behind us. There's lots of keelboats and barges going up and down the river."

Thomas considered those words with a frightful thought. If what the man were saying were true, if he, a grown man, would not last long in the cold river, what about his young son? Chances of anyone on the Clipper even seeing Charles on the extremely wide river were remote, but it gave him a little hope.

"But there are no lifeboats," Daniel protested, reeling in disbelief at the captain's cold words. He wondered, too, if the *Clipper* would slow up to pick up a drowning boy. She was in a race with the *Lady* to St. Louis.

"You don't have to throw me off. I'm going in. I have to find my son!" With those words Thomas released the captain and ran toward the stairs.

"Wait! Thomas!"

Daniel gave the captain and his mate a condemning look and ran after his friend.

Aft again with dozens of frustrated English passengers staring into the darkness, Daniel and several other men restrained a panicked, sweaty, breathless Thomas Bloxham. Dianah was sobbing. Dozens tried to console Thomas and Dianah, including Robert, Hannah, Elizabeth, Katherine, and Henry—who had regained much of his strength.

"Don't do it, Thomas!" Robert said, holding Thomas in a bear hug with his powerful arms. Despite the threat of sure death in the waters of the

Mississippi, Thomas would have jumped into the water had he not been restrained.

"Charles!" Dianah screamed out her son's name over and over again.

There was no answer.

Dianah turned to Daniel, her voice a panic. "Use your priesthood! Dry up this river! Reverse its flow! Tell God to kill the alligators and snakes! Bring back my son!"

Daniel was speechless.

Dianah collapsed on the deck, sobbing.

THURSDAY April 22 – Charles Bloxham, eight years old, fell overboard while drawing a bucket of water. We fear he is drowned. His parents are angry with the captain for not stopping the boat. Thomas Bloxham harbors resentment not only at the captain, but at me and the Church as well. It is a sad day. Thomas still blames God for the loss of his baby back in England, and now this. Passage is tedious, sailing against the current that is very strong, the Mississippi being swollen and very muddy.

FRIDAY April 23 – Thomas Bloxham refused to have a memorial service for Charles. He clings to the hope that he will be will found alive by another vessel. He has threatened the captain, which makes it awkward for all of us. Passed several villages and had a great storm of thunder and lightning. Rain fell heavy. All passengers ran upon a sandbank and were obliged to take shelter from the storm. Provisions here are very dear all along the river. Several Negroes coming on board with vegetables, eggs, apples, pies, etc. We must furnish our own meals as we travel.

Daniel stared at the Mississippi River with a wave a guilt he could not suppress. The river of muscle and dimension, constantly eating into the earth at its banks, brimming with spring runoff, had swallowed up an innocent child, Charles Bloxham. As company leader, Daniel felt responsible for his death and for Thomas Bloxham's deteriorating attitude toward the Church.

Since the disappearance of Charles, Daniel had urged every member of the Mormon company to pray for a miracle. There remained a slight chance that the other steamboat, or even some other vessel such as a barge, had plucked the boy from the cold waters. Although the storms that had plagued their earlier first days of the trip on the Mississippi had passed, Charles' disappearance continued to cloud the minds of everyone in the company. Despite threats, the captain refused to slow the *Lady* down. Daniel felt there must be an unofficial race going on between the *Lady* and the *Clipper,* although that was probably not the only reason for the captain's obstinacy.

Standing aft where Charles was last seen, with black smoke steaming from the smokestacks overhead, Daniel raised his eyes to the gentle, wooded bluffs that lined the river. He could see an egret ornamenting the bank as the steamboat rounded a curve. Spanish moss festooned trees with a brooding grace. A flock of graceful geese flew by. Above him, on the upper deck, first-class passengers were dancing the waltz, polka, cotillion, minuet, and mazurka to orchestra music. Pleasant as these things were, they failed to revive Daniel's spirit. In his gloom he thought of Thomas and Dianah. Their spirits were even lower. They refused to hold a memorial service for their son, clinging to the hope that he was on another vessel, rescued, that he would somehow rejoin them, perhaps in St. Louis.

The grim reality, however, shook Daniel.

Charles was gone.

SATURDAY April 24 – Fine morning, we saw a great number of pelicans, wild geese and ducks. Vivid lightning in the evening. We passed the town of Memphis. Took on wood for the boiler from a farmer clearing land. We have to take on wood twice daily. We have livestock on board. Two wash basins only. A few are sick of bowel complaint from using the muddy water of the Mississippi.

SUNDAY April 25 –Buried a child on shore. Took on more wood. Still no word on Charles Bloxham. We tell everyone we see. We passed about twenty wrecks; this section of the river called a boat graveyard. Held church services.

MONDAY April 26 – Passed Cairo and Cape Girardeau on the left in Missouri. It is a truly interesting scene to pass up the river. We often thought of the crowded population of England, and those who cannot get a foot of land in all their lifetime. Here we travel many hundred miles and see little but forests and no one to occupy it, and the best of land, from New Orleans and beyond.

TUESDAY April 27 – Fine morning, passed a large rock – the Devil's Oven in the midst of the river; high hills on the left bank. The river is often very shallow and it requires much care in managing the boat. Five people were scalded accidentally when condensed steam was released from the boiler.

CHAPTER NOTES

The death of Charles Bloxham on the steamboat is fiction. However, Thomas and Dianah Bloxham did lose a child by that name, either in England, during the trip to Nauvoo, or in Nauvoo. Research fails to yield how and when the child died, and where he died. So the author chose to have Charles die in the steamboat accident. Such deaths were common.

45

ST. LOUIS, FOUNDED IN 1764 BY Pierre Laclede, occupies a strategic position on the Mississippi, just below the Missouri and Illinois rivers. After the explorers, missionaries, and trappers, the settlers came—many by steamboat. It was here that a break in steamboat traffic occurred. Cargoes from the large lower-river boats were reloaded onto lighter-draft vessels for transport upriver. The city's early growth came from the fur trade, and it quickly became the gateway to the West.

To Daniel, the St. Louis levee and wharves bore a strong resemblance to the New Orleans wharves in their confusion and bustle. All along the foot of the wharf, like a row of monstrous wedding cakes, stood more great steamboats with their tall stacks. Black smoke belched out of half of them, slowly dissipating into the otherwise clear blue sky.

In the gloom surrounding the missing Bloxham boy, Daniel could hear bells ringing from the steamboats and sweating Negro stevedores singing and swearing as they rushed bales, hogsheads, and barrels over the gangways. Drays rattled the cobblestones. Beaux in their beaver hats and belles in their crinolines arrived in fancy carriages. Hackney coaches dashed to the water's edge. Clerks scurried about with fluttering notebooks. Floating palaces, keelboats, and barges lined up for miles along the levee, taking on and discharging cargoes and passengers. This was St. Louis, where the Mississippi River met its two most important tributaries, the Ohio and the Missouri. Surely, Daniel thought, there would be no trouble finding a steamboat for a hundred and nine passengers bound for Nauvoo, Illinois.

A hundred and seven. Tragically, Nancy Eagles and Charles Bloxham were no longer in the count. Daniel thought again. A hundred and eight. Hannah's baby.

"Let's split up again," Daniel suggested to his six counselors as they disembarked the *Lady of New Orleans*. "With luck, we may find a boat leaving tomorrow or the next day."

Each man had developed a strong dislike for Captain Andrew Lloyd, who had proved to be a man of greed and no compassion. For the past several days they had spoke of his stubborn refusal to search for Charles Bloxham, and how different the man had been than the captain of the *Echo*.

In their search for a steamboat to take them from St. Louis to Nauvoo, the committee had resolved that the personality of the boat's captain was more important than the boat itself. They hoped there would be several steamboats to choose from and at first glance, that appeared to be the case. Nine could be counted. There were boats painted white trimmed in green, white trimmed in blue, yellow trimmed in black. Several had great semicircle boxes housing the paddle wheels flaunted with painted pictures of landscapes, sunbursts, and other ornate pictures. Some of the sky-reaching smokestacks were cut to resemble out-spraying fern plants.

As the committee members pondered the huge selection, Daniel barked orders. "Brother Harris, you come with me. Brother Cheese, go with Brother Wilding. That leaves Brother Lavender, Brother Jenkins, and Brother Ellison in the third group. My group will take the north end. One of you go south, the other stay in the center section of the wharf. Your assignment is simple. Nauvoo is our destination. But try to find an agreeable captain. And spread the word about the Bloxham lad."

As the three groups went their separate ways, Elizabeth disembarked with Hannah and her children, determined to see this first-rank commercial and mercantile Missouri city and its sights. Other passengers had already told them of St. Louis' prosperity from the fur trade and as an outfitting station for wagon trains set out for the Far West. They and several ladies of the Mormon company were anxious to see the markets, opulent homes with galleries and planted gardens, the Old Cathedral of Saint Louis of France, and the Chouteau Mansion.

More important, they would also spread the word about the missing boy, Charles Bloxham.

Still in deep mourning, Thomas and Dianah went ashore clinging tightly to their four remaining children. Their mood had turned angrier amid talk that the pilot and captain had preserved their professional reputations by getting the *Lady of New Orleans* to St. Louis in near record time, beating the *Missouri Clipper*, which could be seen churning up the river now. Thomas and Dianah had nothing on their minds except to wait for the Clipper to dock, and ask if they had picked a boy out of the river. If the answer were "no," they planned to ask every other vessel coming into St. Louis until they had to leave for Nauvoo. Dianah could not rid her mind of alligators, water moccasins, and other river creatures.

Everyone in the Mormon company realized that Thomas and Dianah were still in the initial shock over their boy's loss, and out of anguish and despair they refused to believe he had actually drowned. James Pulham, who had finally pulled himself out the emotional turmoil surrounding Nancy's death, had tried many times to console the Bloxhams, but they were not ready.

Daniel had assigned several other members of the Mormon company to make similar inquiries and to post "Missing Boy" bulletins all over town. Others were to give the hand-written bulletins to passengers on steamboats departing for New Orleans. Daniel quickly learned that some seventeen hundred steamboats arrived in St. Louis last year.

"At least there is one consolation," Henry Eagles told Thomas as they watched the *Missouri Clipper* approach.

Thomas gave Henry a blank stare.

"The boilers didn't blow up," Henry said. "We could've all been killed."

Henry rubbed the still-tender knot on his head.

Thomas said nothing, but Dianah responded to Katherine. "Your husband is right, Sister Eagles. I guess we should be thankful to have arrived safely here in St. Louis." She thought of the day when several passengers had been scalded by steam. The boilers had overheated because of the race between the two steamboats. Luckily, none of the injured was a Mormon.

As the *Clipper* approached, the pilot and captain of the *Lady* led a robust chorus of taunting cheers, and passed free whiskey to crewmembers. Immediately the crewmembers were hurling foul imprecations at the approaching, losing challenger. Some tossed chairs, fire buckets, axes, and timbers into the air to celebrate their victory.

Thomas could sense how rival pilots and captains were like gamecocks, ready at all times for a fight or a race that might end in a fight. It was no wonder that the captain had not stopped the boat when Charles fell in, that the Lady had taken precarious shortcuts through narrow chutes during the journey. He recalled how shotguns had been brandished by crewmembers each time the *Clipper* had drawn close, meant to menace the rival pilot and captain.

Thomas thought how he would like to get Captain Lloyd alone in a darkened street somewhere in St. Louis and use the butt of a shotgun to cave his head in.

"I'll join you later," Henry said to Katherine, his eyes filled with curiosity.

"Where are you going?" his wife asked with fear-struck eyes. She did not want a repeat of what had happened to Henry in New Orleans.

"I'm going to help spread the word about Charles," he said, flashing his wife a contemptuous smile. "Stay with Thomas and Dianah, or join Hannah and Elizabeth." He pointed to his sister, and let his eyes scan a collection of stevedores, settlers, trappers, and Indians.

"You ought to go with someone," Katherine warned.

"I'll be fine," Henry said. "Give me some of our money."

She handed him a few English coins. "That's all you get." She wished he would go with the other Mormon men, who not only were looking for a Nauvoo-bound steamboat, but shopping for firearms, stoves, and iron to make wagons with.

Henry mumbled to himself and walked away thinking of the forty pounds that members of the Mormon company had given to him and his wife to make up for the money that had been stolen from him in New Orleans. It was only a portion of what he had originally, but he regarded it as enough to stake himself to a new life in America, even if it had to be here in St. Louis instead of New Orleans. If he could find an opportunity, there would be a way to wrest the money from his wife.

Henry Eagles had already heard the rumors of America's abundance, the fertility of the western country, from the hundreds of other deck passengers on the *Lady of New Orleans.* He had spent long hours visiting with immigrants and settlers after he had regained consciousness.

In Henry's mind, America was a land flowing with milk and honey, bearing all the riches of the earth. One option that came into his mind as he saw young adventurers walking alongside their loads—indispensable furniture, seeds and supplies, guns, heirlooms, as well as a horse or two and sometimes a cow—would be to follow them west, along the Missouri River. His mind became overwhelmed with the colors of myth, legend, and opportunity.

Along the water's edge Henry saw a large boat containing several families that had joined together for the trip up the Missouri River, a copy of the *Missouri River Navigator* in the hands of one of the men. The man was reading a detailed account of the channels and the shoals in each section of the river, with here a sandbar and there an eddy. Tow-headed kids played on the wharf while their parents loaded the boat.

Henry's impression of the riches of middle America was further confirmed as he watched steamboats, flatboats, and keelboats being loaded and unloaded with cargo: barrels of flour, whiskey, apples, cider, peach brandy, butter, lard, beef, feathers, and rope yarn. Pork in bulk, bale rope, bagging, venison, bacon, tame fowls, horses, cattle, and slaves. Also bales of cotton, wool, and hides; kegs of salted fish, cases of wine, bags and barrels of spices, bearskins, steel, sugar, fish oil, pepper, rice, molasses, coffee, indigo, logwood, pig copper, furs, and crockery.

Surely, Henry reasoned, there was opportunity for a man like him to become wealthy in farming, shipping, trading, or manufacturing in or around St. Louis. Perhaps he had lucked out. Perhaps there were more opportunities in St. Louis than in New Orleans.

"Care for a plug of tobacco, Englishman?"

Henry turned to face an old trapper dressed in stained buckskins. He had a long, thin, deeply scored red face with high cheekbones, crinkling black hair streaked with gray, bloodshot eyes, and a sharp nose.

"Never tried it before," Henry said, eyeing the old man with suspicion. It would be a long time until he would be able to trust anyone.

"Take a wad, like this." The man opened his mouth to reveal tobacco-stained teeth, several of them missing.

Henry followed the man's lead, flinching at the odd taste.

The old man spat an evil looking spittle onto the ground and laughed. "Where ya headin'?"

"We just arrived on a steamboat. I'm in a group heading for a place called Nauvoo, up north. But I think I'll stay here, or settle somewhere nearby." That's all Henry wanted to reveal. He felt uncomfortable about both the man's questions and the wad of tobacco.

"Ya must be one of them Mormon pukes, then," the man said, his eyes narrowing with hatred.

"Not me," Henry said, regretting he had mentioned Nauvoo. "I'm just traveling with them. Like I said, I want to stay here, or maybe head up the Missouri River."

Henry began to feel sick and dizzy.

"Since you're not Mormon, I'll give ya some advice. Don't buy a used boat from just anybody. There are those who would sell ya a boat made of worm-eaten timber and unsound plank. I've seen dozens of immigrants shove off in craft so poorly and hastily caulked that it would spring a hundred leaks when they had been in the water only a few hours."

Henry regarded the old man with a fetching grin. "When do I spit?"

"Maybe ya better spit now. You're turning green, Englishman."

Henry spit and coughed.

The old man laughed through his gray beard. His buckskin trousers hung loose on his withering legs. "If ya go upriver, ya need to watch for Indians and white outlaws. Indians use hellish devises to lure passin' boats ta shore. They compel white captives ta stand on the bank and plead to be rescued. Once ya go to shore Indians will swarm ya."

Henry spit again with a jerking motion. He shot the man a venomous look, cringing at the tale.

"White outlaws are even worse. They overwhelm even boatloads of immigrants, rob 'em, hold 'em prisoner, torture 'em, then finish 'em off by slittin' their bodies open and stuffin' 'em with stones so they will sink into the river."

The tobacco had given Henry a headache and he blinked hard to adjust his eyes. With a pained expression, full of paranoia and inadequacy, he said, "Maybe I'll stay here in St. Louis."

"Just don't hang around the Mormons. Soon the word will spread around and there will be trouble. Missourians don't like Mormons. You'll learn that soon enough. The only good Mormon is a dead Mormon."

Henry gasped at the threat. "I've got to find my wife. Thanks for the information."

"Have a nice day, Englishman."

Henry drew a heavy breath, spit the wad of tobacco from his mouth, and rambled toward the *Lady of New Orleans*. The chill of an afternoon breeze washed over him as he contemplated what he had learned in such a short time. Coupled with what had happened to him in New Orleans, he suddenly felt overwhelmed and insecure. His stubbornness about staying with the group all the way to Nauvoo was melting.

When Henry arrived at the levee he was surprised to see Daniel and his six assistants huddled together, with other Mormon men surrounding them.

Another steamboat, the *Goddess of Liberty*, was chugging alongside the *Lady*.

"Henry!" Daniel's voice was friendly and forgiving. "We lucked out. We found a boat that's headed for the upper Mississippi. It will take us to Nauvoo. We're going to start transferring our things onto her."

"She looks brand new," Henry said, spitting again, wishing he had a drink of something to rid the tobacco taste from his mouth, like New Orleans brandy.

Daniel responded with a clever smile. "This is her second trip up the river. She was built just this year, all two hundred and forty-eight tons of her."

"Do we leave tonight?"

"No, thank goodness. Tomorrow at two o'clock. That will give us time to buy enough food for the remainder of the trip."

"How many days?"

"We'll arrive there Saturday sometime."

Still hiding his insecurity over his conversation with the old trapper, Henry nodded his head in agreement and bit down on his lip. He had to make a quick decision. If he loaded his personal belongings on the other steamboat, it would commit him for the final leg of the trip. No St. Louis. At least the quick transfer would make it less likely Missourians who hated Mormons would cause much trouble.

Henry stepped onto the *Goddess* as soon as she docked, curious to see her interior, especially the upper decks where expensive cabin passage was accepted.

What he saw astonished him, the same as the hotel lobbies in New Orleans had done: a saloon that was the dominating feature of a magnificent three-hundred-foot long cabin, eight marbled columns, rich carpet, crimson berth curtains, ornamental paintings, ornate chandeliers, furniture of mahogany and rosewood, upholstered with velvet, shining mirrors. From every beam, fretwork and open latticework hung down. Opulent staterooms. Luxurious washrooms, barbershop, nursery, pantry, kitchen, and service rooms.

Henry could visualize himself as a sixteen-dollar cabin passenger gambling in the saloon, feasting on baked pork and vegetables in the dining room, sipping on brandy smashes and gin slings in the barroom, taking a selection of desserts and pastries to his room, and dancing with the ladies to the music of an orchestra.

The sound of men in the Mormon company loading baggage onto the *Goddess* roused Henry from his trance. He heard his name called. He had no choice but to go below and help them.

WEDNESDAY April 28 – Passed many limestone rocks this morning. The whole of the country looks charming. Passed a military station about noon. About 2 o'clock we arrived at St. Louis and it is a fine place. Two large spires on the churches; one building ranging above the rest, it was a hotel called the American Hotel. Such a confusion now on board, merchant clerks coming, inquiring for letters for their houses, drovers coming with their whips wanting to carry luggage, boys with apples, fruit, hardware, jewelry, eggs, etc. In the course of an hour the boat was cleared, passengers went on shore. We changed our English money for American money. We got 5 dollars and 4-1/2 demies for the English sovereign. We had honey for two cents a pound, before from seven to ten pounds for five cents, and the finest geese in the market for fifteen cents each, butter five cents a pound. Here the saints durst not say that they are Mormons for fear of people. About four o'clock the *Goddess of Liberty*, a fine new-built boat carrying 248 tons, drawing two feet of water, came alongside of us. Our luggage was carried from the *Lady of New Orleans* into her. Passage on the Goddess of Liberty was secured for one dollar each including baggage.

46

"FUNNY HOW SOMETHING WITHOUT a head can call your name so loudly."

Robert blinked at Daniel's words as the Goddess passengers began boarding for the two o'clock departure. "What do you mean?"

"Nauvoo," Daniel said. "We'll be there the day after tomorrow. It's within our grasp. Finally, I feel Nauvoo calling my name. In some strange way, Nauvoo feels like home already, and I've never seen the place."

Daniel took a deep breath. The responsibility of delivering the saints to Zion was heavier on his mind than it had ever been, now that it appeared there was no chance of finding Charles Bloxham. Thomas and Dianah, with help from just about everyone else in the Mormon company, had questioned people on every arriving steamboat, keelboat, and barge.

Daniel felt a hand touch his shoulder.

"Hello, Mr. Browett, "I'm Captain Long of the *Goddess of Liberty.*"

Daniel turned to face a medium height man with a knobby nose and a broad flat face. "How did you know my name?"

"You brought more than a hundred passengers to my boat. I made it a point to know your name and look you up. Thanks for the business." The man's blue eyes were gleaming with appreciation. He reached to shake Daniel's hand with a strong, blocky hand and a thick wrist.

Daniel introduced Robert.

"What do you think of the *Goddess?*" the captain asked.

"I hear she's brand new," Daniel said, still giving the captain a quizzical glance, ready to compare him with the captains of the *Echo* and *Lady of New Orleans.*

"You heard correctly. We've run her up to Dubuque, Iowa, once already and back. This is her second trip."

The captain grinned proudly and went on to say that the hull of the *Goddess* was built in New Orleans, and then towed to Ohio where engines and boilers built in Pittsburgh were installed. Chatting in warm, if faintly lordly tones, he told Daniel and Robert that the boat was completed at a total cost of thirty-five thousand dollars. Robert and Daniel stared at the boat's gleaming white paint, trimmed in royal blue, set off by the black chimneys and ironwork. The paddlewheel housing was painted over by a colorful picture of Ruth gleaning the fields of Boas.

Robert said, "It's beautiful. Looks like she will last forever."

Captain Long tilted his head back and laughed. "Not hardly, Englishman. The average life of a steamboat on the Mississippi is only three years before it is either wrecked, sunk, burned or sold as junk."

"Everyone speaks highly of you, captain," Daniel said, probing his memory. "We had bad luck with our last captain, but you have been described by those I have talked to as a man of integrity."

Daniel described their trip from New Orleans and the disappearance of young Charles Bloxham. He glanced at Thomas and Dianah, standing in line with their four remaining children, and a sharp pain went through his heart.

"Unfortunately, that happens a lot," Captain Long said, an irritated look crossing his face. "Too many of our captains have a criminal indifference to the safety of passengers and their boats. Lots of them are fickle, too. They have been known to discharge and order ashore any crewman or officer on board. Many captains are sole owners of their boats and answer to no one, except to civil authorities."

"I guess with no other boat leaving this afternoon up the river we won't be racing another steamboat," Robert said, leveling a gaze at the square-jawed American.

The captain laughed. "No, but I think we'll deliver you to Nauvoo at a good time on Saturday, anyway. But we're going to have to maintain a good watch for underwater snags and rocks. Some of the snags are inaccessible to snag-removal crews that work the river. We have high water this year, and we can't be too careful. The high water will get us past the Keokuk rapids. Sometimes, later in the year, we can't get past Keokuk to Nauvoo. I've got one of the best pilots in the business. Because we're a new boat, I had lots of applications."

"We just want to get our passengers to Nauvoo safe and sound," Daniel said with a faint sarcastic note, suggesting his deep concern.

"I have a proposal," the captain stated, shifting his eyes back and forth at the two men.

Daniel forced a jocular but skeptical tone. "What kind of proposal?"

The captain bored his eyes into Daniel. "I don't have to tell you that deck passage is normally full of pretty rough characters. We constantly have to watch out for gambling disputes and fights between immigrants, and even among the deck hands. Every steamboat has its incidents of manslaughter, murder, rape, swindling, and theft. My proposal is that I want all your Mormon men to act as deputies on your deck. No pay, just authority. I'll announce it, and I'm willing to bet we'll have no problems between here and Nauvoo. What do you say?"

Daniel appeared startled. "What happens if we catch someone thieving something?"

"On the way down, the deck passengers caught a thief. They shaved his head, stripped him of all his clothing excepting his pants, beat him, and chased him from the stern to the bow of the boat threatening him with more beatings. The thief finally jumped overboard and swam to shore."

Daniel thoughtfully scratched his head. "Wow."

The captain's face sobered at the remembrance of nine years of incidents aboard steamboats. "Do you have anyone who can break up fights?"

A look of confident self-assurance passed over Daniel as he smiled at Robert, the former contender for the British heavyweight championship. He also thought of Robert's former sparring mates, Levi Roberts and John Cox. And Henry. Daniel was about to tell the captain about Robert when his eye caught the sight of a group of men walking rapidly toward the wharf, making a beeline to the *Goddess* and the passengers who were slowly boarding.

"Who are those men, captain?" Daniel asked, pointing.

The captain squinted in the direction of the oncoming men. "I know trouble when I see it, and those men mean trouble. I'll find out."

Captain Long intercepted the mob as they approached the passengers. "Need passage upstream?" the captain asked. "We have a last-minute price of twenty-five dollars each for deck passage."

"You've got Mormons getting' on yer boat," a sweaty, broad-shouldered man charged. He wore a black felt hat and a grimy leather coat with fringed sleeves.

Revulsion was plain on Captain Long's face. "That's right. A hundred of them. All paid up for a trip to Nauvoo."

He stole a glance at his passengers, many of them gathering around him out of curiosity.

"A bunch a Joe's rats?" another large, stout-looking man asked. He appeared to be the leader of the group of some fifteen men. Tobacco juice dripped from the corner of his mouth.

Robert stepped forward, eyeing the man. "I'm one of them."

"You one a Joe's rats?"

"I don't like being called a rat," Robert said, his feelings ruffled.

"You're a rat, and I'm a rat killer."

With those words the man charged Robert, brandishing a club that he had hidden behind his back. He swung the club wildly at Robert's head.

Quick as a cat, Robert instinctively lashed out with a series of blows. One to the jaw, one to the stomach, another square on the nose of the man who had charged with the club. The Missourian dropped to his knees, then crumpled to the ground nearly unconscious.

In silent shock, the other mobbers backed away.

With the other passengers quickly gathering around the fracas, Daniel grabbed Henry Eagles by the arm and whispered in his ear. "Give these ruffians your meanest look, Henry. Be quick about it."

Henry took off his cap, letting his wild black hair fall freely over his face. He narrowed his eyes at the Missourians.

Daniel said, "We've got a whole boatload full of mean Mormons, just like this man. And just like the man that knocked out your leader. You want more trouble?" He motioned to Levi Roberts and John Cox. They stepped out of the crowd, their fists balled.

The Missourian wearing the black hat shook his head, then barked an order to the others. "Pick Shreve up. Let's get out of here."

Within seconds, the mob disappeared as quickly as they had come.

Stunned at the quick ending to the altercation, Captain Long spoke to Daniel. "That's a clever way to answer my question. I guess you do have someone qualified to break up fights." He turned to the crowd.

"It's all over, folks. All aboard!"

THURSDAY April 29 – After a cool night preparations were underway about 8 o'clock taking in her cargo. Many Missourians found out we were Mormons. They called us foul names; "Joe's rats" was a common salutation we received. Several Missourians went out of their way to be critical of Nauvoo, giving doleful accounts of "the wretchedness of the place," that all the homes are built of logs and mud, that it has "knee deep" muddy streets, that poverty and starvation awaits us. They talked of the "villainy and roguery" of its inhabitants and the "awful delusion of Mormonism." They said to 'beware of old Joe Smith." At 11 o'clock the fire was kindled and at 1 o'clock the engines were in motion. We went up the Mississippi in fine style. Many villages along the way. Came to Dalton at 3 o'clock, a neat town with two church spires situated on a hill. Took on wood there. Thunder and lightning with heavy rain at night.

A crashing thunderstorm, with thick rain hissing down from skies black at night, had given way to intermittent showers as the *Goddess* steamed out of Hannibal, Missouri—a small village of about twenty homes—after a wood stop. Daniel and Robert found themselves in the pilothouse, invited there by Captain Long.

The captain smoothed his short beard and pointed to the man holding the large wheel. "If you'll watch carefully, you'll notice how the pilot negotiates the river. Downstream he always holds to the channel, following the deepest spots and strongest currents. But we're going upstream, so he holds to the shallow, slack water when rounding the bends. He constantly weaves the boat back and forth in a counter-direction to the channel. That way he avoids the force of the current and saves time, fuel, and wear on the machinery."

The statement caused Robert to heed the incessant *boom, boom, boom* of the high-pressure engines, and the shrill hiss of the scalding steam mingled with the fitful port song of the Negro firemen.

Daniel regarded the pilot, a fair-skinned, big-boned man named Russell White, with respect. The captain had told him earlier that White was the highest-paid crewmember on the *Goddess* because of his skills and experience. Even without a race with another boat, White was keeping the Goddess on schedule even though she was loaded stem to stern with cargo, some of which was destined for Nauvoo. The Mormons there had ordered flour, sugar, molasses, lard, lumber, dry goods, agricultural implements iron, and cotton. There were bags containing U.S. mail destined for the settlement, also.

"Notice that the pilot never holds the same course for as much as a thousand yards," Captain Long said. "He can't relax his attention for even a few seconds. If he did, the *Goddess* might be driven against a bluff bar, stove on a snag, or run aground on a shoal."

White, his strong hands gripping the huge wheel with a width exceeding a man's arm span both directions, bore his eyes straight ahead.

Captain Long pointed to a younger man with straight blond hair, a pink and white face, and a childish thin mouth.

"He's our cub pilot. But he only gets a chance at the boat when the waters are calm and the going is easy. In a few years he will know, just like the pilot, the depth of the water at every place along the river, the strength of the current and eddy, the contours of the river bed, the position of bars, snags, and other obstructions."

The door to the pilothouse opened. The mate, a tall, broad man with a thick neck and big chest, stepped in, his powerful right hand gripping the neck of a child. Daniel had been introduced to the mate earlier, learning that the mate had responsibility for the overall management of the boat. By observation Daniel knew that the mate handled his responsibilities over the crewmembers by brute strength and intimidation, cursing loudly when it seemed appropriate.

"We've got us a stowaway," the mate said.

Captain Long stared at a young boy whose neck was still wrapped by the mate's right hand. "Where are you from, son?"

The boy looked up through locks of blonde hair. He held a hat in his hands. He wore plaid pants and a blue jacket covered a brown shirt. "Hannibal, Sir."

"How old are you?"

"Five and a half." The boy was as calm as morning, and his shoulders were thrown back.

"Do your parents know where you are?"

"Yeh. I hitch rides on steamboats all the time."

"What's your name, boy?"

"Clemens, Sir. Samuel Clemens."

The captain smiled at the boy, and then said to the mate, "Put him off at Keokuk. We have to stop there anyway. The boy can hitch a ride back to Hannibal and be home before sundown."

FRIDAY April 30 – Another steamboat running near us had a boiler explosion. Several injuries; we picked up some of the passengers. Rainy morning. At 11 o'clock we reached Hannibal, Missouri, on the left bank, discharged some goods, and took on wood. I bought a sheep for one and a half-dollars, ready dressed. It made a fine meal for many.

PART THREE

Nauvoo

47

NAUVOO LOOMED IN THE DISTANCE, off the starboard bow of the *Goddess of Liberty.*

Reeling in disbelief that in a few minutes she and her family would arrive at their destination after a two-and-a-half-month trip, Hannah's eyes misted. She thought of all the hardships she had endured. Seasickness. The near sinking of the *Echo*. Henry's treachery. Nearly losing her husband to the cold waters of the Atlantic. Nancy's death. The birth of her baby, Thomas Eagles Harris. Joseph's brush with death, falling overboard. Henry's troubles in New Orleans. And the tragic disappearance of her nephew, Charles Bloxham.

So deep was her memory of those events, coupled with the excitement of nearing Nauvoo, that for the past hour or two Hannah had not taken much note of her surroundings. Packs of wolves darting through the oak and walnut trees lining the river. Black bears and white-tailed deer hiding behind the bushes. Bobcats and cougars slinking through the milkweed, tall grass, and the collection of spring flowers, trout lilies, bellwort, and red trilliums. Bald eagles and Cooper's hawks flying overhead. Wrens, owls, sparrows, blackbirds, warblers, and robins singing in the trees. Ruffled grouse, quail, and pheasants skulking into the serviceberry and redbud bushes. Herons, terns, egrets, geese, teal, and ducks swimming, playing, flying, and landing in and around the steamboat.

"Why is Mama crying?" Joseph asked, his innocent face drawn into a concerned frown.

Even a five-year-old boy could begin to see details of the city called Nauvoo stretched out below the bluffs of the river peninsula, a broad eight-mile curve of the land. Above the bluffs were grasslands stretching eastward, fertile flats that would soon be the farm ground of his father and uncles, Daniel, Thomas, and Henry.

"I think it's because she's so happy," Robert said to his son, drawing his wife to his chest with a powerful arm.

From the recesses of his mind, several images came to him, sharp and clear: a little log cabin on land that he actually owned; cattle branded on one horn with the iron he had brought from England, "R. Harris;" a farm with fields planted with American corn, wheat, vegetables, and fruit trees; and a milk cow, pigs, and chickens roaming near the house.

An American flag fluttered from the Nauvoo landing. Robert compared the sight to the time he was puffed up with pride at the sight of the British flag flying over Squire Hasting's opulent home in Apperley, right after the squire's farm lease elevated Robert to yeoman status. After he joined the Church and retired from pugilism, the squire quickly yanked the lease from him. A new feeling came over Robert. He was now an American. Independent. Free. Soon to be a landowner. He could see himself scooping a handful of dirt, bringing it to his nose, smelling its fragrance. Or standing on a hill, overlooking his land.

A puzzled Joseph spoke again. "Mama, if you're happy, try to smile. Please don't cry."

In a way, Joseph felt like crying himself. He missed his cousin and he was haunted by thoughts of Charles being pulled by the weight of the bucket filling with water into the dark Mississippi.

When Daniel detected a swarm of people gathered on shore singing a hymn, he raised his arms. He began leading the singing of a series of hymns that most knew from memory out of the British hymnal published nearly a year ago. His shoulders back, his chin up, his eyes bright and alert, Daniel wiped at his eyes as the *Goddess* neared the Nauvoo shore. The crushing burden of bringing more than a hundred British saints from Liverpool to Zion was about to be lifted. More tears streamed down his cheeks as he watched James Pulham, standing alone, singing the words of the hymns with the company; Thomas and Dianah huddled with their four children, their hearts still wrenching over the loss of Charles. The singing was audible above the heavy laboring of the engine, the shrill whistle of the safety valve, the crackling of the furnace, the splashing of the huge paddlewheel, and the roar of the scapepipe.

Elizabeth raised her face to the beauty of the surroundings—a peaceful settlement across the placid waters of the river. Homes and shops lining streets that went from the riverfront up a wooded hill in an orderly fashion. A landscape dotted with oak, walnut, cedar, pine, and countless small deciduous trees.

Elizabeth stood breathlessly still, wondering, waiting. She wanted to meet everyone that could be seen on the shore and thank them, hug them, find out who they were. Within that crowd were several friends—the Benbows and the Jenkins to name a few. Where would they sleep tonight? When could they obtain land and build homes? Elizabeth reached down and picked up Lizzy, who had been clutched to Hannah's skirt.

"Look, Lizzy. It's Nauvoo!" There was a stirring in her soul as she said the words and in seconds tears welled up in her eyes. "It's *beautiful,* isn't it?"

Lizzy smiled, first at her aunt, and then at her father. There was strength in Robert's words when he answered for his daughter: "It sure is, dear sister. It doesn't look anything like those Missourians said it did. Lots of mosquitoes, though."

Nearly everyone was fanning the air, swatting at the pesky insects.

"See the man standing on the dock in *front* of everyone?" Elizabeth said, squinting her eyes and pointing. In her mind she guessed that nearly a thousand persons were gathered at the dock where the *Goddess* was slowly steaming.

Hannah's eyes brightened. "Do you suppose that's the Prophet Joseph Smith?"

"I'm positive," said Elizabeth, her eyes moistening again.

While members of his company cried and waved white handkerchiefs at the hundreds of saints waiting to greet them, Daniel Browett took a determined breath as the nose of the *Goddess* touched the landing at the south end of Main Street in Nauvoo, his heart in his throat. Without realizing it, his back straightened, his shoulders squared, and a tear ran down his cheek. His brain went numb with the realization that the trip to Zion was over.

Two emotions swept over him, and they seemed to conflict with each other. A certain weariness touched every fiber of his being, and the tension surrounding his responsibility of being in charge of the Mormon company that was about to step ashore was beginning to drain. However, as he stared at the singing members of the Church on the landing, hundreds of them, Daniel could feel a curious renewal and a broad smile broke out on his face. He prepared to meet the Prophet Joseph Smith for the first time, and to renew his friendship with Theodore Turley and John Benbow.

Yet to see the details of the new city—its streets, homes, gardens, farms, and shops—Elizabeth was viewing a unique spot in the Mississippi River where tumbling rapids swept around the little peninsula. To her, it was beautiful: a place where ancient seas teeming with calcite-producing organisms had laid down layers of limestone. Advancing and retreating glaciers had left rich deposits of sediment. The great river, an offspring of the inland sea and the glaciers, had carved a channel through the limestone and built up a bed of sediment on the curving land. Generations of decomposing plants had enriched the sandy deposits, creating a marshy lowland, overgrown with trees and brush. Less than a mile inland from the river's bend, a gentle rise of some sixty feet led to a bluff and level grasslands stretching eastward.

Somewhere on this fertile little peninsula, Daniel would build Elizabeth a home on land they would actually own, and the thought of that charged her with intensity.

Daniel was not thinking about Elizabeth's new home as he took off his cap and smoothed his blond hair. His eyes were fixed on the man that he and his wife knew had to be Joseph Smith, the Prophet. Theodore Turley and John Benbow were standing next to the Prophet pointing at Daniel, talking into Joseph's ear. For a minute or two, it was as though Daniel had lost sight of the presence of the hundreds of other people. He could only see the tall, powerfully-built, sandy-haired Prophet.

Daniel felt as though he was having some kind of vision of his own. His feet seemed to be lifted off the deck of the *Goddess* and onto the landing by some spiritual power, almost walking in air, paying no attention to anyone other than Joseph, who extended a thick hand.

"Welcome to Nauvoo, Brother Browett," Joseph said with an alert, searching look. He was dressed as though he had just come from an important meeting. He had a fine, black, well-fitting coat, a buff vest, a starched dickey, and a rich-textured cravat. "Thank you for bringing another company of saints from Great Britain to Zion."

In the background, Benbow and Turley waited politely to greet Daniel. They had pointed Daniel out for the Prophet.

The Prophet's voice was soft and low yet resonating, penetrating. As Daniel continued to gaze into Joseph's blue eyes and shook his hand, he felt he was in the presence of a man beaming with intelligence and benevolence, mingled with steady cheerfulness. An unconscious smile painted the Prophet's face. But it was Joseph Smith's eyes that Daniel would never forget. They seemed to penetrate into the deepest abyss of the human heart. Those were the eyes that had beheld God the Father and his Son, Jesus Christ. Those eyes had gazed into eternity, penetrated the heavens, and given the Prophet a comprehension of worlds without number.

Concern was growing on Elizabeth's face as she became aware of the fact that Daniel was temporarily unable to speak. "We're so *honored* to meet you, and to *finally* be in Nauvoo."

Theodore Turley spoke to the Prophet as he greeted the Browetts. "President Smith, this is Sister Browett, Daniel's wife."

"I'm equally honored to meet you, Sister Browett," the Prophet said.

Joseph Smith was the most striking man Elizabeth had ever met. He looked as strong as a giant, six feet tall, and about the same weight as her brother Robert. Joseph had light brown hair, full cheeks, thin lips, and eyes veiled by long, thick eyelashes—even thicker than her brother's. Elizabeth gazed at her husband, who still seemed to be in a trance, his eyes locked onto the Prophet. The Prophet's eyes, in Elizabeth's view, were thoughtful and deep in expression, but not very large.

"Brother Turley and Brother Benbow have told me a lot about you and your husband," Joseph said, his unconscious smile widening. "Your first name is Elizabeth, I take it?"

Elizabeth responded with high-strung eagerness, overwhelmed that the Prophet was speaking to her. "Papa and Mama named me Elizabeth, but around here Sister Browett is *fine* with me." Her heart pounded. The Prophet chuckled, still gripping Daniel's right hand. Daniel broke off staring at Joseph, as the Prophet asked a question. "I know you've endured a long trip, Brother Browett. How are you?"

Daniel's trance dissolved into a warm smile. He swallowed. "Oh, splendid, thank you." Daniel swallowed again, trying to remain emotionally steady as the Prophet's eyes bored into him. "But I wouldn't want to endure it again. It's wonderful to meet you, finally." Daniel shuddered at the thought he would have to tell the Prophet about the death of Nancy and the possible drowning of Charles.

The Prophet's smile widened. "Likewise, Brother Browett. Brother Benbow has spoken highly of you, the way you helped Elder Woodruff with the work in England. Thank you for all your wonderful service as a conference president, clerk, and missionary. Elder Woodruff and the other members of the Twelve have kept me well informed in their many letters." Joseph's eyes glistened with genuine appreciation.

Again, Daniel was speechless for a few seconds. To have a man of the prophetic stature of Joseph Smith compliment and thank him caused Daniel to recoil with humbleness. Daniel's shoulders straightened again, his chin went up, and his eyes glowed. "Thank you. It was wonderful to work with

Elder Woodruff."

Joseph greeted Martha and Rebecca Browett, and then turned to scan the large crowd of English immigrants mingling with the Nauvoo saints who had come to greet them. He said to Daniel, "You'll have to excuse me now. I want to shake more hands and I am sure you want to talk to the Benbows. In a few minutes, please help assemble your company near the landing here. I have some information and instructions that will be helpful." The Prophet shook Daniel's hand again and stepped away. Brigham and Willard were greeting other families already.

As Daniel turned his attention to John Benbow, the thoughts of Benbow's benevolence, kindness, and influence overwhelmed him. It was at Benbow's farm near Castle Frome where Elder Woodruff began the work of converting some six hundred members of the United Brethren to the true gospel of Jesus Christ. Benbow had provided most of the money to print the Book of Mormon in England. After greatly assisting Elder Woodruff in the missionary work in England, Benbow's generosity had helped pave the way for at least forty members of the Church to make their way across the Atlantic to Nauvoo, departing Liverpool last September eighth on the ship *North America*, arriving in Illinois on November twenty-fifth. Theodore Turley had served as company leader.

"Welcome to your new home, Brother Browett." Tears brimmed in John Benbow's eyes as he embraced Daniel. "I think you'll love Nauvoo."

Daniel's watery eyes closed for a moment as he accepted Benbow's embrace. The stark reality of finally being in America, in Zion, swallowed Daniel's emotions and he openly wept. His breath caught in his throat, Daniel again was unable to talk for a few seconds. As he stepped back to contemplate his old friend, Daniel thought that Benbow looked remarkably the same—stocky, medium-framed, square-shouldered, bulbous nose, moustache, long sideburns, deep set eyes, graying brown hair. A month ago, on April first, Benbow had turned forty-one.

"I know all about what you have been going through these past several weeks," Benbow said. "It's a grueling trip."

Benbow looked forward to comparing stories about their ocean voyages. However, he did not look forward to explaining what had happened to his brother, William Benbow, here in Nauvoo.

"I'm grateful it's over," Daniel said, groping for words. "I can't tell you how wonderful it is to embrace you once more." He thought of the day he first met Benbow. It was seven years ago, at the Gloucestershire Fair.

Daniel took a deep breath and for the first time became aware of the pleasant spring day. The sun was shining brightly through intermittent white, puffy clouds. New leaves had formed on a canopy of oak, walnut and elm trees surrounding the landing. Elizabeth was talking with Jane Benbow. Out of the corner of his eye, Daniel could see Robert and Hannah and their children being greeted by the Prophet and his wife Emma.

"I'm sure you have a lot of stories to tell about your trip," Benbow said, fixing on Daniel his warm, brown eyes. "We'll have lots of time to do that, because you and Sister Browett will be staying with us for a few days."

A pleased look crossed Daniel's face. "Are you sure?"

"Positive. It's all been arranged." Benbow gestured toward the steamboat. "Every person stepping off the *Goddess of Liberty* will be assigned to stay in a home of a Nauvoo Church member. See those wagons and teams of horses over there? All of the luggage and the personal belongings you and others have brought from England will be unloaded here at the dock, then loaded on those wagons and taken to the various homes where the English saints will be staying. Brother Joseph has seen to it that everything is organized properly."

Emma Smith's first words to Hannah were of compassion. "I'm sorry you lost a sister during the ocean voyage, Sister Harris."

Struggling to control her four children, Hannah was stunned at the comment. She quickly scanned the wife of the Prophet. Emma was tall, stately, and had dark hair and dark eyes. An indigo blue dress with white ruffles was draped over her square shoulders. "How did you know?" Hannah asked, self-conscious of the way she looked, and probably smelled, as compared with Emma.

"Other passengers have mentioned it to me," Emma said. Her voice was soft and full of concern. "And I feel equally sorry about the loss of your nephew, the Bloxham child. I just met the Bloxhams. It's hard to understand these things, isn't it?"

A pain went through Hannah's heart as she again contemplated the loss of her sister and the disappearance of Charles Bloxham, but she managed to form a little smile to express appreciation for Emma's concern. Hannah clasped a trembling hand to her breast and tried to think happier thoughts. "Yes, It's been hard to understand and accept. I feel especially sorry for Nancy's husband, and for the Bloxham boy's parents."

"God bless you, Sister," Emma said, touching Hannah on the shoulder. Emma turned her attention to other passengers.

Forty minutes passed. Having greeted and spoken to every passenger, including all the children, Joseph Smith stepped aboard a wagon and began to speak. Robert regarded the Prophet with an awe he had given no man previously. His grip had been powerful, coming from a man just slightly larger than himself, a man with a thick neck, a broad chest, muscular arms, and a firm jaw. The Prophet's eyes had wilted Robert and he hoped that Joseph Smith had perceived the new man, the saint, the baptized Robert Harris. He shrunk at the thought that the Prophet may have perceived a vision of the old Robert Harris, Bobby the pugilist, the man who had been selfish and proud.

To Robert, the Prophet's voice was equally penetrating. Joseph began. "My tears have wet my pillow as I have thought of the hardships you good brothers and sisters have put up with on your long sojourn from England, but you are finally here. This is Nauvoo. This is our Zion. We are ready for you. We are anxious to get to know you. We have drained swamps and cut underbrush. Here by the riverfront you can see rich farmland and many homes. My home is the log cabin right over there, by the way…southwest corner of Main and Water Streets. You'll get to know all the streets and the layout of the city very soon, I trust."

The *Goddess* passengers were not aware of it, but the Prophet had spent the earlier part of the day working out details for Sunday's organization of the Teachers Quorum in Nauvoo, and had yet to attend a city council meeting to determine the location of a new burial ground and to decide what to do with the large number of dogs running loose in the city.

"You are a hundred and eighty-five miles north of St. Louis. I hope you didn't meet too many of the unfriendly Missourians there. Any missing persons, Brother Browett?"

A few of the new visitors laughed.

"You are in the Illinois wilderness and this is going to be the finest city in the state of Illinois, thanks to people like you."

Robert felt Daniel brush his shoulder. Daniel quickly whispered, "Do you think the Prophet knows about the altercation we had with the Missourians in St. Louis?"

Robert blushed, hoping that his reputation of being a tough guy, a fighter, had not followed him to Nauvoo.

Joseph spoke again. "We have been scouring the river for the sight of a steamboat carrying English immigrants for nearly two weeks, ever since the passengers from the Sheffield arrived. You folks are the third group to arrive from England via the Atlantic Ocean to New Orleans, then up the Mississippi on a steamboat."

The president of the Church of Jesus Christ of Latter-day Saints went on to relate the arrival of British saints, company by company: first, forty-one Mormon passengers of the *Britannia,* who arrived in July of 1840; next, the *North America,* 201 members, including Theodore Turley and John Benbow, who arrived in October; the *Isaac Newton,* 50 members, December; the *Sheffield,* 235 members, March; the *Caroline,* 88 members, mid-April; and now the *Echo*'s 109 passengers.

The Prophet stated that two other ships, the *Alesto* and the *Rochester,* were on their way. The latter carried the Apostles Brigham Young, Wilford Woodruff, Willard Richards, Orson Pratt, John Taylor, Heber C. Kimball and George A. Smith. The Harmony, under the leadership of Thomas Kington, was scheduled to leave Bristol in a few days.

Daniel reached to scratch his head, contemplating the vast numbers of British saints who had immigrated to America and specifically the United

Brethren converts who were already here. They included John and Jane Benbow, William and Mary Rowberry Jenkins, Robert and Elizabeth Clift, William and Mary Jenkins Parsons, Robert and Elizabeth Holmes, William and Ann Cole, William and Mary Parsons, and John and Grace Ann Parry.

Happiness lined the face of the Prophet as he concluded. "Now you have heard about enough of me for today. I know you are anxious to go with your assigned families, get some rest, clean up, and see our little city here in the American frontier, and begin plans for your own homes and purchase of property. Your host families will teach you how to acquire lots and farm ground."

A short time later a team of black horses, hooked to a farm wagon and loaded with the belongings of Daniel, Elizabeth, Martha, and Rebecca Browett plodded along a dirt road that led from the landing along Main Street. Time allowed John Benbow to give his newly arrived guests a quick tour of the city as he guided the horses up the hill to Mulholland Street, past rustic huts and cabins, then along the site where the Nauvoo temple was under construction.

"The temple committee laid the temple out just last February," Benbow said. "Workers began laying stones for the basement walls the first week in March." He maneuvered the wagon around the four-acre temple block, bordered by streets called Bluff on the East, Wells on the West, Knight on the North, and Mulholland on the South. Daniel learned that the church had paid $1,100 to Daniel Wells to acquire the entire block. He could see trenched-out corners and the semblance of stonework that would make the basement walls of the temple.

"Everyone took the afternoon off to meet the steamboat, but tomorrow the workers will return," said John as everyone got out of the wagon. "And normally there are people at work building cabins and fences, planting gardens, and working in the fields. There are more important things to do right now, and that's to take care of the Daniel Browett company of saints from England."

John Benbow smiled, his eyes glowing. "It's good to have you here, Brother Browett."

Daniel returned the smile. In Daniel's eyes, Nauvoo was vastly different than any hamlet or parish he had ever seen in England. The first thing that struck Daniel was the absence of a church or a cathedral. In England, Gothic-inspired Anglican churches dotted the landscape everywhere, their granite spires and fine stained-glass windows a permanent feature of every parish. Here in Nauvoo, there were no thatched-roof stone cottages, quaint pubs, cobblestone streets lined with shops, or market squares. Not even a castle. The only history that could be written about this place, Daniel thought, was that of wild animals and Indians.

The landscape was different, too. In England, every square acre was used for living or farming. In Nauvoo, there were hundreds – if not thousands – of acres in and around the city yet to see the soil turned by a plow. The trees, large and small, looked similar to those in the Malvern Hills and the Cotswolds: oak, walnut, poplar, aspen, hickory, pecan, locust, elm, maple, birch. In some places the brush was so thick Daniel could not see through it. There were dogwood, hawthorn, willows, and several different berry trees. As in England, wildflowers of every imaginable color were popping out every-where.

"I don't see a church, Brother Benbow," Daniel said, his eyes flitting in every direction.

John Benbow flashed another familiar smile. "We Mormons here are a little like the United Brethren and the Primitive Methodists back in England. There's not one chapel in Nauvoo and other than the temple I don't know of any plans to construct a house of worship. We hold meetings outside. Every Sunday we go to the oak grove you see just below the temple and listen to the Prophet Joseph Smith speak, and others, of course. You'll be amazed at how your understanding of the gospel and the scriptures will expand by listening to the Prophet. I can't tell you how much I look forward to our Sunday meet-ings. You'll find out tomorrow."

Daniel nodded understandingly. "How long until the temple will be completed?"

He was anxious for John and others to explain more about the purpose of temples. He could remember Elder Wilford Woodruff telling him that a temple was a "house of prayer, a house of order, a house for the worship of God, a place where ordinances necessary for exaltation could be administered, such as endowments."

From the summit of a gently-sloping bluff that overlooked the lower portion of Nauvoo and the landing where the *Goddess* had disgorged her passengers, Daniel stared at the excavations and footings, which seemed massive. Benbow had already explained that the temple was going to measure eighty feet wide by a hundred and twenty feet long on its inside dimensions, and reach a height of around a hundred and fifty or sixty feet, counting the tower.

To answer Daniel's question, Benbow raised his eyebrows. "From what I can gather, I think the construction of this temple is going to almost dominate our lives for five or six years. Think of Solomon's temple or Herod's temple—the size, the workmanship. The Prophet wants the temple to be a tribute to the Lord in its quality. The walls are going to be strong and massive, probably four or five feet thick, made with stone. It's too bad you weren't here for the general conference of the Church three weeks ago. The Prophet laid the cornerstones. There were close to ten thousand people watching."

The thought of that many people gathered in one spot in this frontier setting made Daniel's head swim, as did the requirements to build such a large structure. Nauvoo was a city of perhaps three thousand, counting men women and children. In every direction all Daniel could see were little huts and log houses. Where would his Church leaders get the resources to build a temple similar to that of Solomon? Or even similar to the cathedrals in England? Given the poverty of the saints, who would pay for it? Among the Mormons were there adequate architects, stonecutters, quarrymen, sawyers, woodcutters, carpenters, plasterers, painters, glaziers, and tinsmiths? In England, such people were abundant. The legacy proved it—London's Westminster Abbey, the Tower of London, the Gloucester Cathedral, and endless castles.

At least one thought gave Daniel peace of mind. He was excited to offer his talent as a carpenter. He knew how to build more than barrels.

All during Daniel's conversation with John Benbow, Elizabeth had been courteous enough not to interrupt, but true to her character she became a constant chatterbox again, flooding Martha, Rebecca, Jane Benbow and her niece, Ellen, and her nephew, Thomas, with a barrage of her feelings, opinions and viewpoints. She expressed how happy she was to finally be in Nauvoo and how their lives here were going to be filled with excitement and challenge. She scanned the landscape for vacant farm ground. She took a mental note of every hut and log house, envisioning how she wanted Daniel to build their home. She saw years of hard work ahead, true, but she also saw fun in building a new life, a change in the old life they had in England, and fulfillment in being a midwife and herbalist. Selection of land they could actually own and construction of a house could not come quickly enough for her, and restless, impulsive feelings stirred in her soul.

Martha was relieved to be at their final destination, but Nauvoo slightly depressed her. The vast majority of adults she had seen so far, even though they appeared enthusiastic and happy, were far younger than she was. They ranged from Rebecca's age, early twenties, to Daniel's age, early and mid thirties. John Benbow, in his early forties, was almost at the other end of the spectrum. The few older men she had noticed all had wives clinging to them. At fifty-five years of age, Martha had not given up the idea of being married again. She had been a widow for nearly fifteen years. Nauvoo, however, did not seem to offer any hope in that regard.

"What do you think of our humble little city, Elizabeth?" Jane Benbow asked. She was swathed in a bright yellow dress she had brought from England.

"It's *nothing* like I've ever seen in England," Elizabeth said without thinking, still proud of her English heritage. "All I see here is a collection of mud houses and log houses."

Compared to Jane, Elizabeth felt grimy and dressed almost inappropriately in a plain purple day dress. The trip across the ocean and up the Mississippi had been an ordeal for her.

John Benbow defended Nauvoo sharply. "Our city should not be defined by the houses we build, but by the souls we save."

Elizabeth grimaced, and then rolled her eyes at Daniel acknowledging that she had spoken the wrong words. She turned back to Benbow. "I'm sorry, I didn't *mean* it that way."

She wouldn't admit it to him, but she was sorely disappointed that she was going to have to live in a tent or a mud house for a few weeks, then in a log cabin. She had become spoiled in England during the few months she and Daniel had lived in Squire Hastings' opulent stone cottage on the farm they had leased.

Jane provided some solace. "It won't be long before you see more real nice frame houses and even some brick homes."

As everyone boarded Benbow's wagon again and the mules followed a rutty, muddy road five miles east toward Benbow's new farm, Martha patted her daughter, Rebecca, on the hand and put an arm around her. Ever since the bad experience with the sailor on the *Echo*, Martha had watched for any signs that Rebecca might be emotionally scarred. Thankfully, none had been manifest so far, but Martha wondered how Nauvoo was affecting her. England and Rebecca's other three brothers were thousands of miles away. Nauvoo was so different from Apperley, Deerhurst, Tewkesbury and The Leigh that Martha dreaded the prospect that both she and her daughter might become extremely homesick.

SATURDAY May 1 – Passed the city of Quincy about 7 o'clock this morning and in the afternoon we came in sight of the city of Nauvoo. The Prophet of the Lord and three hundred saints met us at the landing. The Prophet Joseph impressed me as a man of good judgment and possessed of an abundance of intelligence; whilst you listen to his conversation you receive intelligence, which expands your mind and causes your heart to rejoice. A number of the Brethren were ready to receive us; they kindly offered their houses. Teams with wagons took our luggage and belongings to houses until arrangements could be made for their final accommodation. Many slept in a large stone building belonging to one of the Brethren. Elizabeth and I, along with my mother and sister, stayed with John Benbow.

48

ROBERT STRODE OUT INTO THE fresh spring air, surveying his new surroundings. His ears rang with the sounds of axes, saws, and mauls as Nauvoo residents cleared land and constructed dwellings: huts, log cabins, and a few frame homes. At a nearby grassy lot, a large black oak, with its dark green, shiny leaves, crashed to the ground, a victim of the need for logs and furniture.

His eyes scanned the horizon. A few homes already took on a picture of permanency with neat picket fences surrounding them. Several one-acre lots were enclosed by zigzag worm fences, others were open. Newly planted plum, apricot, apple, peach, crab, cherry, and persimmon trees formed the makings of new orchards.

"I still feel badly that you and your wife and baby had to sleep in your little hut," Robert said as he and James Pulham followed William Jenkins through upper Nauvoo, looking at potential lots where Robert could build a home. He and Hannah and their four children had slept comfortably on a large cornhusk mattress in a new square-log cabin. William's daughter, Ann Eliza, was less than two weeks old. James had slept in a tent. Hannah was still in the little home, penning a letter to her mother in Apperley.

William shrugged his shoulders in humility at Robert and James. "It's just as warm in the hut as it is in the log house. I should mention that around here we usually refer to those huts as 'wattle' houses. I suggest you build one just like it as soon as you buy your lot. You can live it in while you build your log house." William and his wife had been passengers on the *North America*, along with John Benbow and Theodore Turley.

At breakfast, William and his wife had shared the stories of their conversion by Elder Woodruff, how Mary had sung at meetings where Wilford spoke, and the occasion when the American missionary did not have time to administer to Mary to cure her sore throat. Elder Woodruff sent his silk handkerchief instead, with instructions to wear it around her neck and her faith would make her whole. By the next day she was well again.

"We brought material to make a tent," Robert said. "Your hut is really not much more than a mud house."

William laughed. "In a way it is. It's plastered with mud. Inside is a wall made of willows and tree branches. We placed poles in the ground just a few feet apart, and then took the willows and branches and wove them basket-style through the poles to make the walls. Afterward, we plastered the walls both inside and out with mud. The thatched roof kept us dry."

"How long did you live in it?" James asked, feeling out-of-place with the two married men. He missed Nancy, whose remains were somewhere at the bottom of the Caribbean Sea.

"Just a little over a month. We were in our log house by the middle of November. When we found out we would be hosting some of the ship passengers we fixed it up again. It's not built to last very long, obviously, but we were quite comfortable while we were building our house. With your four children, you'll probably need both a tent and a wattle house, even if it is for a short time. After that, you need to build a log home. You'll have a lot of help, from me and the other English converts."

"The question is—where?" said Robert, continuing his gaze at the Nauvoo landscape. He tried not to be irritated at the swarms of mosquitoes that pestered him. When he inhaled, he had to be careful. Mosquitoes sometimes went up his nose.

"Why not right there?" William said, pointing south, across Ripley Street. "My lot is what we refer to as block twenty-eight of the Wells Addition, all platted as laid out by the Prophet and those who helped him. This area used to be an eighty-acre farm owned by Daniel Wells."

William walked across the road and stood on the property. He gestured with his arms. "This entire four-acre block is available. It's part of the first Ethan Kimball Addition. We're standing on block one of the Kimball Addition."

William took time to point out how straight the streets were laid out, following exact north and south and east and west directions, thanks to a proposal by an inspired Joseph Smith that had passed the city council. The council had divided Nauvoo into four political wards as well. Each ward had a bishop, and each bishop had the responsibility to care for the poor, organize work parties for the temple, and collect tithing. Ecclesiastically, everyone in Nauvoo attended church together in the grove or, in the case of bad weather, broke up into smaller groups to meet in the larger homes. Stake priesthood quorums were organized for deacons, teachers, and priests.

Robert eyed the property with intense scrutiny. It was only four streets east and one street south of the temple lot, which William had shown him yesterday. The block sloped gently to the south. Warm rays of morning sunshine lit many dozens of trees that dotted the four-acre tract of land. William recounted how the Prophet, after his ordeals in Missouri—including the infamous Mormon extermination order—had found a large number of exiled Church members at Quincy, the region's principal town. Joseph Smith arranged for the purchase of the Nauvoo lands on long-term credit from such speculators as the White sons, Isaac Galland, Horace Hotchkiss, George Robinson, and Hiram Kimball. Galland, in particular, had been kind to the Mormon people and charged the saints no interest on the land he was selling.

"I've got a good mind to settle right here," Robert said, hiding a feeling of insecurity that he might be making a decision that was too quick and too irrational. As a fighter, he had been daring and bold. That was his personality. There was a side of him that wanted to make a quick, clear decision, and it was manifest now. But that decision had to be right. He would hate for his wife or anyone else to later criticize his choice for a lot if there were something better. He had seen several choices in the scant time he had spent with William yesterday afternoon and this morning. *Why waste time? It's the second of May, time to plant a garden and build a home.*

"You like this block, don't you?" William said, after explaining that Ethan Kimball was an Eastern investor, and had designated more than three hundred acres of his family's holdings as Nauvoo's first addition. Within the addition, there was an eighteen-block area divided into seventy-two lots.

"I do," Robert said, still pondering. "Don't you, James?"

James nodded. "It's a good spot."

"I'm going to show it to my wife," Robert said, "and I'm going to show it to Daniel and Elizabeth."

If Robert's vision came to pass, he and Daniel could buy up the entire block and each own two lots, then share a portion of it with James. Robert would leave it to Daniel to select their farm ground.

As the men returned to William's cabin, the new immigrants learned more facts about Nauvoo. Native Americans had abandoned the land forty years earlier. The first white settlers had arrived in the 1820s. Land could be purchased on credit from the Church. The city was made up of saints who had streamed in from Missouri, plus members who had gathered from Kirtland and other places such as the New England and Atlantic states, plus some from the South—particularly Kentucky and Tennessee.

"I think I've found our lot," Robert said, locking eyes with Hannah. "It's big. Plenty of room for cabins. Tell your mother."

Hannah smiled at Robert, and then continued with her letter. "I'm telling Mama what an experience it was to meet the Prophet. She should have been here. And I plan to tell her all about the city. Nauvoo is sure a contrast to most places in England, especially Liverpool and London."

"The floodgates are about to open," Robert added. "I think thousands of British converts will come here."

"It's already happening," James said.

"And for good reason," Hannah said, "The gathering is real. Her hand moved quickly across the page with her quill pen.

Dearest Mother,

We feel thankful to Almighty God that we arrived in Nauvoo safe and well, after a long, tedious, expensive journey. Robert and I have every expectation and prospect of being happy and comfortable.

We arrived by steamer packet here in Nauvoo yesterday. The inhabitants, upon the sound of the steamboat's large bells and whistle, came to welcome us. We are temporarily staying with the William Jenkins family—I'm sure you remember them. They are not charging us a farthing.

President Joseph Smith was there to greet us. He was especially concerned about anyone who could not afford to buy a lot or build a house, however meager. Yes, we said, there are some who expended their last shilling getting here. Universal love and kindness prevails. Oh, Mother! How I wish you were here!

The journey up the Mississippi River was pleasant enough, except for one tragic incident. Poor little Charles Bloxham, a child, fell into the river on a rainy day and we are supposed that he has been lost forever. Our hearts ache for Brother and Sister Bloxham. Thomas, especially, is having such a hard time. He seems to blame the Lord for every misfortune.

And, oh, how I miss Nancy! Her husband, James, misses her so much. But his attitude is so good. I pray that someday he may find a new wife, after the proper mourning time, and have a life of happiness. I am told there are many, many widows here, looking for a husband.

About Nauvoo. It is beautiful, set on a hill just above the huge river. Meat is cheap—two pence a pound for choice pieces, one pence a pound for the others. The Jenkins family seems to have plenty of bacon and ham. Fowls one shilling. Eggs two pence a dozen. While meat is cheap, vegetables are high. It is spring and the winter storage vegetables are all gone, except for cabbage, potatoes, and turnips. But everyone seems to have plenty of cornmeal. We must plant a large garden to feed our family. Gardening is on, full drive. We will sow peas, beans, Indian corn, onions, pumpkins, cucumbers, melons, and everything we can find. Flour is under a penny a pound. Sugar five pence a pound. Wood is the firing used, and is not cheap. Milk is two pence a quart. Honey six pence a pound. Potatoes are a shilling a bushel.

Our clothing will last us for a while. But one of the first tasks will be to make new clothing for everyone. We can buy good strong cotton here at five or six pence a yard. Good print at six pence. Thread and pots are the deartest of anything here.

Everyone warns us of the ague, a fever that afflicts people here along the Mississippi.. We hope it will bypass us. Death is always such a worry, and I fear for my new child. I've already learned that this is a hard place to raise children, for a great many children died last year of summer complaint when teething.

We think we will buy a lot not too far from the temple site. Robert says he will build a temporary house out of sticks and mud, and then begin working on a nice home made of logs. Someday, I hope to have a nice frame house, or brick.

Daniel will help Robert make furniture. Right now, we have neither chairs nor tables. Or a bedstead, or a spinning wheel. We have plans to have fruit trees. The peach trees here are beautiful. We will have plums and apples, too. Robert says we must find us a milk cow right away.

I must now conclude, and shall be very glad to know if you received my letter from New Orleans. I shall rejoice to hear from you. Robert and the children unite with me in love to you. Remember me to all our family, and to my friends I left behind. Please take the time to say hello to Robert's brother, John. He prays that someday John will change his mind and join the Church. But we suspect his involvement with the pub, the Ferret's Folly, is a millstone around his neck. And I pray that my two older brothers will join the Church, also. We look forward to the day when you will change your mind, and come to Nauvoo.

I remain, my dear Mother, your affectionate Daughter,
> *Hannah Maria Eagles Harris*

Breakfast at the Benbow home consisted of plenty of bacon, eggs, fried potatoes, and heavy wheat bread with honey.

As they ate, the Browetts and the Benbows exchanged stories about their Atlantic crossings. Like the *Echo* passengers, John related that nearly all the *North America* passengers had been seasick for the first few days out of Liverpool. Sickness had even claimed Theodore Turley, who acted as president of the company, just as Daniel had done for the *Echo* passengers. Benbow told of high winds, angry seas, and a whirlpool that nearly swallowed the ship. Benbow's niece and nephew, Ellen and Thomas, spiced the story up with animated details.

Leaving the women to do dishes, Daniel followed John and Thomas out into the warm sunshine. Daniel was not as impressed with John Benbow's Nauvoo farm as he had been with the Benbow's Hill Farm back in Herefordshire, England. But Daniel knew that, given time, Benbow's eighty acres here in the Illinois frontier would eventually equal or surpass the farm in England for one reason: John Benbow owned it instead of leasing it.

"Eighty acres looks to me to be a lot of ground, a big farm," Daniel said as they strode away from the rustic log cabin they had slept in, out into the flat prairie that comprised of Benbow's farm. "Do you plan on eventually expanding it so you have as much acreage as you did in Herefordshire?"

He wondered how John felt about living in a small, crude log cabin as opposed to the spacious white mansion that he had occupied in England. At least the small cabin was stuffed with nice personal belongings that John and his wife had brought with them. As Daniel had brought his carpentry tools with him, Benbow had brought a few of his farm implements and they could be seen strewn about the yard.

"Perhaps," Benbow answered with a firm resolve, "but a step at a time.

There's a lot of work to do to prepare raw land to raise crops."

John pointed to a few fields that had been turned by the plow last fall, plowed again in the spring, and planted with wheat, barley, corn and vegetables such as potatoes and turnips. Already, work had begun to surround the farm with heavy ditches and thorn hedges. Barns and sheds were under construction.

"I'll be all summer breaking up the rest of the eighty acres. The prairie grass here is thick. One horse can't pull a plow the first time, it takes at least two, or two yoke of oxen. You can't just plow it and plant your crops. The sod has to rot over the winter. I think I'll add another eighty this fall or at least by next spring. I already have my eye on another eighty that I like."

"How did you buy this first eighty?" Daniel asked, contemplating all the things that lay ahead of him to get securely settled in his new environment.

Benbow's heart sank to his knees, and he was stone silent for a few seconds. He knew the question was inevitable, but he had dreaded it. He delayed a direct answer by explaining that his farm was in the northwest quarter of section eleven of Hancock County, and in township six north of range eight west of the fourth principal meridian. The cost, Benbow explained, was a hundred and twenty five dollars, or twenty-five English pounds.

The inevitable question came from Daniel. "Did you buy it from the county, from the Church, or from a previous owner?"

Benbow swallowed hard and looked away, a little tear running down his cheek. "I bought it from my brother, William."

Daniel had not known William Benbow very well. He knew William had been the Hanley store merchant who led Elder Wilford Woodruff from the Potteries in England to the John Benbow farm in Herefordshire in March of last year. It was a key event, because that led to Elder Woodruff's conversion of some six hundred members of the United Brethren, included John Benbow and Superintendent Thomas Kington. Daniel had met William only once, during a general conference of the church for the English saints held in Manchester last August. William and his family sailed to America on the same ship as John and Jane Benbow, and their adopted children, Thomas and Ellen.

"It will be nice to see your brother again," Daniel said innocently.

Benbow cringed. For a few seconds he was unable to form any words. Finally, still looking away from Daniel, his blank eyes staring at the Illinois prairie, he said, "I doubt that will be possible. I don't know where he is."

Daniel's jaw dropped. "I don't understand, Brother Benbow."

"William had his feelings hurt over a variety of things that we don't need to talk about." Benbow still refused to look Daniel in the eye, obviously hurt and embarrassed by what he was saying. "He bought this eighty acres during the winter. I was looking at several choices. To make a long story short, he sold me his eighty and left Nauvoo. He even left the Church. My best guess is that he took his family to Iowa—Fort Madison, I think. He's even talked about going to New York, Buffalo, or Chicago." Those were cities that John and his brother had passed through after the North America had landed in New York City last October.

Daniel scanned John Benbow again, thinking of his own experiences on the Atlantic. A black hat was pulled tightly over John's head, hiding his sad face. Clearly, John missed his brother. "Maybe William will come back, Brother Benbow. Even if it takes a few years. Who knows?"

Daniel thought about what Elder Woodruff had once told him, that Satan would use offensive remarks from others as a tool to discourage people. *If someone hasn't offended you today, you haven't gotten out of bed yet. As "natural men," we are not perfect. We have to toughen up, thicken our skins. Learn to forgive. Learn to apologize. Learn to accept apologies. Be humble and Christ-like.*

"I hope so," John said. "I pray so. I know one thing. I'm never, never going to give up on him."

The brilliant blue eyes of Mary Ann Weston Davis glistened as she watched the British square-rigged *Harmony* being released from the steamship that had towed her down the River Mersey out of Liverpool on this tenth day of May 1841. Staring into the Irish Sea, except for brief glances at Thomas Kington and nearly fifty other Mormon emigrants on board, Mary Ann felt defiant and self-satisfied. After weeks of legal bickering, she had finally won the right to take the few pieces of furniture her deceased husband, John, had made for her shortly after their marriage last year. It was safely packed in the ship's hold.

Mary Ann reached for Kington's hand.

"Thank you again for all your help," she told the forty-seven-year-old former superintendent of the United Brethren, now her Church leader for the duration of the trip to Nauvoo. Thanks to the efforts of Kington and Edward Phillips, a former United Brethren preacher, Mary Ann's vindictive mother-in-law and her lawyers had finally given in. Even though Mary Ann had told Mrs. Davis that she had forgiven her, hard feelings remained. After all, Mrs. Davis was, in part, responsible for the murder of her own son.

"I say, Sister Davis, never in my life have I met a woman as mean and vicious as your mother-in-law," Kington said, his mouth curled in satisfaction that the ordeal was finally over.

Hannah Simmons, Edward's fiancée, smiling and marveling at the green Irish coast that would soon disappear, put her thin arms around Mary Ann. "It's all over now. Relax and enjoy the voyage."

Mary Ann looked at Hannah with misty eyes, touching a handkerchief to her cheek, the handkerchief she had used to wave goodbye to the members of the Church and family members that had seen them off at the Liverpool docks. Sadly, Mary Ann's parents had not been among them. They still harbored anger that their daughter had joined the Church and considered Mary Ann an outcast.

"I'll try," Mary Ann said to Hannah, "but I need to get used to this rocking of the ship. I suspect we'll be seasick soon. That's what everyone says." She was referring to letters she had received from English saints who had already made the trip from Liverpool to Nauvoo. "For your sake, I wish Edward were on board."

"Me too," Hannah said, the sea breeze whipping her yellow bonnet. Edward was still in the Malvern Hills, serving as branch president over two branches, Ashfield and Crocutt, working as a blacksmith trying to save enough money to emigrate to Nauvoo, and taking care of his mother. His goal was to make the trip by late summer with his mother.

"I wonder how all of our friends are doing in Nauvoo?" Mary Ann wondered out loud.

Thomas Kington looked thoughtful as seagulls floated in the air above the ship. A sea breeze passed through the British flag and the more than three hundred passengers standing on the decks, bringing a heavy odor of the ocean. "I'll bet Brother Benbow has a handsome farm all plowed, tilled and planted by now. He's been there since last fall. And my best guess is that the *Echo* passengers have been in Nauvoo for more than a month."

Thomas was wrong. The *Echo* passengers had only been there ten days because of the terrible February winter storms on the Atlantic.

Mary Ann's ashen face gave Thomas and his wife a winning smile. "Just think, they've already met the Prophet. And heard him speak several times. I so look forward to that, Brother and Sister Kington."

Hannah Kington returned the smile. "We do too. And we look forward to our new homes there."

"Is that one of your dreams, to have a nice big home in Nauvoo?" Mary Ann asked Hannah, giving her an affectionate look.

Hannah felt a gush of anxiety. "That would be nice. I'll bet all the houses are new, big and wonderful. You'll need a nice home for all your furniture, Sister Davis. We'll get my husband and Brother Benbow to rally all our friends together and build you a dream home."

"I just hope we don't end up living in some kind of primitive mud house in the wilderness," Mary Ann said with a grim smile.

D

49

DANIEL BROWETT TOOK A DEEP BREATH. For a moment he com-
pared the utter sweetness and joy of the warm, spring Nauvoo day to similar
days in the Malvern Hills and the Cotswolds in England.

Broad oak and elm trees, busy with flitting and singing birds, provided a
canopy of shade from a bright overhead sun in the grove where Joseph Smith
was speaking on this Sunday, the sixteenth of May. In and around the oak
grove blossoms of every imaginable wildflower were blooming, covered with
swarming, buzzing bees. Daniel closed his eyes and let the Prophet's words
penetrate his being.

The sermon touched on free agency and the first principles of the gospel.
Faith, repentance, baptism for the remission of sins, and the Holy Ghost: "but
these were believed by some of the righteous societies of the day, but the doctrine of the laying on of hands for the gift of the Holy Ghost was discarded
by them."

Drawing huge gulps of air, the Prophet spoke in a loud voice to a crowd
of nearly three thousand persons. Daniel wondered how long it would be until
Joseph's voice gave out. Minutes later the Prophet slid into the doctrine of
election, using the ninth chapter of Romans as his basis. Nearly an hour later
Joseph Smith had touched on the fact that all men had the power to resist the

devil, and rocked Daniel with his testimony regarding God the Creator, God the Redeemer, and God the witness or Testator.

"You were right about the Prophet's sermons, Brother Benbow," Daniel remarked as the crowd slowly drifted away from the grove, back toward their homes.

John Benbow returned a gracious smile. It was the third Sunday in a row that Daniel had said the same thing. "Wonderful, isn't it?"

"Beyond words to describe," Daniel answered. "Thanks again for letting us stay with you for so long."

"You're welcome. How do you like your wattle hut?"

"Do you want to know the *truth?*" Elizabeth broke in.

"It's not so bad," Daniel said. "The weather's warm and in a few weeks we'll have our log home completed. We're starting on it tomorrow." Daniel thought about the stacks of logs that had been cut along the river, hauled to their lot, and lay curing in the sun on his lot in the Kimball Addition.

"Need any more help?" Benbow asked. The smile was genuine.

"You've got more work than you can do now with your eighty acres," Daniel responded. "Some of the *Echo* passengers have teamed up to help each other, so we're pretty well organized. Thanks for the offer."

Daniel knew that through the combined efforts of his brother-in-law, Robert, and Thomas Bloxham, John Cox, and Levi Roberts, along with his former partner, James Pulham, they could build six log cabins in just two or three weeks. The six men had decided to band together to do the work.

Benbow smiled again, pleased that Daniel and his brother-in-law had made a quick decision to purchase the lot in the Kimball Addition. And that they had found a forty-acre tract to purchase and farm together so near Nauvoo, just two miles east of the temple site, and not far from his own farm. Benbow was further pleased that Wilford Woodruff's United Brethren converts were sticking together, and working together. Thomas Bloxham's farm was right next to Daniel and Robert's. John Cox and Levi Roberts had selected lots very near Daniel and Robert's. Of course that made perfect sense to Benbow. John Cox's wife, Eliza, was a sister to Levi.

The oddball out was Henry Eagles. It seemed strange to John Benbow that Henry had turned down an offer to work with the other six men, preferring to build his own cabin on his own lot, in a different section of Nauvoo altogether. At least the strange brother was smart enough to settle on a twenty-acre farm with the intention of running a small dairy.

"One piece of advice," Benbow cautioned Daniel with a hangdog smile. "Get as much of your hard work done before summer as you can. That's when folks say the sickly season starts here in Nauvoo, and in most of the settlements along the Mississippi."

"You mean the *ague?*" Elizabeth queried, anxious to draw out any information about the dreaded sickness before it hit them.

"Yep," Benbow said. "Luckily, we missed the sickly season last year because we arrived in the fall. We're not looking forward to the hot summer. We just hope we don't get sick. They say the shakes are terrible. Lots of bad swamp air around here in the summer, so folks say."

"Anything we can do to prevent it?" she asked, her skin prickling at the thought of Daniel, Robert, Hannah, or any of her loved ones shaking in uncontrolled fits of fever. Especially the children.

Benbow shook his head, trying to suppress his annoyance of the hot season. "I don't know, yet. I just had a mind to talk about it today. And I don't know if there's much we can do to treat it. I haven't worried too much about it until now, but we need to find out."

Elizabeth held Daniel's arm. "Daniel, I'll make that little project mine, if it's okay. It goes along with my duties as a midwife and herbalist." She thought about the advice given to her by Elder Willard Richards in England last year following her blessing, to become a midwife and herbologist. Her heart was struck again with a yearning for a child of her own, wondering when it would happen, dampened with the prospect that, indeed, she might be lucky to have only one child.

"I hear you delivered a child on the ship, Sister Browett," Jane Benbow commented.

Elizabeth nodded her head and laughed, telling the Benbows how

Captain Wood wanted to name Hannah's baby boy after the ship. Her laughter was dampened by John's remarks about the ague. It worried her. She had already set herself to learning traditional home remedies from Nauvoo's wide variety of citizens: Drink cold boneset leaf tea for a cold. Tie an asafetida bag around a baby's neck to keep colic away. Relieve chigger bites with tobacco juice or a mixture of butter and salt.

But she had not heard of a cure for ague.

Daniel's exhaustive study of the existing log cabins in Nauvoo revealed that inexperienced builders under primitive conditions had constructed most of them. Pressed to get their families under any kind of shelter, some settlers were living in cabins that had a shabby appearance, dirt floors, unchinked walls, lacked windows and proper doors, and had fireplaces that smoked. He was determined to do better.

The gray of an approaching dawn found Daniel reviewing his cabin plans with Robert, James Pulham, Thomas Bloxham, Levi Roberts, and John Cox. A solid rock foundation—eighteen inches high because it was thought termites would climb no higher—had already been erected on Robert's lot, across the street from William Jenkins. As the first rays of sunshine bore from the eastern sky, Daniel eyed the stack of logs he and Robert had cut. They had their tools: froes for splitting wood, broadaxes for hewing...

"The first thing we've got to do is choose two of the best logs for the sills," Daniel said, his face contorted in deep thought. "They will rest directly on the foundation, on the two longest walls."

The men had already determined that the length of their cabins would be sixteen feet. The width would be fourteen feet. After Robert selected two logs, Daniel instructed the five men to use their broadaxes to hew the logs until they were square on all four sides.

As the men began chopping, an early morning breeze ran downhill singing, pushing through the slits in the tops of the remaining trees on Robert and Daniel's lot, turning them into a woodwind section of a spring orchestra. Nests of bluebirds, towhees, brown thrashers, robins, cardinals, and chickadees swayed in the branches. Birds hid under tall pokeberry. Violets had taken over part of the lot, well established along the streets known as Ripley, Warsaw, and Wilcox that bordered the area the men were working.

After the sills were laid on the foundation, the men selected other logs for use as "sleepers," as they were called in America.

"We have to run the sleepers, which will be the floor beams of Robert's cabin, the width of the building and rest their ends on the sills, no less than six feet apart," Daniel instructed, chewing on his lip. "Otherwise, the floorboards may sag."

"I don't want a sagging floor," Hannah said, her eyes blazing as she stirred oatmeal in an iron pot over an open fire in front of their wattle house and tent, both of which served as temporary living quarters.

Hannah's six-week-old baby, Thomas Eagles Harris, named after Hannah's father, was still asleep inside the tent. Joseph, Lizzy, and Willie were watching the men hew the beam logs into shape. Hannah expected the other wives to bring contributions for the morning meal. Dianah Bloxham, with her four children trailing behind, showed up with corn pones. Eliza Cox and her three children brought preserved apples and milk given to her by her new Nauvoo neighbors. Harriet Ann Roberts and her two children brought frog legs, already rolled in a mixture of flour, salt and pepper, ready for the frying pan. Her son, Henry, nearly five years old, had spent the previous afternoon with playmates Joseph Harris and Tommy Bloxham, whacking frogs with their sticks in nearby marshes to get enough frog legs for breakfast—and stirring up the mosquitoes.

"Pick out some of your best logs then," Daniel said to Robert.

"They're all good," Robert replied, eyeing the pile of logs he had cut from felled cottonwood, yellow poplar, and walnut trees.

Elizabeth came out of her tent with Martha and Rebecca, spreading a display of cheeses. "Don't anyone get *sick* on me," she said. "You brethren have five log homes to build. I suspect Daniel will do ours *last*, if I know him."

Daniel paid little attention to her prattling. He was busy instructing the men how to cut the sleepers all the same thickness so that the eventual floor would sit level. Using Daniel's auger brought from England, the men bored a hole through the center of each lap joint and into the sill below. Then they tapped pegs made of locust into the holes with their mallets to secure the sleepers to the sills. To ensure the sleeper would not move, and to fill the space between the sleepers, Daniel had the men cut some straight-grained oak into lengths that matched the distance between the centers of the sleepers. Daniel hoped that the five families could buy some sawmill planks to use as the floor for their cabins.

"Watch those frog legs," Harriet Ann warned, her eyes twinkling. "Don't let the grease get too hot in your pan, or they'll hop right out."

Minutes later Hannah hollered: "Come and get it!"

After a blessing on the food, the five men scooped out ladles full of over-cooked oatmeal into bowls that Hannah had safely transported across the Atlantic and up the Mississippi. They drowned the oatmeal with fresh cream and honey, grabbed a plate of frog legs, cheese, and corn pones and sat on the sleepers visiting. They talked about a little of everything. The need to build the log cabins as quickly as possible. Speculation as to when Wilford Woodruff would arrive in Nauvoo from England. How the church would handle the settlement of old Kirtland debts and preserve the temple there. Their membership in the Nauvoo Legion. Whether or not the Prophet would convince Stephen A. Douglas that Legion members would be exempt from other military duty in Illinois. And Joseph Smith's sermon last Sunday.

Daniel, James, Robert, Levi, and John were all concerned that a still-angry Thomas Bloxham had not attended the Sunday services with Dianah, but none of them dared confront him about it. Thomas still refused to hold any kind of funeral or memorial service for Charles, clinging to a faint hope that he might turn up somewhere.

Observing that Thomas turned gloomy at the mention of the Sunday services and the doctrine of the Prophet's talk, Robert did his best to cheer him up. "Thomas, are you getting so you can understand the Americans when they speak?"

A puzzled look crossed his brother-in-law's face as he bit into a corn pone. "What do you mean? They talk a little different, true, but I understand them."

"A little different, you say? Some of the people around here butcher the English language."

A clever entertainer, Robert pulled his best frontier face, and mimicked an assortment of words and phrases he'd heard the past few days. He began, "Why I'm a'feared yu'd druther miss yer mornin' vittles than leave the 'lasses out of the pone."

That brought a few laughs from Daniel, Levi and John, but not Thomas. He looked away, remaining distant.

Robert tried again, rising to his feet and taking a fighter's stance.

"The way he fights is a sin to Crockett. I hit 'im one polt. It was what I call a sogdolloger. And that made 'im dance like a ducked cat. I thought he'd be savage as a meat axe but he skedaddled in a fine pucker. He'll be back alright, with a plug-ugly puke from Missouri."

That brought an almost irreverent laughter from the four other men, including Thomas, who merely chuckled at first, then broke out into a good belly laugh with the others.

Thomas said, still chuckling, "You don't suppose right at this minute there are groups of converts from other parts of America who are making fun of the way we British talk?"

In his best English colloquialism Robert spurted: "Ya! 'it 'im again Bobby! 'at's it, at 'im again, it the 'arris blood a croppin' out in ya, it is!"

Dominating the conversation among the women, Elizabeth stood up and pointed at her brother, giggling noisily. "I think that was directed at me."

"Sartinly is, 'er my name ain't 'arris!" Robert quipped.

In a better mood, Thomas laughed again.

Daniel soon had his crew building walls on Robert's cabin. They chose two more logs to go across the end of the house, parallel to the sleepers. After cutting them to the right length, they hewed off two sides until the logs were six inches thick. The other sides were left rounded.

To Robert, Daniel's instructions were almost too technical to under-

Photo of a log cabin replica in modern-day Nauvoo. (Photo by Darryl Harris, April 2002)

stand. His butternut shirt was covered with sweat, and he didn't care. He just wanted a log cabin, complete with a cockloft his children could use as sleeping quarters.

"Next, we need to cut lap joints in the bottom ends of each log. The horizontal cut should be the same width as the sill. Each joint should be deep enough to allow the bottom edge of the log to hide the sleeper. Fit those two logs into place in the six-inch spaces you have left between the first and last sleepers, and the ends of the sills. Now you are ready to begin cutting the dovetails for the corners. Do it carefully, so it looks good on the outside. That way, no pins are necessary; the wall will stand without support for as long as the logs are sound. You can notch the logs as you go, one at a time, fitting each log onto the next. If the top log rocks a little, roll it off, hew out a little more, and fit it again."

As one log was placed on top of the other, the five wives watched their husbands form the cabin walls and washed the dishes—all the while participating in Elizabeth's idea of good conversation. Her topics were many. The introduction of the tomato to Nauvoo vegetable gardens. Opinions about Nauvoo's first mayor, John C. Bennett. The pleasant fact that there were no American saloons or bars in the city. How industrious the men and women were. How inexpensive food was compared to prices in England. The geographic distribution of the people into wards. And how their little cabin homes built under Daniel's strict guidance would be the finest in the city.

Elizabeth also made mental notes about the Malvern Hills women and when she would be expected to deliver children. Eliza Cox would be the first in just a few weeks.

Outwardly, Elizabeth remained a chatterbox. Inwardly, there was something very serious going on in her mind.

How to combat ague.

50

A HEAVY THUNDERSTORM, WITH thick rain drumming from skies gray as slate, began early on this June day in Nauvoo. The rain brought work to a halt on the five cabins. Only Robert's had a roof on it, but only a portion of the lathed roof was shingled. The other four cabins had been completed to the square. The rain was flooding the excavation where basement walls were being prepared at the temple site. Crops of corn, grain, and vegetables soaked up the welcome moisture.

With Hannah entertaining the children inside the wattle house, Robert stubbornly worked inside the leaky cabin frame, splitting shingles out of two-foot locust logs. He glanced up Warsaw Street to see a tall, lone figure sloshing through the mud toward the cabin. Holding an umbrella over his head, the man wore a frayed woolen coat that showed stains of rain and dirt, and a four-day stubble beard that moved as he spoke. "Sorry to bother you." The man thrust forward a hand. "The name's Jacob Kemp Butterfield."

Robert tossed his axe aside and accepted the handshake. From the accent, Robert knew the man was native American. "Don't think I ever saw it rain this hard where I'm from."

Butterfield smiled from beneath a wet hat covering his auburn hair. "That would be England, wouldn't it? You English all talk the same. But I hear

England gets her share of rain."

"You're right. But I never did enjoy the winter rains there. Cold and nasty."

Butterfield gave Robert a dignified smile as the American's eyes flitted from side to side. He stood as though rooted to the ground and spoke in a mechanical tone, telling Robert he had been born in Maine, but after his conversion had lived both in Kirtland, Ohio, and Dearborn, Indiana, before settling in Nauvoo. "I see you have a cozy wattle. So do we. Leaks a little. Yours probably does too. But we'll be able to move into our log house next week. We have a new baby, born in March. Persis Amanda. I suppose you have children."

"Four. Last one was born on the ship, coming over."

Jacob's expression changed. "Have they enlisted you into the Nauvoo Legion yet?"

"Yes. I look forward to the parade on the Fourth of July," Robert said. Both men knew the Nauvoo city charter had authorized the organization of the Legion back in February.

"They'll have you working on the temple too, very soon. They want us to donate one day's labor in every ten days."

"So I've heard. I guess I can work that in, too."

"I think they'll give us time to finish our own homes first. Are you planting crops?"

"Yep. My brother-in-law Daniel Browett and I are farming forty acres east of town near the John Benbow farm. We've been working hard to get the first of our crops in. You a farmer?"

"Teamster. Been hauling back and forth from Missouri. The Saints left a lot behind. We're trying to recover as much as possible," Jacob said, his face wretched with concern.

Both Robert and Daniel had been impressed with the flood of help that came from people they had never met before to break up the prairie sod with ploughs pulled by teams of oxen, mules and horses. In each case, about fifteen acres had been planted with crops that could be harvested yet this year. In

Daniel and Robert's case, they were new English immigrants, working hard to get established. In most other cases, Mormons who had been persecuted and banished from Missouri, the people were trying to recoup their losses by opening new farms, building homes, and supplying themselves food. Everyone sought a peaceful agrarian lifestyle on this new Illinois frontier.

Jacob's tone turned serious. "I came to see you about something important."

Robert shrugged his shoulders. "Everything we've been talking about is important, isn't it?"

Butterfield remained glued to his position. "I came to talk to you about your other brother-in-law, Henry Eagles."

Robert braced himself. "Go on. I'm listening."

"As you probably know, Henry and his wife stayed for a few days with some friends of ours when you folks first arrived here last month. Their place is not far from ours. Anyway, I had an opportunity to meet Henry and tried to get to know him better."

Lightning flashed to the southeast and James waited for the thunderclap. It followed three seconds later with a loud boom.

"That man doesn't like you at all, Brother Harris."

Robert shrugged again. "You're not telling me anything I don't already know. Henry has had a chip on his shoulder for a long time. I beat him in a boxing match back in England. He never got over it. Then there was an incident on the ship."

Robert related the story of Henry hitting him on the head, tossing him overboard, and being rescued by the men on the *Echo*. He also told Butterfield how Henry had refused to become a member of the Church, his failure to learn and understand church doctrine, and his struggles in New Orleans.

Jacob finally relaxed. He walked to a window opening. "I guess I shouldn't have said 'doesn't like you,' it would be more accurate to use the word 'hate.' There is a lot of hate in that man. It scares me and concerns me for you."

"I appreciate your concern but I'm not afraid of him."

"I have a recommendation."

"Let's hear it, Brother."

"The only thing I know of to rid a man's hate out of his spirit is the gospel."

Robert nodded his head in agreement. "There's been a lot of effort made in that direction. My wife tried to get him to listen to Elder Woodruff last year in England. Several times, in fact. Henry's wife tried. Daniel tried. He flat told everyone no, that he had no interest. But he was anxious to come to America when he had the opportunity."

"Has he been to the grove to hear Brother Joseph's sermons?"

"No."

Robert told Jacob about Katherine Eagles' frustrations with Henry, that since they had arrived in Nauvoo Henry had worked as a loner to build his own wattle dwelling and was working on a log house. Henry was already complaining that nearly every family in Nauvoo had their own cow and that prospects of owning a prosperous dairy were minimal.

Jacob took Robert's explanations in stride, and concluded by saying, "The man scares me. The church has a lot of enemies, as you know. I've made some friends that are converts from New York and they call many of the people out here in Illinois and Missouri 'ruffians.' That means that most of those types would be in jail had they stayed back east. They're a pretty rough lot. I hope Henry's wife can keep Henry away from them. My friends say Henry reminds them of some of the ruffians they've met."

Robert nodded in agreement. "I'll see what we can do. There's a lot of concern about Henry in our group. It's obvious he hasn't eaten enough husks yet."

"A reference to the prodigal son?"

"You got it."

"Just don't turn your back. From what he said to me, I wouldn't trust him right now. Just between you and me he has no sense of remorse for what he did to you on the ship. I know all about it."

"Thanks for the warning."

"You're welcome," Jacob said, still holding the umbrella over his head. He unlocked his eyes from Robert and trained them on the gray sky. "See you later. When this rain quits watch out for the mosquitoes. Those who were here last year say they will be out in legions, my friend."

As the American walked away, the storm front passed from the Mississippi River east to the Illinois prairie, the wind and driving rain dwindling, and Robert knew it would die as quickly as it had come. The flashes of lightning and booming of thunder became more distant as he returned to his job of making split shakes for his roof. Within another hour, golden shafts of sunlight pierced the purple and gray clouds overhead

A slight shudder ran through Robert as he slapped at a mosquito and contemplated Butterfield's last words.

The deep gloom of night gave way to a brilliant morning. Purple shadows disappeared from beneath the tall cottonwoods, the spreading oaks, and the tall grasses of the swamps surrounding Nauvoo. Millions of mosquitoes came streaming into the first shafts of sunlight, the females in desperate need of blood so they could reproduce. They had slender bodies, long legs, narrow wings, and mouths designed to furtively slip through the flesh of any bird, animal or human being. These millions of *anopheles quadrimaculatus* females, leaving their male counterparts behind to feed on plants, quickly spread out over the Mississippi River peninsula that years ago had been the site of a former Indian village called Quashquema. Today, just as they did then, they would suck blood from unwilling animals: coyotes, rabbits, groundhogs, raccoons, possums, bears, milk cows, oxen, slop-fattened pigs, mules, jacks, and horses. Or it might be any of the fowl family: wild turkeys, geese, ducks, guineas, chickens, hawks, eagles, owls, herons, terns, shrikes, sandpipers, cranes, blackbirds, robins, or sparrows.

Or humans.

As thin skiffs of white clouds moved silently to the east, dark smoke rose from hundreds of rustic log cabin chimneys as Nauvoo wives set copper or iron kettles to heat over black iron arms in a fireplace or out-of-doors.

Innocent children rose out of their straw-tick beds renewed, rubbing their eyes, ready to spoon tasteless hot gruel into their bowls, chew on tough brown bread, and wash it down with warm milk.

With sunburned faces, husbands and sons began plowing fields, chopping down trees, laying stones in the temple foundation—all plunged in passion over their work. Waves lapped against the Nauvoo Landing where one or two steamboats would land on this day, to be met by men, women, and children in desperate need of their cargo and mail.

On this June day in 1841 in Nauvoo, Illinois, there was not a single person who understood the relationship of the mosquito to malaria, or ague, as it was called. For that matter, there was no one in the Illinois frontier, the upper Mississippi valley, the entire United States, or the entire world who knew it.

Not a doctor. Not a biologist. Not even an Apostle or a Prophet.

In the same way that humans need protein for survival, female mosquitoes need blood for protein for their eggs. During this day, millions of mosquitoes would feed on thousands of human beings, animals, and birds, then deposit millions of eggs in the standing water in and around Nauvoo. Eggs that would quickly turn into larvae.

Mosquitoes have an uncanny ability to produce a new generation in as little as seven days.

With Nauvoo wrapped in the warmth of the morning sunshine, these millions of female mosquitoes began to seek their human victims by the scent of skin chemicals, the carbon dioxide and lactic acid in the exhaled human breath, and the infrared light emitted from human bodies.

There was no escape.

As the morning hours ticked away a minute at a time, swarms of mosquitoes found their way to the bare skin of Don Carlos Smith, younger brother of the Prophet, working in a damp basement printing another edition of the *Times and Seasons*. They noisily buzzed to a home on the east side of Main between Water and Sidney streets, finding Sidney Rigdon, and his wife, Phebe. They bit not only the Rigdons but everyone who was there doing business at the U. S. Post Office, located in his home. The labella tips of female "skeeters" bore into John C. Bennett, the mayor of Nauvoo, under fire for lying to the Prophet. And into members of Brigham Young's family, living in an unfurnished log cabin in a low, wet swampy lot—so swampy that oxen had mired in it the first time the property was plowed.

Even a man lying flat on his back, unable to recover from wounds suffered in the massacre at Haun's Mill, was not spared as he had his leg amputated. The "skeeters" plagued both William Yokum and his doctor, and everyone in the house.

Even the Prophet fought the mosquitoes on this day, trying to keep them away from himself, his wife, Emma, and their children. Especially from their baby, only a year old, also named Don Carlos Smith. They plagued Joseph's old horse called Charley, his two pet deer, his turkeys, and his cow.

The mosquitoes did not discriminate. They attacked saints digging wells, building cabins, and laying rock for fireplaces. Women picking greens and herbs. Children gathering wildflowers. Immigrants from England, Wales, Scotland, and Ireland. And new converts from New England and the South.

They bore into customers near the Amos Davis riverfront store. Five-year-olds Joseph Harris and Tommy Bloxham returning home with six pounds of sugar purchased for seventy-five cents. Eliza Cox, who that day bought a dozen eggs for twenty-five cents and a broom for thirty cents. Ann Gailey, who had purchased six chickens for seventy cents. And Harriet Ann Roberts lugging home twenty-five pounds of flour she had purchased for a dollar.

Mosquitoes menaced Ellen and Thomas Benbow out in the farm field helping their uncle, John. Elizabeth, Martha, and Rebecca Browett weeding their garden. Dianah Bloxham hanging out clothing to dry after a big wash day. Henry and Katherine Eagles on their twenty-acre farm finishing the roof on their cabin. And dozens of men bent over laying foundation stones at the temple site, including Levi Roberts, John Cox, James Pulham, Daniel Browett, Robert Harris, Thomas Jenkins, and John Gailey.

None of the Saints in Nauvoo knew on this beautiful late spring day that female mosquitoes carried and transmitted a blood-borne parasite that infects and destroys red blood cells.

Unknown was the fact that as the "skeeters" drank their wee drams of blood from the Nauvoo humans that the mosquitoes transmitted threadlike structures called sporozoites into the unsuspecting man, woman, or child. The sporozoites quickly made their way to the liver, where they multiplied and formed another kind of spore called a merozoite. As the merozoites entered the bloodstream of its human victims, they began to penetrate red blood cells and devour hemoglobin, the chemical that transports oxygen.

And unknown was the fact that when the blood cells disintegrated, the merozoites, now multiplied by sixteen fold, escaped and infected other blood cells. Worse yet, when another mosquito took a blood meal from another Nauvoo human, those merozoites were transferred to the mosquito, ready to infect *another* unsuspecting human.

The angry humans slapped hundreds of mosquitoes to a premature death during the morning hours. No matter. Millions still survived. By noon, most of the "skeeters" had returned to their swampy homes. But by evening, they renewed their hunts.

The mosquitoes never gave up.

Their survival depended on blood.

51

A LIGHT RAIN HAD FALLEN IN NAUVOO during the early morning hours. The rain left a collection of huts, cabins, and tall trees shrouded in a misty fog. For a while the moisture clung to the trees, the grass, and the June flowers, sparkling in the rising morning sun. The millions of female mosquitoes retreated to their swampy homes. By noon, dozens of otherwise prime, warm-blooded targets—United Brethren converts from England—had converged on the lots just south of the temple lot in Nauvoo. The men were attaching shingles to five cabins.

Near the peak of the roof of his own cabin, Daniel called to Elizabeth. "Happy twenty-seventh birthday, dear."

He switched his attention to Hannah. "And happy twenty-sixth to you, Sister Harris."

"And happy sixth *anniversary* to the four of us," Elizabeth responded, shielding her eyes from the brightness of the noonday sun.

As she fanned the air, swiping at a lone buzzing mosquito, Elizabeth pondered with pride her brilliant decision to have a combination anniversary-birthday-housewarming party on June eleventh. The statement brought vivid memories to Elizabeth of the struggles back in 1834 and 1835 with their parents over their courtship and marriage. Dealing with her and Robert's stiff-necked Anglican father. Hannah's stiff-necked Methodist father. Daniel's confused Quaker mother. And their double marriage, first in the hamlet of Apperley's Methodist chapel, then having their vows repeated in the St. Mary de Lode Church.

The only incident that had marred the festivities so far was when John Cox accidentally cut his hand on a nail helping on the Browett roof. The deep cut bled freely until Elizabeth poured it full of cayenne.

"Count to ten, Brother Cox, and it will quit bleeding before you reach ten."

It did.

She bandaged the wound and John quickly returned to the roof.

Each of the five cabins had been constructed with sturdy ceiling beams below, with planks from the water-powered sawmill laid across them. They formed both the ceiling of the first floor and the floor of the small loft. Daniel had designed the lofts so that the vertical walls extended an additional four feet above the ceiling, then the rafters were placed on a forty-five degree angle so that the roof would shed water easily.

As Daniel and James Pulham nailed the shingles to his roof, Robert split more shingles and tossed them up. John Cox, Levi Roberts, and Thomas Bloxham finished the chinking, using clay that had been mixed with just the right amount of water to make it soft and malleable, but not thin and watery. They forced it into all the cracks between the logs, making the cabin as tight as possible.

With a pleased look on his face that the work was about done, including a rock fireplace, Daniel recalled the events of six years of marriage. His mind was vibrant with memories of meeting Thomas Kington and John Benbow in 1835. Becoming a lay preacher with the United Brethren. Dealing with Robert's stubbornness to be active in any church or embrace any religion. Wilford Woodruff's 1840 arrival in the Malvern Hills and the Cotswolds. His and Elizabeth's conversion. His calling as a district president. And his later calling as leader of a company of Church members to emigrate to Nauvoo aboard the *Echo*.

Soon many of the *Echo* passengers could be seen arriving for the party, joining Elizabeth, Hannah, Robert, Dianah, Thomas, Martha, and Rebecca. They were: James Pulham, John and Mary Cheese, Joseph and Eliza Halford, James and Ann Lavender, James and Hannah Lord, John and Alice Ellison, James and Hanna Lord, and David and Alice Wilding.

Several *North America* passengers also arrived. John and Jane Benbow, Robert and Elizabeth Clift, William and Ann Cole, Robert and Elizabeth Holmes, William and Mary Jenkins Parsons, and John and Grace Ann Parry. And James and Elizabeth Robins, of the *Caroline.*

Children of all ages ran through the grass. The older ones knocked the younger ones down at times. Teenagers pitched horseshoes, ran foot races, jumped for distance, pulled sticks, played with pet dogs, and pitched quoits. They played "Old Cat" with a trimmed stick for a bat and stuffed rags for a ball.

A brown dog chased yellow butterflies. A black and white cat caught a mouse, taunted it, and then ate it for lunch.

The women wanted to gossip about folks back in England, but there were no letters yet to be shared. Several were excited to see the first textiles for sale in Nauvoo—tans, amber, mauve, rose, teal blue, azure, lilac, apple green, cabbage green, purple, wine red, vanilla. Home spinning and weaving would soon be on its way out, a few of them predicted. A couple of millinery shops had been opened, which pleased the ladies.

Rustic tables were set with cooked game: deer, turkey, and grouse. Freshly caught fish waited to be fried on an open fire. Friends had sent a collection of hot breads, preserved fruits, cakes, and pies for the new Nauvoo residents to party on. Elizabeth and Hannah made apple slump, a concoction they learned from New England converts—made by placing raised bread dough around the sides of an iron pot, and then filling the dough with apples sweetened with molasses.

During the meal, serious adult conversation centered around Joseph Smith's recent arrest on old Missouri charges and his subsequent release in a court presided over by Judge Stephen Douglas. They talked about the men's training in the Nauvoo Legion and the upcoming Fourth of July Celebration. And they discussed rumors that Nauvoo Mayor John C. Bennett would soon be dismissed because it had been discovered he had a questionable past. Bennett had an estranged wife and child that he had told no one about. When the facts had come out, Mayor Bennett had tried to poison himself. John Benbow told the other men that he could not believe that Joseph had forgiven Bennett and reinstated him to his position in the Church.

The English immigrants were learning that Satan was already at work to disrupt their Zion. It really didn't surprise them. Neither did an article in the Church-owned *Millennial Star* declaring that all non-Mormon religious sects and denominations shall have "free toleration and equal privileges in the city."

Sitting on the ground with the other men with his shoulders slumped, his handsome but pocked face clouded with loneliness, James Pulham said little during the discussion.

Robert drew a heavy breath, slapped his courage, and spoke boldly in James' direction. "Brother Pulham, we need to find you a new wife. I'm thinking of a scripture in Genesis. *It is not good for man to be alone.*"

Reeling in disbelief that Robert would bring up the sensitive subject so soon after Nancy's death and in front of such a large gathering, James dropped his jaw, locked eyes with the undefeated, former British heavyweight contender for a second, and then looked away. It had only been two months since Nancy died. In England, the official mourning period was six to nine months.

The men sitting on the grass below Daniel's cabin on the south-sloping lot went stone silent.

His face blanched, James broke the awkward silence by changing the subject. "Did you see the size of the trout they brought? They say they're easy to catch. When we get time we'll have to learn how to fish."

John Cox unlocked his interlaced fingers and pointed an arm down the hill. "Just take your bucket to the Mississippi and scoop them up. Some say that's how easy it is."

"You're changing the conversation, Brother Pulham," Robert said. "Folks here say there's more women than men in Nauvoo. You should have a lot to pick from."

"I wonder why that is?" asked Levi Roberts, his face pulled into a look of bewilderment.

"It's really quite simple," Daniel said, gathering his thoughts. "More women than men join the Church, for one reason. I think women must be more spiritual. And a lot of the women here are young widows. They've lost their husbands in accidents or sickness of one kind or another. Many of the new converts are widows. When they heard the gospel from the missionaries they could make the decision on their own to join the Church."

Thomas Bloxham rolled his eyes. "So Mormonism is mostly for women? That makes sense. That's why my wife got baptized, and I didn't."

Daniel contemplated Dianah's husband and favored him with a smile. "You'll be baptized one day, just wait and see. We're never going to give up on you."

"Maybe we ought to talk to Brother Joseph and have him preach the gospel direct to you and to Henry," John Benbow suggested. "You'd feel the Spirit for sure."

"You tell Old Joe to worry about keeping all of you on the straight and narrow," Thomas said, returning a saucy grin and trying to keep an unruffled manner. "I'll be all right without him or his Gold Bible."

Visiting with a nearby circle of women, Dianah grimaced at her husband in a prolonged glance and turned her head in disappointment. She wondered how long the Lord would continue to test her husband's faith. The loss of her newly born child, Isaac, in England right after her baptism, and the apparent death of Charles off the back of the steamboat had caused him to blame God to the point that even talking about it with him was uncomfortable. But John Benbow was right. If Thomas would take the time to listen to the Prophet's sermons, there was a chance he would feel the Spirit and be baptized.

A miracle had happened in the case of her brother, Robert, back in England.

She prayed for the same to happen to her husband.

52

DANIEL APPEARED TO BE SELF-CONSCIOUS and ill at ease when he approached John Benbow. The party was just beginning to break up. "Can Elizabeth and I talk to you in private for a few minutes before you go home?"

"Certainly," Benbow replied, shaking his head emphatically. "Where?"

With imploring eyes, Daniel pointed to the west and a low afternoon sun. "Let's take a walk toward the temple site. It won't take long." Daniel motioned to Elizabeth and she floated to his side in her checkered, mauve, cotton dress, slightly soiled with the activities of day including food preparation, serving, and cleanup.

The three English immigrants strode north on Warsaw Street, turning left on Mulholland. They passed other Nauvoo residents, arms swinging, walking home from the temple. A team of horses pulling an empty wagon went by, rattling, the driver half asleep in the afternoon sun.

Elizabeth took over the conversation. "I heard you warning us again today about the *sickly* season that's coming."

Benbow had no illusions as he leveled his gaze at Elizabeth. "It won't miss us. At least that's what everyone says. I'm afraid a lot of us are going to come down with the ague. I don't look forward to it."

"I've been talking to *everyone* I can," Elizabeth said, making a determined face. "There's a remedy that suppresses fever, but it's *expensive.*"

In the weeks she had been a Nauvoo resident, she had dealt with a variety of health issues among the English converts. The croup at the Roberts home—both five-year-old Henry and three-year old Caroline. Measles at the Cox home—four-year-old Elizabeth. Mumps at the Bloxham home—eight-year-old Lucy, seven-year-old Tommy, five-year-old Emma, and three-year-old Johnny. So far, the worst the Harris children had were insect bites and toothaches. Any day Eliza Cox was expected to give birth to a new baby.

Benbow pulled his eyebrows up in surprise. "What is it?"

"Quinine. It comes from the bark of the Cinchona tree."

"Never heard of it."

Elizabeth gave Benbow a cheery smile. "Maybe that's because the Cinchona tree only grows in South America, mostly around the eastern slopes of the Amazonian area of the Andes Mountains. Natives down there *apparently* have been using ground up quinine bark as a fever depressant since the 1600s."

"That's interesting," Benbow said. He was seeing Elizabeth's serious, reasonable, astute side.

"When Elizabeth mentioned to me that there was a fever suppressant that came out of South America," Daniel said, "a scripture out of the Book of Mormon came to mind. We had come across the scripture during our morning scripture study. It struck us like a thunderbolt. It's from Alma 46:40. *And there were some who died with fevers, which at some seasons of the year were very frequent in the land—but not so much with fevers, because of the excellent qualities of the many plants and roots which God had prepared to remove the cause of diseases, to which men where subject by the nature of the climate.*"

"So you are insinuating that the Book of Mormon people were using the bark of this tree to suppress fevers?" Benbow asked as they arrived at the temple site where men were laying stones for the foundation.

"Yes, I *really* think so," Elizabeth said firmly, working her eyebrows a bit. "I've found out that quinine bark was advertised for sale in *England* as early as 1658 and was made official in the London Pharmacopoeia twenty years later.

The remedy made its way to Spain and the Jesuits began to use it *all over* Europe as they traveled around in their missionary activities. They used it so *widely* that it became known as 'Jesuit's powder.' "

Benbow stood silent in thought for a few moments. "And this stuff really works?"

Eyes twinkling, Elizabeth said, "From what I can gather, it would have saved Oliver Cromwell's life."

Benbow laughed. "The vicious old scoundrel deserved to die, didn't he?" Cromwell had controlled the House of Commons in England back in 1648. He had been a vehement anti-Catholic who opposed King Charles I and had Charles beheaded, and then ruled England and Ireland with an iron first for the next eleven years.

"Perhaps," Elizabeth answered, curling her mouth in amusement at Benbow's laugh, "but the point is that his *health* began to fail. He suffered from chills, fevers and rampant shivering. Because he hated the Catholics, he *refused* the so-called 'Jesuit's powder,' which was quinine. Cromwell died of ague in 1658."

Daniel added: "She's found out that ague is not a native disease to the United States. It is believed that it has been imported with the slaves. Ague has been so bad around here that a few years ago there was a serious question as to whether this part of the Mississippi Valley could ever be settled permanently. I remember Elder Woodruff telling us how sick he had been with the ague when he left his home here to go on his mission to England."

Benbow shrugged his shoulders. "Why are you telling me all this? Are you going to hand me a supply of quinine bark powder to take home with me in case I come down with the fever?"

Elizabeth sighed, her eyes heavy and sad. "Believe me, I'd love to. The *problem* is this. *Demand* for the bark worldwide has grown almost beyond the supply. The bark was so valuable at one time that supply could not keep up with the demand. There have been times the cost of the bark powder has often been matched by its weight in gold."

A premonition was building inside Benbow. "I see. You need money."

"I'm willing to go to all the United Brethren converts and take up a collection." Elizabeth said. "But *you* know their financial situation as well as I do."

Both Elizabeth and Daniel knew that John Benbow remained quite wealthy, even after providing most of the financing for the printing of the Book of Mormon in England, paying the way for forty or more Saints to emigrate to Nauvoo, and buying a large farm.

With a quizzical look, Benbow asked, "You just eat this powder?"

"Mix it with water and drink it."

"How much quinine in each dose?"

"Fortunately, *not much,*" Elizabeth answered. "There are different opinions. Some say to give two little grains of quinine every one or two hours, until the patient hears his ears 'singing.' Others just give ten or fifteen grains at the beginning, more if the case is worse."

John Benbow calmly said, "Out with it. Tell me how expensive."

A wistful look stole into Elizabeth's eyes but she maintained her determination. *"Very.* One ounce costs as much as a good cow." Both knew a good cow cost fourteen dollars.

Benbow grunted. "No other alternatives?"

Daniel locked eyes with Benbow. "Priesthood blessings."

Daniel related how Joseph Smith had used the priesthood to restore the health of members of the Church when they first settled Nauvoo.

Elizabeth listened to Daniel, gnawed on her lip, then added: "Aside from priesthood blessings and quinine, medical books I've seen talk about *laudanum*, but from what I've learned it doesn't help much unless it has *quinine* in it. Some people boil dogwood bark, but it's ineffective. Others try wild things like mixing chimney soot with boiling water and taking it three times a day with sugar and cream. *Rubbish.*"

Benbow laughed at the thought.

"Other than quinine, willow bark works best from what I gather. It will suppress fevers some, but *nothing* like quinine."

Ruefully impressed with Elizabeth's knowledge about ague and the proposed remedy, Benbow kept asking questions. "How do you know you can even find quinine?"

"Once we have our fund raising and collect enough money, I'll put in an order through one of the merchants, like Amos Davis or Windsor Lyon. Maybe we can find some in St. Louis or one of the larger settlements."

"Where did you learn all this?"

"Books. Other people. Doctors. Even a saddlebag doctor that was passing through."

"You've got all the answers, seems like."

They began walking back to Warsaw Street, chasing their long shadows.

"Except one," Elizabeth said, swatting mosquitoes away. "No one knows for certain what causes the ague. Some say the damp air from the *swamps* around here. Others say decaying vegetables. But I find either of those hard to believe." She fanned the air again. Millions of female mosquitoes, with their sensors working keenly, were swarming the Nauvoo peninsula seeking their late afternoon blood feast.

After another pause, and in a different tone, Benbow said, "Are you sure it's worth spending that much money on this powder that's so hard to find? Elder Woodruff had the ague, and he lived through it. He was a bundle of strength on his mission in England."

On the back of Benbow's neck, a mosquito punctured his skin and injected its saliva.

Elizabeth's stomach knotted. "I'm worried about the *children*. Not too many adults die from the ague, but that's not true with children. I'd hate for the Bloxhams to lose another child, or for one of Robert's children to die. Fever temperatures get up to a hundred and seven. That's *dangerous.*" She watched Benbow's face for a reaction.

"You've convinced me, Sister Harris. I'll donate fifty dollars." Benbow reached behind his head to scratch the small wound left there by the mosquito. It was itchy and slightly swollen already.

"Thank you *very* much, Brother Benbow," Elizabeth said, giving the Nauvoo farmer her warmest smile. "I'll collect what I can from the other families and order the quinine *right away.*"

Daniel and Robert settled into an almost daily routine of hitching their team of horses to a wooden plow and turning a ribbon of sod on their forty-acre farm, Township Seven, Range Eight, Section Thirty, east of the temple site. Smak dab in the middle of a blossoming rural community of English saints. There were farms of every size: ten acres, twenty, thirty, forty, eighty.

On this day, the walking plow left a single moist furrow, a path for the plowman. In front of the lathered horses, hundreds of tiny migrations constantly scurried about. Grasshoppers clattering off. Butterflies floating up from blossoms. Mice running in circles. Baby rabbits headed for the woods, turning somersaults in the grass. Gophers darting. Snakes slithering away. And quails flushed out of the tall prairie grasses. Even so, the horses walked quietly. The loudest sound was the tear the stubborn sod made as the roots were cut, torn up, and turned over. The healthy soil had a spring to it, in the humus. Next year it would grow crops for the two new English immigrants.

Robert pulled back on the lines. "Whoa, Bendigo. Whoa, Tapper. Time to rest." He had named the horses after the nicknames of famous British heavyweight fighters. Daniel had no choice in the matter. At least it was a departure from his old habit of naming animals after the English class system. His old dog had been named Duke. A horse, Old Earl.

Daniel halted his two yoke of oxen, loaned to them by John Benbow. He grimaced at the thought there were many workdays left before the sod would all be plowed. The process of turning the fertile but heavy soil was slow. His wooden plow would not scour; neither would the cast iron one that Robert was using. The moist muck clung like glue. On some farms wet soil took two teams of horses or three yoke of oxen to break through the tough prairie-grass roots.

Daniel took off his cap, wiped a perspiring forehead, and glanced at his brother-in-law. "Do you wish you were back in England defending your championship?"

One eyebrow went up from Robert's gaunt handsome face. He took a drink of water from a canvas bag. "You're assuming a lot." He passed the bag to Daniel.

Seeing Robert's amused look, Daniel smiled before he drank. "I think you would have been the champion by now. You could have beat Bendigo Thompson or Ben Caunt. No regrets?" He sat on the sod, his feet in the furrow.

Robert sat beside him and poured some of the water over his head to the music of meadowlarks and bobolinks nearby. "No regrets. I guess Hannah was right. Pugilism is a cruel sport when you stop to think about it."

"Would you rather be slaughtering hogs in Apperley?"

"No way," Robert answered, his voice turning grumpy. "I hated being a butcher." Even though he despised the trade, he had brought his tools from England. He used them rarely, though, mostly as a favor to friends.

"Well, you're a farmer now. Different than back in England though, isn't it?" Daniel thought of a year from now when buds would be bursting from the stems of ripening oats and barley.

Robert laughed with transparent pleasure. "Yep. Back there we had farm servants. Here, we do the hard work." He took another drink.

"I haven't minded it much until now," Daniel said, wiping a forearm across his brow. "The weather's starting to get hot and humid."

Lying on his back in the soft prairie grass, Robert said, "How about you? Rather be back in England making barrels in your shop?"

"It was a good time in my life. But this is better. We own our own ground."

"Think we'll ever get our farm to look as good as Brother Benbow's?"

Daniel snickered. "No. But it doesn't matter. We don't have his money or his experience." He lay on his back, too, gazing at the lazy clouds overhead.

"Oh, well."

"Yeh. Oh, well. We have the same gospel, the same testimony. That's all that matters. Maybe someday we could build our families a home out here on our farm."

"That would be nice," Robert said. "Hannah would love that. Good place to raise our children. Big garden full of vegetables. Big root cellar. Wild honey. Flock of chickens. Livestock. Lots of good neighbors. Close to the Benbow farm. Regular visits from Elder Woodruff. Do you miss him?"

"By Jove, I do," Daniel said. "At least we know his ship made it safety across the Atlantic."

Word had already circulated throughout Nauvoo that Brigham Young, John Taylor, and Heber C. Kimball had arrived. They would report their missions to England next Sunday at services to be held in the grove, the day after a big Independence Day celebration that would be held in the city. Wilford and Phoebe were visiting relatives back east and were expected to return to Nauvoo sometime later.

Daniel and Robert talked about Elder Woodruff while they rested. Daniel recalled the day he and Elizabeth met Wilford and were baptized, the powerful testimony he bore, his relentless desire to preach the gospel, and the way the former United Brethren members accepted the gospel so rapidly. They chuckled at the memory of Robert's stubbornness and the night Robert came home to find Elder Woodruff in his home, at Hannah's invitation, teaching the message of the restoration to a group of people, and the miracle of Robert's conversion. That jogged Robert's memory about the long list of questions Wilford answered for him late that evening in Apperley, England, including Robert's concern over the salvation of little children who had died before they were baptized. Robert recalled how frustrated he had been with his parish priest over Robert's refusal to have Joseph and Lizzy christened.

Robert turned to Daniel with imploring eyes. "Do you know what gives me a peaceful satisfaction right now?"

"What?"

Daniel suspected it could be one in any number of things. Robert's relationship with his wife and four children. The strong testimony that had developed in his soul since his baptism. His life in Nauvoo. Hearing Joseph Smith teach in the grove each Sunday. His new log cabin. The farm…

Robert cleared his throat to answer. The tone was emotional. "The announcement that a baptismal font is going to be built and placed in the basement of the temple. Not just the font, but the fact that I'll be able to be baptized by proxy for the little babies my parents lost in infancy, and my father and mother, even grandparents I've never met."

Daniel returned a warm smile to his brother-in-law. Plans had been made by a Church committee to erect a baptismal font mounted on the backs of twelve oxen in the basement of the temple. "Brother William Clayton says it will be located at the east end of the building and will be made of wood, then replaced with one made of stone later."

Robert stood up and took the lines to his horses. "I don't care if it's wood, stone, or gold. I just like what the Prophet has been teaching about baptisms for the dead. It makes me feel good. It will make me feel even better when the baptisms are done for my deceased family members."

Daniel nodded in agreement, rose to his feet, and began to walk to the oxen. Every day the reason for his immigration was becoming firmly etched in his mind. Build the temple. Build the temple. Every tenth day, both he and Robert contributed their blood, sweat, and tears. More, when they had time.

Robert talked to the horses. "Pull, Bendigo. Let's go, Tapper."

53

THE ABSENSE OF KATHERINE EAGLES at the Independence Day cele-bration troubled Elizabeth. Henry's wife was nowhere to be seen among the English saints as she watched the parade along Mulholland Street on this hot, humid day with Hannah and her children. The women's dresses were as dowdy as could be found. A band leading the parade played patriotic music. Elizabeth gave a half-hearted wave to Brigham Young, Heber C. Kimball, and John Taylor as they went by, smiling, waving. The Nauvoo Legion marched by, wearing a hodge-podge of clothing. She barely acknowledged Daniel, Robert, James, and all the other Legion members she knew.

Elizabeth was feeling a stir in her soul to inquire about Katherine.

Major General John C. Bennett waved at them from atop his big white horse. Elizabeth ignored the wave. "I don't *like* that man," she said. She had heard rumors about how Bennett, a doctor, had fondled female patients.

"Me either," Hannah said quickly.

Elizabeth framed Hannah with a fervent stare. "I haven't seen Katherine since last week. I thought she would be here today." She grimaced, and then tried to ignore her feelings. Perhaps she would see Katherine tomorrow at the grove when Brigham Young and the others reported their missions to England.

The Spirit whispered to Elizabeth. *Find Katherine Eagles.*

"I'll be back as soon as I can," Elizabeth said abruptly.

"Where are you going?" Hannah asked, bewildered. She wondered how she would handle the children alone. Joseph, five, was easily distracted by other children his age. Lizzy, three, had a tendency to wander into the parade path. Willie, two, required constant attention. And baby Thomas was crying, wanting to be nursed.

"To Henry and Katherine's cabin. I need to find Katherine."

"When will you be back?" Hannah knew it was a twenty-minute walk to the Eagles cabin.

"Soon, I hope."

Elizabeth made the walk in sixteen minutes, and would have made it quicker except for the crowds the first few blocks leading out of town. There was no one in the fields or in the huts and cabins she passed. High above the prairie a hawk was flying, as smoothly as water flowing. A mother skunk, moving slowly, tail up, head high like some grand court lady, passed in front of her; behind the mother came a line of four young skunks, each a perfect imitation of the mother. Perspiring freely, Elizabeth passed fields of knee-high grain, hay ripening, and corn growing taller with each passing day.

No one answered when she knocked on Katherine's door. Two cows were penned in a hastily built corral. Chickens scratched in the yard. Three geese, with their wings spread, approached, wanting morsels of grain or house scraps.

"Katherine! Open the door. It's me, Elizabeth." She quickly compared the Eagles cabin to hers. It lacked Daniel's touch and craftsmanship.

No answer.

"Katherine! Open up! I know you're there."

Elizabeth felt her muscles tighten. The last shreds of doubt were withering away. Something was wrong.

The sound of footsteps. A wooden slab door on iron hinges opened to a small crack. A voice.

"What are you doing here? You should be at the parade." The voice was barely audible, full of pain.

"May I come in?"

"Is the parade over?"

"No."

"Henry won't be back for a while?"

Elizabeth sensed trouble between Katherine and Henry. "No. Not for quite a while. We've time to talk, just you and me."

The door opened, revealing a badly beaten woman. A yellow and blue festering bruise closed Katherine's right eye. Her lip was swollen and puffy. She moved slowly, as if her ribs were broken. Elizabeth reeled in shocked horror.

"It's obvious who did this to you," Elizabeth said, touching Katherine on the shoulder. "The question is, why?"

Katherine looked at her visitor through a tearful left eye. "It's been going on for a long time, ever since we got married. Now it's worse, as you can see."

Elizabeth felt ashamed, angry, frustrated and profoundly sad as she scanned the wife of Henry Eagles. The woman had obviously been mistreated for months and no one had come to Katherine's rescue. Elizabeth asked the obvious. "Are you going to leave Henry because of this?" She followed Katherine to a crude wooden bench next to a table.

Katherine shook her head as she sat. "I know Henry's mean at times, but I love him. Besides, where would I go? I can't go back to England."

Elizabeth touched Katherine on her swollen cheek. "But we *can't* let this happen to you again." Elizabeth's voice was tinged with sorrow.

Katherine spoke through swollen lips, staring at the dirt floor. "Henry will change. I know he will."

"Does he love you?"

"He married me."

Elizabeth narrowed her eyes. "The *acid* test for genuine love is respect, appreciation, and admiration. Henry is showing *none* of that to you."

Katherine wiped at her tears and sat silent for a few moments before she responded. "I know. But most days it's not too bad. Caring for Henry makes me feel that life is meaningful."

Elizabeth's mind filled with words that she wanted to scream at the beaten woman. Katherine had sold herself to a rotten man, and was likely to be a volunteer hostage all her life. Katherine had made a mistake in marrying Henry, but would not admit it. Katherine obviously believed that submitting to Henry's abuse ensured his undying love and attachment. Katherine's self-esteem was gone. In Elizabeth's mind, the solution was clear.

"Katherine, you've got to *leave* Henry. I can't *stand* the thought of him beating you again."

More silence from Katherine, then a whimpering voice. "I can't."

"Katherine, you can't be responsible for Henry's actions, but you can for yours," Elizabeth said, shaking her head and gritting her teeth. "As long as you stay with him it's a sign that you condone his behavior. And his behavior in this regard is unacceptable. Leave."

Katherine's next words stunned Elizabeth.

"I can't. I'm going to have a baby."

54

DAYS LATER ELIZABETH RETRACED her footsteps empty-handed. She was clad in a dark red dress that matched her darkening mood. The order she had put in for quinine from Windsor Lyon's Drug and Variety Store, housed in a log cabin, was unfulfilled. A crisis larger than Katherine's beating loomed over not only the English immigrants but over all Nauvoo. Inside the Browett cabin, her husband was on fire with the fever. She burst through the door, finding Daniel in a cold sweat, shaking uncontrollably, and sitting on the edge of the bed. Martha and Rebecca dabbed at his forehead with clean white rags.

"Did it come?" Martha asked, taking a cautious step toward her daughter-in-law, hands open.

Elizabeth felt a constriction in her throat. "I'm sorry. No."

Daniel groaned. "When will I get over this?"

His wife shrugged her shoulders, helpless.

Daniel bent his head and let himself tip over to a reclining position. He had felt well enough a week ago to march with the Nauvoo Legion in the Independence Day parade, but knew that ague by that time was afflicting hundreds of men, women, and children in and around the city. Daniel had conversed with Brigham Young, John Taylor, and Heber C. Kimball during the day, hearing their reports about England and their trip across the Atlantic.

The Prophet Joseph, himself fit and healthy, had given a patriotic speech at the festivities, closing with the words: "I would ask no greater boon, than to lay down my life for my country."

Daniel had even felt normal the next day, Sunday, when Brigham, John, and Heber reported their missions in the grove. But by Tuesday, absorbing the distressing news that Wilford Woodruff was visiting relatives back east and had not yet made it to Nauvoo, Daniel fell sick. Robert followed the next day.

"Soon, we hope," Martha said with numb dread as she wiped Daniel's feverish brow again. She wondered when the ague would afflict her. "Maybe the quinine will arrive tomorrow." Steamboats docked daily at the Nauvoo wharf.

Martha, Rebecca, and Elizabeth had watched in morbid helplessness as Daniel's first symptoms appeared. First came yawns and the desire to stretch sore muscles. His fingernails turned a bluish color. He complained of cold sensations all over his body. It seemed to creep into his system in streaks, and then faster and faster, colder and colder, in successive undulations that coursed down his back. Next came cold chills that made his body shake, followed by warm flashes that turned into a burning fever. Today the fever was turning into a harsh sweat.

"Anything change next door?" Elizabeth queried as she felt tears sting her eyes.

Rebecca somberly answered. "Robert's symptoms are the same as Daniel's. Maybe even worse. Hannah told me a few minutes ago that she thinks Joseph is coming down with it, too."

"Oh, no! Not the children!" Elizabeth rang out. "I'm going next door and see what I can do." Submerging herself in her self-calling as a herbalist, blocking out everything else without conscious effort, she burst out of the door and marched into the Harris cabin.

"Hannah! How's Joseph? Is he sick?" A flicker of her green eyes betrayed a bevy of uneasiness. Was it a naïve streak back in England that made her think she could help sick people? It was easy to think that when her friends and family were healthy, but now…

With a face lit with fear and panic, Hannah answered. "He's been complaining of a dull headache and dizziness. He's been so drowsy I've let him sleep all morning. But I think he's awake now, just barely."

Elizabeth examined the five-year-old boy, finding that he also had an irritating cough that secreted a bloody mucus. His eyes were listless.

"How long has he had this cough?" Elizabeth prodded.

"Just today," Hannah answered, cringing. "Is everyone going to get the ague? And I suppose there's no need to ask. No quinine yet?"

Elizabeth shook her head negatively and shrugged her shoulders, trying to steady her confused senses. "No quinine. And to answer your other question, I hope that *everyone* doesn't get the ague. But many already have it."

She thought about the other English converts and how different their symptoms were. John Benbow had a slowed pulse, and his right arm was so numb that he wanted to rub it all the time. His extremities were cold, and his appetite was poor. His shakes were intermittent but violent.

Benbow's wife, Jane, complained of chills with flushes of heat, and had told Elizabeth that she could hardly breath because of a severe pain in the liver area.

Ague had affected James Pulham in yet another way. Aside from the shakes, his urine was bloody and scant; he told Elizabeth that he had diarrhea every morning.

Robert rolled over in his bed. "Nauvoo is no paradise, sister. Send me back to England." His words came slow, with evident pain.

Elizabeth cringed from inside as she riveted her gaze on her normally robust, healthy brother. For the past three days his shakes had begun at noon; he complained that he was weak and drowsy between attacks, feeling a prickling sensation in the region of his liver.

"Have you eaten anything today?" Elizabeth asked.

"No, but I'm hungry now," Robert answered, trying to straighten his aching frame.

Hannah raised her voice in protest. "I don't think eating is good for you." Turning to Elizabeth, she explained that every time Robert ate something he

would belch several times and complain about feeling qualmish, even nause-
ated.

Robert tried to remain optimistic. "Nothing in your bag of tricks?"

"I could go back to the store and get some mercury compounds,"
Elizabeth answered. "A good dose of it probably wouldn't affect you, but it has
killed more than a few frontier folks who have tried to use it for medicine."

"Thanks for nothing," Robert moaned.

"What about Henry and Katherine?" Hannah asked, her eyes rolling
with disgust at the thought Katherine was still recovering from the wounds
her brother had afflicted upon her.

"I haven't been out there today, but they've both come down with it,
too."

"I hope the fever cures Henry's brain," Robert said in a steely voice, col-
lapsing on his bed.

Ten days rolled by before the quinine arrived. By then Elizabeth was afflicted
with ague, as were Martha, Rebecca, and Hannah. Daniel and Robert, because
of the passage of time and priesthood blessings, were feeling better even before
they began taking doses of the medication. The English immigrants soon
learned that settlements all along the Mississippi were equally afflicted. Some
experienced the fever-chill cycle every day, others every other or third day in
a predictable pattern.

"You just have to learn to work around it and divide your calendar into
'well days' and 'ague days,' " several said. Housewives had to plan their washing, ironing, and baking around times when they expected to be down with
the "fits."

Fortunately, Elizabeth and the English immigrants learned, ague made
pioneer life miserable but it was only sometimes fatal.

"Watch out for the cholera, that's worse for deaths," another warned.

Because of the wide diversity of people in Nauvoo there was a wide difference of opinion on how to treat ague. Elizabeth quickly found out that
Joseph Smith distrusted doctors who dispensed medicine. It probably went

back to the death of his brother Alvin. Instead, the Prophet had surrounded himself with doctors like Willard and Levi Richards who used botanical cures advocated by Samuel Thompson—the Thomsonian method.

"But in no way does the Prophet force others to use methods he personally believes in, or compel them to," another told her. "Our Prophet is a Prophet, not a tyrant; a man of God, not a dictator. He loves his people and wants to be loved; not to hate and be hated."

By the time her first supply of quinine arrived, five deaths were being recorded among the citizens of Nauvoo every week. A funeral was held almost every day.

Elizabeth didn't know if luck would hold out, but for now some of the United Brethren converts suffered from sickness but none had died. She protected her supply of quinine as if it were liquid gold. Thomas Kington's company likely would be here in a week or two. She would need more.

55

ROBERT ABRUPTLY STOPPED WEEDING his garden when he heard the good news from Daniel. "Thomas Kington will be here shortly."

It was a sultry Saturday afternoon, the last day of July.

Robert contemplated Daniel's statement and asked, "How do you know?"

Daniel was feeling a rush of excitement. Thomas Kington, the former superintendent of the United Brethren, was one of his best friends.

"Levi Roberts was riding horseback along the main road east of the city and saw several wagons headed toward Nauvoo. He recognized the Kingtons and Mary Ann Weston Davis. About twenty saints from England in all. Levi told them to come to the temple site. He sent someone to notify the Benbows, and right now Levi is trying to find the Prophet and other Church leaders so that a crowd can be assembled to welcome them."

Robert threw down his hoe and marched inside his cabin to tell Hannah.

Barely thirty minutes later, Daniel and Robert and their wives found themselves standing alongside Joseph and Emma Smith, and John and Ann Benbow. With a couple of dozen other British converts, they watched as seven wagons loaded with more immigrants from the old country approached from the east.

"I can't say how much I appreciate the assistance you brethren gave to members of the Twelve during their missions in England," the Prophet told Daniel and John while they waited for the wagons to appear.

Daniel and John colored at the compliment.

"I've been able to hear some of the reports from Brigham Young, Heber C. Kimball, and John Taylor. We're giving them some time in our meetings tomorrow to tell us more. I look forward to hearing from Elder Woodruff as well. We constantly receive letters from him. He says he will be here in time for our October conference."

"What about Willard Richards?" John asked.

"He should arrive in Nauvoo within two or three weeks," Joseph answered.

The wagons drew closer.

"Brother Kington is the man who organized the United Brethren," John said.

"But it was Brother Benbow who gave it the financial support it needed," Daniel explained, touching John on the arm. "Both men are responsible for placing six hundred souls in a position to accept the light and truth of the gospel."

The Prophet placed an arm around John Benbow. "Elder Woodruff's work among your people there probably will go down in the history of the Church as one of the greatest missionary accomplishments ever, thanks to you."

Benbow shuffled his feet and a tear appeared in the corner of his eye.

Emma Smith began singing a hymn and immediately the crowd, swelling to more than a hundred people, joined her.

"That's Brother Kington there, standing in the first wagon with his wife and mother," John Benbow said in a loud, ringing voice, pointing for the Prophet's benefit.

To John, Kington looked healthy and robust as the wagons drew closer. His former farm manager was a little taller than himself, always stood ramrod straight, and had thoughtful brown eyes and thinning sandy hair. But his elderly mother, Eleanor, looked tired and frail. A closer look revealed that Kington's wife, Hannah, looked that way, too, which shocked him. The last time John had seen Hannah Pitt Kington she appeared as healthy as Thomas. John guessed that the trip had taken a toll on her but that she would recover quickly now that she had arrived at her destination.

"Brother Kington! Welcome to Nauvoo!" Benbow yelled as he waited with outstretched arms.

Daniel recalled the day at the Gloucestershire Fair when he first met Benbow and Kington. Both were confident men, encasing blasts of willpower tempered with generous amounts of spirituality. Benbow proved to have an unselfish loving heart. Kington possessed strong leadership qualities, and like Daniel, had served as a district president after his conversion in England.

Daniel could still picture Elizabeth and himself sitting under a large oak tree at the Benbow farm, listening to Kington explain the details about the United Brethren, plus a brief history of the major religions in England. It was the day he converted from his Quaker faith, and Elizabeth from her Anglican faith, and they started training to be lay preachers with the United Brethren.

Elizabeth also noted the pallid appearance of both Eleanor and Hannah Kington. But Elizabeth keyed on Mary Ann Weston Davis, riding in the third wagon. She approached Mary Ann as Benbow and Kington began their tearful embrace, backslapping and squeezing each other so tightly that they almost lost their balance.

To Elizabeth, Mary Ann looked exhausted but beautiful in her wrinkled powder-blue dress. Beneath gracefully winged dark brows, Mary Ann's large eyes were a luminous indigo blue, heavily fringed with curly lashes, filled with grim reminders of things Elizabeth had little clue about.

Scanning the arriving English saints, however, Elizabeth could not see Mary Ann's husband, John Davis, Daniel's former employee in the cooper shop. An Englishman Elizabeth did not know seemed to be tending to Mary Ann's needs.

With Hannah, Sarah Ann Davis Roberts, and several other ladies watching, Elizabeth swept Mary Ann into a strong embrace only to hear sobbing. "I know you must be so happy to be here," Elizabeth said in a worried tone. "I think I cried the day we arrived, too."

Elizabeth pulled away in an effort to determine if the tears were of joy or sadness.

Mary Ann's stinging eyes rose to meet Elizabeth's and those of Sarah's, John Davis' sister. Shaking her head and blinking away the tears she moaned, "Why couldn't my sweet husband John be here to see this?"

Frowning at the unexpected answer, Elizabeth brought an arm to her chest and gasped. "Mary Ann! What do you *mean?* Where is John?"

There was a prolonged silence as Mary Ann regained her composure. Drowning in sorrow, she told a short version of what had happened in England after Elizabeth's departure. How the mob had chased Edward Phillips out of her cottage and beaten her husband. John's deteriorating condition followed by the fall down the stairs trying to talk to John's evil mother. His ultimate death followed by a sad funeral. And the legal fight with Mrs. Davis.

As Mary Ann's story unfolded, the Prophet Joseph gave his welcome speech followed and began spelling out the assignments of where the new immigrants would stay. Elizabeth had it in her mind to change Mary Ann's assignment from the Levi Roberts home to hers, but decided against pressing the Brethren about it when she remembered the connection between Sarah Ann Roberts and John Davis. She dutifully accepted the assignment to host William B. Smith and his wife, Annie, but quickly invited the Roberts to bring Mary Ann to her home that evening for dinner. She was dying to hear details of Mary Ann's story.

Robert and Hannah were about to take Joseph and Sarah Hill and his wife home, but at the last minute Henry and Katherine Eagles showed up. Henry was displaying his other self. As Joseph embraced his sister, Katherine Hill Eagles, Henry strutted around shaking hands as though he were one of the Mormon bishops, and showing off his pregnant wife.

"Good to see you on this beautiful fall afternoon," Henry kept saying. As they loaded up the Hills' possessions in his wagon he left with the words, "Now won't this be fun? Visitors to the Henry Eagles cabin."

Before the Kingtons left with the Benbows, and after having visited with Eleanor and Hannah Pitt Kington, Elizabeth approached Thomas with a brow that was furrowed with deep lines. "I'm concerned about your wife and mother."

"So am I, Sister Browett. The trip has taken a toll on them."

"I'll be out tomorrow afternoon to see them, after Church services in the grove. I don't think you'd better expect them to come in for the services. They need to rest."

Elizabeth got her wish concerning Mary Ann. It happened over a dinner of boiled potatoes, baked squash, cooked red beets, and heavy frontier bread in the Browett home that evening, Mary Ann told the story of how John had died, the victim of a mob beating. A mob that had been organized by John's own mother, and had included old friends of Henry Eagles. She related how she had been forced to sell the household furniture John had made for her. Luckly, she had managed to keep and bring to Nauvoo a long dresser with three shelves, beautiful sets of dinner dishes, and a knife box.

Mary Ann went on to relate how she had stayed in the home of Joseph and Ann Hill after John had died. She described how she felt when John had been buried in a quiet corner of the Tirley graveyard. Edward Phillips, who had been chased out of the house by the mob the day they had beaten John, had been scheduled to leave England a week or two after she left, Mary Ann added. John Hyrum Green and his family were on the same ship, the *Caroline*.

"I guess one good thing about the things I had to sell was that it bought me passage on the *Harmony*," she said wistfully. "It was hard to leave my family."

"I'm sure it was," Elizabeth said. "It was difficult for all of us."

"My mother was especially brokenhearted," Mary Ann continued. "Father seemed distant, which was strange because I was always his favorite child. I know it was because I joined the Church. I gave my sisters some books to read and to remember me by. They cried when I left, and kept clinging to my neck knowing they would probably never see me again. Teams were hired to take us to Gloucester, but I walked most of the way from Tirley. At one point I sat down in the road, overcome with grief and sorrow over the death of my dear husband. I might have stayed there if others had not come back for me."

After she finished with her story, Mary Ann began asking questions about Nauvoo and the people she had known back in England. Elizabeth, Daniel, Martha, Rebecca, Levi Roberts, and Sarah Ann Roberts took turns filling her in. Mary Ann seemed pleased that the United Brethren converts were sticking together and thriving rather well in their new surroundings.

"Most of our farms are located out in the country," Daniel explained. "But some of us live here in town, by the temple." He led a discussion about wattle huts and log homes, promising Mary Ann that the English saints would soon build her one of her own.

Mary Ann was especially curious about one person. Henry Eagles. She had recognized Henry's old friends in the mob that had beaten her husband. "What about Henry Eagles? Is he mixing in quite well with you folks?" She laced her words with tight sarcasm.

The mention of Henry's name made Elizabeth think of poor Katherine and the fact that she had disclosed her pregnancy.

There was an awkward silence as Mary Ann sat waiting for an answer to her question. Finally, with a vision of a badly beaten and bruised Katherine Eagles still in her mind, Elizabeth shook her head.

"Not really," Elizabeth said. "Henry hasn't changed all that much."

To Thomas Kington's English eyes, Nauvoo and the Illinois countryside were a startling contrast to Herefordshire. After loading seven hundred pounds of baggage and belongings into Benbow's wagon, Thomas and John talked about the vastness of the prairie, the inexpensive farm ground, and the lack of aging and stately church and government buildings as they rode to the Benbow farm.

The first thing that struck Thomas, however, was the similarity in the way thirty-five-year-old Benbow managed his American farm. It was organized and neat-looking, just like the Hill Farm back in Herefordshire near Castle Frome. He had already crossed the farmland with irrigation ditches and planted thorn hedges. His dwelling, barns, sheds, garden, and orchards were beautifully arranged. Zigzag worm fences protected crops from grazing animals.

"How many farm servants do you have?" Thomas asked as they began unloading luggage the Kingtons would need during their short stay with the Benbows.

"None," came the reply.

Benbow explained how he had done most of the work with his nephew, Thomas Benbow, but that the English immigrants assisted each other with most of the heavy tasks. He had also hired part-time help when it was available. Benbow told Kington how the American system differed from the British system not only as it applied to farming but everything else.

"How's the work progressing in England?" John asked.

"People are not being baptized as quickly as they were when Elder Woodruff was there, but the Church is making progress. Many of the new converts are making plans to come to Nauvoo." Kington inwardly laughed as he remembered his first impression of Wilford Woodruff when he met Woodruff in March, 1840, at Benbow's Hill Farm in Herefordshire. He had half expected an Apostle to be a tall man in long, flowing red robes and a red hat similar to that of a Catholic cardinal or the Archbishop of Canterbury. Traveling in a richly decorated blue and white royal coach drawn by six matched white horses, complete with trumpeters, footmen, arm guards, and a personal secretary. Nothing of the sort. Wilford was short, plain, simply dressed, and traveled without purse or scrip, like the Apostles in the New Testament.

Kington said that prior to leaving the old country, he and William Pitt had opened a branch of the Church in Bristol. That English city had always been near and dear to his heart because it was the place where John Wesley had begun his outdoor ministry a century earlier. Those efforts led to the formation of the Methodist Church.

John approached his old farm manager and gave him another warm embrace. "It's good to see you again, old friend. I've missed you."

Thomas returned the embrace then stood back and sized up his former employer. He had let his moustache and sideburns grow a little longer, Thomas thought, perhaps because there had been no time to trim them. A tear came to the eye of the former superintendent of the United Brethren congregation. "Just look at what all this has led to," he said, contemplating his now complete trip and the prospect of settling into a peaceful life among the saints. "The further light and truth we were seeking has brought us thousands of miles from what we thought was home, hasn't it?"

John's eyes misted also. "Yes, it has. And it is good."

Elizabeth was worried about Eleanor and Hannah Kington. Elizabeth wasted no time in getting to the Benbow farm Sunday afternoon after attending a fast and testimony meeting in the grove. Accompanied by Daniel, Mary Ann Weston Davis, and William Pitt, Elizabeth found Eleanor and Hannah Pitt Kington resting comfortably in the Benbow cabin but still complaining of exhaustion. Even though she feared hearing about their trip from England to Nauvoo might turn into a "competitive suffering" debate between members of the different emigrating Mormon companies, Elizabeth was determined to hear to details of the journey. Perhaps there would be a key as to why Eleanor and Hannah were so sick.

After examining the two women, Elizabeth turned to face Thomas Kington. "I need to know *all* about your trip," she said in a serious, somber voice.

Ann Benbow served ashcakes—corn meal cakes made by sweeping the hearth clean and laying the cakes on the hottest part of the hearth, and covering them with ashes.

"The first part was probably the worst," Thomas began, as he tipped his head down and grimaced. He sat on a wooden bench in the Benbow home, brushing off ashes to take his first bite of Sister Benbow's ashcake. "As soon as we came into open waters from the Bristol Channel we encountered heavy seas. Anything that was not tied down was bandied about, scaring all of us."

"That's an understatement," Mary Ann added, her tone excited. "I thought we were going to die. The waves crashed over the ship so bad the captain made us stay below. They closed the hatches and locked us in."

"That happened to us, too," Daniel said, nodding.

"We were all very seasick," Mary Ann continued. "We couldn't eat anything for several days."

"Were you and your daughter-in-law sick, too?" Elizabeth asked Eleanor.

In a weak voice, Thomas Kington's elderly mother responded, fanning an arm at a swarm of mosquitoes. "Yes, of course. It was just like Mary Ann said."

"How long until you could *eat* again?" Elizabeth asked. Into her mind came the morbid memory of how Nancy Eagles Pulham had dehydrated and died aboard the *Echo*.

"Just a few days," Hannah Kington answered for her and her mother-in-law. "I can't say our normal appetites returned, but we ate."

As Elizabeth took in Hannah's statement, Thomas continued his narrative. "Just off the banks of Newfoundland, the weather was so severe that our main mast broke off below the deck, and the jib boom was also broken. We had to limp back to Wales to seek refuge. We were able to get our repairs done in Milford Haven."

"We were delayed there a whole week," Mary Ann stated, her head shaking back and forth. "The monotony was terrible."

"But that's when we started eating again, because we were in port," Hannah told Elizabeth. "It was a beautiful harbor, by the way."

"From Milford Haven to just off the coast of Canada, the rest of the trip wasn't too bad," Thomas continued.

"But a terrible storm hit us again," Mary Ann said, grimacing. "It was like a hurricane."

"We survived the storm, but a nearby schooner was driven into the Beauport Rocks," Thomas Kington added. "She was damaged quite severely."

"How were you feeling when you arrived in Quebec?" Elizabeth asked the two women.

"We both lost some weight." Hannah said. "And we were weak, of course."

It was at this point that sixteen-year-old Ellen Benbow could not restrain herself. "Well, you didn't have a whirlpool just about swallow up your ship," she said.

"What do you mean?" Hannah Kington asked, her dim eyes opening a little wider.

"Now, now," John uttered, pointing a threatening finger at his niece. "I don't think the Kingtons want to hear about the whirlpool."

"Of course we do," Thomas responded, his curiosity piqued.

Elizabeth rolled her eyes at Daniel. They had heard the story a dozen times.

"It was more than a year ago when we boarded our ship, the *North America*," Ellen said, beginning to speak at a rapid clip. "Not far out, this really big storm came up, causing a gigantic whirlpool in the ocean. It took us round and round. It made a big hole in the ocean and our ship was caught in it. Really and truly! The only thing that saved us was that Uncle John and the other elders prayed together. They prayed for two or three days. We all thought that Heavenly Father wasn't listening, because we were still in the whirlpool. Auntie gave up and told Uncle John that he just as well quite praying. She lost hope. Didn't you auntie?"

Ann Benbow grimaced and nodded her head. "Yes. I hate to admit it, but I did."

Ellen talked in John's direction. "Next comes the part about Uncle John's dream. Uncle just looked Auntie in the eye and said, 'We are going to be saved. We are going to get out of this.' But Auntie kept saying, 'Oh, John. Don't say that! We can't get out of this!' And that's when Uncle said, 'I saw it all. The Lord is coming to our rescue.' "

Elizabeth stole a glance at John Benbow. A tear streamed down his cheek, just like every other time this story had been told.

"That's when Uncle jumped up, and rushed to the other berths to tell his friends about his dream. He dreamed that he was walking along the shore of the sea when he saw this terrible man with a whip beating the water. The waters of the sea were surging and boiling and heaving all around so that no one could get near it. Suddenly, in Uncle's dream, Uncle saw a man all dressed in white walking toward them and as he came near, he stopped and called out, 'Lucifer, come out of that water!' The terrible man turned and looked, and on command dropped the whip and slunk off. Then in Uncle's dream the sea immediately turned calm and peaceful."

"She's telling the truth," Ann Benbow said, reaching for her husband's hand and squeezing it. "We all went upon the deck to watch and wait, to see if the dream would come true."

"Oh, it did, all right," Ellen smiled. "After a while the whirlpool began to fill in at the bottom. Soon it forced our ship right to the top. The ocean became beautiful and calm, like nothing had ever happened. We had beautiful sailing after that. Right through the Cabot Strait north of Nova Scotia, into the Gulf of St. Lawrence. Then we turned southwest toward Quebec City."

Daniel felt impressed to tell the story of the *Echo*—the storms, the ship turning on her side, the loss of the sailor, the desire on the part of Henry and others to turn back, the prayers, and the calming of the sea. Afterward he said, "I believe there is a common fabric woven into all of this. There is no doubt in my mind that Satan opposes the gathering of the saints to Zion. He has raised his ugly hand during every migration that I am aware of, and he'll continue to do it. There is a war going on between good and evil. It started in heaven and will continue right up until the beginning of the millennium. Satan doesn't want our temple to be built. But I think he'll lose. The temple will be built."

Both John Benbow and Thomas Kington interjected their testimonies in agreement as Elizabeth studied Eleanor and Hannah again. When Kington finished there was a momentary reverent pause within the Benbow cabin. Elizabeth broke it when she inquired, "Brother Kington, continue with your story, please. What transportation did you use to leave Quebec City?"

"For twelve shillings each I bought tickets on a converted tugboat, the

Canada, which took us farther south, up the St. Lawrence River to Montreal."

"Anything of a *peculiar* nature during the trip?" Elizabeth asked, still searching for any clue.

Mary Ann's eyes flared. "Oh, indeed. The *Canada* was full of vermin. The bedbugs were absolutely terrible. The ship's officers never let us topside during the entire four-day trip. We were practically eaten alive."

Elizabeth made a mental note, wondering if the bedbugs could have transmitted some type of disease. She would ask Elder Willard Richards, the physician, who would be in Nauvoo within just a few days. Or she might ask Patty Bartlett Sessions, who lived next to Windsor Lyon's store.

Kington cleared his voice and continued. From Montreal, his Mormon company paid two shillings six demies each to ride second-class on a local ferryboat, the *Princess Victoria,* nine miles up the St. Lawrence to LaPrairie. From there they secured passage on the new Champlain and St. Lawrence Railroad train, which took them to St. John.

For Elizabeth's benefit, Mary Ann reported, "That train ride was almost worse than the storms in the ocean. It shook us to pieces. Thank the Lord it was only fourteen miles. But step-by-step we were getting closer to the United States. From St. John we rode along Lake Champlain on an absolutely beautiful steamboat called the *Burlington.* It was just wonderful, compared to everything else. The decks were like drawing rooms. The cabins were like boudoirs, choicely furnished, and adorned with prints, pictures and musical instruments. Captain Sherman was marvelous. He treated everyone with dignity. I think Brother Kington's mother and wife enjoyed that part of the trip."

"I slept the whole way," Hannah said, shrugging her sagging shoulders. "I missed seeing Burlington, Vermont, where we entered the United States."

"The steamboat took us as far as Whitehall, New York." Kington added, "but from there we had to travel west to reach the Great Lakes and make our way to Nauvoo."

"You mean you missed New York City?" Ann Benbow inquired with imploring eyes. "That was the best part of the trip, as far as I'm concerned. I loved the brick buildings and the others painted white, with doorsteps painted yellow. The streets were wide there, but not so well-flagged and paved as in England. I remember buying a red apple and how delicious it was."

"Yes, we missed New York City," Kington explained. "It was several hundred miles south and we were headed west, anxious to get to our destination. We traveled by canal boat along the Champlain Canal to Waterford, New York, and from that point along the Erie Canal, across the upper tier of several New York counties until we reached Buffalo. We traveled three hundred and fifty-seven miles. The trip took several days. Traveling was smooth, but I'm sure it was wearing on my mother and my wife, and on all of us."

Thomas did not mention that the canal boat passed by Palmyra, New York, the birthplace of Mormonism. He was probably unaware of that historical fact.

"You forgot to tell about George Fidler and Elizabeth Clift getting married in Whitehall," Mary Ann injected. She rolled her eyes and added, "Both sets of parents, by the way, opposed the marriage. But they did it anyway."

Elizabeth giggled at the distraction, then motioned for Thomas to continue.

"We arrived in Buffalo on the sixth of July. We were fortunate to catch a lake steamer called the *Chesapeake,* bound for Chicago. We loaded all our baggage and departed on the eighth of July. The trip on the Great Lakes lasted five days. We traveled southwest on Lake Erie, stopping at Cleveland. From there we proceeded west then north to Detroit, then entered into Lake Huron."

"Lake Huron seemed to take us farther away, instead of closer to Chicago," Hannah reported to Elizabeth. "The farther north we traveled, the worse the storms were. Both of us got sick again."

Elizabeth shook her head in morbid silence.

Kington threw his hands apart in a helpless gesture. "I didn't have the heart to tell Hannah and my mother that the route from Buffalo to Chicago meant that we had to go north, around the state of Michigan, six or seven hundred miles north, in fact, then turn back to the south when we entered Lake Michigan. Maybe that's why a few of our company chose to leave us at

Mormon immigrants arriving in New York saw this view of the piers along South Street, Manhattan.

Detroit. They decided they had enough and went to Kirtland."

"Did you lose *more* weight on that part of the trip?" Elizabeth asked.

"Seems to me they did," Thomas stated.

"I was particularly discouraged when we got to Chicago," Hannah said disdainfully.

Before Elizabeth could ask why, Thomas explained. "There did not appear to be any definite mode of transportation for large groups of people, which surprised me for a city of that size. Folks there bragged the city had grown from between four and five thousand people. There were scheduled coaches and mail transports out of Chicago, but they were too expensive, and not large enough to accommodate us. We still had thirty-two saints in our company."

"So what did you do?" Daniel asked.

"I found out that a lot of freight wagons went between Chicago and the closest access to the Mississippi River. That was a place called Dixon on the Rock River, which empties into the Mississippi. So I made a deal with a freight company. We had to wait a couple of days for enough available wagons, but we loaded our baggage onto several wagons and followed the winding roads to Nauvoo. We could have gone to Dixon and from there to Rock Island and caught a steamboat going down the river to Nauvoo, but this worked out fine. We didn't have to reload our baggage again."

John Benbow nodded his head in agreement. His company had done the opposite last November. They had to buy boats, which were expensive. The boats had gotten stuck in the rapids on the Rock River. Passengers had to get out and walk around the rapids while the men tried to get them unstuck in the freezing water. The hardships caused hard feelings among the company members, which had marred the last leg of their five-thousand-mile journey.

Elizabeth studied Eleanor and Hannah again. "Either way would have contributed to your *exhaustion*," she concluded.

"We were both happy to finally be here," Hannah said. "I think I'll sleep for seven days straight."

With that remark she fanned at the mosquitoes buzzing around in the

Benbow cabin, and sunk deeper into her chair.

CHAPTER NOTES

Details of the Thomas Kington Company were gleaned from a paper entitled "Thomas Kington, Wellsville's Unknown Resident" (unpublished), by Don H. Smith, Pullman, Washington. According to the Mormon Immigration Index, the *Harmony* departed 10 May 1841 from Bristol, England, and arrived in Quebec 12 July 1841. Some of the LDS passengers were James Barnes and his wife, Robert Clift and his wife, Eliza; another couple with the last name of Clift; Reuben, Rhoda, Sylvester, and Daniel Collett; George Fidler; William Gardener; Granger; Brother and Sister Green; Paul Harris; Brother and Sister (Joseph?) Hill; John Hunt and his wife; Mary Ann Weston Davis; C. Moore; Hannah Simonds; and John S. Smith and his wife.

Information about John Benbow's trip on the *North America* came from A History of John Benbow by Arthur B. Erekson, 1988.

56

OUT OF BREATH AND A FLARE OF WORRY on her face, Hannah burst into the Browett cabin on a late September day. "It's time," she called out sharply.

Elizabeth put down her heavy iron and met her sister-in-law with a prolonged stare.

"You mean *Katherine?*"

Hannah nodded, holding a hand against her heaving chest. "Where's Daniel? Can he find a ride for us?" She loathed the thought of returning to Henry and Katherine's cabin on foot, two miles away, where Katherine lay writhing on her bed with labor pains.

"Daniel took Martha to Hyrum Smith's place to get their patriarchal blessings; I don't expect to see them for another hour or so."

Elizabeth put on her shoes and grabbed a satchel that contained her midwifery things. She had used her midwifery skills for the first time in Nauvoo eleven days ago when she assisted a Sister Haight in the birth of her son, now named William Van Orden Haight. "What about Robert? Can he take us?"

Hannah shook her head. "He's somewhere with a few other members of the Nauvoo Legion, training to be a bodyguard for the Prophet." Robert, John Cox, and Levi Roberts had been chosen for the special assignment from among the English immigrants, along with several other native Americans converts.

"How far apart are the labor pains?"

"About ten minutes."

Since it was Katherine's first child, both Hannah and Elizabeth knew the birth was not imminent, but there was a sense of urgency nevertheless. They ran out on Mulholland Street, looking to hitch a ride with someone.

"How's Henry taking this?"

"He's not there."

Elizabeth quickly mulled over reasons why Katherine's notorious husband was not at her side. "Did he take the job in the Pineries?"

Daniel had reluctantly recommended him on the strength that Henry was a good worker when he wanted to be, and the separation from Katherine would be good. Hard-working men were needed in the northern Wisconsin forests to cut lumber for the temple.

Hannah answered quickly. "No. Katherine said something about his having some business in Warsaw. I think he's trying to get a loan so he can start a dairy business here in Nauvoo."

Elizabeth choked back an angry scream at the thought that Henry might be in Warsaw doing business with people who were lining themselves up as enemies of the Mormons. There were enough trials and afflictions without Henry contributing to them. July and August had not been good months for the Saints. Several had died. The Prophet's youngest brother, Don Carlos Smith, only twenty-six years old, had passed away on August seventh from complications of working in a damp cellar, editing the *Times and Seasons*. Ironically, the Prophet's fourteen-month-old son, also named Don Carlos, died a week later. Death had become so widespread that Sidney Rigdon had begun to preach "general" funeral sermons. Elizabeth was thankful that none of the United Brethren converts had died, and held her fingers crossed than none would in the coming months. She credited her scant supply of quinine and priesthood blessings.

On a brighter side, work on the temple was progressing nicely. William

Weeks had begun carving twelve oxen for the temple font. Joseph Smith had preached against doctors and medicine. Daniel and Robert's crops on their forty-acre farm were doing well. The Browett and Harris tables had already been graced with a wide variety of vegetables. Wheat, barley, and corn had been harvested and an acre of potatoes was nearly ready to be dug.

"Sister Browett, Sister Harris—where are you going?"

The voice was familiar as Elizabeth lifted her green eyes to a passing wagon. It was William Pitt, who had arrived in Nauvoo only a few days ago. She gave a quick answer. "Can you give us a ride out to Henry Eagles' house?"

"I don't know where he lives, but I guess you'll tell me."

"Thanks bunches," Hannah said as she and Elizabeth plopped into the wagon seat. "You remember Katherine, Henry's wife? She's having a baby. Elizabeth is a full-fledged midwife now."

"I don't relish the thoughts of seeing Henry again," William said with a loathing voice. He recalled the time at the Gloucestershire fair when Henry and his friends had bullied him, John Cox, Levi Roberts, and Joseph Hill. That was five years ago, in 1836.

"Don't worry," Hannah countered. "He's not there."

At that moment, Henry Eagles was sitting in a grog shop next to the Warsaw Hotel reading an article that that had been printed in the *Warsaw Signal* a week earlier, written by T. Sharp, Editor:

Difficulty at Montrose.

> *We understand that on Monday last at Montrose, there was a military training at which the Mormons and citizens united indiscriminately. After the troops were paraded Joe Smith and Gen. Bennett came over from Nauvoo and attempted to inspect them. Upon this Mr. Kilbourn invited the citizens to withdraw from the ranks which was accordingly done. The Mormons then insulted them, causing much excitement, and at the time our informant left a row was anticipated. Now what right, we*

ask, has Joe Smith to go intary officer? Is this not proof positive that he wishes to organize a military church? Else why should he regulate the parades of the saints; but why should he, a citizen of Illinois, have so much interest in the military improvement of his followers who live out of this State? We see in this thing the essential spirit of Mormonism, which is — treason to the Government. Joe Smith, in the government of his followers wishes to place his authority above that of the State. He is not content therefore that the laws of Iowa should interfere his authority, and threaten violence because his authority is disregarded by those not members of his church....

A smile played on Henry's lips as he read the article. He downed a jigger of whiskey and asked the grog shop owner for another, no thought of his pregnant wife entering his mind.

"If I were you I would get out of the Nauvoo Legion," the man who poured his drink said.

"Think I'll do just that," Henry said in an emphatic but placating voice. Even though the whiskey clouded his thinking, he could recall being told that every able bodied man between the ages of eighteen and forty-five was required by Illinois law to serve. Besides, he had reasoned, if he refused to serve, it would draw immediate attention to himself.

"For an Englishman, you're pretty smart. We like you. Sometime I'm going to introduce you to the man that wrote that article."

"Mr. Sharp?"

"Yep. You'd be interested in what he says about your church."

Henry cut him off with an irate protest. "Not my church. My wife's. I'm not a Mormon."

"I notice you've never been here on Sundays. You must be in church in Nauvoo."

A look of annoyance flared on Henry's face. "Look mister, I'm telling you, I ain't Mormon."

"Would you like to meet Mr. Sharp?"

57

WILFORD WOODRUFF'S HEART BROKE when he heard the news he had missed October conference in Nauvoo. Earlier in the day, Wilford had insisted that his hired teamster, J. B. Collins, push his lathered team of four horses as hard as he dared. Now, having learned at Hoppers Mill that conference was over, Wilford told Mr. Collins to slow his horses to a steady walk. They would still be able to reach the city by nightfall. The news that Hyrum Smith's seven-year-old son had died in Nauvoo also distressed Wilford.

As he continued his journey across the Illinois prairie, Wilford recalled the events of his life since he had returned from his mission to England. Arrival in New York on the twentieth of May. Travel by boat and rail to Portland, Maine. Reunited there with his wife, Phoebe, and his new son, Wilford Junior, born more than a year ago on the twenty-second of March. He and Phoebe crying in each other's arms as they mourned the death of baby Sarah Emma, who had passed away while Wilford was in England. Reading in New York newspapers of the arrest of Joseph Smith by the governor of Missouri, and how it had depressed him. Spending a restful vacation with his wife's family in Maine. Traveling to back to New York with his family to prepare for the trip to Nauvoo.

His ten-day stay in New York City had been marked again by impressions from reading the papers there. News about England concerned him: the war against China raged on with British troops attempting to enter Canton. Parliament had dissolved over great internal commotion, and a new ministry had been elected amid continuing poverty and want. Thousands were reported starving to death there. Banks were breaking, factories were shut down, merchants were taking out bankruptcy, millions were unemployed, and the bread lines were getting longer.

The news about the United States hardly seemed better. Congress seemed divided against itself. The cabinet could hardly hold together. President Tyler had just vetoed the banking bill. Wilford read of ships sinking, steamboats blowing up, fires, earthquakes, storms, murders, lying, swearing, and theft.

To Wilford, evil was an awful storm gathering everywhere.

In contrast, he had read the *Millennial Star,* the Church publication from England, and letters from Parley P. Pratt and Orson Hyde. Peace returned to his heart. Despite opposition, the work of the gospel in England appeared to be in high gear. Orson Hyde was on his way to Israel. Other members of the Twelve were anxiously waiting for Wilford's return to Nauvoo. Sadly, Wilford learned of the death of Don Carlos Smith.

After writing several letters to friends in London, reading an article in the New York Herald about the success of the mission of the Twelve in Great Britain, and spending a few days ministering among the Saints throughout the state, Wilford and his family had left New York City on September ninth. He had to cope with more than five hundred pounds of luggage. Traveling with four other adult members of the Church, they traveled to Albany up the Hudson River. They reached Buffalo and the shores of Lake Erie by a combination of river steamboat and rail, seeing Niagara Falls on the way. Leaving Buffalo September twentieth on the *Chesapeake,* paying a fare of twenty dollars for himself and his wife, enduring three hundred other passengers and a load of jackasses, geese and pigs, the Woodruffs reached Chicago eight days later, having covered slightly over a thousand miles. The trip had been marred by rough water, high winds, seasickness, a near shipwreck with the steamship turning on its side, and waves that swept animals overboard.

In Chicago, Wilford hired a team and wagon owned by J. B. Collins to carry him, his wife and child, and luggage that had accumulated to eight hundred pounds, across Illinois to Nauvoo. They had averaged about thirty miles a day and now Nauvoo was in site, looming to the west as the October sun threatened to disappear from the sky. Wilford didn't know it, but the John Benbow farm lay one mile east of the road he was traveling.

"Do you think there'll be a welcoming committee?" Phoebe asked her husband with a half smile. She knew better than to ask. Letters they had forwarded to Joseph Smith and Brigham Young could only give estimates of an arrival date.

Wilford put a husky right arm around his faithful wife and pulled her tightly toward him. "No, but Brigham will have a comfortable bed for us."

The wagon reached Nauvoo a few minutes later, lumbering along Mulholland Street past log homes occupied by Daniel Browett, Robert Harris, and other English immigrants that Wilford had converted. A peculiar feeling came over Wilford as he realized that two years ago when he had left Nauvoo there were scarcely a dozen homes established. Now it appeared there were more than two hundred. Next came the Nauvoo temple construction site, which gave Wilford a spiritual lift. He studied the partially built basement walls as the wagon trudged onward. People who were not already in their homes were scurrying to get there. There were so many new people that no one seemed to recognize Elder Wilford Woodruff, a member of the Council of Twelve Apostles, even when Wilford stopped the wagon to inquire where Brigham Young lived.

When Wilford knocked on his fellow Apostle's door at a quarter past six, Willard Richards and Heber C. Kimball answered the door. After a round of warm embraces, Willard explained that the two Apostles were at the Young home to give Brother Brigham a blessing because he had been ill. That fact concerned Wilford, but Willard's next words shocked him to grief.

"I have some bad news, Brother Woodruff. Brother Thomas Kington's wife died of the ague Monday. Her funeral was today. Had you been here a day earlier, I'm certain you would have been the main speaker at her funeral. Brother Kington's mother died earlier. I guess that's a double dose of bad news for you. Sorry."

A warm October morning sun cast a cheery brightness over Nauvoo. Under that bright sun, Wilford met with the Prophet Joseph Smith and members of the Quorum of Twelve Apostles. There were only two quorum members absent. Parley P. Pratt was in Great Britain; Orson Hyde was in the Holy Land.

Although he enjoyed giving a report of his mission, emphasizing his work among the United Brethren, and giving credit to Thomas Kington and John Benbow, Wilford's heart was heavy as he thought about the passing of Hannah Pitt Kington and Eleanor Kington. Both had been victims of ague. Both had been especially susceptible to the terrible fever because of their weakened condition. The trip across the Atlantic and thereafter to Nauvoo had taken its toll.

In the afternoon, Wilford sent word that he wanted to meet with Brother Kington as soon as possible. Within two hours Kington had accompanied the Benbow family into Nauvoo and was waiting at the Browett cabin when Wilford emerged from his meeting.

"I'm so sorry to hear about your wife and mother," Wilford said as he gave his old friend a prolonged embrace with gentle slaps on the back.

Wilford drew back and contemplated Thomas's sorrow-laden face and the dull suffering look of his eyes. The former United Brethren superintendent had made an extreme sacrifice in following the command to gather to Zion. Except for his friends, Thomas was alone in a new land.

"Thank you, Elder Woodruff," Thomas said as he returned the embrace, fatigued at the events of recent weeks, but intensely awake. He paused, trying to control his emotions. Losing control, he began to weep.

Benbow approached the embracing men and put his arms around both of them. His weather-beaten face had turned grave and sad, recalling the day-by-day struggles of the two dying women, their morbid deaths, and their funerals.

Daniel drew a heavy breath, gave Wilford a strong embrace, and wiped away a tear. His emotions were so mixed he didn't know if the tear was a continued result of mourning in Kington's behalf, or happiness to see Elder Woodruff.

Several minutes later, when Elizabeth greeted Wilford, she couldn't help herself as she began to babble about how responsible she felt for the death of the two women. She told how she had used quinine to reduce the fevers, every combination of herbs, recommended rest and mild foods, but nothing had seemed to work.

Kington recomposed himself. "Sister Browett did everything she could. Everyone did."

Wilford swallowed hard. "God bless you Sister Browett. And God bless you, Brother Kington. God will sustain you in this loss. Somehow you will get over this. Life will go on. Rich blessings will follow."

As the gathering turned from a funeral-like atmosphere to a reunion of sorts, Wilford greeted one-by-one the other English immigrants who had gathered at the Browett home, names that he was familiar with. People that he had taught, converted, baptized. William and Ann Fenner Cole. John and Eliza Roberts Cox. Martha and Rebecca Browett. Robert and Hannah Maria Eagles Harris. Joseph and Mary Ann Marsden Hill. Robert and Elizabeth Cole Holmes. William and Mary Rowberry Jenkins. John and Grace Ann Williams Parry. William and Mary Jenkins Parsons. William and Caroline Smith Pitt. Levi and Sarah Davis Roberts. James and Elizabeth Lambert Robins.

Just before Wilford greeted Thomas and Dianah Bloxham and James Pulham, Elizabeth whispered something into his ear. She informed the Apostle of the loss of nine-year-old Charles Bloxham off the back of the steamboat and the death of Nancy Eagles Pulham on the *Echo*. Wilford came to two conclusions as he expressed his condolences. James was well adjusted, happy, and eager to get on with his life. Thomas Bloxham, on the other hand, appeared to be resentful, even bitter toward the Church and the whole process of the gathering to Zion. These were the thoughts that crossed his mind as dozens and dozens of other English immigrants streamed toward him to say their hellos.

Three weeks later, on a Saturday, Wilford found himself greeting even more immigrants from England, including twenty-seven-year-old Edward Phillips and his mother, Mary Ann Pressdee Phillips, and John Hyrum Green, his wife, the former Susannah Phillips, and their children. They had crossed the Atlantic on the *Caroline,* landed in Quebec, and followed nearly the same route from there to Nauvoo as Wilford had done.

It was Edward Phillips who had constantly repeated the phrase over and over again about the United Brethren congregation: *It seemed to me that we had come to a precipice and could go no further until Brother Woodruff placed a bridge over the precipice and we went on with glad rejoicing.*

He repeated the saying as he greeted Wilford.

Edward's words were laced with the truth, but Wilford remained humble. "It was because of good people like you that the work went so smoothly."

Edward had been put in charge of two branches in England, Ashfield and Corcutt, with George Brooks as his assistant. Elder Woodruff had ordained him an elder last fall during a conference. More than once, Edward had contended with mobs. He remembered with vivid detail the day he was chased out of Mary Ann and John Davis's home in Tirley.

Robert and Hannah accommodated the Greens for a few days. On a cool but pleasant late October afternoon, the two families watched as their children played in the brown grass that separated the Harris and Browett cabins. Ann Green, at six, was a year older than Joseph Harris and could out-run and out-jump him. Lizzy, at three and a half, proved to be a good playmate to Charlotte Green, who had just turned three. William Harris, at only two, had a hard time keeping up with them. Hannah's baby, Thomas Eagles Harris, born on the ship, was only four and a half months old and had to be held by his parents. Susannah's youngest, William Robert Green, however, was ten months old and could walk with assistance.

John Hyrum Green cast his unbelieving eyes at the endless Illinois prairie as Robert took him for a stroll. "Everywhere I look I see the evidences of harvested fields, productive gardens, and a happy faces," he said. "The prices for food, compared to what we were paying in England, is cheaper here. Two dollars and twenty-five cents for a hundredweight of flour, corn at twenty-five cents a bushel, bacon from seven to eight cents a pound, and butter only ten cents a pound."

Robert pointed to an empty lot. "If you're interested, that lot is available and so is the next one over there," Robert said.

"Wouldn't it be fun to raise our families together here in Nauvoo?" Hannah added. "They're about the same ages and it would be good for them to play together."

"I think it's a wonderful idea," Susannah responded, letting her dreams run wild. "And what if we saved the other one for my brother Edward?"

"All you have to do is say the word and it's done—as long as someone else doesn't get it first." Hannah was pleased they were interested. She bounced her baby and kept an eye on the younger children.

Hyrum felt a warmth overtake his heart. "Wouldn't it be funny if some of them married each other some day?" Charlotte had fallen down and Hyrum watched as Robert's son, Joseph, helped her to her feet. He gave her a gentle kiss on the cheek.

"Nothing wrong with that," Susannah said, her eyes glowing. "I'm going to like Nauvoo, and I already like my new neighbors. Always did. Always will."

CHAPTER NOTES:

Joseph Harris married Charlotte Green in 1855 after both families settled in Kaysville, Utah. They are the great-great grandparents of the author of this book.

58

ROBERT WAS BUTCHERING A HOG and Hannah was making soap as Daniel and Elizabeth slowly walked from Hyrum Smith's home to their own log cabin on a frosty morning. Red robins bobbed ahead of them, too busy to sing. It was fall. Squirrels ran ahead of them, scolding Daniel and Elizabeth for disturbing their harvest. Their bulging cheeks made them look like old men with toothaches. Yellow touch-me-nots looked faded. A sharp, cold breeze blew from the northwest, running wildly through fallen leaves. Someone's milk cow huddled in a ravine, her back arched and her tail to the wind.

The cooler weather was not on Daniel and Elizabeth's minds, however. They had just received their patriarchal blessings. Their souls felt a peculiar warmth, similar to the day they had been baptized by Wilford Woodruff a year and a half ago.

They found Hannah bent over an outdoor cooking pot on the south side of the Harris cabin, partially protected by the wind, stirring her mixture of lard, water, and lye. A crude ash hopper, lined with paper and filled with hickory ashes, stood next to the cooking pot.

"You sure go through a *lot* of soap, Hannah," Elizabeth stammered, observing the mixture that looked to her a lot like chicken gravy. It would look more like jelly or cooking custard in a few more minutes. Remaining fumes, normally irritating, were being whisked away by the wind. Another fire heated a larger iron pot where dirty clothes were at a low boil.

"You would too if you had two children in diapers," Hannah answered with a pleasant laugh. Six-month-old Thomas was asleep in a wooden rocker, hidden by bundles of blankets. Willie, nearly two, stood staring at the fire that heated the soap mixture. Her other two children, Joseph and Lizzy, were watching their father butcher the hog.

If only I had children in diapers, Elizabeth thought. *Am I the only woman in the world who is unable to give her husband a child?*

"Keep saving me your extra grease," Hannah pleaded. "Bacon, mutton tallow, beef tallow, anything. It all works about the same." Hannah touched Willie on the head. "Don't get too close yet. It's still not safe."

"With Robert butchering a hog, perhaps you should think about loaning us some of the fat," Elizabeth said with a forced smile, trying to contain her jealousy.

"Oh, I almost forgot about that," Hannah said, fighting the reflex to shiver. "I guess we will have a lot of cracklings when he gets done. Are you just returning from Brother Hyrum's place?"

Daniel's eyes brightened. "Yes. We'd like to tell you and Robert about our blessings. You need to schedule yours right away. Can you come over tonight after dinner?"

Hannah nodded as she added dried herbs and wildflowers to her mixture. "I'm sure Robert would love to." She eyed her crude wooden molds. "Want me to bring you a bar of soap?"

That evening, Daniel and Elizabeth exchanged uneasy looks as they opened the door to find Henry and Katherine Eagles standing at the door with Robert and Elizabeth. Katherine cradled her infant in her arms, born the day Hannah and Elizabeth arrived breathless but eager to help.

"Hope you don't mind us crashing the party," Henry said as he thrust his right hand toward Daniel, shaking his hand.

"Not at all," Daniel answered, his face blank, wondering which hat Henry might be wearing—the white one or the black one.

"I didn't tell you they were coming to our place for dinner," Hannah said. Her look was apologetic. "Henry seems to be interested in learning about patriarchal blessings, too."

Elizabeth rolled her eyes and pointed to her wooden chairs. Martha and Rebecca strolled toward the Browett home from their next-door cabin Daniel had just built for them. As they entered, Rebecca fired Henry a scandalous look.

When everyone was seated, Daniel began. "Patriarchal blessings have been given almost since the restoration of the Church. As you probably know, the Prophet's father was the first church patriarch."

From a smug smile, Henry interrupted. His accent was still very British. "Old chaps, I hear the wording he used in his blessings were pretty wild."

Hannah, who was seated next to Henry, threw a bony elbow into her brother's side. "Be polite, Henry. We're not here to listen to your babbling. Let Daniel teach us."

Inwardly frowning at Henry, Daniel continued. "Having Brother Hyrum Smith place his hands on our heads and, through the Spirit, declare our lineage and give us a blessing was a special spiritual treat, as far as we are concerned."

Elizabeth beamed, nodding her head in agreement.

"We are both of the Tribe of Ephraim," Daniel explained, "as are most of the members of the Church. To me, the blessing I received is going to be like a star to follow. I'm going to treat it like a personal revelation, given to me through an ordained servant of the Savior. I want it to be an anchor to my soul, and if I am worthy, neither death nor the devil can deprive me of the blessings."

"Don't say death," Elizabeth sputtered. "Why do you say that?" For the first time in her life, she had an eerie premonition about her husband.

Daniel returned a puzzled look to his wife. "I didn't mean anything by it, except that all of the ordinances of the gospel, especially baptism, mean that we have a reclamation from the first death which was brought on by the fall of Adam and Eve. My blessing, I think, will help keep me on the path toward entrance in God's highest kingdom, the Celestial Kingdom. Especially if I heed the Holy Ghost."

"All I have to do is make an appointment with Brother Hyrum?" Hannah asked, her interest piqued.

"Yes," said Elizabeth. "Do it soon. It was a *wonderful* spiritual experience."

"Totally unnecessary, I do say," Henry said flatly, his eyes darting around the room.

"Henry, please," Hannah said, feeling an unwelcome shiver. She glanced at Katherine, who hung her head.

"That's the trouble with you Mormons," Henry added, looking dubious. "You know, you think you have the answer to everything, and you don't want to hear the other side. You can't quite muffle me. I have the right to say what I want. America is a free country, right? We have freedom of speech, don't we?"

Robert narrowed his eyes at his brother-in-law. "All right, Henry. Everyone here is a guest in my house, so I give you permission to speak. Make it short. Say your peace, but don't get me riled up. You know what I mean, don't you?"

The remark caused Henry to pause for a few seconds, contemplating Robert. He did not want another fight, but he felt he could say what was on his mind without risking a serious altercation. He continued.

"Old man Smith told a lot of Mormons in their blessings that they would have power to translate themselves from land to land and from country to country, even from one planet to another. What rubbish."

"Henry," Daniel interrupted, "I'm certain Joseph Smith Senior was talking about resurrected beings who inhabit the Celestial Kingdom. The heavens contain millions, perhaps billions of planets. There has to be some kind of ability to travel in the heavens. How do you suppose Heavenly Father and Jesus Christ traveled from their celestial sphere to appear to Joseph Smith in the sacred grove?"

Henry's tone lowered to a guttural rumble. "Joe Smith pretends to have restored everything. There's nothing in the Bible that says patriarchs gave blessings to Church members. The old patriarchs like Jacob merely gave blessings to their sons. That's all. They didn't tell them which tribe they came from. If I got a blessing, Hyrum would no doubt declare me to be Ephraim, just like you. But Joe Smith teaches that rebellious people are not of the bloodline of Ephraim. So which is correct?"

Robert was shocked at Henry's astuteness. He turned to Katherine. "Has Henry been studying the Bible and the Doctrine and Covenants? Or is he learning this rubbish from enemies of the Church?"

Henry placed a hand over Katherine's mouth. Katherine stared blankly at Robert, then cast her eyes obediently downward, turning her attention to her baby.

Henry stood, his tone now dangerously defiant. "It's not rubbish, old chap."

Robert stood and faced Henry. "What a churl you are. I say it's rubbish." He took a menacing step forward.

"Let's go home, Katherine. I've made my point." With those words, Henry took three steps toward the door, opened it, and waited for his wife to walk outside.

The door slammed.

Hannah shook her head in astonishment. "I was hoping to have a pleasant evening with my brother. I guess it was too much to ask."

"It won't be the end of it," Robert said, seating himself again. "He will question everything about the gospel from now until eternity."

"I'm afraid you're right," Hannah said, turning her gaze to Rebecca and Martha, who appeared shocked but eager to learn more about patriarchal blessings. Daniel began talking again, starting with his opinion that more blessings would end up not fulfilled than would be fulfilled, simply because the people receiving them would probably not fulfill the conditions.

"On a *happier* note," Elizabeth said, deliberately changing the subject, "I hear Mary Ann is getting married right away."

Hannah appeared startled but pleased. Marriage would be the perfect solution for the young English convert who had lost her husband, John Davis, in the tragic mobbing and beating last year in England. "Oh, I hadn't heard. Who to?"

Elizabeth's green eyes danced. "Brother Peter Maughan, another English convert of Cumberland. He came to America on the Rochester, with Brigham Young. If you'll remember, Brother Maughan was in the *same* wagon train when they arrived here in Nauvoo. That's how they got acquainted."

"Young and handsome, I suppose," Hannah returned.

"Widower with *six* children," Elizabeth responded, giggling now. "The youngest is only seven months. They're going to live in the Orson Hyde home, at least until Elder Hyde returns from his mission."

"I don't know whether to feel happy for Mary Ann, or sorry for her burden."

Daniel said, "Mary Ann will do fine."

CHAPTER NOTES:

Mary Ann Weston Davis married Peter Maughan on November 2, 1841, in Nauvoo. Maughan's first wife, the former Ruth Harrison, died March 26, 1841, in Alston, Cumberland, England. According to the Peter Maughan history, his first wife died of complications giving birth to their sixth child.

59

PLURAL MARRIAGE. POLYGAMY. Abraham. Isaac. Jacob. The words had rung through Wilford Woodruff's mind all throughout the night, robbing him of sleep. The crisp December air whipped through cracks in his log cabin.

Wilford fumbled for a lantern and lit it. Squinting at his surroundings, he saw only the Spartan interior of the modest home he had purchased in October for eighty-five dollars, and the few items of furniture he had retrieved from storage in Montrose. A meager Christmas had been celebrated two days earlier.

Phoebe stirred, rolled over, and resumed her deep sleep.

A quick dousing of water to his face did little to ease his anxiety. Wilford stared out of the small window, into a dark void, trying to force negative images out of his mind. *Joseph Smith has a second wife. Will it be long until members of the Twelve are expected to actually practice this ancient doctrine? Will Phoebe accept it? Can I?*

Under the light of the lantern the thirty-four-year-old Apostle reached for his journal, an old habit now. His first inkling was to record how he had felt during an all-day session, when Joseph had confided with the Twelve concerning another sacred revelation. Joseph told them that the Savior had revealed to him that plural marriage as practiced by the ancients was as much a part of the restoration as baptisms for the dead, the priesthood, and the Book of Mormon.

Wilford filled his quill with ink and touched the quill to the paper. His fingers froze. *I will breach a trust if I write about the plural wife doctrine. Joseph asked each of us to keep the matter a secret for a while longer, until we feel that members of the Church can accept it.*

He put down the quill and heaved a sigh, recalling, as best he could, the Prophet's words. *Plural marriage is the law of Abraham, or the works of Abraham. We cannot receive the promise made to Abraham without entering into the "New and Everlasting Covenant" of marriage. The ancient order must be restored as it was in Abraham's day. The Lord's servants through the ages have practiced polygamy. No man can receive a fullness of the celestial glory and eternal life except he obeys the plural marriage law. A fullness of salvation cannot be obtained without it. It is the purest and most exalting and elevating principle that God ever revealed to man.*

Staggering to his feet again, Wilford paced, chilled by the cold floor on the soles of his bare feet. He stared again at his slumbering wife, and at his child, bundled in a homemade crib. He fought a rising trepidation. During the day the Spirit had borne witness to him that everything Joseph had taught was the truth, as it always had done when he had listened to the Prophet teach. *Am I doubting, now? What dire repercussions will come to my Church as we eventually embrace this ancient doctrine?*

For an instant, Wilford's eyes focused on his own shadow, cast against the log wall by the dim lantern. *No, never. I will not doubt.*

His jaw tightened as he blew out the lantern and knelt by his bed to pray. *Give me strength, Heavenly Father.*

He remained on his knees for more than an hour. The peace he was pleading for came gradually, but forcefully. As he ended his prayer and cuddled next to Phoebe, a feeling of triumph settled over him. There would be no more doubt. *If my will is swallowed up in the will of the Savior and the Father, perhaps I will be worthy of exaltation.*

He drifted into a peaceful sleep.

60

January 1842

THE LATE JANUARY DAY BEGAN WITH a cold sunrise, no color in the clouds. There was only a dazzling silver disk in a gray muslin sky. A biting wind blew out of the west.

Yesterday's brief thaw had sharpened the icicles that hung in a harpstring row from the roof of his log home. Just for fun, Wilford Woodruff brushed his hand across them. They fell with a musical shattering.

Wilford rode hunched over aboard his gray gelding from his home just below the temple site to the John Benbow farm, five miles east. He couldn't help but think of the time the Lord had told him to leave the Potteries area of England and travel south to the Benbow farm in Herefordshire in 1840, nearly two years ago. That's when he first met John Benbow and began the process of converting the United Brethren congregation. Entering the Benbow house now, he found a parlor full of United Brethren converts waiting for him to preach a Sunday sermon at their sacrament meeting.

As he spoke, he scanned his English friends, taking in each pair of eyes separately. He couldn't help wondering how each of them might react if the time came for Joseph to reveal the doctrine of plural marriage to the entire

Church membership.

Wilford locked his eyes first on Thomas Kington. Thomas had just married a widow, Margaret Pizel Meyers, three weeks earlier. A profound thought came to Wilford. *Plural marriage could become a great blessing to widows who might otherwise have no chance of marrying a worthy Mormon man here in the Nauvoo community.*

Next, Wilford scanned Daniel Browett, sitting beside his giddy wife. The couple was clearly frustrated that after six years of marriage they had no children. Was there a biological problem wit his wife? Another profound thought came to Wilford. *Plural marriage could become a tool to assist Heavenly Father to bring spirit children into the world, and provide them homes where they can be taught the restored gospel.*

Rebecca Browett. High strung, young, thin-boned. Single. Would she accept plural marriage if a proposal came? Or would she hold out for a man who had never married?

Robert Harris. Four children in only five years of marriage. *He may set a record for the most children of all my converts. He doesn't need another wife.*

John Hyrum Green. *Like Robert, prolific. Wife pregnant again with number five.*

William Pitt. The musician. First child born two weeks ago. *Sick wife. What if she were to die?*

Levi Roberts. First child born only a week ago. Wife healthy.

John Cox. First child due in two to three weeks. Wife beaming.

Thomas Bloxham. Not baptized. Still angry because of the death of his newborn son in England, and the drowning of his son off the back of the steamboat.

Edward Phillips. Engaged to marry Annie Simmons. *Why wait, Edward?*

John Benbow. Two teenage adopted children. Older than most of the other United Brethren converts. Plural marriage? *Prediction: probably not.*

Over refreshments of hot cider and applesauce cake, the conversation turned casual, yet focusing on the Church.

"Things seem to be quiet in the Church this time of year," Benbow said with a calm look. "All of the men here have said they enjoyed taking part in the Prophet's review of the Nauvoo Legion last week. What news do you bring to us?"

Wilford drew a deep breath, and then exhaled. *If he only knew what I can't tell him.*

"Nothing startling," Wilford said. "The Prophet Joseph is doing a brisk business at his little red store. John Taylor will become the new editor of the *Times and Seasons* next week. And I will become the new superintendent of the printing office at the same time."

Wilford didn't mention that he had bought a larger home with a quarter-acre lot, plus two more lots. That his cow had produced a nice heifer calf two weeks ago. Or that he had helped butcher twenty hogs for the Nauvoo House last week.

"Congratulations," offered Jane Benbow.

"Thank you. And by the way, Joseph told me to thank both of you again for the loan you gave him."

John beamed outwardly. "Tell him he's welcome. He knows that. I'm always happy to assist building up the Kingdom. We all need to learn that we can't take our money with us when we die."

Wilford changed the subject again. "The baptismal font is not too busy right now. The weather's too cold." He spoke of the giant wooden baptismal font in the temple, placed on the backs of twelve wooden oxen, each symbolically representing one of the Twelve Tribes of Israel.

"I can't wait to bring the names of my parents and deceased brothers and sisters, and be baptized for them," Robert said, wincing at their memory.

"Me, too," Hannah added, thinking of her father and her sister, Editha.

Wilford let his imagination run wild as he responded. "As do all of us." Wilford thought of the millions, no billions, of people who had inhabited the earth and had never been baptized.

Someday, he thought to himself, he would like to make certain great leaders in American and world history were given saving ordinances. Joseph Smith, he remembered, had taught as much as two years earlier that those who died without such ordinances must hear the gospel in the hereafter before they could be saved.

At the August funeral service of a high councilor Joseph talked of baptism for the dead, and again at the general conference that Wilford had just barely missed. During the same day-long training in which the Prophet had taught the plural marriage doctrine, he had also expanded on baptisms for the dead. *The objective is to offer salvation to all humankind. Except a man be born of water, and of the Spirit, he cannot enter into the Kingdom of God.*

"Do you enjoy your work mission, Daniel?" Wilford asked, changing the subject again.

Daniel was one of nearly three hundred workmen that had been called to quarry rock and haul stones to the temple site during the winter months. Wilford knew Daniel's talents as a carpenter would be used immensely during the next two or three or four years. Conversely, there were no Mormon chapels being built in Nauvoo. Not one.

"Hard work, but worth it," Daniel commented, drenched with self-satisfaction.

The Prophet had recently declared that the Church would hold no general conferences until they could be held in the temple. Daniel shook his head, contemplating all that had to be done. In addition to the thousands of pieces of limestone that were being blasted out of the quarry, more than a million board feet of lumber would be needed. Besides masons, carpenters, sawyers, woodworkers, plasterers, painters, glaziers, and tinsmiths would be needed. Cranes would have to be built.

Daniel speculated that walls for the first level would start to go up by spring. Stakes in the out areas, beyond Nauvoo, had already been dissolved. Members were moving closer to the city, or in it, to be ready to meet the labor demands of the gigantic project.

"Your farm is going to end up looking similar to the Hill Farm near Castle Frome," Wilford told Benbow, whose eyes began to glisten at the compliment. Wilford thought how he missed the Hill Farm and all of England, especially the friends that had remained there.

"Thanks. I wonder who's running it now?" the Englishman said, scratching his chin. "I just received a letter. The man who ended up with it, Richard Oakey, just died."

Wilford's face registered no surprise. He had predicted a fateful end to the man because of the underhanded way in which he had convinced the landowner to terminate Benbow's lease.

John Benbow was better off in Nauvoo.

CHAPTER NOTES

According to Wilford Woodruff's journal, he rode to John Benbow's home on Sunday, January 30, preached at his home, and spent the evening conversing with several of the brethren.

61

June 1842

ROBERT AND DANIEL HAD PLOWED all day. They had used a borrowed team of horses from John Benbow because both Tapper and Bendigo
had become lame, due to overwork on their forty-acre farm. When they
returned the horses late that afternoon day in June, neither man knew that
Joseph Smith was visiting the Benbow farm. And little did Robert suspect that
Joseph would challenge him to a wrestling match.

"Your reputation precedes you, Brother Harris," Joseph said, wrapping a
huge hand around Robert's. "Perhaps you will be the only man ever to whip
me. After all, you would have been the British heavyweight champion.
Right?" He was dressed in a clean white shirt, brown trousers, and riding
boots.

To Robert, the grip felt stronger than Henry's. Tired, sweaty, conscious
of his soiled shirt, Robert scanned Benbow's barns and sheds, looking for
someplace to hide. He could not breathe. *Only man ever to whip me? Is the
Prophet challenging me to a pugilism match, or wrestling?*

Joseph glanced playfully at John Benbow, Porter Rockwell, Brigham
Young, Wilford Woodruff, and then at Daniel. "Cat got your tongue, Brother

Harris?"

Robert stared at the ground, sinking lower and lower.

"This is the way Brother Joseph unwinds and gets his exercise," Porter explained, giving Robert a calm look of apology. "There's no harm in it."

Robert exhaled slowly, filled with uncertainty. "I'd rather not."

Porter laughed. "Brother Harris, I promise not to tell you about the time Howard Coray wrestled with the Prophet."

Joseph looked uncomfortable. "Now, Port. You needn't tell stories."

Porter held up a hand. His smile turned mischevious. "No, but I will anyway. Brother Coray reluctantly agreed to wrestle with the Prophet. Brother Joseph took a lock on his right leg, and broke it three inches above the ankle. But the next day Brother Joseph went to Brother Coray and gave him a blessing, and the leg healed right away. So don't worry, Brother Harris. If you get hurt, a blessing will follow." Porter threw back his head and laughed again. He didn't tell Robert that Coray had been outweighed considerbly.

Robert pulled a face.

Joseph gave Robert an easy smile. "Your assignment in the Nauvoo Legion is to be one of my bodyguards. It'll be just a friendly wrestling match. If you're thinking of bare fists, forget it. I'm playful, but not crazy."

Shifting his weight from one foot to another, Robert thought how much he, along with Levi Roberts and John Cox, enjoyed his training, even though there had been no specific assignments come their way yet. All the bodyguards felt they had let the Prophet down during the recent sham battle of the Nauvoo Legion, when Mayor John C. Bennett tried to assassinate the Prophet. No one knew about it until later. The prophet's spiritual awareness had saved him.

"Give it all you've got, Brother Harris," Rockwell said with a sober smile. "Brother Joseph has never been beaten. Not even at stick pulling."

Robert cast his pleading eyes toward Daniel.

Daniel's blue eyes were clouded with concern. He could not quite picture his brother-in-law wrestling with a prophet of God. He preferred to think of Joseph as a busy Church leader and effective administrator. In March,

Joseph had issued the Wentworth letter summarizing thirteen points of Mormon belief, written a long letter decrying the evils of slavery, organized the Relief Society, took over as editor of the *Times and Seasons*, help organize the Masonic Lodge in Nauvoo, baptized eighty people on a single day, and authorized more baptisms for the dead.

In April, Joseph had authorized several newspapers to publish the Book of Abraham, preached a powerful sermon against fornicators and adulterers, and lashed out at the unvirtuous activities of then-Mayor John C. Bennett. On May 19, following Bennett's disfellowshipment, Joseph had been elected to serve as mayor, as if he didn't have enough to do leading the Church. He had spent much of the month of May encouraging the rapid building of the temple.

Daniel shrugged his shoulders and rolled his eyes.

Robert glanced at John Benbow, who had recently been ordained to the office of high priest, and who had just a few days ago been baptized six times in the new font by Wilford Woodruff for six deceased members of his family.

John's voice was light and crisp. "The Prophet and the Brethren are here wanting my advice on a land purchase. There's some ground northwest of here that will be needed for more converts who are gathering to Nauvoo, owned by a Mr. Shelton from New York. My advice to you, Brother Harris, is to get your balance."

Still speechless, Robert's eyes finally met those of his friendly challenger, six-foot tall, two hundred pounds, age thirty-six, still in his athletic prime. Robert had turned thirty last December. "I don't know," he stammered.

"Just pretend the Missouri authorities are hiding in the trees," Joseph said, pointing to a nearby grove of trees. "Give me all you have. If they see that I can defend myself, they might hightail it home. They've been trying to arrest Porter and me ever since someone tried to kill ex-governor Boggs in Missouri a few weeks ago."

The remarks caused Brigham Young to laugh. "I think Brother Joseph has met his match. I'll take Brother Harris. How about you, Brother Porter?"

"I know the rest of ya don't bet, but I'll put my money on Brother

Harris." Porter Rockwell reached into his pocket and pulled out a dollar and a half eagle. "You're all alone on this one, Brother Joseph." He slowly ran his fingers through his beard, waiting for an answer.

"Put your money back in your pocket, Brother Rockwell," Joseph said. "There's no one here who will make a real bet."

"None who dare in front of you, you mean," Porter said with an awkward smile.

"What about you, Brother Browett?" Brigham asked. "How do you think this will turn out?"

"Can there be such a thing as a draw?" Daniel asked.

Porter grinned and took off his hat. "Well, that's enough posturing. Let's see you two wrestle."

"What are the rules?" Robert asked, his face still sober and confused.

Joseph laughed heartily, patting his firm stomach. "Whoever ends up on top wins, Brother Harris." Joseph crouched, braced himself, and took a step toward Robert.

Robert tossed a pathetic glance at Daniel, shrugged his shoulders, and waited for the Prophet to make the first move.

Joseph lunged, hoping to capture Robert in a bear hug. Quick as a cat, Robert backed away.

"You're fast, that's for certain," said Joseph, smiling.

Robert returned the smile, trying to relax.

Joseph lunged again, trying for Robert's leg, missing. "Very fast, indeed."

Robert reasoned that he could probably evade Joseph's every move, but that would only prolong the outcome—whatever that might be. He knew he had to engage. When Joseph lunged this time, the two men collided. Joseph's broad shoulder ground into Robert's sternum. A split second later the two men were in a bear hug, straining for an advantage. In a locked position, they circled to the left, then the right.

Robert quickly concluded that Joseph Smith was stronger than any man he had ever fought. By instinct, however, he was wrestling the Prophet with every ounce of energy. The bear hug became a battle of sheer strength. *I hope*

I don't have to go home and tell Hannah I killed the Prophet.

Slowly, Robert could feel Joseph gaining an advantage. Robert squeezed until his face was blue. It wasn't enough. He felt himself tip backwards. The two men crashed to the ground with Joseph on top.

Joseph's words startled Robert as the Prophet relaxed his grip and rolled away. "Brother Harris, you passed the test."

Robert gave a grim sigh. "Test? What test?" *Does he think I let him win?*

"I'm thinking of a scripture in the Book of Abraham," Joseph said, smiling at his foe's puzzled look.

Robert shrugged his shoulders.

Joseph motioned to the others. "Sit on the grass with us a moment."

"What do you mean, the Book of Abraham?" Robert asked, watching Daniel sit beside him. Wilford, Brigham, John, and Porter formed a semicircle in front of the Prophet.

Daniel nudged his brother-in-law with a bony elbow. "The translation from the papyrus, remember? We've been reading it in the *Times and Seasons.*"

Robert looked unsettled as he tried to remember.

Brigham came to Robert's rescue, arching his eyebrows with intrigue. "Brother Joseph purchased four Egyptian mummies in 1835 from a man named Michael H. Chandler. The mummies had been exhumed on the west bank of the Nile River opposite the ancient city of Thebes sometime between 1817 and 1821."

Brigham thought it was more than a nifty coincidence that the mummies were found about the time Joseph received his first vision.

Wilford could sense Robert's bewilderment. He took over the explanation. "Chandler found a book of papyrus clutched to the bosom of one of the mummies. During a tour on the East Coast of America, Chandler inquired of everyone he could talk to that might know of someone who might translate the Egyptian writings. He was lead to our Prophet, Joseph Smith."

"To make a long story short," Joseph said, "As soon as I examined the papyrus I knew that Abraham was the original author and I began to translate it. We now call it the Book of Abraham."

Robert twisted the ring on his finger, trying to relax. "You mentioned a test."

"It has nothing to do with our wrestling match. There is a scripture from the third chapter of the Book of Abraham. *And we will prove them herewith, to see if they will do all things whatsoever the Lord their God shall command them.*"

Robert raised an eyebrow, searching for the connection.

"Brother Harris, a great purpose of life is to come here and prove ourselves," Joseph said. "You passed the test, at least so far. You hearkened to the gospel message brought to you by the Lord's messenger, Elder Woodruff. You gave up the world, the chance to become the heavyweight champion of Great Britain. After wrestling with you today I am impressed to tell you that you would have won the championship. You're the strongest man I have wrestled. By now, you would have been wealthy and famous. Instead, here you are in Nauvoo, a poor dirt farmer. But I perceive you are a happy dirt farmer with a beautiful wife and four wonderful children. You're keeping the commandments and trying to endure to the end. I'm right, aren't I?"

Robert's eyes welled up with emotion. "Yes, Brother Joseph. You're right." *Amazing. One moment this man is pinning me to the ground. The next moment he is teaching me more about the gospel.*

"Let me tell you more about the Book of Abraham."

Daniel felt a familiar tinge of wonder that evening as he tried to explain what he had learned from his almost-private session with Joseph Smith at the Benbow farm. He spoke slowly, in a serious, formal tone.

During the day, Elizabeth had been to the William and Wilson Law's gristmill for flour, and to the general store for tallow, flaxseed, peppermint, mustard, sugar, and calico. She planned on having Rebecca sew a calico dress for Hannah's birthday which was only days away. Of course that meant her own birthday was nearing, and their anniversaries.

Daniel crinkled his blue eyes at Elizabeth, touching her hand. "All along I supposed that the Savior, through the Prophet Joseph Smith, had merely restored a New Testament Church."

Elizabeth blinked. "That's not true?"

Daniel had always been struck by his wife's steady manner and her vision of always helping people. In February, she had helped deliver a daughter to John and Eliza Cox, a girl they had named Mary Ann, after the woman who was now the wife of Peter Maughan. In April, Elizabeth had been there to assist Susannah Green with her new baby, a son that John Hyrum named Robert, in honor of his friendship with Robert Harris.

She seemed to always be learning more about healing from Willard Richards. Yellowroot tea or red sassafras bush root tea to get rid of worms in children. Chestnut leaf tea four times weekly for whooping cough (or take a teaspoon of alum powder and honey mixed together when coughing starts). Blackberry roots or lady-slipper plants for diarrhea. The list seemed endless.

Yesterday Elizabeth had mentioned how troubled she was that her supply of quinine was exhausted. The fever season was nearly upon them and there seemed to be none available.

Daniel smiled at her question. "Yes and no. Joseph taught us that the Church had been organized even in Old Testament times, beginning, of course, with Adam."

"I never thought of it that way, " Elizabeth said, a puzzled look crossing her face.

"Think of everything that happened during the restoration of the gospel. Joseph Smith received the keys to the Aaronic Priesthood from John the Baptist, who was actually the last of the Old Testament prophets. And Joseph received the keys of the higher priesthood from Peter, James and John, but they restored a priesthood authority known to and held by the Old Testament Prophet Melchizedek. Every other angelic ministrant who came to him to restore keys and authority came from Old Testament times."

"But what has this to do with what Joseph taught you about the Book of Abraham?"

With an appraising look at Elizabeth, who was biting her lip, Daniel said, "I've concluded that the Lord moves in mysterious ways. It's an old conclusion, of course."

"What?"

"The way in which the Savior restored the knowledge of the Abrahamic covenant is amazing."

"What do you mean?"

"The Savior could have appeared to Joseph like he did in the first vision and talk to him-face-to-face about the Abrahamic covenant, but he didn't. There's good reason why he didn't."

"Why?" Elizabeth asked faintly, wishing she already knew.

"Number one. The Lord is not going to show himself if there is another way. Joseph Smith is a human being just like the rest of us. He walks the earth by faith, just like you and me. He has to work out his salvation and prove himself to God, just like you and me. True, he is a Prophet who has already seen the Savior several times. But I believe the Savior doesn't show himself unless he absolutely has to."

"I agree, but I *still* don't understand where you're going with this."

Daniel's voice was calm. "Reason number two. The information about the Abrahamic covenant had been preserved in papyrus from the old times. All the Lord had to do was give it to him. It is no coincidence that the mummies were discovered about the time Joseph had the first vision, and that Michael Chandler sought out Joseph Smith. Joseph immediately knew that the papyrus book, clutched in the bosom of one of the mummies, was sacred."

"So you think that was a *clever way* for the Lord to get the book to our Prophet?"

"Very."

Elizabeth nodded. "I agree."

"But if the Abrahamic covenant is so *important,* why isn't it explained in full detail in the Old Testament?"

This time Elizabeth wrinkled her face. "Good question."

There was a pause.

"What is the answer?"

Daniel pressed. "I thought you might think of it yourself."

Another pause.

Daniel's blue eyes twinkled. "Think harder."

"Does it have anything to do with how the Bible was edited, translated, and re-translated?"

Daniel was pleased with his wife's answer. "Exactly right."

Daniel was thinking of what Thomas Kington had taught them in England. A pagan Roman emperor, Constantine, had collated the Bible, rejecting much of the original writings. Following him, bishops and monks added, deleted, and revised as they pleased—whatever gave them more control over the people.

Daniel had long concluded that the Bible was a product of tumultuous times, evolving through countless translations. Details of the Abrahamic covenant could easily have been lost. First Nephi chapter thirteen, verse twenty-eight came to his mind. *Wherefore, thou seest that after the book hath gone forth through the hands of the great and abominable church, that there are many plain and precious things taken away from the book, which is the book of the Lamb of God.*

"So now that we have it, exactly what is it?" Elizabeth asked. "It's not that easy for someone like me to understand. What did the Prophet say to you today?"

"It all centers around the family."

Elizabeth looked impressed. "How so?"

""Let's start from the beginning. Just like us, what did Abraham have to have for his salvation?"

Elizabeth opened her olive green eyes as wide as possible. "The gospel."

"Yes, but what part of the gospel first?"

"Baptism?"

"Correct. Baptism is the covenant of salvation. Next, Abraham had to have the higher priesthood conferred upon him. Then the Lord was prepared to bless him. Jehovah, who is Christ, told Abraham that Christ would come through his lineage, and that Abraham's posterity would receive certain lands as an eternal inheritance."

"But what does that have to do with us?"

"We are the seed of Abraham. Abraham's book says that when we receive the gospel we shall be counted as the seed of Abraham, and that all the families of the earth will be blessed. The richest of those blessings is life eternal."

Elizabeth was still puzzled. "I *think* I'm getting it."

"Let me help you some more," Daniel said, his blue eyes taking in the woman he loved so much. "Joseph told us that the Lord had restored the Abrahamic covenant in perfect accord with the purpose and message of the Book of Mormon. It was not the Lord's purpose to merely reestablish the organization of the New Testament church, simply because salvation and exhalation is not found in the organizational structure of the Church. It is found in the in the covenants. It order to have the covenants of salvation, the true priesthood and the true Church had to be properly restored."

"That makes sense."

"Joseph told us that the schoolmaster to the covenants is the Book of Abraham. He admonished us to learn from that book how father Abraham sought after and received the fullness of those blessings. We need to keep our copies of the *Times and Seasons* and study the book just as we study the Book of Mormon and the Bible. It won't be long, Joseph told us, until the Book of Abraham will be printed and distributed to the membership of the Church."

Elizabeth touched her chin. "It still seems like something is missing."

"Oh, the Prophet admitted that."

"What do you mean?"

"He said there was one final piece of the puzzle."

"Give it to me, please."

"All he said is that it had something to do with marriage. When the time comes for him to reveal this information to the Church, it will all fit in nicely with the Abrahamic covenant."

"What do you think it is?"

"Something about the eternal nature of marriage, and the eternal nature of families. That's what I think."

Daniel thought of the stillborn son that had been born to the Prophet's wife, Emma, last February. What he didn't know was that Joseph already had a second wife, and had taught the endowment ceremony to members of the Twelve. All these things tied into the Abrahamic covenant.

"Did Brother Joseph say anything about John C. Bennett?"

"Not a word."

Elizabeth thought it curious that one day Bennett claimed that Joseph Smith authorized him to have illicit relationships with women other than his wife, then turned around and signed a statement saying the claim was false.

62

July 1842

THE MAN HIDING IN THE TREES was stocky and dark. His wide shoulders were thrown back and his chin tucked hard against his chest. His dark hair was slicked back with grease. Dark stubble shrouded his strong jaw.

Martha Rebecca Browett had no clue the man was there. Alone, she meandered aimlessly along Mulholland humming a tune, clutching the items she had purchased at Lyons Drug Store. The sun had set along the river. There was barely enough light to see the road.

She had enjoyed her walk to the store on this late day in July. Her journey had taken her past the temple, down the hill past new frame and new brick homes, and to the store where she had purchased wine red cotton cloth and white flax cloth to sew a dress for Thomas Kington's new wife, Margaret. She was in no hurry to get home. For a time she had strolled along the Mississippi. She had enjoyed the humming of the bees, the chirping of birds, and the ducks feeding along the banks, doing their quacking. Buttercups, columbine, wild roses, bluebells, daisies, and wild peas adorned her way.

Turning left from Water Street, she trudged up the gently sloping hill toward home.

"Rebecca."

The mention of her name startled her. She took a step backward. From the darkness, deep in the trees, a voice came, saying her name again.

"Who's there?"

The dark figure of a man approached. His dark eyes seemed to scorch the earth before him. Rebecca placed a hand over her heart and gasped. "Henry? Henry Eagles? Is that you?"

"Yes. I need to talk to you." Henry wore a dark red shirt, black trousers, and a dark gray cap pulled over his swarthy face.

"You scared me," she said, still wary. She thought of a similar incident aboard the *Echo*. "If you need to talk to me, come to my house tomorrow when Daniel can be there."

Henry shook his head. A guttural rumble came from his mouth. "Our conversation needs to be in private." He paused. "I like your yellow dress. You look beautiful tonight."

Rebecca shuddered and took another step backward.

"Do you often think of marriage? Do you think of men?"

Sudden visions of her terrifying night on the *Echo* swept over her, when the sailor named John Poole attacked her. She had the impulse to run.

Too late. Henry gripped her arm. It was a powerful grip, sure to leave bruises.

"Let me go, please."

"Rebecca, I want you to be my wife. I told you that once before, remember? I really mean it this time."

"You're crazy. You're already married. Please let me go."

A smirk came over Henry's face. "Surely by now you've heard about spiritual wives. You've read John C. Bennett's stuff, haven't you? If Joe Smith can have more than one wife, I can, too. I choose you."

Rebecca nodded, her trembling fingers revealing her fear. "Yes, I've heard about Bennett. He's an unscrupulous rogue. Let me go." *Jesus, too, had his Judas.*

"I think you dream every night about marriage. This is your chance."

Rebecca closed her eyes and cringed.

"What's your answer?"

"Can't I have some time to think about it?" She assessed the tightness of Henry's grip.

"You don't need time."

Rebecca's resolve stiffened. "And who do you suppose will perform the marriage?"

"In spiritual wifery, we just mutually consent."

"I don't consent." Her tone was icy now.

With surprising quickness, she jerked her arm away from Henry. She started to spin, to run away, but it was too late. She felt Henry's fist strike her on the back of her neck, pounding her to the ground. Her reflex was to crawl away. Her elbows and her knees burned as she clambered along, her mind hunting for options. She screamed. She froze as she saw Henry again, this time standing in front of her. Barely conscious of her own actions, she screamed again.

Henry's meaty hand covered her mouth.

An unexpected voice from the night: "Who's there? What's going on?"

Henry jumped up and disappeared into the trees. Rebecca rose to her knees, sobbing. A man and a woman bent over her.

"Are you going to be all right? Who was that man?"

Daniel and Robert didn't wait until morning to confront Henry. They rode Tapper and Bendigo along a dark road leading east to Henry's small farm. They found him in a dimly lit log barn, his head pressed into the flank of a cow. A rag bitch—a tin cup filled with bacon grease and a twisted rag wick—provided the light.

"Little late for milking, isn't it Henry?" Robert said, simmering with rage.

Henry appeared both bewildered and horrified that his failed secret marriage attempt had resulted in Robert and Daniel's appearance so quickly. He had been sipping on homemade bald face, whiskey fresh from his still without any aging.

Robert stood over Henry. "Nice Brogans you're wearing. Two-dollar work shoes are too good for you. They're covered with manure already."

"Leave me alone," Henry said slowly, emphasizing each word.

All friendliness had long disappeared from Daniel's face. "I think those were Rebecca's words, exactly," he grumbled.

"Let's just forget it, shall we? I meant no harm. Just some buffoonery. I'm sorry. You have to forgive me, right? That's your gospel in action."

Even the cow flinched at the speed in which Robert jerked Henry off his feet and pressed his face to his. "You're a real work of art, Henry. I speak for both the Browett family, and for me. Hannah, too. If anything like this happens again, it will be your nose, your ribs, your jaw, and even your neck. Got it?"

He picked up his brother-in-law and threw him over the corral fence.

Daniel was speechless.

Robert's voice hissed. "Vengeance is ours, saith Daniel and Robert. That's the gospel in action, Henry. And don't you forget it."

No answer.

"Let's go home, Daniel. I don't think he'll bother Rebecca again."

"I guess we can blame John C. Bennett for all this," Daniel said. Reins loose on his neck, Bendigo was picking his way home along the dark road.

"Give Henry an inch, and he'll take a wife." Robert's tone was one of disgust.

There was silence for a few minutes. Only the clip-clop of the horses could be heard.

"I guess you can't blame Henry for being confused," Daniel said. "Bennett would confuse anyone."

"I don't think Henry's too confused. He knows why we were there. He knows why we left him laying flat on his back."

Daniel laughed. "What I mean is that he didn't have the benefit of someone like Wilford Woodruff explaining all this to him."

"He ought to be baptized and come to Church," Robert said emphatically. "It's his fault for staying away."

Both men began to review in their minds what Wilford had told a priesthood gathering of the English converts recently. True, the doctrine of plural marriage had been restored by the Prophet. True, Joseph had more than one wife, the most recent being Eliza R. Snow. True, Joseph had known about the doctrine for many years. True, an angel had told Joseph that unless he put the doctrine into practice immediately, he would be destroyed. True, a few select members of the Church were going to be asked to engage in the practice.

False, the charge that Joseph was living as man and wife with every woman to whom he had been sealed; most were sealed for eternity only—not time, or life on the earth. False, the notion that the practice is "spiritual wifery." Spiritual wifery was a non-Mormon practice in another area of the country. True, plural marriage was God's law, practiced under strict guidelines; it was a commandment.

"What do you think will happen now?" Daniel asked.

"Henry will get on a ship and return to England."

Daniel chuckled. "Not Henry. I mean with this plural marriage controversy."

Bennett had recently published his tense, self-revealing account entitled, *The History of the Saints; or, An Expose of Joe Smith and Mormonism*. Daniel had read it. He used these words to describe Bennett: friend of Satan, slippery, ambitious, egotistical.

"It's not for me," Robert said, staring into the darkness.

"What if the Brethren asked you to practice it?" Daniel thought of Jacob's warning in the Book of Mormon: *Behold, David and Solomon had many wives and concubines, which thing was abominable before me, saith the Lord.*

"Me? Not a chance. Elder Woodruff said that a very select few would be asked. Besides, Hannah would kill me."

"Not Hannah." Daniel also thought of Jacob's explanation as to when the Lord approved polygamy, a few verses later: *For if I will, saith the Lord of*

Hosts, raise up seed unto me, I will command my people; otherwise they shall hearken unto these things. To him, the message was clear. God only approved of plural marriage when he commanded it.

Robert was joking, but the thought of having to ask her to approve plural marriage brought him a feeling of emptiness. "Yes, Hannah. She has her own mean streak. She's related to Henry Eagles."

"I've never seen her mean streak. I don't think you have either."

"True. But if I brought another woman home… Even if she were Church approved."

Henry's head was back against the flank of the same cow. Bent but not broken, his mind was working. Rebecca was off limits, but there were other women available. *What's good for Joe Smith, is good for me. Joe is lying, anyway, about his wives. He's even taken married women to wife. Why can't I? Some Prophet, this arrogant Joe Smith. I hate Robert and Daniel. I'll get even. I swear.*

Lanterns in both Browett cabins and in the Harris cabin were burning bright at midnight when Daniel and Robert returned. They found Rebecca resting comfortably, with Martha, Elizabeth, and Hannah pacing, talking. While Daniel and Robert were gone, they covered a lot of ground. At first they talked about Henry's encounter with Rebecca. That led to John C. Bennett: expulsion from the Masons in mid-June; excommunication papers; and his anti-Mormon articles.

Other subjects: William Law's defense of the morality of the Saints. The July Fourth celebration. Two men fined for selling whiskey during the parade. Joseph speaking to eight thousand Saints. Plural wives. Polygamy. Plural wives. Polygamy.

"Is my brother still alive?" Hannah asked, as all three women stepped out to meet them, away from Rebecca's ears. Crowded stars arched overhead, the night air warm.

"If he comes around here again he'll wish he wasn't," Robert said, his laugh bitter. "How's Rebecca?"

"Badly shaken, but getting over it."

"She's going to have another mental scar forever," Elizabeth said. The color was drained from her face with worry.

"Who were the people who scared Henry off?" Daniel asked.

"Two couples, out for an evening walk."

"Did you get their names? I need to go thank them."

"Jacob Kemp Butterfield, and his wife, Louisa. They've lived in Nauvoo for a year and a half. Originally from Maine. He's a teamster. Robert's met him before, not long after we arrived in Nauvoo. The other couple was Joseph Horne, and his wife, Mary. They just moved here from Quincy. He's English, born in London, but his parents raised him in Canada, a place called Little York, I think."

"Let's go see them tomorrow," Daniel said.

Martha Browett dropped her chin. Since she had accepted the gospel in England, she had been taught that she should work to obtain all that her Father in Heaven has in store for her, in heaven. But back then, no one told her about polygamy.

Daniel and Elizabeth breakfasted at eight, with the air heavy with the scent of roses she had planted around her log cabin. Their breakfast was corn fritters, eggs, and milk. Elizabeth was still a stewpot of worry, her face lined with weariness from the previous night's events.

"I have to ask you this question," Elizabeth said, probing. The thumping of her heart made speech difficult

Daniel's face registered no surprise. "About polygamy? Would I take another wife if the Brethren asked?"

Elizabeth's jaw dropped. She had not expected Daniel to talk about the subject so willingly. It had been mutually off limits by silent acclamation before today. She blinked, smoothed her hair with both hands, and thought of her next words, slowly and primly.

"It would break my heart." Her eyes misted.

"And mine," Daniel answered without hesitation.

"But if the brethren asked?"

Daniel took a while to answer. He gazed into his wife's sad green eyes. She dabbed at them with her apron.

"I don't know," he said honestly. "It would have to be a matter of prayer, and fasting."

Elizabeth bowed her head and stared at the floor. She wiped her eyes again. "I feel so terrible that I have not given you a child yet."

"Elizabeth. Please. It's not your fault."

"I think about my blessing from Brigham Young every day. At least one child. That's what Willard Richards said Brigham's blessing meant. A mother in Zion."

Daniel reached for his wife's hand. He squeezed it.

Elizabeth looked mournful. "Perhaps another wife could give you a child."

"Elizabeth, that's enough for now. I love you."

More tears. "I love you, too."

Silence.

63

September 25, 1842

BEFORE DANIEL DESCENDED INTO the well he had helped James Pulham dig, he peered down what looked like an auger hole. Once he reached the bottom and looked up, the hole appeared to be no larger than an American coin, like a half-cent piece. The deeper the hole had been dug, the more eerie the feeling it gave Daniel.

Daniel began helping James with the well the day he learned James had proposed to Harriet Barnes Clifford, a widow. She was also a United Brethren convert. She and her husband, Elijah Clifford, had arrived in Nauvoo the same day as Mary Ann Weston Davis. Elijah, however, had succumbed to cholera in May. A wedding between James and Harriet was scheduled for next week.

Yesterday, forty feet down, they had hit water. Today, their plan was to dig another six to eight feet to make certain they had a good strong vein and a lot of storage space in the bottom of the well. When the hole became so deep that they couldn't throw the dirt out, they had started another hole, in the center. Dirt from that hole went to the first shelf. In this case, a third shelf had become necessary. Then a large bucket and a mule. Tomorrow, they could start lining the walls of the well with rocks, using the reliable keystone method.

"Ready!" Daniel yelled at the top of his voice.

The hollow sound vibrated through the well chamber. James sent his borrowed mule into motion.

He had tried using a horse the first day. It was too dangerous. The horse pulled too fast.

Daniel watched the large wooden bucket, filled with mud, begin to move upward. He prayed the rope would hold. He prayed the sand streaks would not cause a cave-in. Foot by foot, it disappeared to the top. A minute or two later, the bucket started back down.

The process began when James and Daniel laid a wagon wheel on the ground and scribed a circle around the rim. The first day they dug the height of a man. After that, the digging was slower. They found there were three ways to dig: on their side, up against the bank; on their knees; or go into the hole almost upside down. The walls had to be straight, or the bucket would hit the sides and chunk out rocks as they went. Even a small rock could kill a man standing in the bottom if it hit him on the head.

Using a shovel with only a one-foot handle and a short-handled mattock, they had reached forty feet in eight days.

Hands held high, Daniel caught the bucket. In the suffocating dampness, he filled it again. "Take it up!"

The conversation Robert was having with Edward Phillips and John Hyrum Green reminded Robert of conversations he used to have with his father back in England. It centered on livestock. His father, highly opinionated, had almost forced his opinions of everything on everyone. Robert found himself doing the same thing, over a worm fence, on this rather humid September day. The two newcomers to Nauvoo were like sponges, however, eager for the information. They regarded Robert as an expert, because Robert's father, grandfather, and great-grandfather had been livestock traders and butchers in Gloucestershire, England.

"What about pigs?" Hyrum asked.

"Easy to raise," Robert answered. He tried his best to sound frontier, rather than English, in his accent. "You can make pets of them. They're quick to learn your voice. Sows have piglets twice a year. But around here, wildcats, wolves, and fox are tough on little pigs, just like they're tough on any little animal, like lambs. We didn't have that problem in England. Keep one hog around that you don't castrate. You need one real mean old boar hog. They'll tend to keep the predators away. Be sure to mark your hogs. Notch their ears in some peculiar way, so's you can tell which ones are yours. Fatten your hogs up in the summer. They eat anything. Even chestnuts. But don't give them too many chestnuts. Makes the meat too flabby, and not much grease. Get them slaughtered in November. Pack the meat in boxes, salt it good, and let it stay for two months. Then take the meat out and wash it, hang it, and let it dry. It will keep a long time."

In a strange way, almost, Robert hungered for his father, to talk to him, to listen to him. This, even though they had not gotten along over the matter of his marriage to Hannah, and over the subject of religion. He had always taken his father for granted, a warm presence, cloying in his affection, annoying in his domination. In his mind's eye, he could still see his father and mother's headstones in the Deerhurst Anglican churchyard. And his brother William's. He had died at age thirty-five. The Savior's revelation to Joseph Smith about baptism for the dead was one of Robert's favorite gospel subjects. It gave him peace.

Cattle.

"When cattle get sick, they'll eat ivy sometimes. They'll get to where they don't want nothing to eat but that. And then that makes them sicker. To get them over that, put some milk, soda, and salt in a bottle. Shake it up and pour it down 'em. They'll vomit, and it makes 'em better."

Edward Phillips took a mental note. He had been a married man for several weeks now. Heber C. Kimball had performed the marriage between him and his long-time sweetheart, Annie Simmons, at Camp Creek, just northeast of downtown Nauvoo. Edward had a hard time deciding which was more important, focusing on beginning his married life in Nauvoo as a farmer, or paying attention to all the stressful distractions. Missouri authorities had tried to arrest Joseph Smith for the shooting of ex-Governor Boggs in Missouri. Joseph was now in hiding. Joseph had made a prediction that someday the Mormons would be driven to the Rocky Mountains. Sidney Rigdon, Joseph's counselor, influenced by John C. Bennett's statements, had said some things in opposition to Joseph. Nauvoo residents had been politicked by gubernatorial candidates. Thomas Ford had been elected. Nauvoo had been redivided into ten wards. Wilford Woodruff and others were still sick with the ague. Elizabeth Browett had not been able to find any quinine all during the sickly season.

Meat.

"Before you kill a beef for winter, put it in a pen and feed it corn twice a day for two or three months. The corn will make the meat sweet and tender. Cure the meat, wrap it in cheesecloth, and hang it in your smokehouse. Eat what you can fresh, and dry the rest."

Oxen.

"You likely will have to train your own pair of oxen. Make sure you castrate them first. Bulls make poor work animals. A yoke of oxen needs to be three of four years old before you start training them. Put a yoke on them and let them go with it on for a while. Next thing, attach a little log to the yoke, just a light one, until they get used to pulling. Then put on a bigger log. After a while you can hook them to a wagon, but even then it takes a long time to train them."

Sheep.

"Keep a few sheep around, if you can afford it. Hannah, Elizabeth, Martha, and Rebecca can help your wives card the wool, spin it, and weave it on a loom to make cloth for your homemade clothes. I hate shearing sheep, though. As an animal, sheep don't keep too well. They're apt to take cold in the spring, even get pneumonia. If they get worms, burn hickory and give the ashes to them. Cornmeal with turpentine works pretty good, too. Put a bell on your sheep. Wildcats, wolves, and dogs are bad on sheep. The bell keeps them away, mostly."

Geese and ducks.

"They'll thrive around your place, keeping the bugs down. They're rough on gardens. They like tomatoes, watermelons, cabbage, and bean blossoms. Your wives'll want a few around for the feathers. You can get half a pillow's worth of feathers off a goose. To pluck the feathers, put the head right back under your arm, hold both feet with one hand, and pull the feathers opposite the way they lay. Soon you'll get a big pile of feathers. You can pick them once a year. They get used to it. Duck eggs ain't bad to eat. Goose eggs are strong. When I first got here, neighbors gave me five goose eggs. I put them under my own setting goose and do you know what? She rolled 'em right out of the nest. I don't know how she knew the difference from her own eleven, but she did."

Robert's little audience kept making mental notes.

On September twenty-fifth, the only member of the Council of the Twelve Apostles still on a foreign mission departed Liverpool as company leader on the *Medford,* presiding over 214 members of the Church, emigrants from Great Britain. His journey had taken him farther than any of the other Apostles. He had sojourned in Germany, learning the language there. He had eaten snails on an island in the Mediterranean Sea, wept in the Garden of Gethsemane, prayed on the Mount of Olives, dedicated the Land of Israel, and walked the streets of Jerusalem.

Now Orson Hyde was on his way to Nauvoo.

He had no idea that his life would soon be entwined with the Browett family.

64

ROBERT WHEELED WHEN HE HEARD his name called. He was mid-sentence in his conversation with Edward Phillips and John Hyrum Green.

"Uncle Robert! Come quick! The well fell in!" The urgent voice belonged to nine-year-old Lucy Bloxham.

Daniel! James!

Led by Robert, the three men broke into a dead run. When they arrived at the well site, the bay mule was standing still, hooked to a rope that disappeared into what once was a hole. Wide-eyed children, with curious long faces, milled around.

"Shovels! We need shovels!" Robert yelled. He ran a half block north, grabbed shovels from his place and from Daniel's, and began digging with Edward and John.

As he dug, Robert screamed at the children: "Joseph! Tommy! Lucy! Find everyone you can! We need help!"

Elizabeth Browett was a mile and a half away at the Thomas Bloxham cabin, checking on Dianah's new baby, born five weeks earlier.

"It's nice to have a restful day at home," Dianah said. "Be sure to thank Hannah and Daniel's sister and mother for tending to my children today."

hill to see how Elder Woodruff is doing. He's still in bed with the fever. I guess I stayed too long."

A teary-eyed Harriet Clifford emerged from the reddish haze of the crowd. "James didn't show up," she said in a low, mournful voice.

Daniel was speechless.

"We've still got people looking," Robert said. "We didn't think to send someone to Elder Woodruff's home."

"We better keep digging," said Levi Roberts.

The diggers found the body of James Pulham at one o'clock in the morning. In his grief, Daniel concluded that James must have descended into the well, down the ladder, after he left, either to scoop one more load into the bucket, or to inspect the walls.

None of the children had actually seen him go into the well. They only heard it collapse.

Still suffering from the ague, Wilford Woodruff preached the sermon at James Pulham's funeral, four days later.

CHAPTER NOTES

The reader is reminded that James Pulham is a fictitious character. Accidents such as the one at the well, portrayed in this chapter, were a constant threat on the American frontier.

65

December 1842

DANIEL BROWETT RAISED HIS AXE and drew a heavy breath. With a powerful thrust, he sent the axe head through a cottonwood log, splitting it in two. With his cap drawn low across his forehead, a woolen scarf wrapped around his neck, and his black wool coat wrapped around his body, he steadied another log and took aim. The ground was frozen hard, and the air sharp as a splinter. The late rising sun reddened the horizon to the color of plum juice.

"Brother Browett?"

Daniel whirled to see a man approaching, his breath visible. The snow crunched loudly under the weight of his boots. He was of average height with red hair mostly hidden under a top hat. He was a stranger.

A right hand was extended, glove off. "We've never met. I'm Orson Hyde. I went to the wrong cabin first. Your sister and mother directed me here. Rebecca and Martha, is that right?"

"Yes, that's right. Nice to meet you," Daniel said with a cheery smile, puzzled that the Apostle would be here alone, looking for him. "I heard you had arrived in Nauvoo. Welcome, and Merry Christmas."

"Our company came through New Orleans, just like yours. Quite the city."

The remark stirred Daniel's remembrance. "Quite the city. I agree. And quite the riverboat trip?"

A friendly nod. "I'm here on official business, Brother Browett, substituting for Elder Richards."

"I hope his trip to Springfield is successful," Daniel said. Willard served as personal secretary to Joseph Smith.

"We all do, for the sake of the Church, and the Prophet. I'm here on an errand from the Prophet. Can you meet with him and Elder Woodruff this afternoon?"

"Today?"

"Yes, this afternoon."

"What time?"

The Apostle pulled out his pocket watch. "Four o'clock."

"Can you tell me what this is about?"

"No."

Daniel gasped. *What does the Prophet want with me?* He shrugged his shoulders and managed a faint smile. "Tell them I'll be there."

Orson Hyde shook Daniel's hand again. "Merry Christmas, Brother Browett. And happy birthday. Elder Woodruff tells me your birthday was yesterday, on the Sabbath. Twenty-nine years old?"

Daniel nodded, amazed that Elder Woodruff had remembered.

"You're still young. I'll be thirty-eight next month. How many children?"

"None. But we're trying."

Orson sensed Daniel's embarrassment. "See you soon. Don't be late."

A bewildered Daniel Browett watched the Apostle trudge up the street, and turn left toward the temple site, where church services had been held in its incomplete basement floor since the end of October. He discarded his axe and went into an empty house to change clothes, his mind a perfect blank.

Elizabeth was making her rounds. Levi's wife, Harriet Ann Roberts, was due in a month. Their two children, Henry and Caroline, had colds. John's wife, Eliza Roberts Cox, was due in two months. So was William's wife, Mary Rowberry Jenkins. Harriet Clifford was recovering from the flu.

Elizabeth was a busy woman. Two days earlier, on a Saturday, she had delivered Thomas Kington's first child by his new wife.

The cold, empty cabin added to Daniel's anguish. He stirred the fire with an iron poker, sending sparks spiraling upward. He added two logs, and held his hands outward, warming them, still struggling with his ice-fogged brain. *What do they want? What's Wilford up to?*

Later, as Daniel began his walk to the Red Brick Store, located on the south side of Water Street, a new snowstorm began to blanket the city. Sparrows played in a neighbor's raspberry patch, the vines acting like a springboard. The wind blew, pushing flakes of snow horizontally across his face. He shivered. A man could freeze to death in this weather. He saw only one other man along the way, Jacob Kemp Butterfield, the teamster. An empty dray trailed behind a team of bay horses, their long winter hair blowing in the wind. Hunched over, Daniel waved and shuddered a friendly hello.

According to his pocket watch, it was exactly six minutes to four when he stood in front of the Red Brick Store. Here, the Relief Society had been organized March seventeenth, 1842. A year later the Young Gentlemen and Young Ladies Relief Society had been organized in the same building. Except for a clerk, there was no one on the first floor. A rarity attributed no doubt to the bad weather. Daniel was directed to the stairs.

The second floor consisted of a large council room and Joseph's office. Daniel found three men in the office: Joseph Smith, Wilford Woodruff, and Orson Hyde. Without his hat, Orson's red hair was bright as a fox's tail.

Daniel, Wilford, Orson, and the Prophet exchanged pleasantries for eleven minutes. Joseph had spent part of the day, just like Daniel, chopping wood. The Prophet's mind, however, was naturally preoccupied with the delegation he had sent to Springfield.

"I'm sure the burden is great on you," Daniel said, referring to the lengthy legal battle over the charges from Missouri that he and Porter Rockwell had tried to kill Boggs. Daniel thought about Joseph's seclusion at the time when Emma was ill with fever, and the times that the Church despaired of her life. His case was at this moment being presented to a judge in Springfield.

"I've got quite a delegation in Springfield," Joseph said. "Willard Richards, William Clayton, Heber C. Kimball, Henry Sherwood, Peter Haws, Alpheus Cutler, and Reynolds Cahoon. They're armed with affidavits and all sorts of legal papers. I'm confident I'll be acquitted."

Daniel gave a polite shrug. *I don't think the Prophet wants to give me a private update of his legal battles.*

"How's your little boy, Elder Woodruff?" Daniel asked. Little Wilford junior had been sick with the croup in November.

"Just fine now," the Apostle said. "Tell Sister Browett thanks again for all the help she's been."

"I will," Daniel said, with a proud smile.

Joseph Smith made a visible head motion to Wilford.

"We have an assignment for you, Brother Browett."

"I suspected something like that."

Wilford's smile was guarded. So was a muffled chuckle. "How well do you know Sister Harriet Clifford?"

"Elizabeth and I have been trying to help her all we can. She's very lonely, and heartbroken. Two deaths in a matter of a few months takes a toll." Daniel swallowed hard, fighting back tears as he thought of his cousin, James Pulham.

Wilford stole a look at the Prophet. "We're quite concerned about her."

"I'm glad."

"We have a proposed solution."

Daniel took a deep breath.

Wilford cleared his throat. "I have a few questions first." He paused. "Are you keeping all the commandments?"

The question caught Daniel off guard. "Yes, I think so."

Other questions followed. A testimony of Jesus Christ, and of his role as Savior and Redeemer? Honest? Sustain Church leaders? Faithful to the

Prophet and his teachings? Keeping the covenants made at baptism? Paying tithing? Treating your wife and family with respect? Attending church?

Daniel's answers were favorable.

"On that basis," Wilford said, "We have an assignment for you. Can you take Sister Clifford as a second wife?"

A groan escaped Daniel's lips as his heart sunk to the floor. His skin prickled. His hands felt dry and cold. He thought about Elizabeth. The day they were married in the little redbrick Methodist chapel in Apperley. Their honeymoon in Bath. And their second marriage, at the insistence of her Anglican parents, in the St. Mary de Lode Church in Gloucester. *This will devastate her.*

Daniel squirmed in his chair, and began an abstracted stare at the wall.

Joseph Smith sat without speaking, his eyes shining and enormous.

After several seconds of stone silence, Wilford spoke again.

"I know it's a difficult question for you to answer right now. You'll need to think and pray about it, and discuss it with Sister Browett. I'm certain you know something about the doctrine of plural marriage. Let me review it with you."

With a super-human effort to clear his mind from all that was rushing through it, Daniel leaned forward, clasped his hands, and took a deep breath.

Elder Wilford Woodruff, with Joseph sometimes adding an amplifying sentence here and there, began at the very beginning. The revelation had come to Joseph in the Kirtland years. Plural marriage was part of the restoration. It was practiced by the ancients, recorded in the Bible. Plural marriage was a commandment to the Church, from God. Marriage is an institution ordained of God. Marriage and the family are intended to last forever, to survive death. Marriages performed by priesthood authority are for time and all eternity. Plural marriage is a religious principle, not a social experiment or a sexual aberration. Unauthorized practice of the principle was condemned in the Book of Mormon. The idea of having more than one wife, certainly, is in sharp contrast with what the Saints have been taught to believe. Therefore, it is naturally difficult to accept. Those who entered into plural marriage are expected to demonstrate loyalty and devotion to spouse, and to observe the highest standards of fidelity and morality.

Wilford and Joseph's explanations took the better part of an hour.

"We don't expect you to give us an answer today," Wilford said. "Again, you need to seek your wife's approval and blessing. You need to fast and pray about it."

Inwardly, Daniel cried out in agony. "I understand."

"We need to take care of our people. There's no one more qualified than you to take care of Sister Clifford."

Daniel left the Red Brick Store in shock. The wind felt stronger. The cold felt colder. His legs felt like stone. The crunching of the snow was deafening as he walked. There was a thundering in his ears. He drew a heavy breath, the frigid air stinging his lungs. *Why me? What will Elizabeth think? I hardly know Harriet.*

He tried to gauge Elizabeth's reaction. She would oppose it. She would cry. She might want to move away. She might throw the frying pan at him. She might privately seek out the Brethren and give them a piece of her mind.

He thought of Harriet. He truly felt sorry for her. Saints who had endured the hardship of emigrating to Nauvoo from England had a special place in his heart. Especially those who lost a husband or a wife after their arrival, like Thomas Kington. He pictured Harriet Clifford in his mind: ordinary looking, deep-set sad brown eyes, dark brown hair, round face, medium height and weight.

Daniel tried to gauge Harriet's reaction, too. Like Elizabeth, she might reject the whole idea. She would regard it as a marriage by assignment. Perhaps she was not over her grief about the death of James, or even the death of her first husband. Could she get along with Elizabeth? And his mother, and sister?

Another puzzling thought crossed Daniel's mind. *Would Robert be asked to do the same thing?*

Merry Christmas.

66

Daniel was relieved to find his cabin still empty. It gave him time to pray and to think. His ten-minute prayer was full of pleadings. To understand the law of plural marriage. To gain a testimony of it. For the Spirit to confirm whether or not to accept the assignment to marry another wife. To have the courage to talk to Elizabeth.

Afterward, feeling a little better, he changed his clothes and returned to his wood chopping. Each time his axe split a block, he thought of Elizabeth. The news would fracture her, split her apart. From her skull to the tips of her toes. Inwardly, he expected some kind of answer as he swung the axe. Nothing. Only a stupor of thought.

She returned just before dark, after five.

Elizabeth greeted Daniel with a kiss. "I thought you'd have a *large* pile of chopped wood done by now. Where've you been?"

Her words stabbed at him. Unintentional, of course. He didn't know how to answer. "I'll be in for supper in a few minutes. What are we having?"

She pushed her lips forward in thought. "I'll warm up yesterday's stew. I've got enough bread. I'll have to bake some more tomorrow. Unless I have too many calls to make. Maybe I'd better do it *tonight*. Huh?"

I'll let her get the loaves into the oven before I tell her. Daniel nodded his approval and steadied another cottonwood log. "I'll work up my appetite."

Daniel's whole body was stiff and cold when he went inside, despite the log splitting. The aroma of the stew did little to revive his spirits, nor did the warmth of the hearth. He slowly pulled off his cap, coat, and gloves, tossing them aside.

"Hang them up," Elizabeth commanded without looking up from her breadboard. She was kneading dough and making loaves, sprinkling a little more flour over them. "And light a couple more dips."

"Yes, dear," he said meekly. He found two tallow candles, lit them, and set them on the table. He needed to curry her favor, not aggravate her over a little thing like not hanging up his hat and coat.

"Wait until I get these loaves into the oven. Then we'll eat."

Daniel sat on his bench in front of the hearth, elbows on his knees, face in his hands. *How will I begin?*

"The Roberts children have *nasty* colds. I hope they're better in time for Christmas."

Daniel grunted.

A puff of flour exploded into the air as Elizabeth turned her loaves. "I recommended bayberry tea for their sore throats. If Sister Roberts can't find any at the store tomorrow, I may have to *loan* her some of ours. She has plenty of ginger, cloves, and white pine to mix with it. She's starting them on golden seal, too. Sister Cox said the peppermint sure helped with her child's colic. And the rhubarb did the trick as a mild laxative."

The fire began to warm Daniel. His brain, however, remained in a damp fog.

Elizabeth continued to ramble. It was her habit to ramble, especially when they were alone at night. Daniel always played the polite listener, as though he had a ticket to a lyceum. "Elder Richards, bless his heart, helps all he can with advice. He constantly tells me how the Prophet and Brigham Young *dislike* regular doctors. Claims they want to cure you or kill you, makes no difference, as long as they get your money. I suppose the doctors *hate* me.

Doing most all this for free. I suppose Joseph's dislike of doctors goes back to the time when the Smith family lost Alvin. I heard about that. Seventeen years ago it happened. I don't see *why* they administer calomel, anyway. It's nothing but *poison*. Elder Richards says the Prophet keeps telling him that Mr. Thompson's botanical cures could just as well be an addition to the gospel. The theory compliments the Word of Wisdom so very nicely. I guess the Prophet wants a qualified herbalist to tend to the needs of the Legion. Have you heard that? *Good idea,* don't you think?"

No answer.

"I've told you about Priddy Meeks, haven't I? Priddy believes that evil spirits are the cause of every pain, ache, and misery we endure here on earth. I agree. Remember Elder Woodruff telling us that he *never* had the ague until the Lord asked him to go on his mission to England? He nearly *died*. Satan didn't want him to go on that mission. No wonder. *Look* what he accomplished. He thinks eighteen hundred converts resulted from that mission already. Six hundred from the United Brethren alone. Good thing he had lots of help from the other Apostles, and you, and Brother Kington. And John Benbow."

Daniel remained silent. He hoped Robert and Hannah would barge in, just to visit. Or his mother and his sister. Or he could delay the subject until tomorrow. Or the next day. Or the next. *They didn't give me a deadline.*

Elizabeth paused, contemplating Daniel's silence. "You're not *saying* much. Are you feeling well? Brigham Young gave me his recipe for composition tea. Four ounces each of powdered poplar bark and hemlock, two ounces each of ground ginger and cloves and cinnamon, and an ounce of cayenne. Want to *try* some?"

"Fine." He had to answer one way or another, or she would ask him again. He wondered why Brigham didn't use bayberry in his tea. Daniel liked bayberry.

She placed the loaves in the oven, and then reached for her teapot. "Brigham likes it with cream and just a dash of sugar. I'll fix *yours* that way."

Silence again.

"Sister Clifford feels a *lot* better. The flu really had her down. Poor thing. Losing her husband and cousin James so soon together."

A silent groan. The thought of James made him weep inwardly again. The mention of Sister Clifford's name shook him back to reality. His heart pounded. *Get it over with.*

Elizabeth used her ladle to fill two bowls with partridge stew. Daniel said the blessing. He chose his words carefully.

A confused look came to Elizabeth. "What did you mean," she asked, *"give us understanding of the Lord's new commandment?* Is there a new commandment I don't know about?"

Daniel blew on his stew, assessing Elizabeth's astute question. His gaze settled on her face, noting her pallor and the darkening smudges under her concerned eyes. "You haven't met Elder Orson Hyde yet."

"Do you mean to say that you have?"

"He came by today while I was chopping wood."

"So he's the source of this new commandment you mentioned in the blessing of the food?"

"No. Of course not."

"I don't suppose he was making a *social* call."

"No. Official business. While Elder Richards is out of town, Elder Hyde is handling some of his duties."

"Such as?"

"He said the Prophet wanted to meet with me."

"With *you?* Just you? What on earth for?"

"I met with not only the Prophet, but with Elder Woodruff and Elder Hyde as well. In the upper room of the Red Brick Store."

A premonition was building inside Elizabeth. She hung her head and fell silent.

Daniel brought the first spoonful of stew to his lips. He sensed Elizabeth knew where the conversation was heading. He chewed his food slowly.

"Would you rather talk about this tomorrow?"

Elizabeth turned away, hiding her tears. She thought of happier days, in

England. Their honeymoon in the ancient Roman spa town of Bath. Working together as lay preachers in the United Brethren congregation. Leasing land from Squire Hastings. Her next words were barely audible. "Never would be better."

There was a long pause. "Are you okay?" Daniel asked, painfully aware of her feelings.

She rose from the table and took a few feeble steps toward the hearth. "Are you *really* considering doing this, or do you have a choice?"

Daniel's eyes filled with tears. "They asked that both of us present it to the Lord in prayer."

Another long pause. Elizabeth flexed her fingers and stared at them. Her face had turned from a deep pink to a bright red. "I'm to pray to ask if it's okay to give up half my husband to another woman?"

Daniel didn't know what to say. So he said nothing.

Elizabeth's stern features hardened. "I'm going to bed. Enjoy your stew. Sleep in front of the hearth. I want to be alone."

Daniel stood at the table, staring at the two untouched bowls of food. *I didn't even get a chance to say Harriet Clifford's name.*

COMING SOON: *Volumes Three and Four*

Volume Three, entitled *Trials and Tribulations*, tells about Robert, Hannah, Daniel and Elizabeth's lives in Nauvoo. It was being written as this volume was being printed. You will soon find it in your favorite bookstore. Volume Four, *The Separation*, will deal with the period of time that our main characters are separated for the first time in their lives. Robert and Daniel serve in the Mormon Battalion. Hannah and Elizabeth are left behind, in Winter Quarters.

ABOUT THE AUTHOR

Darryl Harris received his B.A. degree in communictions from Brigham Young University in 1966, after attending Idaho State University. He was graduated from Marsh Valley High School in 1959, and was raised in the small Idaho communities of McCammon and Arimo.

He served as a missionary in the Northern Far East Mission (1961-62) and the Korean Mission (1962-64).

After being employed by the *Deseret News* in Salt Lake City and *The Post-Register* in Idaho Falls, and Evans Advertising Agency in Salt Lake City, he began his own business, Harris Publishing, Inc., in 1971. His firm has ninety employees and it publishes twelve different magazines, many of them national. Some of them are: *SnoWest, SledHeads, Houseboat, PDB (Pontoon and Deck Boat), Riverjet, Potato Grower, The Sugar Producer, Mountain West Turf,* and *Idaho Falls.*

His Church callings have included bishop, counselor in a bishopric, mission president (Korea Seoul), stake mission president, and area public communictions director (Southeast Idaho). He married the former Christine Sorensen in 1965. They reside in Idaho Falls and have five children and fifteen grandchildren.